BLOOD
OF THE
CHOSEN

Praise for

Ashes of the Sun

"Wexler's post-apocalyptic world is rich with history and fascinating in its inventive combination of magic, alchemy, and technology. This standout series opener is a winner: intricate, immersive, and irresistible."
—*Booklist* (starred)

"Wexler demonstrates a talent for worldbuilding... Familial tension, magic, and politics combine to kick this series off to a powerful start."
—*Publishers Weekly*

"*Ashes of the Sun* exists in the grey space between science-fiction and fantasy, creating a world that felt fresh yet familiar at the same time... [It] evokes the expansive feel of some of my favorite sci-fi shows... I'll be eagerly waiting to see how it unfolds." —*Fantasy Book Critic*

"*Ashes of the Sun* is an enormously fun, thought-provoking novel that is an outstanding launch novel for a series. Highly, highly recommended."
—*SFFWorld*

"There are monsters to fight and relics from a now-vanished, more advanced civilisation, which makes for some colourful worldbuilding... The prose and pacing are strong, bolstered by impressively vivid action scenes." —*SFX*

"Wexler's best work yet... *Ashes of the Sun* has scale and pace, and tension and batshit cool scenery, and I enjoyed it a hell of lot. (It's also queer as hell: that's always a nice bonus.) And I can't wait to see what comes next." —*Tor.com*

"A real high-octane, dystopian fantasy thrill-ride... There are some extremely exciting showdowns, skirmishes, and fights against grotesque monstrosities... This novel acts as a complete standalone yet there is still so much to see and explore in Wexler's world." —*Grimdark*

By Django Wexler

Burningblade & Silvereye

Ashes of the Sun
Blood of the Chosen

The Shadow Campaigns

The Thousand Names
The Shadow Throne
The Price of Valor
The Guns of Empire
The Infernal Battalion

BLOOD
OF THE
CHOSEN

Burningblade & Silvereye
Book 2

DJANGO WEXLER

An Ad Astra Book

First published in the UK in 2021 by Head of Zeus Ltd
An Ad Astra book

9 7 5 3 1 2 4 6 8

A catalogue record for this book is available from the British Library.

Cover illustration by Scott Fischer
Map and chapter ornaments by Charis Loke

ISBN (HB): 9781788543224
ISBN (TPB): 9781788543231
ISBN (E): 9781788543217

Printed and bound by CPI Group (UK) Ltd, Croydon, CR0 4YY

Head of Zeus Ltd
First Floor East
5–8 Hardwick Street
London EC1R 4RG
WWW.HEADOFZEUS.COM

For Mom

Cast of Characters

(as of the end of *Ashes of the Sun*)

Yora's crew in Deepfire

Yora—daughter of the famous failed revolutionary Kaidan Hiddenedge, and leader of a group of thieves and rebels opposed to the rule of **Dux Raskos Rottentooth**. Killed by **Tanax** in the centarchs' ambush of her group.

Gyre Silvereye—also known as Halfmask for the mask he wore to hide his missing eye. See the series recap.

Sarah—an arcanist and scavenger. Badly wounded by blaster fire in the centarchs' ambush, losing an arm.

Nevin—a thief and **Sarah**'s boyfriend. Disappeared after the centarchs' ambush.

Ibb—a scavenger. Abandoned the group for civilian life when **Kit**'s assignments proved too dangerous.

Harrow—a scavenger and animal handler. Tunnelborn, with a crush on **Yora**. Killed by a ghoul construct on one of **Kit**'s assignments.

Lynnia Sharptongue—an elderly alchemist and a close friend of **Yora**'s, with many connections to the underground.

Kitsraea Doomseeker ("Kit")—a famous scavenger, secretly working for the ghouls of Refuge. Ultimately traveled with **Gyre** and **Naumoriel** to Leviathan's Womb, and was mortally wounded in the confrontation atop the Leviathan. **Gyre** transferred her mind into the construct's analytica, and she currently inhabits its swarm of construct bodies.

Government of Deepfire

Dux Raskos Rottentooth—appointed governor of Deepfire for the Republic. Venal and corrupt. **Maya** exposed his involvement in a smuggling ring, and he fled Deepfire ahead of orders for his arrest.
Guria Fairshot—head of Deepfire's Auxiliaries and **Raskos**' right-hand man. Arrested after **Maya** exposed Raskos.

Ghouls of Refuge

Naumoriel—Minister of the Exterior for the city of Refuge. Obsessed with restoring the Leviathan and using it to destroy the Order, he tasked **Kit** with finding the necessary arcana. Ultimately killed by **Gyre** to prevent the Leviathan from being unleashed on humanity.
Elariel—**Naumoriel**'s young assistant and **Kit**'s handler.

The Twilight Order

Maya Burningblade—agathios to **Jaedia**, later a full centarch. See the series recap.
Jaedia Suddenstorm—a centarch. Master to **Maya** and **Marn** and former agathios to **Basel**. Kept away from the Forge and Order politics. Ambushed and taken over by a "black spider," she traveled to Leviathan's Womb with **Nicomidi** before being confronted by **Maya**, **Tanax**, and **Beq**. Broke the black spider's control to save Maya and was saved by her in turn, but lapsed into a coma afterward.
Marn—agathios to **Jaedia**. Captured by *dhakim*, and later rescued by **Maya**. Sent to the countryside to recover.

Baselanthus Coldflame—a Kyriliarch of the Council, leader of the Pragmatic faction. Master to **Jaedia**. Originally installed the Thing into **Maya**'s body.

Nicomidi Thunderclap—a Kyriliarch of the Council, leader of the Dogmatic faction. Master to **Tanax**. Revealed as a traitor to the Order, and allied to the spider-controlled **Jaedia**. Killed by her at Leviathan's Womb when he outlived his usefulness.

Prodominus Scatterbolt—a Kyriliarch of the Council, leader of the small Revivalist faction. Has a reputation for eccentricity.

Evinda Stonecutter—a centarch, well respected and politically neutral.

Va'aht Thousandcuts—a centarch, member of the Dogmatic faction. Originally took Maya from her home and destroyed **Gyre**'s eye.

Tanax Brokenedge—agathios to **Nicomidi**, later a full centarch. A rival to **Maya** on their first mission as agathia, but became an ally once his master's treachery was revealed. He and **Beq** are the only ones who know about the link between **Maya** and **Gyre**.

Varo Plagueluck—a scout and friend of **Maya**'s. Notorious for his disaster stories.

Bequaria ("Beq")—an arcanist and **Maya**'s lover. Went to Leviathan's Womb with **Maya**, and knows about her link with **Gyre**.

Series Recap

At eight years old, Gyre is playing with his five-year-old sister, Maya, when their vulpi farm is visited by the centarch Va'aht Thousandcuts, who announces that Maya must come with him to join the Twilight Order. Maya doesn't want to go, and Gyre tries to stop the centarch, stabbing him with a small knife. Va'aht cuts out Gyre's eye in punishment before taking Maya away.

Twelve years later, Maya is agathios to the centarch Jaedia Suddenstorm, with few memories of her early life. While on a mission, she encounters a mysterious black spider in control of a human body, which seems to recognize her and calls her *sha'deia*. Concerned, her mentor leaves on a secret assignment, while Maya is sent out with a team of trainees including Tanax—a student of Jaedia's enemy Nicomidi Thunderclap—Varo, and Beq.

Meanwhile, Gyre works with a team of rebels—including the elderly alchemist Lynnia and arcanist Sarah—in the city of Deepfire, fighting against the Dawn Republic and the local Dux Raskos Rottentooth. Privately, he searches for the legendary Tomb, the dead city of the ghouls, hoping to find power to overthrow the Order. Kit, the only person who has ever found the Tomb, comes to offer him a deal: He and his friends will help her secure the Core Analytica, and she will guide him to the Tomb.

Gyre's group accepts the mission, but the search proves dangerous. Some of his friends are killed, and Raskos' forces raid their base. To convince Gyre to stay with the plan, Kit introduces him to her handlers, the ghouls Elariel and Naumoriel. The Tomb is the supposedly extinct ghouls' hiding place, which they call Refuge. Naumoriel promises Gyre power if he secures the Core Analytica.

After a first assignment tracking down slavers, Maya's group is sent to Deepfire to assist Raskos against the rebels. Maya distrusts Raskos and, snooping, discovers evidence he is working with Nicomidi. She and Beq sneak out into the city and meet with Sarah, who tells them about a secret warehouse that holds the spoils of Raskos' corrupt dealings. When they return, Raskos asks them to spring a trap on the rebels.

Kit has discovered the trap and convinces Gyre to go for the Core Analytica—stored in the warehouse—rather than help warn the others. Maya attempts to talk the rebels down and promises to investigate Raskos, but his troops start a fight and a bloodbath ensues. Sarah is badly wounded, and most of the rebels are killed. Furious, Maya rushes to the warehouse, looking for proof of Raskos' crimes.

When she gets there, she meets Gyre and Kit, and they end up fighting. Gyre is no match for Maya's power, but she lets them escape without the Core Analytica. Excessive use of her power has left her feeling ill, and when Tanax catches up, he tells her that she's under arrest for treason. Jaedia has gone rogue, killing Order forces, and Maya is under suspicion.

Gyre discovers that the ghouls have abandoned him and Kit has given up hope. He convinces her to take him to Refuge to ask for another chance. They find their way to the city, where they're captured by Naumoriel. He agrees to give Gyre the power he needs to fight the Order, though at great cost—Gyre receives implanted augmentations, enhancing his combat abilities.

Maya spends time in a cell, feverish and delirious. When she recovers, Nicomidi offers to clear her charges if she agrees to renounce Jaedia and drop any investigation into Raskos. Maya refuses and instead issues an ancient challenge to trial by combat, which Tanax, newly promoted to Centarch, must meet. During the duel, Maya discovers her gear has been sabotaged by Nicomidi in an attempt to kill her. She wins anyway, though, and Nicomidi flees, indicating his guilt.

Gyre and Kit, with the reluctant help of Sarah and Lynnia, break into the palace in Deepfire and steal the Core Analytica. Naumoriel takes Gyre and Kit to a mountain fortress called Leviathan's Womb, where the greatest of the ghoul war-constructs is near completion. The Core Analytica is the last part needed to activate it. Kit suggests to Gyre that they double-cross the ghouls and take it for themselves.

Maya and Beq set out to find Jaedia. Tanax joins them, badly shaken by his master's treason. They follow a trail that also leads to Leviathan's Womb, where Jaedia has been joined by Nicomidi. Jaedia is under the control of the black spider, and she kills Nicomidi when he's no longer useful. She nearly kills Maya, but Jaedia fights off control long enough for Maya to destroy the spider. Wounded, Jaedia asks them to go into the mountain and stop the Leviathan from being activated.

Gyre, Kit, and Naumoriel enter the fortress, with Maya and Tanax on their heels. Naumoriel leaves the two humans to fend the centarchs off, and the ghoul goes to the Leviathan. Gyre defeats Tanax, but Maya fights him to a standstill before Kit stabs her from behind. Kit removes the power source for Gyre's augments, disabling him, and promises she'll return after seizing control of the Leviathan. After she leaves, Maya, badly wounded, restores Gyre's power source and begs him to stop the Leviathan. Gyre agrees, realizing his private revenge against the Order can't include the mass destruction the Leviathan would cause, and goes after Kit.

Aboard the colossal construct, Naumoriel sees through Kit's betrayal and mortally wounds her. Gyre sabotages the Leviathan, enraging the ghoul, but Gyre's augments let him kill Naumoriel. He carries the dying Kit to the Leviathan's control system, which transfers the user's mind into the giant machine and its attendant swarm of smaller constructs.

Outside the fortress, Maya and Gyre talk, but both remain

committed to their beliefs—in support of the Order or against it. Still, they hope they can meet again. Maya, Tanax, and Beq head back to civilization. Gyre is joined by small constructs, now remotely controlled by the disembodied Kit, and he plans to return to Refuge and find another way to bring down the Order.

BLOOD
OF THE
CHOSEN

Chapter 1

G yre sat on a boulder and shaded his eyes, looking down the length of the little valley.

It was a beautiful day in a beautiful spot. Summer was shading into fall, putting a hint of chill in the air, but the afternoon sun was still warm. A shrunken stream wound snakelike between tufts of grass and stands of hardy mountain bushes. And of course there were the serried ranks of the Shattered Peaks, snowcapped mountains stretching off into blue infinity.

The problem is, it's a beautiful spot that looks just like every other beautiful spot in the plaguing mountains.

"You think this is the right valley?" Kit said from behind him. "They all look the same to me."

"Me too." Gyre sighed. "We're in the right area, but..."

"Well, we can always check the next one. And the one after that." Kit's voice was chipper. "I'm in no hurry. You're the one who's dying."

Gyre frowned. "Who says I'm dying?"

"Just, you know, in general. Since you still have a fragile, aging human body."

"Weren't you the one who offered to give up half of eternity last night for a taste of my baked potato?"

"I'm trying," Kit said in a tone of wounded dignity, "to practice positive thinking."

Gyre lowered his hand and turned. Kit's voice was coming from a construct, a spiderlike thing half a meter high with an oval central body and eight limbs that could function as either legs or manipulators. It was made of striated black muscle laid over a metal skeleton, the fibers stretching and pulsing as it moved. In the past week, Kit had become quite adept at controlling the thing, and Gyre even thought he could see some of her body language in the way it carried itself.

Kit wasn't *in* the construct, of course. It was more like an appendage, along with hundreds of others, connected to the Core Analytica in the now-crippled Leviathan. Gyre had transferred Kit's mind into the great construct while she lay dying, and now its swarm served as her surrogate bodies. There were three basic types: a roughly human-sized version for heavy work and an even larger variety for hauling cargo, in addition to this small scout.

"And the most positive thing I can think of is that I'll get to watch everybody get old and die, while I don't have to," Kit went on. "It's very comforting."

"I think I read a fairy tale where that was considered a curse," Gyre said.

"I don't see why. I'm going to have such a good time outliving the shit out of all of you."

"Fair enough. I suppose one takes one's fun where one can find it."

"Exactly."

Gyre got to his feet, brushing dust off the tail of his coat. He patted his side, and the little construct swarmed up his leg and onto his back, tiny claws gripping. It settled on his shoulder, where he'd grown used its modest weight.

The boulder stood at the head of the valley, where the slopes grew too rocky to climb. Gyre was headed for a tall, flat section of cliff, which he desperately hoped looked familiar. A week or so previously, he'd emerged from the ghoul-built tunnels running under the mountains somewhere in this area, but finding the exact spot had proved to be more difficult than he'd hoped.

There. After a week, soft earth held no footprints, but a patch of bare rock showed a long, unnatural scrape. Naumoriel had come with them, in a cart-sized war-construct, and its traces were harder to obscure. *This has to be it.*

He hiked closer, legs straining at the slope, and ran his fingers along the wall of rock.

"Well?" Kit said from his shoulder.

"You said you could open it," Gyre said.

"I said I *think* I can open it," Kit said. "Assuming this is actually a door at all."

"Try."

"Just so we're clear, if I *do* get it open, someone is going to notice."

"I know." He and Kit had learned the hard way that you couldn't sneak into Refuge.

"Okay. Here goes."

Nothing obvious happened. From what Kit had explained, ghoul constructs used invisible energy to talk to one another across short distances, and she could use this channel to convince some of them to do what she wanted. Gyre waited, holding his breath. The little construct on his shoulder shifted its weight.

"Is it—" he began.

"Quiet. This is tricky." The construct gave a credible impression of the sound of Kit clicking her tongue. "There we go."

A hole appeared in the side of the mountain, part of the rock face sliding aside to reveal a long, curved tunnel. Gyre let out his breath and closed his eyes for a moment. *Finally.*

"Good work."

"Better get inside," Kit said. "I don't know how long it'll stay open."

Gyre strode forward. Patches of faintly glowing moss provided only a sliver of light—ghouls and their constructs could see in almost total darkness. Fortunately, Gyre could as well, through his silver eye. *Provided I have a ghoul to charge me back up again.* The energy bottle at his hip had barely a third of its power remaining.

The tunnel was perfectly smooth, bored by tireless, painstaking constructs, stretching back and away into the stone until it vanished around a curve. There was only one way to go, so Gyre started walking. Behind him, the door slid closed.

"So we made it," Kit said in the silence that followed. "Now what?"

"Now we see if the ghouls are willing to talk to us."

"And if they're not?"

Gyre sighed. "Then we probably get cut to pieces by constructs."

"Well. *You* do. I'll have to find someone else to hang out with."

"You're getting good at this positive thinking, you know that?"

They heard the guard-constructs coming before they saw them, a heartbeat-fast slap of leathery feet on stone. A pair of the things came around the curve of the tunnel, sprinting as fast as a warbird at full gallop. Like Kit's little spider, they were built of dark, pulsing muscle wrapped around a metal frame. These were soldier-constructs, roughly humanoid, bodies reinforced with steel plates. Bracers on their arms carried long, curved blades.

Gyre held up his hands, hoping they were smart enough to understand the gesture. He took a deep breath and shouted, "Please! I need to speak to Elariel!"

The things didn't even slow down. Gyre swore and went for his sword.

At the same time, he concentrated and heard a *click* from the base of his skull. The world suddenly went slow, as though everything was underwater. Shadows fanned out ahead of the two constructs, fading from almost solid to wraithlike—projections of where the things would be a few moments from now, possibilities for how they could change course. Kit's spider leapt from his shoulder, falling slowly with its legs spread wide.

At Gyre's side, the energy bottle grew warm. *I don't have much time.*

When Gyre himself moved, he felt normal, but he knew the *dhaka* energy running through his limbs drove him at tremendous speed. He sidestepped the first construct, bringing his sword up at an angle that let the thing's momentum do most of the work. The ghoul blade sliced neatly through muscle and steel, taking the guard's arm off below the shoulder. Gyre spun behind it, twisting into a downward chop that removed its other arm, then swung horizontally into the second construct, bisecting it at the waist. Black blood sprayed against the wall.

With another moment of concentration, Gyre disengaged his augmentations, and the world of shadows faded. Time abruptly resumed its normal course. Kit's spider skittered aside, and the disarmed construct turned awkwardly, dark fluid dripping from its stumps. Its companion fell apart into two halves.

"Listen to me," Gyre said. *Someone has to be able to hear.* Naumoriel had been able to find them as soon as they'd gotten close to Refuge, hadn't he? "I need to speak to Elariel. I don't want to threaten Refuge, I swear. I was with Naumoriel when he left." The construct lurched forward, and Gyre jumped away. "Plague it, you gave me this sword! Can anyone hear me?"

More footsteps echoed down the tunnel. *Sounds like at least half a dozen. I can't fight them all.* He felt the wall against his back and raised his blade again.

The disarmed thing in front of him abruptly stopped. Gyre once again held his breath, listening to the approaching footfalls grow louder.

"Gyre Silvereye." A woman's voice, with a heavy accent, issued incongruously from the construct. It wasn't Elariel—this ghoul sounded older, and definitely less practiced with the human tongue. "You will come to Refuge for questioning at once. Surrender your weapons to the approaching guardians."

"Understood," Gyre said as five more soldier-constructs sprinted into view. He looked down at Kit's spider. "See? I told you they'd let us in."

"Oh yeah," she said as the armored things surrounded them. "This just gets better and better."

It took the better part of a day to walk to the ghoul city, although truth be told, by the time they got there Gyre had lost track of the hour completely. The constructs set an exhausting pace, but he was glad for their escort—the tunnels branched and twisted, and there was no chance he and Kit would have found their way alone. But the soldier-constructs never hesitated, and eventually they reached a massive pair of doors, which grudgingly pulled apart to admit them.

"So what are we telling them about me?" Kit said in Gyre's ear as they followed the constructs in. " 'Cause let me say up front if they want to come out and mess with my new brain, they can forget about it."

"I'll have to play it by ear," Gyre said quietly. "What Naumoriel was doing was criminal, according to the ghouls, so they may not be happy about you." He frowned. "You remember the rendezvous, if something goes wrong?"

Kit snorted. "I'm not sure I _can_ forget things anymore. And anyway I've got a body there already."

Gyre nodded. He was still getting used to the idea that Kit could be carrying on a conversation with him while simultaneously performing another task dozens of kilometers away. _At least if the ghouls_ do _take exception to her and take this body to bits, she'll be fine._ The same, of course, did not hold true for him.

Beyond the doors was a larger cavern. _Much_ larger, bigger even than the dock at Leviathan's Womb. Refuge, the last ghoul city, looked at first like a night sky full of dim, twinkling stars. Through Gyre's silver eye, he could make out more of the shape of it—a vast cave, kilometers wide and hundreds of meters high, studded with enormous columns and rock formations. The stalactites and stalagmites couldn't be natural, but they had been sculpted to have a rough, organic look, pillars of rock the size of tenement blocks hanging from the ceiling or thrusting up from the cavern floor. Those formations, Gyre knew from previous visits, were honeycombed with rooms and tunnels. Nearby, a small river cascaded out of an opening high in the cavern wall, splashing in a torrential waterfall into a broad pool.

It was a staggering sight, a testament to the power and skill of the ghoul engineers and *dhakim*. Gyre was almost certainly the only human to have seen it since the Elder War, four hundred years previously. As far as the world knew, the ghouls and the Chosen had wiped one another out—that Refuge had survived was a secret the remaining ghouls would do anything to protect.

There wasn't much time to admire the view. His escort pointed the way, and they passed quickly through a series of arched doorways and spotless, faintly glowing tunnels. Though Refuge was a ghoul city, actual ghouls were few and far between, and it was constructs they passed in the halls. They came in all shapes and sizes, from tiny messengers smaller than Kit's spider to great lumbering crabs carrying heavy burdens. Eventually Gyre's escort halted and a closed door slid open. Gyre went inside, Kit still clinging to his shoulder.

"Gyre Silvereye." It was the voice that had spoken to him through the soldier-construct. "Please sit."

The room held only a couple of chairs, with the polished, extruded look of most ghoul furniture. One of them was occupied, so Gyre went to the other, giving a polite bow before he sat down.

The ghoul in the other chair acknowledged him with a bare nod. Like all her kind, she was humanoid but decidedly inhuman in appearance: taller than Gyre, slim enough to look rangy by human standards, and covered all over in dense brown-and-white fur. Her eyes were enormous, filling half her face with huge pupils and narrow whites, and she had long, expressive ears that twitched as she spoke. She wore no clothing, apart from a small metal coil threaded through the base of one ear. Gyre couldn't say if it was decorative or arcana. When she smiled at him, her teeth were white and finely pointed.

"My name," she said, with the careful diction of someone speaking a language they'd studied but not used much, "is Tyraves. I am the new Minister of the Exterior."

"Gyre," said Gyre. "But you knew that. Thank you for letting me back into the city."

"It was judged that you may have important information," Tyraves said. "If you are forthcoming with it, this will be easier for you."

"I'm happy to tell you anything I can," Gyre said. "But I would like to speak to Elariel."

"Elariel"—Tyraves pronounced the name with distaste—"is currently standing trial for her part in the crimes of my...predecessor, Naumoriel." Her sharp-toothed smile broadened. Gyre didn't sense much humor in it, and her ears were flattened back against her skull. "Tell me of your association with them. Start from the beginning."

"That may take some time."

Tyraves' tongue darted across her pointed teeth. "Neither of us is going anywhere."

Fair enough. He'd expected something like this, although now that he was faced with the reality of Tyraves' unsympathetic features, the plan he'd come up with on the road back from Leviathan's Womb was starting to feel distinctly shaky. *A little late to back out now, though.*

He laid out the story for her with only a few careful edits, from when Kit had recruited him to the final trip to Leviathan's Womb. How he'd fought off the Order's attempt to stop them, defeating his sister, Maya, and another centarch—

"Two centarchs." Tyraves' ears twitched. "You fought off two centarchs on your own?"

"Only thanks to Naumoriel's augmentations, of course."

"Hmm." Tyraves leaned forward in her chair and reached out with one hand, laying her thin fingers on Gyre's arm. His flesh rose in goose bumps as *something* raced through him, the soft breath of *dhaka*. The ghoul's eyes widened a little. "I see."

"Is something wrong?"

"No." She sat back, ears flattening again. "What Naumoriel did to you was...extensive. I doubt anything like it has been attempted since the war. I am surprised, frankly, that you survived."

Gyre shivered. "It certainly wasn't...pleasant."

"I imagine not." She steepled her hands. "So you repelled the Order attack while Naumoriel was aboard the Leviathan, installing the Analytica. Then what?"

"Then..." Gyre hesitated. *This is the tricky part.* "I'm not sure, exactly. Something went wrong. There was an explosion, and the Leviathan fell against the dock. By the time I got aboard, Naumoriel was dying."

In reality, the explosion had been Gyre's own doing, as had Naumoriel's death. Seeing exactly what the old ghoul had planned to unleash against the Republic, and with his sister's desperate plea ringing in his ears, Gyre had disabled the Leviathan. Ever since, he'd spent his nights wondering whether he'd made the right choice.

But Tyraves doesn't need to know that.

"Old fool," she said, and muttered something scathing in her own language. "We are saved the trouble of a trial for *him*, at any rate." She leaned forward again, her ears standing straight. "But as far as you are aware, the Order agents never came in contact with Naumoriel?"

"Definitely not," Gyre said. "We fought on the dock, and he was already on board."

She pursed her lips. "Still better if you had killed them. Or better yet if the place had collapsed and killed you all. But perhaps disaster has been avoided."

"I don't think there's any risk to Refuge," Gyre said. "For all the Order knows, we were just scavengers who dug up a big find."

"That is not your determination to make," Tyraves snapped. "The Geraia has entrusted me with the responsibility of keeping our city safe. What steps that entails is my decision." She sat back, hands folded. "But there remains the question of what to do with you, now that you've conveniently brought yourself back here."

"I want to talk to Elariel. Please."

"She is in no position to help you."

"Even so." *She's the only ally in this place I'm likely to have.*

"Hmm." Tyraves tapped her fingers on the arm of her chair, thoughtfully, as if weighing her curiosity against the inconvenience of his request. "Perhaps. Wait here."

The wait turned out to be at least an hour, while Gyre's certainty that he'd made a disastrously wrong choice steadily increased.

I didn't have to come back here. No doubt the ghouls would have tried to track him down, but the augmentations combined with the skills from his career as a thief and revolutionary would have made it easy to hide. *Get away from Deepfire, away from the mountains.* There were more than enough cesspools in the Splinter Kingdoms for a mercenary to disappear into.

But that would have meant giving up. Gyre had come to the mountains in search of the lost city of the ghouls, hoping that it would give him the power to destroy the Order that had stolen his sister and taken his eye. What he'd found went far beyond his wildest hopes, and to turn away from it now...

Enough. He clenched his fists. *I've already thrown the dice. Now it's just a matter of seeing the roll.*

Kit waited on the chair while he paced back and forth. She didn't speak—he had no doubt the ghouls could listen, if they cared to—but the little spider-construct was surprisingly reassuring. *I'm not alone. Not completely.* Tyraves hadn't raised an eyebrow, either. Constructs were such a part of the fabric of ghoul life that they were practically invisible, and Kit's body wasn't big enough to be dangerous.

Eventually, the door slid open. The soldier-constructs had been joined by a transporter—a chair on construct legs, essentially. Gyre climbed aboard, and the thing took off at a gallop, speeding with uncanny grace through twisting corridors and up endlessly spiraling ramps. Gyre got brief glimpses of the city through passing windows and had the impression that they were ascending, winding their way up toward the top of the massive cavern. The tunnels grew more elaborately adorned, featureless smoothness giving way to intricate carvings and soft, mossy carpets. There were even other ghouls about, walking in small groups surrounded by guardian constructs or carried in chairs like his own.

When the transporter came to a halt, Gyre found himself in front of a new set of doors, carved with a stylized frieze depicting the city. More soldier-constructs guarded them, massive things twice the size of the rest. Tyraves was waiting for him, and at her nod he gingerly slipped down from the chair.

"The Geraia is in session," the ghoul said. "Elariel is with them, in case her testimony is required. You may speak to her, but do not interrupt the proceedings."

The Geraia, Gyre had gathered, was something like the ghoul's version of the Senate, and so he was expecting the chamber of the Senate in Skyreach—a semicircle of chairs, with a central rostrum for a speaker. Instead he found himself walking into something more like an arena, a circular floor ringed by more construct guards. Around it were box seats, each separated from its neighbors by columns, stacked one above the other at least ten levels above the floor.

Gyre guessed that membership in the Geraia must be based on age, because the ghouls in the boxes looked ancient, fur gone gray and patchy. Many were housed in customized constructs, like the one Naumoriel had used, connected to them by tubes and wires. Someone was talking in the liquid gabble of the ghoul language when Gyre entered, but the speech came to a halt as a murmur ran through the room. Gyre felt wide, rheumy eyes on him as he crossed to a small table, where Elariel was sitting hunched over, looking miserable.

A bell rang, low and deep, and someone else was talking up above. Gyre heard Tyraves reply, waiting near the door, but it was all incomprehensible. Elariel looked around, her ears going rigid with shock at the sight of him.

"*Gyre?*" The word was a hiss. "What are you doing here? I thought..." She lapsed into her own tongue for a moment.

"I figured I'd drop in and see how you were doing," Gyre said, taking the seat beside her. Overhead, an argument seemed to be in progress.

"You can't *be* here," Elariel said. "This is the *Geraia*. There hasn't been a human here since...since *ever!*"

"It's a historic occasion, then." Gyre grinned, fighting down nerves. Elariel's ears twitched, and she smiled briefly, then shook her head.

"There is no way you're getting out of here alive," she said.

"From what Tyraves was saying, neither are you."

Elariel straightened up. "I was always prepared for that. Even if my master had succeeded." She looked sidelong at Gyre. "They told me that he died. I don't suppose..."

"He's dead," Gyre said. "I'm sorry."

"He didn't expect to return. He would regret only that he couldn't bring the Leviathan to life." Her ears drooped, but she kept her shoulders square. "And Kitsrea?"

"Dead," Gyre said. *Best keep it simple for now.* "I was the only one who escaped."

"And you came back here. Why? You must know they'll kill you this time."

"I have a plan. Sort of. But I'm going to need your help."

"I'm not sure there's much I can do." Elariel gestured at the guards all around. "Before you got here they were debating if I merited a quick execution or a painful punishment as an example to others."

"There must be some of them who agree with what Naumoriel was trying to do." Gyre craned his head in a circle, catching many of the old ghouls looking down at him. "Naumoriel was old enough to remember the war, and some of these look even older."

"If you mean they want revenge on the Chosen and the Order, of course they do," Elariel said. Her ears quivered angrily. "But they're cowards, afraid of the slightest risk. They've hidden under this mountain for so long they can't imagine doing anything else. My master hoped to push them, make it impossible for them to remain concealed, but..."

"What if I offered them a way to strike back, without any risk to Refuge? Do you think they would take it?"

"I think they won't listen to a human, any more than you would listen to a... a talking loadbird."

"A talking loadbird would get a lot of attention *because* it's a talking loadbird," Gyre said. "If I try to explain my plan, will you translate for me?"

"You mean *here*? Now?"

"When else?"

"I don't have any authority to speak here," Elariel said, her ears drooping again. "It's against the rules of the chamber, unless I'm called on to answer a question, and even then—"

"What are they going to do?" Gyre said. "Execute you?"

"I..." Elariel stared at him with her huge, dark eyes, the tips of her ears slowly rising. "I suppose you're right." She gave a small, sharp-toothed smile. "Just don't blame me when they dissolve your living brain in a vat of acid."

"Can they really do that?"

"Oh yes. *Dhaka* can be used for some very *imaginative* tortures."

"Good to know," Gyre said. "Okay. Let me get their attention, and then do your best to translate."

She nodded, and Gyre got to his feet.

Time to find out if this sounds as good as it does in my head. He took a deep breath and shouted as loud as he could manage.

"*Members of the Geraia!*"

The murmur of conversation running through the hall cut off abruptly. As the echoes died away, an old woman's tremulous voice said something sharp, and there was a scattering of laughter.

"She asked what the beast was braying about," Elariel said under her breath. " 'Beast' in this case specifically in the sense of an animal bred for labor, like a—"

"I get the gist," Gyre muttered. "Just follow along." He cleared his throat and said, "I apologize for the interruption. I understand that my presence here is unprecedented. But I believe that my experience has been equally unprecedented, and I have a proposal I would like to put to you."

It was actually an advantage sometimes, Gyre thought, not to speak the language. People were shouting back at him, but they were easy to ignore. He plowed forward, Elariel repeating his words in her own tongue.

"Naumoriel planned to reactivate the Leviathan and use it to crush the Republic and the Order. You have condemned his plan as dangerous for Refuge, and you are right to do so. If I had not been able to defeat the agents of the Order, they might have caught up with him and found proof of your city's existence."

"You're not helping your case," Elariel hissed as the shouts from above grew louder.

Gyre swallowed and went on. "But even if he failed, I think that Naumoriel understood the problem. The problem is humanity. Here I stand, after all, in a place where no human has ever stood before."

A ghoul shouted something back, to more laughter. "He says that can be fixed," Elariel translated unnecessarily.

"You could kill me, certainly. But you cannot avoid dealing with humanity. There are too many of us and too few of you. Fortunately for both sides, we don't need to be in conflict!" Gyre spread his hands. "I know, in the past, humans served the Chosen. But the Chosen are dead and gone. All that's left is a shadow, a dead hand locked around humanity's throat. A corpse-claw called the Order.

"That's where Naumoriel went wrong. If he'd succeeded with the Leviathan, he might have crushed Skyreach, maybe even broken the Order. But he could never have destroyed humanity entirely, and he would have succeeded only in teaching the survivors to hate the ghouls even more than they already do. Eventually, they would find their way here, and they would destroy you."

"You...threaten us?!" The words were halting but recognizable. A ghoul on the third tier was on her feet, hands on the rail as she glared down at Gyre. "Here...in our own domain...you speak of destroying...*usss*?" She gestured emphatically with one hand. "We... destroy...*you*. Tyraves!"

"I'm not here to threaten!" Gyre shouted before the Minister of the Exterior could move. "I'm here to make an offer I think will help both ghouls and humans. My people don't *want* to be slaves to the Order any longer. If we could, we would throw off the legacy of the Chosen and all their prejudices with it. I've seen what your arcana can do, your *dhaka*. If humans knew how much you could help them, they would line up to be your allies."

A big, barrel-chested ghoul in the lowest tier boomed an answer that got applause. Gyre glanced at Elariel, who translated, "He says that the humans would line up to plunder our living city like they plunder our dead ones."

"Some might," Gyre admitted in answer. "You need to remain hidden for now, of course. But I think you're selling humanity short. So here is my offer, which carries no risk to Refuge. I will go back into the human world. I have connections among those who want to overthrow the Order. Give me supplies—weapons, medicine, money—and I can gain influence among them."

He turned in a slow circle. "The Order's control is based on *fear*. Everyone knows that the centarchs are unstoppable. But with your help, I fought them and *won*." This was the key, the point that had burned itself into Gyre's mind. "The Order has a vast reach, but in reality they are spread thin. Only the knowledge that no one can oppose them keeps them in power. Break that—break it *even once*—and the whole edifice will crumble like a rotten stump and take the Republic with it. And then we can build something in the wreckage. A new human society, in partnership with the ghouls.

"And if I fail, what of it? Give me nothing that can't be explained as scavenged, and even in the worst case, nothing will lead back here. The Order will never suspect anything until it is too late. What, in the end, do you have to lose?"

The hall was getting quieter, he thought, as he approached the peroration, while Elariel's voice rang louder. As he finished, there was a moment of silence. Then the deep-voiced ghoul spoke, and it was not Elariel but Tyraves who translated.

"What," she said, walking over to their table, "would you actually do? Where would you go?"

"To Khirkhaz," Gyre said immediately. It was another thing he'd gone through, over and over, since leaving Leviathan's Womb. "In the far south. They'll be looking for me in Deepfire. Khirkhaz is on the other side of the Republic, and I have contacts there. There's a group called the Commune who have been fighting the Republic and the Order for years. If I can bring them something that can fight centarchs, they'll embrace us with open arms."

Tyraves turned to Elariel and barked something in the ghoul tongue. Elariel straightened up, ears vibrating angrily.

"No, he did not tell me his plan," she said. "But I think he is right."

"Elariel should come with me," Gyre said. "As a liaison."

Her eyes widened as she translated this. Tyraves looked between them, then up at the ranks of the Geraia. Murmurs were once again running between boxes, and Gyre hoped he wasn't fooling himself that it didn't sound entirely unfriendly.

"We cannot...ally...with humans." The old ghoul woman's face was a rictus, her eyes fixed on Gyre. "The Corruptor...would not allow it. We would all...be destroyed."

Gyre glanced at Elariel, hoping for some clarification, but she just shook her head frantically, listening to the chatter. For long minutes, Gyre stood with his arms crossed, feeling absurdly helpless. Finally the deep-voiced man spoke alone, and Elariel froze, her ears flattening. *That can't be good.*

"Gyre Silvereye," Tyraves said. Her tone was acid. "The Geraia is displeased at your presumption in coming here today. However." Her lips twisted unhappily. "There is a certain amount of curiosity as well. We tentatively accept your proposal."

Gyre let out a long breath. "Thank you. You won't regret it."

"We will not, whatever happens. Be assured we will make certain of that." Tyraves turned to Elariel. "As you requested, Elariel will accompany you as a . . . liaison."

"Perfect," Gyre said. But Elariel was still staring down at the table, her knuckles white.

"In order to be certain the security of Refuge is not compromised, precautions will be taken. She will be altered, so as to better carry out her mission." Tyraves gave a nasty smile. "By our laws, Elariel, this cannot be done without your consent. Do you give it?"

"What do you mean *altered*?" Gyre said. "And what happens if she won't consent?"

"If she refuses this assignment, then she will face her punishment for endangering the city, and die in the manner the Geraia feels most appropriate."

"That's stretching 'consent' a little far, don't you think?" Gyre said, feeling a sudden knot in his stomach. *Definitely not good.* "Elariel, I don't know what they want to do, but—"

"Your opinion is not required, *human*," Tyraves said. "The Geraia has spoken."

"I—"

"It's all right," Elariel cut him off. "I'll do it." She looked up at him, wide eyes liquid and ears drooping, with a forced smile. "It's got to be better than dying, right?"

From the ugly grin on Tyraves' face, Gyre wasn't certain he agreed.

Chapter 2

"B asel wants to see me," Maya said. "He hasn't said why, but I'm sure
it's an assignment."

Maya held Jaedia's hand, feeling the rough patches on her fingers,
calluses that matched Maya's own. Her master's hand was warm, and
her breath was gentle and steady. But her bright blue eyes remained
closed.

She lay on a bed in the Forge hospital. Like the rest of the Twilight
Order's fortress, it was built on a massive scale, with halls big enough
for hundreds. At the moment, Jaedia was the only long-term patient,
tucked in a corner behind hanging curtains. Maya sat by her bedside,
as she had every day.

They'd all been wounded after the fight at Leviathan's Womb, but
Jaedia's injuries weren't the kind quickheal could mend. Maya had
saved her life by burning the black spider's threads from her body, but
she'd been unconscious ever since, and the Forge's doctors seemed
helpless.

Maybe we need a dhakim. Whatever had been done to Jaedia was certainly a product of *dhaka*, though the Order's records contained nothing like it.

Maya touched the Thing, the nameless arcana embedded in the flesh above her sternum, then frowned. It had always been a sort of good-luck charm, but over the last few months, it had *reacted* when she drew on *deiat*, first when she'd fought Gyre in Deepfire and then again when she'd saved Jaedia's life. The Thing had grown hot enough to blister the flesh around it, and Maya had felt feverish and ill afterward. The doctors of the Forge had nothing to say about that, either.

"I have to go," Maya whispered. She squeezed Jaedia's limp hand. "Please just... wake up, if you can." She swallowed. "I miss you."

Just give me that, Maya thought. Not a prayer, precisely—the common people might beg for favors from the absent Chosen like the imaginary gods of old, but the Twilight Order knew there was no one left to ask. *Even so. I found her. I saved her. Please just let her wake up.*

Slowly, Maya got to her feet. Quickheal had closed the wound in her abdomen, but it still ached, and the too-tight skin pulled awkwardly. At least she was back in her uniform, with her haken on her hip.

All right, *Maya. Enough.* She pulled herself up and shook her head. *No more wallowing. There's work to do.*

Beq was waiting for her outside the hospital, perched on a stool, her nose buried in a thick, leather-bound book. Maya stood next to her and coughed politely.

"Mmm?" Beq said.

"Should I come back at a better time?" Maya said.

"What?" Beq looked up, eyes going wide, then shot to her feet. "Maya! No, of course not—I mean, I was waiting for you, so—"

Maya couldn't help but grin. "Beq. Beq!"

"Yes!" Beq squeaked, and took a breath. "Sorry."

"It's all right," Maya said. She leaned forward and kissed her, briefly but firmly.

Beq—Arcanist Bequaria, in full—was dark-skinned enough that she didn't show a blush easily, but her forehead creased adorably when she was embarrassed. She had a dusting of dark freckles and long, braided hair the color of leaves in high summer. Her eyes were a deep blue, oddly distorted behind the pair of elaborate arcana spectacles she always wore.

"I just don't get the chance to read much," Beq said. "They won't let us take books from the library into the field, and while I'm here there's always work to be done. And this is a treatise by Arcanist Rafini Screwloose, and I think this may be the only unexpurgated copy—"

"I'm sure it's fascinating," Maya said. "How are you feeling?"

"Me? I'm fine." Beq stamped her foot to demonstrate. "Nothing serious."

"The doctor said I should be okay," Maya said. "Just some aches and pains, but that'll pass."

"Good," Beq said. "That's good. I was . . . worried." She hesitated. "What about Jaedia?"

"The same," Maya said, swallowing a lump in her throat. "She seems all right, but she hasn't woken up. The doctors here will take care of her."

"You don't have to leave, you know," Beq said quietly. "The Council can't make you."

"I know." Maya kissed Beq again. "But Basel needs my help. He wouldn't ask if it weren't important."

"Probably not." Beq sighed. "If you're going out again, though . . ."

"Don't worry," Maya said. "If he's sending me somewhere, you're coming with me."

"Good." Beq's forehead creased further, and she looked down, fiddling with the dials that controlled her glasses. "That's good."

"You said that already."

"Yeah."

There was a long pause.

"I'd better go up," Maya said. "I'll see you afterward?"

Beq nodded and grinned.

Of all the things that had come out of the events of the last few months, Maya reflected as she climbed the endless circular stair at the heart of the Forge, her relationship with Beq was the most unexpected but perhaps the most welcome. It felt tentative, experimental—Maya had never so much as kissed anyone before—but at the same time she felt like she could no longer imagine her life without it. And Beq, thank the Chosen, seemed to feel the same way. They hadn't talked about it much, but they both seemed to want more than some sweaty, inexperienced fumbling in a camp tent.

Though I certainly want that also. Maya, having been stuck in the hospital since their return, had to admit to feeling a certain amount of…impatience in that regard. *Maybe once I'm done with Basel…*

She shook her head again, trying to clear it of pleasant distractions, as she climbed one last ring of stairs to the Forge's highest level, where the Kyriiarchs had their offices.

Baselanthus' office was familiar territory. It was small, by Forge standards, and crammed full of broken arcana. A few chairs sat in front of an unmetal desk cluttered with papers.

Maya thought the Kyriiarch himself looked older than he had the last time she'd been here. In spite of his sagging jowls and flyaway gray beard, he'd always seemed energetic and vital. Now he looked tired, his crimson eyes deep-sunk in their sockets. He sat back in his chair as Maya came in.

"Kyriiarch," Maya said, coming respectfully to attention.

"Please," Basel said. "No need for that. How do you feel?"

"Better," Maya said. "The doctors say there've been no difficulties. I need to work on regaining some flexibility, but otherwise I'm fit for action."

"I'm very relieved to hear it," Basel said. "And Jaedia? No change?"

"No," Maya said softly.

"I'm sorry I haven't had a chance to visit her," Basel said. "She was always chiding me about getting too caught up in"—he gestured grimly to the papers on his desk—"all this. But needs must, you know."

"You can see her once she wakes up," Maya said.

"No doubt." Basel smiled gently. "As you may have guessed, I have a request for you."

"Of course," Maya said.

"You'd better sit."

Maya took one of the chairs. Basel shuffled his papers for a moment, then sighed.

"I read your report with interest," he said. "As did the rest of the Council, naturally. Everyone agrees that you and Tanax acquitted yourself well in extremely difficult circumstances."

"Thank you," Maya said.

"A few of the details were... unclear. You convinced this rebel, Gyre Silvereye, to sabotage the weapon he'd come to steal?"

Maya swallowed. The fact that Gyre was her brother was the one thing she'd left out.

"I don't believe his intentions were bad," she said. "I think he was... misled. I made things clear to him."

"And he obviously succeeded, since no monstrosities from the Plague War have emerged from the mountains," Basel said. "But it leaves us with a great many unanswered questions."

"I have quite a few of those myself," Maya said. "Most of all regarding the plaguespawn that controlled Jaedia. And what Nicomidi thought he was doing there. He told me the Chosen spoke to him, and that they would return."

"Mmm." Basel leaned back in his chair. "The man may simply have gone mad, for all we know. That's usually the answer when someone claims the Chosen are speaking to them. But I agree it merits investigation. And the plaguespawn... well, rest assured that is the Council's highest priority. But we have few leads."

"There's really nothing in the records?" Maya said. "No one has encountered such a thing before?"

"The records are vast, and we have not searched every corner," Basel said. "But there is certainly nothing in any of the standard indices."

There can't be nothing. Maya set her jaw. The black spider had told her it was merely an *instrument. Whose instrument? Does that mean there are* more *of them out there?*

"I understand your frustration," Basel said. "Believe me, I want answers as much as you do."

"I know," Maya said. "It's just... that thing hurt Jaedia. I want to understand why."

"For the moment, the fact that you killed it will have to be good enough."

"Yes, Kyriliarch." Maya took a deep breath and calmed herself. "What do you need from me?"

"There are several unusual features to this matter," Basel said. "The first is that the request comes not from me, but from Kyriliarch Prodominus."

Prodominus? She'd only met the Revivalist leader a few times, and he'd never shown a particular interest in her.

"Kyriliarch Prodominus could have asked me directly," Maya said.

"He could have," Basel agreed. "I suspect he thought you would be more inclined to listen to a request from me."

"And he asked for me specifically?"

"He did."

"Do you know why?"

"No," Basel said. "Which is another unusual feature."

"And what does he want?"

"He declined to explain, other than that it would be dangerous and involve a considerable journey. Which, needless to say—"

"Is also unusual," Maya finished, smiling slightly. "I get the idea. But *you* are asking me to do it?"

"I am asking you to at least hear him out."

"May I inquire why?"

Basel sighed and steepled his hands. "These are fraught times, Maya. The Pragmatics are in the ascendant, for the moment. The Dogmatics are obviously in disarray after Nicomidi's betrayal, and I daresay we'll have his seat for one of ours before this is done. But we must move carefully. An open break on the Council would be bad for all of us, especially while the investigation into Nicomidi is ongoing. What he told you..."

"I thought you said he was mad."

"It's a possibility. But we must at least consider the theory that he had...confederates. Others who believed that, in some fashion, they can communicate with the Chosen."

"Which sounds a lot like the Revivalists," Maya said. "You don't trust Prodominus?"

"At this point, I don't trust anyone on the Council," Basel said. "If this group exists—which it may not, of course—then Nicomidi demonstrated that they are willing to act against the interests of the Order as a whole. That is extremely dangerous."

"I understand," Maya said. "You want me to spy on Prodominus."

"Not...exactly." Basel gave a slight smile. "I hope it does not offend you, my girl, if I say you are not an *ideal* spy. You are too...forthright. But if Prodominus has asked me to request your aid, he can hardly complain if you give me a full report afterward. Whatever he's doing, it's better that we know about it than not, don't you think?"

"I suppose. Unless his task is going to harm the Order."

"I rely on your judgment," Basel said. "*You*, I trust to keep the Order's interests foremost."

Maya felt a glow of pride at that, and sat up a little straighter. "Thank you, Kyriliarch."

"I am sorry to ask this of you, Maya," Basel said. "I know Jaedia wanted to keep you away from the Council and its rivalries, and I fear this may drag you further in. But..."

"Jaedia would understand," Maya said. "I can't hide from the rest of the Order. Nicomidi made that clear when he tried to have Tanax kill me in the arena."

"I suppose he did." Basel leaned forward again. "You'll help, then?"

"I'll do what I can."

"Thank you, Maya. I will let Prodominus know to expect you." He gave a broad smile. "You've made me very proud, you know. I'm sure Jaedia would say the same."

"Thank you, Kyriarch." Maya swallowed a lump in her throat. "I certainly hope so."

Prodominus' office was at the opposite end of the same floor, down a dusty corridor. A lonely sunstone burned on the far wall, throwing a pool of light around a half-open door. Maya paused on the threshold to straighten her uniform.

"That you, Burningblade?" said a gruff voice from inside. "Come in."

Prodominus' office was just as much a mess as Baselanthus', but with a distinctly martial flavor. A complete suit of Legionary armor stood in one corner, off-white and insectoid, and several blaster rifles in various stages of disassembly were laid out on a workbench. Another table held a wide variety of glasswork, beakers and pots and spiraling tubes. A heavy trunk full of hundreds of tiny bottles sat on the floor.

Prodominus himself sat with his feet up on a desk covered in books, each volume thick with paper-strip bookmarks. He was a big man, made to look bigger by the wildness of his hair and beard, which were orange-red and shaggy. The grin he turned on Maya was nearly lost in the tangle.

"Kyriarch," Maya said, coming to attention.

"Old Basel passed along my request, then." Prodominus sat up, chair creaking dangerously. "Have a seat if you like."

"Um." Maya looked around. "Where?"

The Kyriarch peered at the mess. "I think there's a chair under those cavalry sabers. Just chuck 'em on the floor."

Maya obediently picked up the bundle of antique swords and deposited them as gently as she could. The chair was gray with dust, and she had to fight the urge to wipe it with her sleeve before sitting.

"Thank you for coming, first of all," Prodominus said. "I know you don't have to listen to the crazy old Revivalist, so I want you to know I'm accounting this a personal favor."

"I'm happy to take on any task that's to the benefit of the Order," Maya said.

"Aren't we all? It's figuring out which those are that's the trick." Prodominus studied her for a moment. "Your report from the ghoul ruin made for interesting reading. But that was good work you did."

"Thank you, Kyriliarch."

"I take a personal interest in ghoul arcana." Prodominus waved at the worktable full of glassware. "*Dhak*, of course, but not the sort that requires a *dhakim*. There's a surprising amount you can do with just potions and powders. The scavenger you fought, the one who defeated you and Tanax. Is that how he did it?"

"In part." Maya hesitated for a moment, not sure how much to say. "He had explosives, certainly, and something that produced smoke. But he also used a blade that could penetrate a panoply field, and he seemed to be immune to most manifestations of *deiat*."

"Hmm." Prodominus' jaw worked as though chewing something tough. "Someone's been raiding some *deep* caverns."

"Is that what you want me to work on?"

"No, that's more in the nature of a side project," the Kyriliarch said. "This is a bit more urgent. Tell me, have you ever heard of the Archive?"

"I'm assuming you don't mean the archives here at the Forge."

"You assume correctly. The Archive is a Chosen facility, a repository of information about everything related to their empire and arcana. There were originally many copies, we think, but only one survives."

"I've never heard of such a thing," Maya said.

"It's not common knowledge, even among the Order."

"Why? It seems like it would be extremely useful."

"It would be, if we could get to it. The Archive is on the Forsaken Coast, across the Shattered Peaks. The nearest working Gate is a few days' walk, and the area is thick with plaguespawn."

Maya's eyes narrowed. "I wouldn't have thought a few plaguespawn would be a problem for a party of centarchs."

"It's not just a few. There are packs of them, and they're bigger and meaner than they ought to be. There have been six expeditions to the Archive in the last century, all led by centarchs, and only three of them came back."

"Plaguespawn don't form packs," Maya said. "Unless there's a *dhakim* controlling them."

"Indeed. There's *something* out there that doesn't want us around." Prodominus frowned. "That's why the Council keeps the place quiet. Otherwise too many young hotheads might take it into their minds to go get themselves killed."

"But you want me to go, I take it?"

"Quick on the uptake, you are." Prodominus sighed and leaned back in his chair. "I have a question I need answered, and the Archive is the only way. As far as we can tell, the more people we send over, the more attention they draw and the stronger the response. The best chance is to take a small team and hope to make it there and back without getting noticed."

"Why me?" Maya said. "Baselanthus said you requested me specifically."

It felt bold, coming right out with it, but Basel *had* told her to get whatever information she could. Prodominus looked at her silently for a moment, then gave a huge shrug.

"The information I need may bear on the business with Jaedia and Nicomidi," he said. "Or it may not, but I want to be prepared for the possibility. Outside the Council itself, only you and Tanax know the whole of that story, and he's already on another assignment. For the moment, the Kyriliarchs want to keep those cards close to our chest, which means not bringing in anyone new. Which means you."

Maya sat up straighter. *It has something to do with Jaedia.* "What do you need me to find?"

"We have a piece of Chosen arcana. We think it's important, but we don't know precisely why. The Archive will be able to tell us."

Prodominus rustled through the paperwork on his desk and finally came up with a sheaf of pages, bound together with string on one side. He tossed them to Maya. Flipping through, she saw drawings of a half-spherical device embedded with crystals. Three sharp prongs curved up like claws from its flat surface. There were careful sketches, inset with close-ups of details and markings. According to the accompanying text, the thing was small enough to hold in one hand.

"Where did you find it?" Maya said, turning the pages. "And why do you think it's important?"

"For the moment I'll have to keep that to myself," Prodominus said, looking uncomfortable. "Council business. You'll have to take it from me that I've got my reasons."

"Will we be able to find it in the Archive with just this? It's hard enough to dig anything useful out of the stacks here, and they were designed by humans."

"The Archive is a bit easier to use," Prodominus said. "It takes a fair charge of *deiat* to activate, though, so you'll have to do it yourself."

"I see." Maya looked back down at the pages, trying to think.

"Can I count on you?" Prodominus said. "I know it's a little bit—"

"Unusual," Maya said with a private smile. "But I'll do it." *Baselanthus is right. There's something odd here, and we're better off being on the inside than the outside.* "Can I choose my own team?"

"Of course. Not too many, and make sure it's people you trust."

"I have a couple in mind," Maya said. "When do you want me to leave?"

"As soon as you can. I'll authorize whatever you need from the quartermasters."

Maya got to her feet, papers at her side as she came to attention. "Then with your permission, Kyriliarch, I'll go and get started."

"Of course." Prodominus' expression was hard to read behind his beard. "Good luck, Burningblade."

"Varo!" Maya said. "Over here."

Varo threaded his way through the tables in the great checkerboard-tiled atrium of the Forge's logistics level. There were enough seats for hundreds, but only a few tables were occupied. Still, Maya gathered curious looks. The lower levels of the fortress were the domain of the Order's support services, the arcanists, scouts, archivists, and quarter-masters. Unable to wield *deiat*, they were nonetheless vital to the Order's mission, and Maya thought it was ridiculous that many cent-archs considered them beneath notice.

She and Beq sat at a square table, and Beq was already studying the packet of papers she'd gotten from Prodominus, several extra lenses over her eyes to let her focus on fine details. Varo pulled up a chair beside her and dropped into it with a sigh.

"It figures," he said without prompting. "I get sent away on another assignment *just* when you two get to do something really interesting."

"Deepfire wasn't *interesting* enough for you?"

"Eh." He waved vaguely. "It's just a city. Now, ghoul ruins are *really* exciting."

"Frankly," Beq said without looking up, "we could have done with a little less excitement."

"Any mission where everyone makes it back alive is a good mis-sion," Varo said. He ran a hand over his scalp, which was freshly shaved and scrubbed to a light brown sheen. "That's what my friend told me one time, at any rate. But he fell into a den of kite snakes and we had to amputate both his arms, so maybe he would have disagreed after-ward."

"I missed you," Maya said, laughing. "At least *you* seem to have made it back intact."

"Oh, I always do, more's the pity." Varo poked Beq in the shoulder. "Good to see you, too."

"Right," Beq said, still peering at the papers. "Good to ... you know. Thing."

"Leave her be," Maya said. "I need to ask you something."

"If it's about the story with the cannibal barbers—"

"Not like that," Maya said, suppressing a grin. "I've got an assignment.

It's supposed to be a really nasty place, out on the Forsaken Coast. I'd like it if you'd come with us, but I'm not going to order you. My guess is we'll be in serious danger."

"Ah." Varo sat back in his chair. "Who else is on the team?"

"It will just be the three of us," Maya said.

"That's all right, then. You two can take care of yourselves." He gave a resigned sigh. "I'd hate to have some other poor bastard join up and get killed."

"Nobody got killed last time," Beq said, flipping a page. "Maybe you've broken your streak of bad luck."

"Never say that," Varo moaned. "It's bad luck."

Maya laughed and turned to Beq. "So do those drawings tell you anything?"

"Not...much." Beq looked up at last, touching the side of her spectacles. Lenses clicked and flipped out of the way. "There's some pieces that look familiar, but I don't know enough to say what they might be doing. There's something odd going on, but without the actual thing to look at..."

"I suppose that's why we're going to this Archive." Maya quickly summarized their objective for Varo, while Beq became increasingly excited.

"I can't *believe* the Council has a source like this and doesn't tell anyone," Beq said. "Can you imagine what we could ask it? We could finally find out what the point of an Ackman junction is, or how to activate the third sequence of the—"

"I'm a little more interested in the *packs* of plaguespawn," Varo said. "Prodominus was certain of that?"

"He was," Maya said. "But you'll like this part. He's given us full access to the stacks here to prepare, including the restricted sections." She produced Prodominus' letter with a flourish. "We've got the run of the place."

"Well, *that's* something." Varo looked at the Kyriliarch's illegible signature. "He must really trust you."

"I'm not sure *why*, but he seems to," Maya said. "If you're coming, Varo, we'd better get started."

The restricted section was at the back of the stacks, walled off from the rest by a heavy barred grating. One of the archivists read the letter from Prodominus, lips pressed together in disapproval, and went to get a ring of keys. The grate swung open with a groan, and the archivist glared at the three of them like they were children being given the run of the sweet shop.

"Don't remove anything," she said. "Call for a copyist if you need to. Don't try to return anything to the shelves, you'll only lose it, just stack it on the table when you're finished. And *please* be careful with the materials. Some of these books are very fragile." Her gaze fixed on Maya. "And if you even *think* of using any fire—"

"I understand," Maya said, spreading her hands. "We'll be careful."

"Hmph."

The archivist stalked off, and Maya and Beq exchanged looks. Varo was already moving ahead, a glowing sunstone in hand. The ceiling was low, and heavy metal shelves crowded in on all sides, thick with dust. There were books, of course, but also curled scrolls in ivory cases and pages loosely bound with twine.

"What *is* all this stuff?" Maya brushed the gray off of one spine and read, "*Notes on the Proceedings of the Twenty-Third Senate?* Why would the Council care if people read that?"

"Probably nobody remembers," Varo said, holding up the sunstone as he peered at the books. "Stuff gets shoved in here because some Kyriliarch thinks it ought to, and no one ever goes back and looks at it again."

"My master in the arcanists was always angry about it," Beq said, her voice full of quiet reverence. "He said that we end up redoing work that had been done a hundred years ago because the Council never bothered to let anyone read it."

"This goes on forever," Maya said. "What are we looking for, exactly?"

"The reports from the previous expeditions, to begin with," Varo said. "And anything about the region. I'm hoping there's at least a decent map."

"Should be over this way," Beq said, pointing around a corner.

Maya, who had not spent any time with the intricacies of the Forge's filing system, quickly found herself reduced to the role of passive observer. There was a small table, and Varo and Beq quickly filled it with a stack of loose-bound reports, as well as some proper books that Varo said might come in handy. They set to reading, Varo scribbling notes on a fresh sheet of paper.

"This sounds like one of yours," Beq read aloud. "'At the end of a day's travel, Scout-Trainee Festig complained of pain in his left foot. After removing his boot, we discovered a scorpion had taken up residence and had stung him repeatedly. His foot commenced to swell to three times its normal size, and on observing the putrefaction moving up his limb Centarch Ghisa Ragewell was forced to remove it.'"

"Amateur." Varo sniffed. "Checking your boots for scorpions is the first thing they teach you as a scout. Standards clearly weren't as high in those days." He paused. "Mind you, it didn't help one of my friends. The plaguing thing was hiding in the privy, and it stung him right in the—"

Beq snorted laughter.

"You want to talk about *swelling*," Varo muttered. "Course, he wasn't complaining."

After a few attempts to read something herself, Maya decided she was better off leaving them to it. She started walking back and forth along the shelves, occasionally reaching out to rub the dust away from an obscured title, not really expecting to find anything.

What's wrong with me? She felt restless, unsettled. The prospect of being in the field with her friends *ought* to have been attractive. And she *was* looking forward to it, especially the chance to spend some time alone with Beq. *Varo, at least, can be relied on to butt out when I need him to.*

But there was more. *Prodominus said this might have something to do with what happened to Jaedia and Nicomidi.* He'd refused to explain any further, but he clearly knew more than he was telling. *Why? Why bring me into this and not tell me everything?*

There's still too much I don't understand. The black spider, Nicomidi's madness, the strange plaguespawn and constructs that had torn each other to pieces in front of the ghoul ruins. *And Gyre.* He'd fought her once, back at Raskos Rottentooth's warehouse, and his alchemical tricks had been no match for *deiat*. But the second time, on the docks beside that mammoth *thing*, he'd been like a different person entirely.

And he has a silver eye. There were rumors of *dhakim* who could replace lost limbs, but she'd never heard of someone getting an *eye. So is he working* with *the black spider, or against it? How many sides are there?*

She hadn't heard anything from him since they'd parted. Not a surprise, of course. But somehow she'd half expected he'd come in from the cold once he thought things over. *He stopped that ghoul weapon. He's not a bad person, I know it.*

Her hand paused on the shelf, midway through wiping away a layer of grime. The title of the book, picked out in flaking silver leaf, was *A Basic Dictionary of Formal High Chosen.*

For their everyday language, Maya knew, the Chosen had relied on the same tongue that humans now spoke throughout their former empire. But they'd had another tongue, old even by Elder standards, that they'd used for sacred or ritual occasions, now called High Chosen. *Who put a dictionary in the restricted section?* Maya went to move on, then paused. *Maybe...*

She pulled the book out, turning the ancient pages with care. Even so, the edges crumbled under her fingers.

The black spider called me sha'deia. First in Bastion, where she'd found it attached to Hollis Plaguetouch, and again when she'd confronted Jaedia. It wasn't a word Maya knew, but it had the sound of High Chosen. *It said I might be "the one." The one what?*

It took her a while to struggle through the dictionary's arcane organization, and longer to cross-reference lists of meanings. High Chosen was hellaciously complex, words changing their function depending on prefixes, context, or even the speaker. Maya dug out a sheet of foolscap and scribbled notes, and after half an hour of swearing and crossing things out she'd managed to compile a short list of reasonable guesses.

Sha'deia:

Precious Seed.

Reserved Child.

Maya's fingers brushed the last line, and she swallowed. Her other hand came up, unbidden, to touch the Thing.

Beloved Daughter.

Chapter 3

The door to Elariel's chamber slid open. It was dark inside, even for
Refuge. With his silver eye, Gyre could see a person-sized bundle
of sheets on the bed, curled up and facing the wall.

"If that's you, Tyraves," Elariel mumbled, "go away and fuck yourself
with a jagged iron pole."

"That's . . . quite an image," Gyre said. "But it's me."

It had been three days since the end of the trial. The ghouls had
taken Elariel away and given Gyre a small sleeping chamber, with a
soldier-construct watching the door in case he had any illusions about
his status. Most of his time had been spent haggling with Tyraves
over the logistics of his expedition. Money had been the simplest of
his needs—the ghouls could forge Republic thalers easily. Alchemical
ingredients, too, she'd been happy to provide, but the core of Gyre's
requests had proven more contentious. Blades like his own silver
sword that could cut unmetal armor and the fields that offered protection against *deiat*; these were the keys to facing the Order in battle,
but they were also the hardest to explain away as scavenger finds. In

the end, Tyraves had grudgingly agreed to part with a limited number of each.

"I'm sorry I haven't been to see you sooner," Gyre said. "They said you were still recovering from your procedure."

"Recovering from my procedure," Elariel said, voice thick. "That's one way of putting it."

"Are you all right?" Gyre let the door close behind him. Moss overhead started to glow weakly. "Can I help?"

"I'm not all right, and no one can help," Elariel said.

"Okay," Gyre said. "But they want us to leave today. Do you think you're going to be up to it?"

Silence. Gyre blew out a breath and crossed the room, squatting beside the bed.

"Elariel," he said gently, laying a hand on her shoulder. "I don't know what happened—"

"Don't *touch* me!"

Elariel twitched like a landed fish in her blanket cocoon, and Gyre hastily backed away. She managed to thrash herself off the bed entirely, landing on the floor with a *thump*, and fought wildly to escape from the tangled sheet. Gyre's eyes widened as she emerged, kicking the bedding away and sitting with her back to the bed, breathing hard.

The Elariel he remembered, with red-brown fur, huge eyes, and long, pointed ears, was gone. In her place was...

...a human.

She looked to be twenty or so, with milk-pale skin and hair the color of the old Elariel's fur. Something about her face still held a trace of her former self, eyes a little too wide, ears slightly pointed. Her once-sharp teeth were now flat and perfectly white.

"Elariel?" Gyre said. He couldn't help a note of disbelief, but regretted it immediately. Tears welled in her eyes, and she angrily knuckled them away.

"Yes, it's me." Her voice, at least, was the same. "Just...*altered*."

"Chosen defend," Gyre muttered.

"It's only logical," Elariel spat. "If I'm going to go far from Refuge, and there's a chance I could be killed or captured, we can't have my corpse raising too many awkward questions. I'm sure Tyraves was laughing at the irony."

"Are you..." Gyre shook his head. "Is it permanent?"

"I suppose they could change me back, but why would they want to?" She drew her knees up to her chest and hugged them. "They're not going to let me back into Refuge, whatever happens."

She hid her face, and her shoulders shook with quiet sobs. Gyre waited until the silence grew too awkward to bear.

"I'm so sorry," he said. "When I asked for you as liaison, I didn't think—"

"Of course not," Elariel said. "How could you know? You're just a *human*."

Another silence, even more awkward.

"I'm sorry," Elariel said. "It's not your fault. This is...better than being tortured to death, obviously. I just..." She sucked in a breath. "You have no idea how painful the last few days have been."

"I think I do, actually," Gyre said. He closed his eyes for a moment, and his mind filled with Naumoriel's knives and his own hoarse screams.

"I suppose you might," Elariel said, looking up. Her eyes were red from crying, but she set her jaw decisively. "You said you're ready to go?"

"More or less."

"Then let's get the *fuck* out of here." Elariel clambered to her feet. "I don't want to—What?"

Gyre looked deliberately away. She was naked. Of course, she'd always been naked, all the ghouls were, but their thick fur made it less...obvious.

"We're going to need to get you some clothes first," he said.

"Oh." Elariel looked down at herself. "I suppose it'll be colder on the surface."

"That's...one reason." He caught her inquisitive expression and sighed. *I may have some explaining to do.*

*   *   *

In the end, the ghouls came up with a crude wardrobe for Elariel, to which Gyre added his own traveling cloak. *We can buy something better in Deepfire.*

The supplies he'd asked for were too heavy to carry on foot, so Tyraves agreed to deliver them to a spot on the western road in three days' time. That would give them a chance to secure transportation and a few other things he needed. For the moment, he carried only a satchel packed with thalers and a half dozen energy bottles.

Tyraves rode with them in a transporter through the long, curving tunnels, coming to a stop near an apparently impenetrable rock face. At a gesture from her, it slid apart far enough for them to slip through, revealing a hint of morning sunlight. The ghoul turned away, shielding her eyes.

"Human," she said. "I don't pretend that I believe this absurd venture will succeed. But I trust you will try your hardest to justify the unprecedented faith the Geraia has placed in you."

"Give them my thanks," Gyre said.

"Elariel knows how to reach us with a message," Tyraves said, pointedly not looking at Elariel herself. "But she should not bother unless you have good news to report. Expect no further help from Refuge until you have proven your worth."

"I get the idea," Gyre said, temper fraying a little. He held his hand out to Elariel. "Let's go."

They slipped down from the transporter. Kit's spider, silent since Gyre had entered Refuge, still clung to one shoulder. He hoisted the pack full of thalers on the other and headed for the sliver of daylight. Elariel followed, blinking and rubbing her eyes.

They emerged into a narrow mountain valley. The door waited only moments before sliding closed with a shallow *boom*, leaving no trace of its presence behind.

"It's ... bright." Elariel kept one hand over her face.

"Your eyes should adapt, if they're human now." Something poked Gyre not very gently in the back of the neck. "Yes, Kit, go ahead."

"Oh-my-*fucking*-Chosen-defend-son-of-a-stinking-plaguepit," Kit said, all in a rush. Her voice rose into song. "Gisela was a lusty lass, her breasts were big as mountains, and I'll tell you 'bout her—"

"Is this *really* necessary?" Gyre interrupted.

"*You* try spending four days in enforced silence," Kit said. "I'm never going to make fun of those monks up on Mount Shiver again. You know they do that for *years*? I'd go mad. *Mad*."

"Don't you have other bodies to keep yourself occupied?"

"I've got a dozen at the rendezvous point, but they're just waiting. *Bor*ing." The spider skittered higher up Gyre's shoulder. "I could barely stop myself from giving you advice when you fucked everything up."

"Thank you," Gyre said, "for your forbearance."

"Excuse me," Elariel said. "Your construct is talking."

"I know," Gyre said.

"All right," Elariel said, with the air of someone carefully remaining calm. "It's just that they don't, as a rule. And I wanted to make sure *I* wasn't going mad. Under the circumstances it wouldn't surprise me."

"You're not mad," Gyre said wearily. "Let me make reintroductions. Elariel, Kitsrea Doomseeker. Kit, Elariel. Elariel looks human now, and Kit's a construct. Everyone clear?"

"No," Elariel said. "Not remotely." She looked more closely at the little spider. "You told me that Kit was dead."

"I am!" Kit said. "Kind of."

"When Naumoriel tried to activate the Leviathan, there was an explosion," Gyre explained. He felt a twinge of guilt at the lie, but he wasn't sure Elariel would appreciate his role in what had happened. "Kit was dying. Naumoriel had explained how the Leviathan's control system worked, the transfer of a mind into the Core Analytica, so I thought it was worth a try."

"Sure," Kit said, "why not take your mortally wounded lover and shove her into an ancient machine of uncertain effectiveness? What could go wrong?"

"Well," Elariel said, "to begin with, if the transfer had failed partway, you could have been left a twisted wreck, in eternal agony—"

"Believe me, *I have thought of that*," Kit said.

"It worked," Gyre said. "The Leviathan is still crippled, of course, but its construct swarm still functions."

"That's...fascinating." Elariel shook her head. "And you are... yourself? Fully intelligent?"

"I mean, as far as I know," Kit said. "How would I tell?"

"There were always debates about whether an Analytica of sufficient complexity could support a true mind," Elariel said. "But of course, what defines 'mind'? Self-recognition? Surely too simple. Perhaps some tests—"

"Gyre, promise you won't let her take me apart," Kit said.

"You have other bodies."

"It's the principle of the thing."

"I'll do my best," Gyre said. "But for now you're going to have to leave us and head to the rendezvous."

"*Bor*ing," Kit singsonged.

"In Deepfire they'd think you're a plaguespawn, and being taken apart would be the least of your problems."

"Yeah, yeah." Kit released her hold and dropped agilely to the ground. "If you're not there on time, I'm going to assume you're dead and find someone else to amuse me."

"Thanks."

The little construct scuttled off, losing itself surprisingly quickly in the rocks.

"I don't remember her being so..." Elariel made a vague but evocative gesture.

"You didn't know her as well as I did," Gyre said, shifting his pack. "Though being dead has definitely made her...more so."

Elariel tentatively lowered her hand from her eyes, blinking in the bright sunlight, and looked around curiously. It was, Gyre realized, probably the first time she'd been aboveground and unprotected in daylight.

"It's very...blue," she said after a moment.

"The sky?"

Elariel nodded. "I hope you have some idea where we are, because I certainly don't."

"More or less," Gyre said. "At the bottom of this valley, we ought to be able to see Hunter's Gap. We can be in Deepfire by nightfall."

"Deepfire." Elariel looked uncertain. "We have no other choice?"

"It's the only place around here we'll find the supplies we need," Gyre said. "And I still have contacts there. Believe me, I don't like it any better than you do." He wasn't sure how far the legend of Gyre Silver-eye had spread, but in Deepfire the chance of someone recognizing him was high. *Cross that bridge when we come to it.* "We won't be there for long."

"All right." Elariel took several deep breaths. "I am...in your debt, Gyre. After everything my master did to you, you...saved my life. I hope to make myself as useful as I can."

"It was the right thing to do." Gyre scratched his head, embarrassed. "Come on. Let's get walking."

It took considerably longer to reach the city than Gyre had expected, thanks to an amateur mistake on his part. He'd secured basic clothing for Elariel, but he'd forgotten to ask about *shoes*. Elariel herself hadn't even considered footwear, since ghouls had tough, calloused feet and generally went without. Her new, human soles were as soft as if she'd spent her life in a carpeted palace. It took only a few minutes of picking their way down the slope before she was badly scraped.

Gyre tried to improvise, ripping up his spare shirt and winding the rags around Elariel's feet, but it didn't improve matters much. The ghoul did her best, but the pain was visible on her face, and she left a trail of bloody marks on the rock. Too much of that and she wouldn't be able to walk at all. Gyre called a halt.

They were to the north of the city, on the same road he and Kit had taken on their first, desperate trip to Refuge. "Road" was an exaggeration, of course—it was nothing more than a vague track, descending from the outside lip of the Deepfire crater. At the head of the valley, part of the crater wall had collapsed, forming a low point called Hunter's Gap. A set of crude stone steps had been hacked into the rock to make the way easier, but it was still a considerable climb.

There was no way Elariel was walking up those steps, and Gyre could see she knew it. Her face paled.

"Go ahead," she said. "I'll... make my way up more slowly."

"Don't be stupid," Gyre said. "I'm not leaving you out here alone."

"But..."

"Here." Gyre knelt in the dust, cupping his hands behind his back. "Get on."

The ghoul looked on the verge of tears. "I..."

"I'm sorry if it's undignified, all right? There's nobody to see."

"I'm not concerned for my *dignity*. I'm supposed to be helping, not some sort of... burden." Her brow furrowed. "Perhaps..."

"Just get on, all right?"

Elariel nodded and climbed gingerly onto his back, wrapping her arms around his neck. He caught her legs, careful of her injured feet. Gyre rose and shifted his balance, then set off up the valley, sticking to the flattest part of the path.

It made for an exhausting climb. Just reaching the stairs had Gyre's legs burning, each step sending waves of pain through his thighs. He was sweating freely. The switchbacks loomed, somehow taller than in his memory.

"Here," Elariel said in his ear. "This will help."

Her hand pressed to his cheek, and a wave of cool relief ran through him. The pain in his legs vanished, and his breath came easier.

"What did you do?" Gyre said.

"A touch of *dhaka*, nothing more."

Dhaka. Elariel was a *dhakim*, like all ghouls. It was easy to forget. "Ah. Thanks."

She heard the hesitation in his voice. "Should I not have done that?"

"Just warn me first, next time."

"I understand." She settled her head on his shoulder as he started up the steps. "I have a great deal to learn about humans. Among ghouls, feeling another in pain and not taking it away as a matter of course would be considered insultingly rude."

"You can't do anything about your feet?"

"Working *dhaka* on oneself is extremely dangerous," she said. "It can create a sort of . . . loop. It's hard to explain. But it's an easy way to die."

"Blisters are probably preferable," Gyre said. "I don't need to tell you not to use *dhaka* where anyone but me can see, do I?"

"I understand that much, at least," Elariel said. "You humans inherited the foolish notions of your Chosen masters."

"No argument," Gyre said. "And that's what we're trying to change, but we don't want to get strung up as *dhakim* beforehand."

The sun dropped toward the horizon as Gyre worked his way up the steps. Elariel took away his pain twice more. Without her help he would have had to give up and rest until morning. As it was, the sky was a deep purple when they crested the Gap and staggered onto the more gentle downslope of the Deepfire crater. The city was a cluster of distant lights, sprawling to either side of the sullen red glow of the Pit, like the aftermath of a giant axe blow into the earth.

Fortunately there was a hostel not far from the gap, a ways outside Deepfire proper. Gyre staggered in well after dark, Elariel still clinging to his back. The proprietor, a leather-skinned old woman, barely gave them a second glance. *No doubt she's seen sorrier bunches straggle in.* Gyre paid for a room and a late dinner but collapsed into bed before the latter even arrived.

In the morning, he woke up and found himself unable to move. He'd expected to be stiff, but this was much worse. When he tried to bend his leg, it only trembled, and his arms were little better. He managed to sit up and tugged at his trousers, finding thick black bruises blossoming all along his thighs.

"Elariel." Gyre tried not to let the panic into his voice. "*Elariel*. Wake up, please."

"Mmlrg." Elariel, lying on the small room's other bed, rolled over. She'd stripped naked again. "What...oh." She put her hand to her forehead. "I thought I was having a nightmare for a moment."

"You're not dreaming, and I can't move my legs," Gyre said. He lowered his voice to a whisper, aware of the thin walls. "You did something with *dhaka*. What happened?"

She let out a sigh and rolled out of bed.

"Would you put your shirt on?" Gyre said.

"Why?" She knelt next to him and put her hands on his thigh. "Is someone likely to come in?"

Gyre shook his head and tried to keep his eyes on her face.

"Your muscles are all torn up," she said. "There are fractures in the bones, too. I think...perhaps I went too far. Without pain, you exerted yourself past the point of damaging your body."

"It couldn't be helped," Gyre said. "We had to get over the Gap somehow. Can you do anything so I can at least walk?"

"I can speed your healing. And take the pain away, but—"

"Can you leave me a *bit* of pain? Enough to remind me to take it easy?"

Elariel nodded. A moment later, blessed relief swept over Gyre, leaving only a dull ache.

"I am sorry," Elariel said. "I am not...experienced with these matters."

"It's...aah...all right." Gyre managed to swing his legs off the bed and winced. *Maybe I should ask for a* little *less pain*. He gritted his teeth instead and got to his feet. "We don't have much walking to do anyway."

"I assume you have an agenda in mind?"

"Indeed." Gyre let out a pained breath and hobbled to the door. "First stop, breakfast."

After breakfast Gyre managed to flag down a rickety two-wheeler cab with a tired-looking loadbird in a harness. The driver looked like she was at the end of a long shift and merely raised an eyebrow at the disheveled appearance of her two passengers. Gyre told her to take them to the West Central district and quieted her objections to the long ride by handing her twice what the trip was worth.

That set the tone for the rest of the morning. The bag full of thalers functioned like a magic key, opening doors that ought to have stayed shut and closing mouths that ought to have asked questions. The smoke-drooling chimneys of the manufactories disappeared, replaced with respectable stone apartment buildings and glass-windowed shops. Traffic was heavy, pedestrians fighting for space with carts pulled by loadbirds and thickheads, with the occasional rider on a swiftbird or even a pony pushing through. As always, the smell of the dung was staggering if you weren't used to it. Elariel wrinkled her nose in distaste.

Their first stop was a shop that catered to well-heeled scavengers, where Gyre was unlikely to be recognized. The proprietor looked like he was on the verge of calling the guards when they entered, but a glance in the bag rapidly changed his tune. Gyre dropped hints to the effect that he and Elariel had narrowly escaped disaster, losing all their gear but securing a big payday, and the shop owner was only too happy to help them "replace" their wardrobes.

An hour later, and the two of them walked out wearing brand-new outfits, clean and well fitted, leather padding still soft and supple. Sets of spares and other useful gear—including underthings for Elariel, a concept he'd had to quietly explain to her—he arranged to have delivered to the west gate on the morning of their departure.

"It pulls when I move," Elariel said, twisting awkwardly to try to look at herself. "And it's always *pressing* on my skin. How do you humans stand this?"

"We get used to it, I guess."

"It comes of not being properly equipped for your environment." Elariel sniffed.

"Probably. But we're all in the same boat now." Her face fell so abruptly Gyre winced. "Sorry. I know it's hard."

Gyre's hand came up to scratch at his old scar, and he stopped himself with an effort. He'd gotten a black silk eye patch, secured with a jaunty red band, to cover up the ghoul-made eye. It still left him more recognizable than he would have liked, so he'd added a new hooded cloak, pulled up to keep his face mostly shadowed. *Now I just look like someone trying to hide. Wonderful.*

There was nothing to be done, though, without the closetful of disguises he'd left behind at Lynnia's. Fortunately, while there were Auxie patrols on every corner in West Central, there was plenty of traffic to keep them occupied. *It's still Deepfire, after all. I'm hardly the only one-eyed man, or the only person who wants to keep out of sight.*

He walked around the block, watching the crowds carefully for tails, before heading off in another direction. After crossing another two streets, he paused to put his back to the brick wall of a shop selling meat pies. Elariel pressed in beside him, her shoulder against his. He glanced at her, surprised, and found her breathing hard. Sweat beaded on her forehead.

"Is something wrong?" he said. "Is it your feet?" She had new boots now, specially fitted, but they still might need breaking in—

"I'm fine," Elariel muttered.

"You're not."

"It's just…" She looked at him, eyes a little panicked. "There are so *many* of you."

Ah. That made sense. There were no crowds in Refuge, unless you counted constructs, which the ghouls did not. And her visits to Deepfire had avoided people, for obvious reasons.

"It's all right," Elariel said. "I need to get used to it."

"We can take it slowly," Gyre said. "Stay here a moment. I'll get us something to eat."

The meat pies were delicious, soft and flaky, the filling hot enough to burn. Gyre broke his open and demonstrated how to blow across it. Elariel sniffed, then took a cautious bite. In a few moments, she'd finished the whole thing, unselfconsciously licking her fingers.

"You never tried the food when you were up here?" Gyre said.

"I couldn't exactly go out to the corner stall," Elariel said. "Besides, who knew humans could make something so...good." She stared down at her hands and shook her head.

"The secret," Gyre said, "is that not *everything* is made out of fungus."

Their next destination was a stablemaster's office, serving the same sort of deep-pocketed clientele as the previous shop. The actual stables, with their unruly, stinking animals, were on the edge of town—this was more like a quiet parlor, with leather chairs and a well-stocked bar, where gentlemen could make an agreement to outfit an expedition. Now that he and Elariel looked the part, a smiling young woman in a riding outfit with dark blue hair piled in a tall bun came right over.

"Welcome," she said. "You look like someone who knows what he's after."

"I do indeed," Gyre said. "Hardshells. How many have you got?"

"Hardshells?" She sounded taken aback. "Three. But—"

"I'll take them. With full tack and wagons. Are they trained for caravanning?"

"Of course," the woman said, then shook her head. "Are you certain, sir? If you're planning to go far into the mountains, hardshells are not a good choice. They're slow in the cold, and they take slopes poorly—"

"Let me worry about that," Gyre said.

"Very well," she said, going stiff. "And how long will you be requiring them?"

"Oh, I won't be bringing them back."

That set off a whole new round of questions and objections, which Gyre finally silenced by counting stacks of thalers out of the bag until the stablemaster's jaw was hanging open. She finally agreed to deliver the beasts, with wagons and tack, and stood blinking as Gyre grinned at her and left the shop.

"Is it not usual to purchase beasts?" Elariel said, following close behind. "I thought that was the purpose of this establishment."

"I imagine they do more hires than sales," Gyre said. "And hard-shells aren't useful for scavengers. But *we* are not going farther into the mountains."

"I will trust your judgment," Elariel said. "So we have...clothes and beasts of burden for transportation. What remains? Provisions?"

"We can handle that tomorrow morning, as we're heading out," Gyre said. "Next up is securing the rest of our cargo." He sighed. "Which is, unfortunately, going to be the hard part."

Lynnia's was a two-story stone building, narrow and deep, with a slate roof and neatly painted facade that screamed respectability. To the authorities, she was an elderly spinster who took in occasional boarders for pin money. Only those well-connected to the world of scavengers and smugglers knew there was a well-equipped alchemist's lab buried under the house, and that the concoctions Lynnia brewed there were the best in the business.

Unfortunately, Lynnia hadn't forgiven him for his role in Yora's death, and Gyre wasn't sure she should. *I'm a long way from forgiving myself.* Yora had been almost a daughter to her.

He pinched the bridge of his nose, trying to think of something to say. Elariel, behind him, shifted uneasily.

"Is something wrong?" she said.

"This may be...tricky," Gyre said. "Just follow my lead. I know how to handle Lynnia Sharptongue."

He knocked, and there was a rustling inside, then the step-drag sound of Lynnia walking on her bad leg. The door opened and she looked up at him. She was a tiny thing, really, wrinkled and spotted, her black hair hacked short. The signs of her craft were there for anyone who knew how to look, fingertips stained with acid, eyebrows patchy from explosive mishaps.

"Hello, sir," she said. "Are you looking for lodging?"

"Lynnia, it's me." Gyre pulled back his hood.

"Gyre." Her eyes narrowed. "You promised me I'd never see you again."

"I know," Gyre said. "I'm sorry. But I need your help."

"Course you do," the old woman grumbled, digging in her pocket.

Gyre hesitated a moment, which turned out to be a moment too long. Lynnia pulled out a small clay ball, already smoking. She held it in front of his eyes, where it burst in a great, silent flare of light, singeing Gyre's face and leaving him blinded by flickering afterimages.

"Think Lynnia's a pushover, do you?" As Gyre clutched at his real eye with both hands, one of the alchemist's heavy boots connected with his knee, and a spike of agony sent him toppling forward. "A soft touch? Just turn up with a sob story and she'll let bygones be bygones? I told you last time that it *was* the last time, boy, and I meant it."

Gyre struggled for breath, lying just inside her front door. From the feel of it, Lynnia was now standing on his back, and something sharp pricked against the side of his neck.

"Wander in here with a new pretty girl on your arm, asking for *help*." She spat on the floor beside his head. "Get tired of the last one already? Or did you get her killed too?" Her weight shifted, bringing fresh pain. Her voice was right in his ear. "Now, pick yourself up and get off my doorstep before I call the Auxies—"

"Please get off him." Elariel's voice.

"Back off, girlie. Just 'cause you've got a nice ass doesn't mean I won't stick you—"

There was a sudden silence, and then a clatter as Lynnia hit the ground. Free of her weight, Gyre rolled over and gasped for breath, still unable to see anything except flickering blue and green.

"Lynnia?" He coughed. "Elariel, what happened?"

"She was hurting you," Elariel said, a little panicky. "I didn't know—"

"Is she all right?"

"She's just sleeping."

Gyre relaxed slightly. He pressed his palm against his real eye and flipped up the eye patch so he could see out of the silver one. Lynnia lay on the floor beside him, a paring knife in her hand, breath whistling through her nose. Elariel hovered in the doorway, hugging herself.

"Shut the door," Gyre groaned, gathering his aching legs under him. "The last thing we need is the Auxies wandering by—"

"Lynnia?" Another woman's voice, and a tread on the stairs. "What in the name of the Chosen is going—Lynnia!" Gyre turned in time to see someone in the kitchen doorway. "What have you done to her?"

"Hi, Sarah." Gyre held up his hands. "This is, um, not how I envisioned this going."

Sometime later, the four of them sat in Lynnia's parlor, with Gyre and Elariel on the couch and Lynnia and Sarah in the facing armchairs. Lynnia was sunk deep into the cushions, aggressively drinking tea and clutching a modest bump on her head. She was still glaring daggers at Gyre, but at least she'd put the actual knife away.

Sarah, on the other hand, seemed pleased to see him. She was a big, cheerful girl with a mass of red curls a few shades lighter than Elariel's. She was looking much better than the last time he'd seen her, the burns and bruises mostly healed. Shiny coin-sized scars dotted her face and neck, and her left arm was gone just below the shoulder, courtesy of a blaster bolt she'd barely survived during the Order ambush.

"It's good to see you," Sarah said. "We were worried."

Lynnia snorted.

"*I* was worried," Sarah amended. "After I made you... those things." Her eyes went to Elariel.

"It's good to see you too," Gyre said. "This is Elariel, and you can trust her."

Elariel gave a respectful nod, and Lynnia snorted again.

"I take it the bombs worked?" Sarah said.

"To perfection," Gyre said. "Thank you."

"I read about the attack on the Spike," Sarah said. "They tried to keep it quiet, but rumors got around. Was that you?"

Gyre spread his hands, mock-humbly.

"Is this going to be like last time?" Lynnia snapped. "Where you breeze in with a bag of thalers and demand the impossible overnight?"

"In fairness, you did manage last time," Gyre said. "But it's a little bit more than that. I'd like to buy your stock."

"My stock?" Lynnia narrowed her eyes. "My stock of what?"

"Everything," Gyre said. "Explosives, quickheal, bone-break potion, whatever you've got. I have a wagon leaving the city tomorrow morning, and I need to fill it. Money is no object."

"Money is no object," Lynnia repeated in disbelief. "People like to say that, but it's never true."

"It's true this time. Charge me double, I don't care."

Lynnia's lip curled, but he could see warring emotions in her face. She hadn't gotten to be the best alchemist in Deepfire by passing up a good deal.

"I don't have enough to fill a wagon," she said. "Not even close. And I can't just magic up more on a moment's notice."

"Buy out your competitors," Gyre said promptly. "Tell them you'll outbid their clients."

"You can't be serious," Lynnia said. "You want to buy up every alchemical in the city?"

"As many as I can get my hands on." Gyre opened his bag and started counting stacks of thalers onto the coffee table. He stopped when Lynnia leaned forward in her seat. There was already enough money on the table to buy the house they were sitting in and a few on either side.

"You..." Lynnia's lips twitched. "Fuck it. Fine. I'm not made of fucking stone. But don't think this means I've forgotten what you did."

"I know." Gyre shook his head. "I don't expect you to forgive me. But I'm doing my best—"

"I don't give a shit. Yora's still dead." Lynnia got up abruptly. "I'm going to write a few notes. Sarah, are you going to be all right with him?"

"I'll be fine," Sarah said.

Lynnia muttered and shuffled out. They heard her descending into the workshop, and Gyre let out a breath.

"Sorry," Sarah said. "She's... well. You know her."

"I do. And she's not wrong, about what I did."

"Yes, she is," Sarah said. "For her Yora will always be a little girl. But she knew the risks. We all did. We went ahead anyway because we thought we were doing the right thing."

"Yeah." Gyre hesitated for a moment. "Do you still believe that? That we were doing the right thing?"

"Of course I do. What Raskos and his goons were doing to Deepfire—"

"Not just Raskos. The whole system. The Republic and the Order. We used to talk about... something better."

Sarah sat up straighter, taken aback. "I suppose I still believe in that, too. I just haven't had much occasion to think about it lately."

"I may have... something. A chance. I don't know how much of one. But if it works, then... who knows."

"Does it involve your mysterious new friends with the unlimited bank account?" Her eyes flicked to Elariel.

"It does. And some of our *old* friends from the south." This was a code phrase for the Khirkhaz Commune.

"Ah." Sarah raised her eyebrows. "That's where you're taking this wagonload of alchemicals? South?"

Gyre nodded.

"And, what? I'm assuming this isn't just a social call. You want me to make you more arcana bombs?"

"Actually," Gyre said, "I was wondering if you wanted to join us."

There was a long silence. Elariel shot him a surprised look, while Sarah herself chewed her lip thoughtfully.

"If you want a peaceful life from here on out," Gyre said, "then by all means, stay away from me. No one can ever say you haven't done your part. But I thought I'd ask, just in case you were—"

"Bored?" Sarah said. "I'm bored out of my fucking mind. Amnesty or not, everyone in the underworld knows the Republic is watching me, and there isn't much legitimate work for a one-armed arcanist. Lynnia pretends I earn my keep here, but truthfully it's charity." She let out a long sigh. "That's the problem, Gyre. I don't want charity from you, and I'm not sure what good I could do. If you need an arcanist, there's a few still working I could recommend."

"You're the one I trust. And..." He paused, stomach twisting a little, and lowered his voice. "I don't want to make promises I can't keep. But it's possible that we might have a...solution for your problem."

"A solution?" Sarah looked blank, and Gyre tapped his cheek just below his silver eye. Sarah's eyes went very, very wide, and her voice was a whisper. "You're not serious."

"Like I said. It's not for certain. But there's a chance."

"I'll take it," Sarah said. "When do we leave?"

"In the morning," Gyre said. "But I need you to understand that if you're getting into this, you're going to be all the way in."

"I always am," Sarah said. At Gyre's expression, she sobered slightly. "Just promise me this is a project that Yora would have approved of."

"I like to think so," Gyre said. "In concept, if not in execution."

"Then I'm all the way in," Sarah said. "I'll ride herd on Lynnia's shipment in the morning."

"You trust her?" Elariel said.

They were in the square in front of the Tinker's Gate, one of the half dozen in the southern face of the crater. The Tinker's wasn't the busiest, but the square that led into it was crowded enough, with several wagons and their teams loading up and a steady stream of riders and pedestrians. Gyre watched the northern entrance impatiently.

"Sarah?" He glanced at Elariel, who stood behind him in the shadow of a column and out of the press. "Absolutely."

"You'll have to tell her who I am," Elariel said quietly. "*What* I am. She won't..."

"She'll probably want to ask you all kinds of questions," Gyre said.

"I thought humans hated us," Elariel said.

"*Most* humans, probably. They just believe what the Order tells them. But Sarah was one of us. Plus she's an arcanist, and all arcanists are a little mad for anything Elder." Gyre perked up. "Ah, here they come."

At the other end of the square, traffic made way for a small caravan. Three hardshells, each pulling a substantial enclosed wagon, pushed through the mess of loadbirds and thickheads. The smaller animals instinctively gave the larger ones a wide berth.

The hardshells resembled a common tortoise, but enormously larger—the top of their curved shells was above Gyre's head, and their own protruding head about level with his shoulder. Four massive legs, green-brown and dusty, were in slow but constant motion, moving the creature along at a gentle walk. Their scaled shells were painted in jaunty colors, the first one blue, the others red and green.

Hardshells couldn't gallop like a loadbird, but they were tireless and fantastically strong and could live on almost any fodder. Their chief downside as beasts of burden was cost—the slow-breeding animals were always in high demand, and priced accordingly. The blue-painted one was on a simple lead tied to a ring in its nose and held by a sullen-looking young man. Wagon wheels creaked and rattled on the irregular ground of the square.

"Supposed to get a signature," the boy said as he came over. He held up a sheet of paper.

"Of course." Gyre signed with a flourish. "Any advice for handling them?"

"Just point 'em in the right direction and take a nap," the boy said. "That's about all there is to it."

"Do they have names?"

"We call 'em Blue, Red, and Green," he said. "But you can call 'em whatever you like—they don't listen anyway."

"Well," Gyre said. "I promise to take good care of them."

"Make soup out of 'em if you want, it's no skin off my back. Long as I don't have to clean up their shit anymore." The boy yawned and wandered away.

Next to arrive was the rest of the gear Gyre had ordered at the outfitter's shop, brought in a two-bird cart by an obsequious porter angling for a tip. Gyre was happy to oblige, and helped the man load the trunks into the front wagon, the hardshells watching them with chelonian disinterest. No sooner had the porter retreated, bowing gratefully, than Sarah arrived with another wagon, this one operated by a pair of decidedly less helpful teamsters.

She whistled at the sight of the hardshells and their burdens. "You weren't kidding. This is quite an expedition."

"Big bastards aren't worth shit in the mountains," one of the porters opined. "Better off with a thickhead every time."

"Thanks," Gyre said. "Just stack everything in the wagon."

The load Sarah had escorted wasn't the only one. Several more arrived over the course of the next half hour, attended by messengers from most of the city's major alchemists. They contained chests of explosives packed carefully in unspun wool, barrels of quickheal in waxed paper packets, stacks of glowstones, tubes of glue and solvent, and every other product Deepfire's best minds could come up with. Toward the end, a Moorcat Combine courier arrived with the bill, which was big enough to make Gyre wince. He counted out stacks of thalers into the uniformed young woman's waiting trunk until she was satisfied, then hefted the now much lighter sack over his shoulder.

"So what's the third wagon for?" Sarah said. The first held their gear and provisions for the journey, while the second was packed with alchemicals.

"You'll see," Gyre said. "Let's get moving. The last thing we need is the Auxies deciding we're the world's most obvious smugglers."

The blue-painted hardshell had three cushioned seats strapped to the forward slope of its shell. Gyre scrambled up, and Sarah took the seat beside him, nimble in spite of her missing arm. Gyre leaned over to offer his hand to Elariel, but she shook her head and got in the wagon behind them, where she could be out of sight.

Gyre gave the line attached to the tortoise's nose a flip, making the ring jingle. That got it moving, and by gentle tugs he managed to point it in the right direction. Behind him, Red and Green lumbered into motion as well, trained to follow the leading wagon as the stable-master had promised. Before too long, Deepfire's modest gatehouse passed overhead, and they were on their way down the long, serpentine road.

It was already getting colder, away from the Pit—they'd hurry to descend from Deepfire's artificial warmth to a more congenial altitude without spending too long in between. Gyre kept the rope in hand, but there wasn't much to do. Blue followed the road, and the others followed Blue. *Maybe the kid was right about a nap.*

"Did Lynnia give you trouble?" Gyre asked Sarah as the city disappeared behind the mountain.

"Surprisingly little. She muttered something about young idiots running off when they should know better, but I think she knows I can't stay with her forever." Sarah glanced back at the wagon trundling along behind them. "What about your friend? She seems shy."

"She's had a rough time," Gyre said. "We're going to have to take it slowly."

"Fair enough." Sarah looked out at the mountains for a while. "So are you going to let me in on the big secret?"

"It'll be easier if I can show you," Gyre said. "We don't have far to go."

Sarah pursed her lips but accepted that, and they passed an hour or so in idle chat. Gyre could only imagine what Sarah was feeling, having uprooted her whole life on the strength of a few minutes' conversation and his promise that he might be able to help her. They'd never been close, back in the old days, but she'd always gotten along with anyone. It was a talent Gyre had come to appreciate.

Eventually they came to a fork in the road. The main path turned to the left, swinging south to join up with the Republic Road. That highway ran through the Splinter Kingdom towns of Meltrock and Drail before reaching the great border city of Obstadt. Most trade with the Republic ran that way, legal and illegal. It would be the most direct route to his destination, a long, long road from Deepfire to Khirkhaz in the far south, but a well-trodden one. A Republic courier swapping out swiftbirds at post stations might hope to cover the distance in less than a week. Unfortunately, the odds of successfully crossing half the Republic with *this* cargo were small. Even the border check at Obstadt would be impossible.

Straight ahead, meanwhile, a smaller road continued down through the mountains to the west. As far as Gyre knew, it didn't have a name other than the west road. It led into the valley of the river Seta and the plains of the western coast. That was a region of scattered towns, farmsteads, and fortresses, not so much Splinter Kingdoms as no kingdoms at all. It would take longer—Gyre would count it lucky if they got to Khirkhaz in less than a month—but they'd trade the dangers of Republic patrols for wandering plaguespawn and local warlords.

Since we can certainly defend ourselves, it seems like a better bet. He tugged the rope, and with a groan and a rattle, the wagons moved off the rutted dirt path of the main road and onto the less-used track.

Sarah raised an eyebrow at their choice of route, and raised it further when Gyre pulled them off the road entirely, swinging into a narrow valley. There wasn't even a track here, just a bit of flat ground leading up to a rocky cliff.

"I don't mean to tell you your business," Sarah said as the cliff approached, "but are we supposed to be going somewhere?"

"We're just meeting up with the rest of our cargo," Gyre said. He tugged the rope to halt the wagon, then slid down and cupped his hands. "Kit? You there?"

"Kit?" Sarah said. "You mean *Doomseeker*? She's here?"

"After a fashion," came Kit's voice. "You took your sweet time."

There was a low rumble, and part of the rock face slid open, revealing a smooth ghoul-built tunnel beyond. In the entrance were a dozen of Kit's spider-constructs in all three sizes. They scuttled out into the open, the big ones pulling neat gray boxes behind them. *My supplies. Let's hope Tyraves kept her word.*

"It's all right," Gyre said, looking back at a sudden clatter. "They're— Are you okay?"

Sarah had slipped off at the sight of the constructs and managed to tangle a leg in the ropes. Now she hung upside down from the hardshell's back, her arm dangling.

"Is this some kind of newfangled exercise routine?" Kit said, her chuckle coming from the closest construct.

"Right," Sarah said, grabbing hold of the net to right herself. "Gyre Silvereye, you have got a *lot* of explaining to do."

Chapter 4

Jaedia lay still, eyes closed, breathing soft and unhurried. Maya tried to convince herself that her mentor looked better, that there was more color in her cheeks, but the truth was that nothing had changed. There was no reason to think she'd suddenly wake up now, or tomorrow.

Or ever. Maya shook her head, rejecting that thought out of hand. *She* will *wake up.* And if it was tomorrow, or the day after, Maya wouldn't be here with her when she did.

"I'm sorry," she said, taking Jaedia's hand between her own as she always did. "I have to go. Basel needs my help. I know you'd understand." She *would* understand. Jaedia had always been willing to put the needs of the Order before her own. "But I'll be back, don't worry. And maybe..."

Maya swallowed, finding the rest hard to say out loud. *Maybe we'll find something. Maybe whatever this arcana is will be related to the black spiders, or the Archive will have more information, or* something. *Anything that will bring you back to yourself.*

She sat there, holding Jaedia's hand, for a long time.

Behind her, the curtain rustled and she heard a cough. Maya put her mentor's hand down and slipped out of the curtained enclosure into the empty vastness of the hospital floor. She was surprised to find that it was Tanax waiting by the door, arms crossed, looking awkward.

"I'm sorry," he said. "I didn't mean to interrupt. I can wait, if—"

"It's all right." Maya let out a breath, trying to push away thoughts of Jaedia. *Focus on the mission. The rest can come later.*

"I wanted to be sure I saw you before you left." He frowned. "I'm sorry I can't accompany you. The Council has asked me to see to Senate business in Skyreach."

"That sounds important."

"I suppose it is." His frown turned to a grimace, and he glanced over his shoulder. "Just between us, it's mostly operating sunstones and flitters for a bunch of old men who look at you like you're part of the furniture."

Maya chuckled. "Careful. I might have to include that in my report to the Council."

It was how he'd threatened her, on that first mission. Tanax winced, then grinned.

"I wanted to lend you something." He dug in his pocket and came up with a small glass-and-unmetal sphere.

"Your watch charm?" Maya raised an eyebrow. It was a rare bit of arcana. "Are you sure?"

"It was a gift from Nicomidi," Tanax said, lips tightening. "I think you will get more use out of it than I will."

"Thank you, then." Maya tucked the little thing away.

"I just want you to know…" Tanax shifted awkwardly. "Things have been…unsettled. The Council is in an uproar, and I don't know how matters will fall out between the Dogmatics and the Pragmatics. But…if you need help, you can rely on me. Whatever happens."

"Thank you for that, too," Maya said, trying not to smile at his obvious discomfiture. Tanax had had some inflexible notions about the dignity befitting a centarch drilled into him at an early age, but he was trying his best.

"Well." He cleared his throat. "Best of luck. Come and see me when you return, if your schedule permits."

"I will."

He gave a formal nod and slunk out of the hospital. Maya looked back at Jaedia's enclosure, then shook her head.

Focus. It's time to go.

Varo and Beq were waiting for her in the Gate chamber at the heart of the mountain.

The Gate network was the Twilight Order's greatest asset, letting the small number of centarchs travel easily across the Republic and beyond. But it was also a vulnerability, in theory—anyone who could wield *deiat* could travel straight into the center of the Order's home base.

Of course, that would mean a centarch had turned traitor to the Order, which until recently had seemed unthinkable. In the wake of Nicomidi's treachery, however, Maya was not surprised to find the Gate chamber under heavy guard. A full squad of Legionaries waited against the walls, in off-white unmetal armor with blaster rifles over their shoulders. They were led by a fully armored centarch, who nodded silently at Maya as she came in.

There were three Gates here, side by side. They looked like broad archways, big enough to admit a carriage, made of many strands of iridescent unmetal braided together. They narrowed as they arced upward, until at the apex the connecting thread was no wider than a pencil. When they were inactive, there was nothing visible through them but the rest of the empty stone room.

Varo was already wearing his pack, a hefty thing strapped around his body and topped with a tightly coiled bedroll. He had a heavy machete on one hip and a blaster pistol on the other. Other bits of arcana and useful tools hung on straps. Beq was, if anything, even more heavily loaded, still rummaging in her pack to check that everything was in place. She looked up and grinned at Maya.

"You're going to have to carry all of that, you know," Maya said. They'd decided taking mounts would only increase the risk of attracting unwanted attention.

"Better to wear out my legs than be short something and not have it a week out from the Gate," Beq said.

"You'd think so," Varo said. "But when you're running from a ravenous crocopede, you might regret—"

"I'll manage," Beq said, shutting the pack and pulling it over her shoulder. She was stronger than she looked, and Maya never tired of watching the play of muscles across her back. Her green hair was gathered in a ponytail, only a few wisps escaping at the nape of her neck.

"Fair enough," Varo said. "I don't have to outrun the crocopede, after all, I just have to outrun *you*."

"I'll handle any crocopedes we come across, how about that?" Maya said. "Are you two ready?"

"I think so," Beq said. "I wish we knew a little more about this Archive. I'd have a better idea what to bring."

"Prodominus says we know all we need to," Maya said. "All we can do is trust him."

"Famous last words," Varo said.

"That's about enough," Maya said. "Here goes."

She touched the haken on her hip, drawing a slender thread of *deiat* through it. As always, opening herself to the fire of the sun felt like a sudden warmth throughout her body, as though narrow rays of bright daylight were shining on her. One ribbon of power went into her panoply belt, the silvery fabric she wore around her midsection under her shirt. The field came up, imperceptible except for the faint blue tinge it laid over her vision. It would stop nearly any attack, though at the cost of a serious drain on her power.

The other filament of *deiat* went to the Gate, the central one of the three. Only a centarch—or a Chosen, had there been any left—could draw power from *deiat*. Arcana like blasters relied on sunsplinters, which could store a centarch's power, but something as complex as a Gate required a direct connection. Through the link, Maya sent a mental pattern that corresponded to another Gate, far away across the Shattered Peaks. At once the arch filled with a thick white mist, swirling but always opaque as a curtain.

Maya stepped forward first. Jaedia had trained her to be alert at these moments. Since you could never see through a Gate to the other side, there was always a danger of ambush. She kept a hand on her haken, passing through the mist without so much as a tingle, and emerged on the Forsaken Coast.

It was earlier in the day here, the sun only a handsbreadth above the horizon. The Gate stood on a windswept hillside, set into a rocky scree broken by a few hardy shrubs and the occasional stunted tree. More hills rose in all directions, and just ahead a small stream winked in the sun. There was no sign of plaguespawn, and Maya loosened her grip on her weapon.

A moment later Varo and Beq emerged, and Maya withdrew her power from the Gate. The mist vanished and they were alone, a thousand kilometers from the Forge and who knew how far from the nearest outpost of civilization. They stood in silence, surveying the landscape.

"Pretty," Beq concluded, "in a desolate sort of way."

"Looks dry," Varo said. He unrolled a thin leather map. "I don't know how much to trust this thing—it was drawn two hundred years ago. But according to the notes from the last expedition, we should head down out of the hills to the west. It's a bit farther, but it'll be easier than hiking over rocks. I suggest sticking to the stream as long as we can."

"Seems sensible," Maya said. "Lead the way, and keep your eyes peeled. This place is supposed to be thick with plaguespawn."

Prodominus had given her the impression that she'd be hacking her way through a tide of malformed monsters, but the reality turned out to be more prosaic. The stream was nearly dry, only a half-meter trickle, and its wide, rocky bed provided a convenient track. Varo led the way, occasionally drawing his machete to hack down a bramble, but other than that none of them touched their weapons. Maya saw no plaguespawn, and the only animal she spotted was a hawk circling so high overhead it was only a speck.

There were also no people, and no sign there had ever been any. It was an odd feeling. On Maya's travels with Jaedia, they'd passed through plenty of wilderness, but they'd almost always been following some kind of track, some indication that humans had come this way before. There were felled trees, roadside shrines, even graves of unlucky travelers. Here there was nothing but the Gate itself, which quickly vanished behind them. It was as though they'd stepped into another world, where the Chosen and their human servants had never built a continent-wide empire.

At noon, they stopped in the lee of a cliff face to rest and eat travel rations, dried meat and hardtack. Beq crunched her way through the double-baked biscuits with a long-suffering air, while Varo seemed to positively relish his.

"So how long has it been since people lived here?" Maya asked Beq. "It feels so empty."

"Hard to be really certain," Beq said. She coughed, and gulped from her canteen. "This was one of the first regions to break away from Republic control, less than fifty years after the war. The Legions were busy closer to Skyreach, and the local duxes just took power for themselves. After that, there was a little trade through the mountains, but it gradually dried up. For the last couple of hundred years, the only people who've come here from the Republic have been centarchs, and they haven't reported meeting anybody."

"When things get hard, the instinct is always to hunker down and protect your own," Varo said. "First every province for itself, then every city, then every town and every family. But a family can't hold off plaguespawn forever. Eventually someone makes a mistake, something gets inside the walls, and then there's no one to call for help."

Maya raised her eyebrow at this unusual bit of sincerity from the scout. He shrugged and went back to his biscuit.

That's why the Order is so important, though. The centarchs—and the Legions they maintained—kept the Republic together. *Without us, who knows if there would be any people left* anywhere. It was a bleak image, a continent full of nothing but plaguespawn. Forests growing up in the abandoned villages, rabbits and deer fleeing their unnatural predators through fields gone to seed.

We do what we have to. In her mind, Maya realized, she was directing the argument at Gyre. In the ghoul ruins, he'd accused her and the Order of being tyrants, using their power to rule over what was left of humanity for their own ends. *And maybe some of us do. But a few like Raskos or Nicomidi doesn't mean we can tear down the Order and let* dhakim *do as they please.* Otherwise the Republic would end up like *this*, fracturing into smaller and smaller pieces until the last of humanity was submerged under the tide of darkness.

It was a melancholy line of thought, and she was glad to abandon it and pick up her pack again. They refilled their canteens and kept on following the stream, which wound between two rocky hills and then spilled out onto lower ground. Here, dry, yellowing grass grew almost to Maya's hips, stretching into the distance west and south. Varo turned them north, parallel to the line of hills, and Maya could see the shadow of a forest rising in that direction.

"Still no plaguespawn," she muttered an hour later. "Either the reports are wrong, or our luck is phenomenal."

"Maybe the reports are just out of date?" Beq said. "Plaguespawn are attracted to humans, and there aren't any left. They could have all just moved on."

"The last expedition was only thirty years ago," Varo said. "And they ran into enough that two centarchs had trouble holding them off. Things can't have changed *that* much."

"Let's hope for phenomenal luck, then," Maya said.

Whatever it was, it held until nightfall. Varo found them a campsite in a copse of low trees, still a few kilometers from the edge of the forest. They set up their tents on the small patch of bare ground, and the scout carefully dug a pit for a fire.

"Looks like a spark in the wrong place would send the whole plain up in smoke," he said cheerfully. "So watch what you're doing with that thing."

Maya lit the flames with the tiniest pinch of *deiat*, then threaded a bit more into the watch charm, enough to activate it until morning. She set it on a rock near the tents; any substantial movement crossing its perimeter would set off the alarm. Varo grunted in appreciation, busying himself boiling water to soften up their evening meal.

Maya and Beq were sharing a tent. This had just sort of happened, when they were planning the expedition—someone had written down they'd need two tents for the three of them, and no one had objected. It was a silly thing to get worked up over, since it wasn't as though they hadn't shared before. But that had been out of necessity, and making it part of the plan felt... different.

The problem, Maya thought, lay in the fact that she wasn't really sure what this thing between them *was*. It wasn't like she had a deep well of experience to draw on. She'd spent her childhood traveling from village to village with Jaedia, and each region had its own peculiar rituals around courtship, marriage, and raising children, none of which Maya had ever really felt *applied* to her. She was a centarch, and therefore apart. Centarchs could have lovers, of course. She was even fairly sure Jaedia had managed some discreet assignations, which she hadn't recognized at the time. But few of them seemed to take things further than that, either within the Order or without.

Whatever the reason, Maya couldn't deny that her heart beat a bit faster when the light faded completely and Beq announced she was going to bed. Varo said he was staying out a bit longer, and so Maya left him by the dying fire and slid through the flap on hands and knees. The two-person tent the quartermasters had given them wasn't large, but it was big enough for them both to spread out their bedrolls side by side.

"Did I tell you about how I nearly killed Tanax when we were on the road to Grace?" Maya said.

"There's been a few times you nearly killed Tanax," Beq said. "You'll have to be more specific."

"You and I were going off alone, right? And this was just after the first time we kissed. I had...built up this whole thing in my head. We'd have two weeks by ourselves."

"I didn't even think about that," Beq said. "Which is probably for the best, because I'm not sure I'd have been able to say a word to you if I had."

"And then Tanax invited himself along," Maya said. "And we ended up staying in caravan tents *anyway*, and it was just...driving me a little insane."

"Oh no." Beq laughed out loud, covering her mouth with her hand. "Poor Maya."

"It was pretty plaguing frustrating."

"We did manage to get some time alone, if I recall," Beq said, sitting cross-legged. "Once we got back to Grace."

"And *you* nearly spent the night playing with the Thing instead of—"

"I did not." Beq adjusted her spectacles, lenses clicking. "Not the *whole* night."

"Anyway," Maya said when she stopped laughing. "This sort of feels like a do-over, you know?" It was hard to read Beq's expression in the dark, and Maya wondered abruptly if she'd gone too far. "Not that we have to. It's been a long day—"

Beq groaned. "Just...come here, would you?"

She woke to find the translucent walls of the tent glowing with the gray light of early morning. Beq, naked under the thin sheet, was curled up against her, spectacles neatly folded on the bedroll beside her.

"Good morning," Maya said as her eyes flickered.

"Mmmph." Beq gave a sleepy smile. "Morning."

The business of dressing in the narrow confines of the tent, clothes stiff with yesterday's sweat, was less than exciting. Still, by the time Maya emerged into daylight, she was feeling considerably better than she had the night before. Varo was already up, his tent packed, chewing on dried meat as he looked contemplatively at the forest ahead of them.

"The maps seem accurate so far," Maya said. "How much farther to the Archive on this route?"

"Not far, but I don't know how rough the ground is," Varo said. "Might be there by tonight, might be tomorrow morning."

A part of Maya regretted that their objective was so close. *I wouldn't have minded another few nights.* But that was foolish. *I'm not a child sneaking around behind someone's back. Beq and I can fuck all we like at the Forge, without worrying about getting ambushed by plaguespawn.*

The forest was shadowy and cool, in spite of the daylight, and a lack of undergrowth made for easy walking. Varo, consulting an arcana compass, turned their steps northwest, up a steady slope.

"There's... something," Beq said abruptly. She adjusted her spectacles, lenses clicking. "Up there. Moving— There!"

Maya saw it too, a tall, dark shape running with fluid grace. *Has to be plaguespawn.* She checked her panoply belt and drew her haken.

"I'll take it," Maya said. "Watch the flanks."

With a *whoomph*, her weapon ignited, an orange-white bar of pure fire extending from the haken where a real sword's blade would be. Maya took up the fighting stance drilled into her by hundreds of hours of practice and waited as the dark thing ghosted forward through the trees.

Like all plaguespawn, it looked as though it had been assembled in a butcher's shop out of scraps—skinless, with splintered, repurposed bones held together by ropes of pulsing red muscle. This one was vaguely humanoid, bipedal and two-armed, though the resemblance ended there. Its ropy arms were lined with bones of different shapes and sizes, and claws made from snapped-off ribs extended from where its hands should be. It had no skull, just a queerly misshapen lump of meat for a head, with no mouth and three mismatched eyes blinking out at odd angles.

Somehow, it was more disturbing to watch than the plaguespawn that approximated wolves or bears. Its legs moved oddly, multijointed and too flexible. The thing seemed to realize it had been spotted, and gave up its stalking approach in favor of a head-on charge, pounding across the forest floor.

Maya let it get to twenty meters off, then closed her free hand into a fist. Fire blasted up from the forest floor, a white-hot pillar she intended to incinerate the monster outright. The plaguespawn reacted quickly, vaulting to one side. Its flesh was lightly charred, but it kept coming, arms spread wide.

Fast little plaguepit. Maya held her ground, then sidestepped at the last moment, slashing sideways. Her haken cut through the thing's upper arm with a curl of smoke and the scent of burning meat. The limb fell twitching to the forest floor. The creature dug in a foot and slid to a halt, bringing its other claw around in a swipe that drew shimmering sparks from the panoply field. Maya felt a rush of cold as the panoply belt drew *deiat* out of her, and she pivoted into a horizontal slash that cut the vile thing in half. Black blood spurted as it fell in two sections, still squirming.

"You okay?" Beq said. She had her blaster pistol out, watching the woods.

"Fine," Maya muttered. The plaguespawn's three eyes were still looking up at her, and the intelligence in their gaze made her uncomfortable. A quick blast of flame turned the head into charcoal.

Something's wrong. Plaguespawn were dumb, knowing only the hunger to kill and create more of their kind from the dead flesh. That was how humanity had kept them at bay all this time. *But the plaguespawn at the ghoul ruins weren't like that.* They'd moved like a pack, with a single purpose. *Because the black spider was controlling them with* dhaka.

This one had been alone, but it had fought smarter than it had any right to. *It should never have gotten a hit in.* Maya looked up from the blackened corpse and frowned.

We could turn back. If someone *was* controlling the plaguespawn, that someone now knew they were here. *But can I really tell Prodominus and Basel that I gave up and came home because I had a bad feeling?*

"What now?" Varo said, straightening up and holstering his pistol.

"Keep moving," Maya said. "But carefully."

The real attack came in the late afternoon, when the forest was striped with long shadows.

They'd continued uphill for the rest of the day, eating lunch on the march. Hills rose ahead, and the ground became rocky.

"If this map is right," Varo said, "the Archive is at the top of a hill a few kilometers farther on." He frowned at the terrain and the looming shadows. "I don't like the thought of being caught in one of those gullies."

"We could camp here," Beq suggested. "Make the climb with more daylight left."

Maya cocked her head, considering. As she did, she caught a flash of motion, a dark patch sliding through light and shadow. She drew her haken without thinking, blade igniting.

"Something's here," she hissed.

"I see it," Beq said. "On the right."

"Ah," Varo said. "I was about to say it's on the left. So—"

Plaguespawn charged from every point of the compass.

There were at least a dozen of them. Most were similar in shape to the humanoid Maya had dispatched earlier, but quicker canine forms ran beside them, heads little more than enormous yawning jaws studded with mismatched teeth. They bounded through the trees like a pack of hounds.

The three of them stood back-to-back without need of instructions. The *crack* of blaster fire rolled over Maya, mixed with the *booms* as the bolts exploded in showers of wood and earth. Beq had dropped to one knee, taking careful aim, and her first bolt blew one of the humanoids apart in a shower of torn flesh. Varo sent two bolts chasing after one of the wolf-things, swore, and adjusted his aim to catch another as it gathered itself to leap.

Maya raised her free hand and flame blasted out of the earth, tendrils leaping and twisting to catch the plaguespawn as they tried to dodge.

Humanoids and wolf-things alike were roasted, but they kept coming, even as their flesh blackened and flaked away from their bones. Several collapsed, but the rest closed in. A wolf-thing leapt, and she met it with a sweep of her haken that cut its jaw in half. Another came at her from below, nipping at her heel as a real dog might, distracting her while a pair of humanoids closed in from either side. Maya spun toward one, slashing it to pieces, and hurled a bolt of flame into the other that sent it staggering back, burning.

Varo had his machete out, meeting another humanoid and hacking chunks out of it. Beq was still firing, plaguespawn wreckage strewn in front of her, but two wolf-things had gone wide to flank her. She turned to engage one, and Maya leapt at the other, cutting it apart.

"Varo, down!" Beq shouted, and the scout ducked. She nailed the humanoid he'd been fighting, sending flaming chunks of it to rain down on the fallen leaves. Varo shook black blood from his machete and looked around for another opponent.

"I think we're clear," Maya said. She closed her fist, and flame erupted from several plaguespawn that were still twitching. "Chosen fucking defend, those things are fast."

"They tried to flank us," Varo said. "Plaguespawn don't do that."

"Unless someone's controlling them," Beq said, and shuddered. A *dhakim* had nearly killed them all in the tunnels under Grace. "Maya..."

"We should get out of these woods," Maya said. "I sure as plague don't want to be here after dark."

"That…may be more difficult than you think." Varo pointed back the way they'd come, and Maya saw dark shapes filtering through the trees. *More of them. A lot more.*

"We need to run," Maya said. "Now. Ditch the tents."

"Where?" Beq said, shrugging awkwardly out of her pack.

"Up to the hills," Maya said. The light was already failing, and her haken blade cast weird, shifting shadows. "If we can find a cliff or something to put our backs against, we'll have a better chance. A cave, maybe." There was movement ahead of them now, too. "I'll lead. You guys keep them off me from behind. Ready?"

Beq nodded, and Varo gave a breathless grunt.

"*Run!*"

They ran, dodging between the trees. The plaguespawn behind them broke into a sprint as well, the canines bounding ahead with distended jaws open wide. Beq half turned and fired on the move, sending fountains of dirt into the air and blasting apart one of the monsters.

In front of them, a trio of humanoids set themselves in Maya's path. She threw herself at them, feeling one set of claws scrape against her panoply as she cut the first monster down. A quick gesture sent a ring of fire blasting outward, knocking the other two off their feet. Maya closed her fist and incinerated one and Varo shot the other. But more shadows were moving through the darkening trees, and more wolf-things paced them on either side.

We need something. The upward slope was cutting into Maya's speed, and she was gasping for breath. The rocky hills were black shapes against the horizon. *There has to be a cliff. Plague it, just a big rock. Some way to keep them from getting behind us.* She could hold them off if they came from only one direction. *Maybe.* Her connection to *deiat* felt strained, fraying, the blasts of fire and hits to her panoply adding up. *I can't keep going forever.*

Then another group rushed her, and there was no time for thought, only action. Her sword blurred into a livid crimson line, slashing through shadows that twisted and tore and fell back sizzling. One of the canines got too close, its jaw closing around Maya's ankle, and her panoply strained. For a moment it felt like she'd plunged into ice water, *deiat* draining away rapidly. Maya slashed the thing's misshapen head off, but its grip didn't slacken, and she had to blast it with intense fire before it charred and fell away.

"Maya!" Beq's shout. Maya spun.

The latest wave had brought them to a halt. Beq slid into a crouch, firing rapidly at the canines coming up from behind them. Varo, beside her, worked hurriedly to replace the drained sunsplinter in his blaster with a fresh one. Bodies and fragments of bodies piled up, forming a steaming barricade. The arcanist looked over her shoulder and yelled a warning. She raised her blaster and fired, the bolt zipping past Maya's head to explode against a humanoid in mid-leap. Behind Beq, though, something moved among the corpses, and Maya answered with a scream of her own.

"Look out!"

One of the canines Beq had shot was still coming. It wormed its way through the bodies of its fellows and pushed off in a final leap, jaw open so wide that its twisted head was levered almost in half. Beq turned back, bringing her blaster around, but not quickly enough. The thing's maw snapped closed, driving inch-long fangs into her back and side. Beq screamed as it bore her down, her blaster going off as it fell.

Maya lashed out with a blast of fire that turned the humanoid in front of her to gray ash. She ran for Beq, but Varo was quicker, his blaster bolt exploding against the wolf-thing and sending pieces of it flying. Maya skidded to a halt in a spray of fallen leaves, rapidly summoning a circular wall of seething flame to buy them a moment's respite.

"Beq!"

"I'm...okay." Beq pushed herself on her elbows. "I just—" Her eyes rolled up in her head and she fell backward, limp against the forest floor. Maya's guts gave a horrible lurch.

Varo knelt beside her, prying the remains of the plaguespawn's jaw away from the wound. It was hard to see anything under the torn clothing, but a horrifying amount of blood pulsed out. Varo swore, grabbing the first bit of cloth that came to hand and jamming it against Beq's gory midsection.

"She needs quickheal and stitching *now*," Varo said.

Bastard plaguing fuck. The flames around them were guttering out, and beyond was a dark circle of plaguespawn, waiting for their chance. *Fuck fuck* fuck. *We should have turned back after the first one, there was clearly something wrong, you stupid fucking girl you've killed her and everyone else—*

"*Maya!*" Varo shouted. His hands were slick with crimson.

Do something. Maya struggled to fight through the moment of paralysis. The grip of her haken was slick in her hands, and her heart felt like it was going to break through her ribs. *And she's bleeding, there's so much blood—*

There. The sun was almost gone now, the shapes of the hills darker shadows against the purpling sky. One looked closer than the others, and Maya turned to face it, not sure what direction she was running anymore.

"Can you carry her?"

"Not for long," Varo said, "and she's bleeding—"

"If we stay here we're all dead," Maya growled. "Grab her and get ready to move."

"Shit." Varo picked Beq up, hoisting her over his shoulder and trying to keep the cloth pressed tight at the same time. "Okay—"

"Now!"

Maya let the wall around them die. She slashed with her haken and pulled on every bit of *deiat* she could muster, sending a wave of writhing, coruscating flames rolling out in front of her. The trees went up like torches, the blaze spreading upward until the canopy took fire. Wild, hot winds sent spirals of burning leaves in all directions. Ahead of them, there was a gap in the line of plaguespawn, the creatures incinerated or blown away. Maya forced herself into motion, exhausted legs screaming. The Thing was burning hot in her chest, as though in echo of her flames.

The plaguespawn were coming in from either side. Maya slashed again, two walls of nearly solid fire blooming ahead of her, leaving a narrow gap between them in stark, flickering orange-white. Her mouth felt like it was coated with ash, and every footfall took an eternity. She wanted to look back, make sure Varo was following, but she didn't dare—if she tripped, put a foot wrong, she would fall, and that would be the end.

The lines of fire extended ahead of her and guttered out behind, a brief corridor of safety, getting smaller and darker as Maya's strength waned. The hill she was running toward loomed ahead, but it didn't matter anymore—even if they got there, she'd have no way to hold the monsters off. But to stop would be death. *Just one more step. One more. One more.* Plaguespawn ran beside her on the other side of the walls of flame, easily keeping pace.

There was a light ahead. For a moment Maya mistook it for one of her own fires, spreading faster than she could run. But it waved back and forth, like a lantern carried in nervous hands, and it was soon joined by another. *Who—*

The barricade appeared out of the darkness so suddenly that Maya nearly slammed into it. It was made of unmetal, iridescent in the light of the fires, several large, jagged sheets of it assembled into a makeshift wall. It would have been a commonplace thing, back in the Republic. *But nobody's supposed to live out here.*

One of the sheets was pulled aside, and a dark shape raised a handheld lantern. Maya blinked and looked over her shoulder to find Varo coming up behind her, gasping for breath. Past him, the flames were dying out, and the plaguespawn—

—were retreating. Slinking back into the darkness, until there was nothing out in the woods but dancing shadows.

More figures were gathered in the narrow gap in the barricade. The one with the lantern stepped forward.

"Excuse me," she said. There was a note of terror in her voice, mixed with quiet determination. "But are you...outsiders?"

Chapter 5

The plaguespawn skittered through the grass. Its back was lined with small bones that flexed and cracked as it moved, and its single eye was surrounded by a ring of distressingly humanlike teeth.

In the shadow-world of his silver eye, Gyre watched and waited. When it gathered itself for a leap, shadows raced ahead of it, showing its most likely path and every possible variation. It was fast as a snake but still seemed to move like it was trapped in tar, sailing slowly through the air with its clawed forelegs waving. Gyre sidestepped, letting it come within inches. It landed in the grass, spinning almost instantly to try again.

"Stop playing with the plagued thing, Gyre," Kit said. The foot of one of her large constructs came down on top of the plaguespawn and crushed it into a smear of black goo.

With a sigh, Gyre sheathed his sword and felt the *click* in his skull as time rushed into its normal course. He checked the energy bottle at his hip—still half-full—and looked up at the big construct. The things didn't have faces, and he always found it awkward trying to figure out where he should focus his attention.

"I was just practicing a little," he said. "It's been too quiet."

"I'll spar with you if you need practice," Kit said. The spider-construct raised its forelegs in a parody of a boxer's stance. "Come at me! But later. I'm all finished with the water barrels."

Their three wagons were pulled up by the bank of a small stream. The three hardshells, Blue, Red, and Evil Bastard, were contentedly munching on the sun-dried tufts of grass. All around, to the horizon, the plain spread in gently undulating folds, green stalks fading into gold as fall advanced. Here and there, a tree broke the monotony. In the distance, the river Seta glowed like a vein of molten silver winding toward the sea.

Elariel was nowhere to be seen, probably tucked up in the little nest she'd built in the back of the first wagon. Sarah stood in the stream, stripped down to just rolled-up pants and a chest wrap, pouring a bucket over herself. She shook her head, spraying water everywhere, and gave a whoop.

"Chosen defend, that's cold!"

And Kit—well, Kit was all around them. They'd brought a dozen constructs in total—two of the biggest, taller than Gyre, plus four roughly human-sized units and six of the cat-sized ones that could sit on his shoulder. Folded up, they all just about fit in the third wagon alongside Tyraves' supplies, which was useful when they needed to hide from prying eyes. When no one was about, though, the constructs kept pace with their little caravan, keeping watch and scouting ahead. At the moment, the other large construct was carrying barrels of water back to the wagon, with the smaller, more agile units assisting with latches and rope ties.

Traveling with Kit definitely has its advantages.

Gyre had expected the Seta plain to be empty, but he hadn't appreciated *how* empty it really was. Since they'd come down out of the mountains, passing a single walled town called Dustheap at the foot of the pass, they hadn't seen anything larger than a farmhouse. Kit had become adept at spotting the plaguespawn that were drawn to their passage. They'd yet to run into one large enough to give her trouble. Gyre only drew his sword to give himself a workout.

When they did encounter other humans, they didn't seem eager to make anyone's acquaintance. The farmhouses were nothing like the ramshackle, sprawling building Gyre had grown up in, with loose wooden pens for vulpi amid fields of vegetables. Each one was a miniature fortress, with an earth-and-log palisade protecting a yard full of animals and a central house with high walls and no windows. Fields had watchtowers and crossbow-armed watchmen, who often turned their unfriendly gazes on Gyre's wagons until they were out of sight.

Inside the Republic, the efforts of the Legions and the centarchs mostly kept the land clear of plaguespawn, apart from occasional incursions. The larger Splinter Kingdoms tried to do the same, though often with less success. Out here, though, in this land claimed by no nation, each small group just did their best to survive whatever wandered by.

"We moving on?" Sarah wandered up from the stream, shirt still damp.

"Yeah, Kit says she's about ready. Get Blue moving?"

Sarah nodded and pulled herself up onto the hardshell. At a tug of the rope, the big beast snorted and started its steady, tireless amble, jaw still working on a mouthful of grass. Gyre waited beside it, watching to make sure that the others joined the convoy. Red took up its position readily enough, but the third hardshell—the one formerly known as Green—was reluctant. Gyre grabbed its rope carefully. He still had a scab on his arm from the incident that had led to its redesignation as Evil Bastard. A few tugs got it started, and Gyre watched for a moment before jogging back to climb up on Blue. Once you got them going, the hardshells would follow contentedly along indefinitely.

He scrambled up beside Sarah and settled into the woven seat on the hardshell's back. One of Kit's small constructs came up with him, planting itself at the very apex of the creature's shell like a mountaineer proudly astride a peak. The rest of her bodies were out in the grass, pacing them on either side.

"You can see, even though those things don't have eyes," Sarah said.

"Mmm," Kit said noncommittally, guessing where this was going.

"And you can hear. Can you smell?"

"Not really."

"What about touch?"

"Some. I know when the arms are pressing on something."

"Do they feel pain?"

"Not especially. I'm *aware* of damage, but—" Kit shifted on her perch. "What are you planning?"

"Nothing!" Sarah said, trying to look innocent. "Just a little experiment."

"*Gyre*," Kit whined. "She wants to dissect my body."

"You've got so many bodies," Gyre said lazily. "Surely you can donate one to the cause."

"Just because I don't feel pain doesn't mean I *like* being taken apart," Kit said. "That's it, I'm going to go ride with Elariel. *She* doesn't want to disassemble me."

The little construct scuttled down the hardshell's back, then leapt to the first wagon and disappeared inside through a hatch in the roof. Gyre and Sarah looked at one another and chuckled.

"I'm still not used to that," Sarah said wonderingly. "She's really in there, isn't she? I didn't know Kit that well, but...it certainly seems like her."

"As far as I've been able to tell," Gyre said. "Elariel will explain to you all about personality simulations and self-reinforcing adjustable matrices if you ask her, but I don't recommend it."

"Noted," Sarah said, though her eyes were bright. "Though Elariel doesn't seem keen on talking to me at all."

"Elariel is..." Gyre sighed. "I don't know."

The ghoul had hidden herself in the wagon since they'd left Deepfire, not even coming out in the evenings for dinner. Gyre wasn't sure quite what to do about her. *She looks miserable.*

"I can only imagine what she's been through," Sarah said. "Changed into something else, kicked out of her home...no wonder she's depressed."

"She was better when we were in Deepfire. Maybe it's having another human around that's bothering her." Gyre shrugged. "Or maybe it's the boredom. Too much time to think."

"That can do strange things to a person," Sarah acknowledged. She looked at him sidelong. "You were going to finish that story."

Gyre had been filling Sarah in, gradually, on what had happened since he left Deepfire. It felt strange, sharing his secrets so openly. She'd agreed to help sight unseen, though, so it felt only fair that he bring her up to speed.

"I can't believe you actually found the Tomb," Sarah said. "Ibb and I had a bet, did I tell you? Over whether you'd give up or get lost and die in the tunnels."

"Which side did you take?" Gyre asked.

"I forget."

"Do you know what happened to Ibb, by the way?"

"He's okay. Went straight. Family man, husband and kids, no funny business." Sarah gave a one-shouldered shrug. "I always felt like he was more in it for the thrill than anything else."

Gyre smiled, remembering. It had been a good crew. Sarah and Ibb, Harrow and Yora. *Then I introduced Kit and screwed everything up.*

"I keep telling you it's not your fault," Sarah said quietly. "We weren't a...a social club. Even before...what happened, we were stealing from Raskos and the Auxies, and everyone knew that meant our lives were on the line."

"Yeah." Gyre forced a smile. "Anyway. We made it to the valley—"

He took the story through to the very end—his confrontation with Maya and the other centarch, Kit's betrayal, and his final face-off with Naumoriel. Dragging Kit's broken body to the ghoul machines afterward, hoping something could still be saved.

"You really think she deserved that?" Sarah said, glancing at one of the big constructs walking beside them. "After what she did to you?"

"I don't know," Gyre admitted.

"And you trust her? Now?"

"I do," Gyre said. "I understand her a little better, I think."

"Well." Sarah sat back, rubbing at her stump with her good hand. "I don't want to second-guess. But can I ask you something?"

"Of course."

"Why did you stop Naumoriel?"

There was a brief silence. Blue gave a mournful *chuff* and tore a bite from a stand of grass as they passed. The wagons behind them creaked along.

"Not that I think it was the wrong decision," Sarah said. "But the way you used to talk... I don't know. Yora wanted to get rid of Raskos, maybe make life in Deepfire a little more fair for the tunnelborn. But you always sounded like you wanted to break the Republic across your knee."

"I did. I still do. But..." Gyre sighed and leaned back in his seat, staring up at the wisps of clouds passing overhead. "Maya was right. There are some things you can't sacrifice. Yora wouldn't have burned down Deepfire just to get Raskos, and I couldn't let Naumoriel loose on humanity just because he'd take down the Order and the Republic. It can't *just* be about revenge. It has to be about what comes after."

"That's what you told the ghouls," Sarah said. "You think you'll find that in Khirkhaz?"

"I'm hoping to find... something," Gyre said. "Someone willing to work with me, at least. Yora had contacts there, and I sent some messages ahead by the old routes. When we get there... we'll see." He raised an eyebrow at Sarah. "Sorry you signed up for this yet?"

"Nah. It beats moping around Lynnia's kitchen. And I got to meet a real live ghoul." Sarah glanced back at the wagon. "Or I might get to, eventually."

Gyre closed his eyes, letting the autumn sun beat down on him. Blue put one foot in front of the other, and the wagon rolled on.

* * *

They had three big tents, which Kit had become adept at putting up, small constructs working together to tie knots and plant poles with impressive speed. Gyre and Sarah each had one to themselves, and the third remained folded, since Elariel preferred the dark, enclosed space at the back of the wagon. The ghoul hadn't even emerged when they'd stopped for the evening.

"She's eating something in there, I hope?" Gyre said to Kit, whose small construct waited nearby as he unrolled his bedding.

"Hardtack and jerky," Kit said. "We brought plenty."

"Does she actually talk to you when you're in there with her?"

"Not really," Kit said. "A lot of times I feel like she doesn't even notice me."

That made sense, Gyre reflected. In Refuge, constructs were always just *there*, going about their inscrutable business. You probably learned to ignore them.

"I'm starting to worry about her," Gyre said. "She seemed like she was coming out of herself a bit in Deepfire, but lately..."

"Can you blame her for being miserable?"

"There's being miserable and there's wallowing in misery."

"She deserves a good wallow." The small construct raised a limb, and Gyre guessed that if Kit had had eyes he'd be getting a sharp look. "You'd wallow, too, if you'd had your body radically and agonizingly changed against your will." In case the point wasn't clear, the construct tapped its carapace.

"Fair enough," Gyre said. "Was it agonizing? For you, I mean."

"Honestly," Kit said, "what with having my guts ripped open, it's hard to say. There was just a lot of agony going around."

"I'm sure." Gyre hesitated. "I did offer to turn the thing off for good afterward."

"'Sorry you're a disembodied construct now,'" Kit said, imitating

Gyre's accent, "'but it's okay, right, because I offered to kill you!' Forgive me for not being thrilled."

"All *right*," Gyre said. "You're not ever going to let me forget about this, are you?"

"Never. I mean, would you?" The construct did a little excited hopstep. "As for Elariel, I think she's still just getting used to her new body."

"How so?"

"Well, for starters, she's masturbating a lot. And I mean a lot by my standards, which are—"

Gyre rolled his eyes. "You're just envious."

"Fucking right I'm envious. You know what I would give for a good frig right now?"

"Okay. New topic, please. I saw some rabbits this morning. When we head out tomorrow, any chance you could run them down?"

"Sorry. Still thinking about the time I—"

"*Kit.*"

"Yeah, yeah. Rabbits." She heaved a sigh, and the construct did a very credible impression of a resigned shrug.

There were rabbits to be had the next day, it turned out. Kit managed to grab them and Gyre spent some time skinning and gutting them. The hardshells would gladly snap up the entrails, he found, especially Evil Bastard. By the time they camped for the night he had them ready to stake up beside the fire.

"I didn't know you were a cook," Sarah said.

"Not much of one," Gyre said. "But a few bits and pieces. There were a lot of times when a rabbit was the only meat I was likely to get."

"It *smells* amazing, at least."

"That's what I'm counting on." After nothing but hardtack for a week, fresh meat would be hard to resist. He'd made the campfire in a spot where the aroma would drift into the wagon.

Sure enough, the small door eventually opened, and Elariel emerged, blinking owlishly in the firelight. She was wrapped in a blanket, like an off-color monk's robe.

"It smells..." Elariel sniffed again and licked her lips. "Can I have some?"

"Of course," Gyre said. "It's not quite ready. Have a seat."

The ghoul shuffled over and knelt beside him, across the fire from Sarah. The arcanist smiled at her, and Elariel forced a grin, shrinking a little into her blanket. Gyre caught Sarah's eye, and she nodded.

"Gonna go and see a... something about something else?" She shook her head. "Never could remember the stupid phrase. Piss. I'm gonna go piss." She got up and went out into the darkness.

"She doesn't bite, you know," Gyre said to Elariel. "And I've told her everything. You don't have to hide."

"I'm not hiding," Elariel said. "I am just..."

"Just?"

"Hiding, I suppose." Elariel pulled up her knees and put her chin in her hands, watching the rabbits as fat dripped and popped. "I do not know how to speak to humans."

"You talk to me."

"You have been to Refuge. You saw my people as they truly are. Not always... praiseworthy, but not the monsters of your storybooks either. I do not think other humans will be so understanding."

"I think Sarah will surprise you."

"Mmm." Elariel's eyes were fixed on the food. "Are they ready yet?"

"Just about."

Sarah returned and helped Gyre cut the rabbits into quarters, while Elariel watched wide-eyed. Gyre bit into his portion, pulling the tender meat from the bone, and the ghoul tentatively followed suit. Soon she was devouring the thing with gusto, cheeks splattered with juices.

"Humans," she muttered as she ate, "are made *all* wrong. Even your teeth are wrong."

"Ghouls have different teeth?" Sarah said.

"They are sharp enough to tear," Elariel said. "Not that we do. Meat is uncommon. Most of our food is fungus."

"I can attest to that," Gyre groaned.

"And you normally have . . . fur, right?" Sarah said.

"Of course." Elariel licked a bone clean and tossed it into the fire, and then reached for another chunk of rabbit.

"There are these . . . things we often found in your ruins," Sarah said, shuffling closer. "About this big, like little half circles, sometimes with bits of bristle on them. Alyn Darkfinder wrote a treatise proposing they were a religious artifact, but—"

Elariel barked a laugh, spraying rabbit juice into the fire. "Those are brushes for cleaning your teeth!"

"I knew it!" Sarah crowed, slapping her thigh. "Darkfinder always wants everything to be *so* important."

"Cleaning teeth is important," Elariel said, grinning. "Growing new ones can be quite painful."

And they were off, Sarah asking an endless series of questions about ghouls, and Elariel laughing at her occasional misconceptions. Between them they occupied the rest of the evening and polished off the rest of the rabbits, and Gyre retired to his tent with the satisfaction of a job well done. He was a little surprised, though, when Elariel came out of the wagon first thing in the morning, shading her eyes against the sun.

"I thought I might ride outside today," she said, then looked at the ground. "If there's room, of course."

"I don't think Blue will mind," Gyre said. "Climb aboard."

Sarah, once she made sure Evil Bastard got in line properly, jogged over and pulled herself up. She grinned at Elariel and settled into the rope chair.

They were well south of the Seta by now, working their way up a range of low hills. Beyond that was another wide, flat valley, the Ghir, and then the mighty Absom. Then, finally, they would reach the border of the Republic, and Khirkhaz.

There was a track to follow, the wheel ruts of previous vehicles marking a clear, flat route that wove between the heights. They saw more signs of human habitation here, with most of the higher promontories bearing some kind of walled compound. Just in case, he'd asked Kit to keep her larger units inside the wagon.

"This must be a very warlike land," Elariel said as they bumped along in the shadow of a tall watchtower. "I suppose that was always the way of humans."

"I doubt there's been a soldier here for two hundred years," Sarah said. "There could be bandits, but it seems unlikely. Not enough traffic for even bandits to eat."

"Then why are there so many fortresses?" Elariel pointed. "See, there's another."

"Plaguespawn," Sarah said. "Each of those is probably just a few families. All the walls are to keep plaguespawn out."

"Plaguespawn," Elariel mused, then said something in her own language. "They are truly so dangerous?"

"It's not so much that they're dangerous as that they're relentless," Gyre said. "A gang of farmers with spears can kill most plaguespawn, if they find them. But the bastards just don't give up. They keep coming, year after year, and eventually they catch you with your guard down. Even where I grew up, in the Republic, there were patrols and militia alarms when one was spotted."

"Plaguespawn don't bother your people?" Sarah said.

"They try to enter Refuge from time to time," Elariel said. "Small, fragile things. The constructs destroy them."

"I asked Naumoriel about plaguespawn once," Gyre said. "The Order tells us that the ghouls created them, along with the Plague itself. He just laughed at that."

"The Chosen and their slaves are eager to blame us for everything wrong with the world," Elariel said bitterly.

"It's not true, then?" Gyre said. "Do your people know where they came from?"

Elariel was silent for a long moment, and Gyre worried he'd offended her. When he glanced over, though, she just seemed lost in thought.

"There are...stories," she said eventually. "Legends. You have to understand how much was destroyed in the war. Ninety-nine out of one hundred of my people did not survive. What you saw, at Refuge, was only the barest remnant of what we once were. A great deal of knowledge was lost along with the cities the Chosen melted to slag. But some, those who remember the war, call the plaguespawn..." She broke off, muttering something in her language, then translated, " 'the Corruptor's children.' "

"The Corruptor?" Sarah said. "Is that some sort of god?"

"Not exactly," Elariel said. "More like a cautionary tale. I explained to you, Gyre, that *dhaka* cannot be used on the *dhakim* herself? The Corruptor was one who tried, and the consequences were... dire. Our own people had to cleanse everything he had touched. Afterward, his name was stricken from our history." She shrugged. "Some believe that his spirit lingers, ready to snatch the unwary. Stories for children."

"That old woman at the trial told us we wouldn't succeed," Gyre said. "That the Corruptor wouldn't allow it."

"Pomarkiel," Elariel said. "She is considered eccentric, even among the Geraia."

"But why would this evil spirit oppose trying to overthrow the Order?"

Elariel sighed and glanced nervously at Sarah. "Before the war, there were efforts to help the three races live in closer harmony. *Some* believe that the Corruptor hated these attempts and thought that ghouls alone should survive. They say that's what led to his experiments. His name can be a... symbol for those who detest your kind." She shook her head. "It's nothing anyone younger than four hundred takes seriously."

"Four hundred." Sarah whistled. "If humans lived to be four hundred, maybe we'd be a little better at planning for the long term."

"There is a saying that short lives make for wastrel behavior, and vice versa," Elariel said. "It's pithier in my language. But the reverse can also be true. Naumoriel was unique among our leaders in despising the Geraia's... abundance of caution."

"How do these Geraia get chosen, anyway?" Sarah said.

Elariel launched into a long explanation—it was, apparently, quite complicated—and Gyre let his attention drift. The track was tending downward again, wagons rolling and bumping over the rocky ground. He couldn't see far ahead through the hills, but he could picture the map, and they were making excellent time.

If only I were more sure of what we were riding into. He'd sent messages to the Commune, but there hadn't been time for a reply. Yora had been on polite terms with the rebels, and her crew had occasionally smuggled alchemicals into the Republic for Communard buyers, but that was all. *There's no guarantee we're going to get a warm welcome.* He *hoped* that three wagonloads of weapons and supplies would buy a little goodwill. *We'll see...*

By evening, they'd emerged from the hills. Kit's constructs had once again found some meat—wild goat, this time—and Gyre did his best with the butchering and cooking. His best probably wasn't very good, but his audience seemed appreciative. After dinner, Elariel disappeared into the rear wagon and returned with a smooth, oblong ceramic box. She settled down with it in her lap and looked nervously at Sarah.

"I thought...it was time I offer this," she said. "But you should understand the risks."

"Risks?" Sarah said. Then her eyes widened, and she leaned forward. "Is that..."

Elariel nodded. The box clicked at her touch and the top swung smoothly open. Inside was an arm. It looked like a limb from one of the ghoul constructs, black muscle wrapped over metallic bones, with more metal plating on the outside. Unlike the soldier-constructs, which were only approximately humanoid, effort had been made to mimic actual human shape and musculature.

"Chosen defend," Sarah breathed. She peered at the intricate gearing of the fingers. "You just happened to have this with you?"

Gyre cleared his throat. "I asked Tyraves to include it. Just in case you decided to take me up on my offer."

"That's the Halfmask I remember," Sarah said. "Always thinking ahead." She shook her head. "Will it...work?"

"It will require *dhaka* to attach, of course," Elariel said. "And it must be adjusted, to match your body."

"Right." Sarah laughed, a little giddily, and held up her intact arm to compare. "I was just thinking it looked a little small."

"Please listen," Elariel said. "This will not be easy. I am not an expert in workings of this sort, and I have no equipment to assist me. There will be a great deal of pain, and I dare not blunt it while encouraging your nerves to bond. We will try, adjust, and try again. The result may not be perfect. I cannot guarantee... anything." She paused for breath, not looking Sarah in the eye. "Given all that, do you wish me to make the attempt?"

"She's not kidding about the pain," Gyre said. "When Naumoriel put in my eye and the rest of the augmentations..." He shuddered.

"I believe you," Sarah said, looking down at the prosthetic. "But... of course I want to do it. Any arcanist would give their right arm just to examine that thing, let alone use it." She frowned. "Figuratively. You know what I mean."

"And in your case I believe it is the left arm," Elariel said.

"Anyway. Yes. I trust you, Elariel. You can do this."

"You have no reason to trust me," Elariel said in a small voice.

"I'm choosing to do so anyway." Sarah grinned at her. "So how do we get started?"

That night, Gyre struggled to sleep through the sound of screams.

His tent was on the other side of the wagons, but it made little difference when Sarah worked herself up, alternating between full-throated shrieks and strings of high-volume profanity. He lay on his side, trying not to think back to his time strapped to Naumoriel's surgical machines. Several times he decided to go over and put a stop to it—*it has to be going wrong, for her to sound like that*—but each time he got no further than kicking the sheet away. *Because what would I say to them, really?* No one knew the danger more than Elariel herself.

The next day, Sarah was tucked up in the first wagon by the time Gyre woke, and she didn't appear for breakfast. Elariel rode beside him on the hardshell, tight-lipped and tired, and they passed the time in silence. Even Kit, for once, seemed subdued.

At lunch, however, Sarah came out of the wagon and yawned, wearing only pants and a chest wrap. Her face was hollow and her eyes bloodshot, but the ghoul arm hung at her side. The place where it joined her stump was wrapped in bandages, with angry red flesh peeking out.

"Good morning," Gyre said. "Afternoon. Are you..." He stopped, because "all right" seemed silly in light of what he'd heard last night. But he couldn't think of anything else, so he said it anyway. "All right?"

"Nope," Sarah said. Her voice was hoarse. "Not at all. But I can do *this*."

She closed her eyes, her face a mask of concentration, and the arm bent at the elbow, then relaxed.

"Congratulations," Gyre said.

"Thanks." Sarah let out a breath. "Tonight Elariel says we're going to work on the fingers."

The second night was as bad as the first, but the following day Sarah excitedly showed off her ability to make a fist. From that point on, things slowly improved. There were fewer shrieks of wordless pain, and Sarah's gaunt features began to fill out again. During the day, Elariel sat beside her on the hardshell and gave her little tests—picking up stones, or closing her eyes and guessing which finger the ghoul was pressing on. Bit by bit the arcanist improved, to her own evident delight. By the time they came to the river Ghir, she was doing tricks.

"Watch this!" She tossed a smooth stone in the air, then another, dexterously keeping them both aloft like a circus juggler. "I don't think I could do that *before* I got shot. And I *definitely* couldn't do this." She caught both stones and tightened her hand into a fist with a *crunch*. When she opened her fingers, fragments of rock and dust filtered through them.

"Remind me to be careful shaking hands," Gyre said.

"I don't recommend shaking any hands," Elariel said. "Not until you have more practice. But I think we're finished with the primary adjustments."

"Can you try putting a shirt on?" Gyre said. "We're going to have to go through a town today, and it'd be nice not to have to hide you in the wagon." He raised his voice. "Kit, speaking of which."

"Ugh," Kit said, through her nearest construct. "Weeks of tramping across empty plains, and as soon as we get near anything interesting I'm supposed to stay under cover."

"Sorry," Gyre said. "If it helps, I don't think it'll be that interesting. I'm not planning to spend the night, but this is the only bridge, unless we swing a hundred kilometers out of our way."

Sarah ducked into the wagon to change and then pulled herself back up onto the hardshell. She still used her real arm for that, Gyre noted. "How does this look?"

The loose shirt hung a little oddly on the contoured plates of the ghoul arm, but not so much that it was blindingly obvious. A casual observer might assume she was wearing a bracer under her clothes, which was odd but harmless.

"Not bad," he said. "You'll need a glove, too, of course. If we ever get somewhere with a tailor, we might be able to get you something that'll pass a little better, but it'll do for now."

The Ghir was closer than Gyre had guessed, hidden by the depths of its banks. After another hour it came into view, along with the bridge. This was a construction of Chosen make, a gentle, freestanding unmetal arch that soared effortlessly from one bank of the river to the other, half a kilometer away. More human-scale buildings were crowded around both ends, including wooden forts. They weren't large, by any means, but it was still a bigger collection of humanity than they'd encountered in weeks, and it made Gyre relax a little.

Then, as the hardshells brought them closer, he stiffened. One of the houses was canting sideways. As he watched, it leaned drunkenly against its neighbor, then collapsed entirely, wooden splinters and dust flying.

"What the plaguing fuck?" Sarah said.

Gyre closed his real eye, letting his silver one focus. He could make out the small shapes of people fleeing the destruction. Another house was already in ruins, and something large shifted in the rubble. His breath caught as it reared up, a red-and-white monstrosity of muscle and bone.

"Plaguespawn," he said. "A big one."

"There's a fortress," Sarah said. "So where are the guards?"

Gyre couldn't see anyone trying to fight back. He shook his head.

"Maybe dead, maybe fled." He checked his sword in its scabbard. "I'm going to help. Catch up when you can."

Elariel was wide-eyed. Sarah took Blue's control rope and gave him a cheerful grin. "Good luck!"

Gyre dropped to the dirt. Blue and the others kept plodding along, the wagons rumbling past at a steady pace. He took a breath and concentrated, hearing the *click* inside his skull, and the world of shadows descended.

What Naumoriel had done to him went beyond his eye. As the old ghoul had said, it was no good seeing what might happen without the speed to do anything about it, and so he'd wormed silver wires into Gyre's flesh and wrapped them around his bones. When he drew from the energy bottle, the world seemed to slow, and Gyre moved with impossible speed. He ran in great floating leaps, each footstep raising a spray of dust.

The plaguespawn was partly covered in the debris of fallen houses. It was the size of a pony, but lower to the ground and with limbs on every side of its irregular body. A central stalk sprouted a dozen eyes, surrounded by four meaty, bone-tipped tendrils that whipped out like maces to smash anything nearby. More tentacles hung under its body, trailing splintered bones as sharp as knives.

Gyre could see a couple of people lying in the street, either dead or senseless. Another corpse lay in the wreckage of the house, pulped and grisly. The plaguespawn's tendrils battered at a corner where the wall was still standing, and Gyre could hear screams. *Someone must be in there.*

He drew his silver blade, leaning into a turn as the wind of his passage stung his cheeks. He didn't bother to swing the sword, only held it out diagonally and set his arm against the shock, letting his momentum do the work like a lancer on a charging warbird. The ghoul-made weapon sliced through flesh and bone with ease, carving away two of the plaguespawn's limbs and opening a long cut through its side. Gyre was past before the black blood spurted, digging in his heels to stop in a long furrow of dirt. Smoke rose from his boots, and the energy bottle at his side was fever hot.

The plaguespawn lurched as its severed legs fell away. As Gyre hoped, it stumbled in his direction, leaving the wrecked house. The monster didn't turn—the thing didn't seem to have a "front"—but extracted itself, clumsily, and lumbered into the street, trailing black blood. All four tentacles reached for Gyre, twisting themselves into elastic coils before springing toward him with lethal speed.

Fast as they were, in the world of shadows he was faster still. Gyre started toward the thing, twisting and sidestepping in an elegant dance, letting the tentacles skim past him and chopping through them as they went. One by one they fell away. Then he was past, leaping up to land atop the thing's body and severing its eyestalk with a single stroke. As it staggered, Gyre plunged his silver sword straight down, stabbing right through the monster. It shuddered and slumped sideways.

When he was certain it was dead, Gyre let the world of shadows fade with a *click*, fighting the moment of disorientation that always came afterward. His energy bottle was mostly drained, but that wasn't a problem—he had a half dozen spares, and Elariel could recharge them. He hopped down from the corpse, wobbling a little, and sheathed his sword.

What was left of the ruined building looked set to collapse at any moment, and he could hear sobbing from under the debris. *Plaguefire.*

That sounds like kids. He picked his way closer but didn't dare shift anything. *I need Kit's spiders.* He looked up and found the caravan already at the outskirts of town, but—

They *don't look friendly.*

A dozen riders on warbirds had arrived, flanking the wagons. They were heavily armored, with steel breastplates, helmets, and bracers over thick leather. Each wore a sword and carried several thin three-meter lances in a quiver beside their bird's rump. Even their mounts were armed, great curving metal tines supplementing the warbird's natural talons and a spade-shaped steel blade covering its beak.

Sarah and Elariel, sitting on Blue's back, looked bewildered but unharmed. Gyre stepped away from the wrecked building and raised his hands peaceably as two of the riders broke off and cantered over to him. Their leader pulled up short, controlling their bird with expert clicks of the tongue, and opened their helmet visor. It was a woman with bright red eyes, her imperious expression enhanced by an abstract blue tattoo that covered most of her face.

"Identify yourself," she snapped.

"My name is Gyre," Gyre said. He nodded gently at the caravan. "Those are my wagons and my companions. We're merchants bound for the south."

Her lips twisted at the word "merchants." "I am Ichtricia, First Lance of the household of Comes Androkos. You may address me as Lance Ichtricia."

"A pleasure to meet you, Lance Ichtricia," Gyre said.

She looked past him at the broken houses. "What happened here?"

"Plaguespawn," Gyre said, pointing at the corpse. "When my companions and I approached, we saw it attacking the village. It looked like people were in danger, so I ran ahead and killed it. If your soldiers can help, I think there are survivors in that building there—"

"You killed it," Ichtricia interrupted. "Alone."

Gyre gave his blandest smile. "I carry some arcana weapons for just this sort of occasion."

"Are you aware that you are within the borders of the Kingdom of Ehrenvare?"

"I can't say that I am," Gyre said. "If there's an entry tax I should have paid, I'd be happy to—"

"Ignorance is no excuse before the law, of course." Ichtricia lowered her visor. "Gyre the merchant, you are hereby detained on the authority of King Cadmus of Ehrenvare. You stand accused of slaying a plaguespawn of greater than fifty kilograms, in violation of the edict reserving such sport exclusively for the royal family or those with their explicit writ. You and your companions will be taken to Ehren City to face His Majesty's judgment. Please remove all of your weapons, slowly."

She had one of the long, thin lances in her hand, aimed at Gyre's throat like the world's largest knitting needle. Gyre found himself with absolutely nothing to say.

Chapter 6

Maya woke in a tangle of bedsheets, gasping for breath. Her mind was a blur of horrors, Beq lying unmoving beside Jaedia in the Forge hospital, Varo telling stories about his dead friends while a black spider crawled slowly up to the back of his neck. Gyre, one eye blazing with silver fire, chasing her through the ruins of their childhood home.

Now she lay in warm semidarkness, soaked in sweat, her stomach roiling. For long moments, Maya forced herself to wait and breathe. There was pain in her chest, around the Thing, and when she explored it with her fingers she found the skin there flushed and puffy. *Again.* The worst had been the first night she'd met Gyre, when fever and weakness had racked her for days, but on several occasions since, the Thing had gotten hot enough to burn. *Is there something wrong with it, or something wrong with me?*

Never mind. Doesn't matter now. Where's Beq? She'd been bleeding— *so much blood*—but if Maya herself was safe, surely she was too. They had bandages, plenty of quickheal. *Please, please, please...*

She sat up, too fast, and her stomach heaved. Maya managed to get clear of the bedroll before vomiting a thin stream of bile. When she was done, she found her things piled at the foot of the bed, her canteen among them. She washed the taste from her mouth, drained the rest, and felt a little better.

"Hello?" she said weakly. "Is anyone here?"

"Hello." The voice was soft, muffled. "Can I...come in?"

"Who's there?" Maya said. "Where's Beq?"

A door opened, admitting a little light. Maya made out the figure of a girl of fifteen or so in a shapeless brown dress, her purple hair in a complicated braid. She slipped into the room, fidgeting nervously.

"I'm sorry," she began. "I'm not...that is, you are..." She paused, took a deep breath. "Outsiders. I've never met an outsider."

"I'm Maya," Maya said, trying to slow her racing heartbeat and put on a pleasant expression. *She looks terrified.*

"I'm Calla," the girl said.

"Calla, please. My friend, the other woman who was with me. Is she"—*not dead, she can't be dead*—"all right?"

Calla nodded, and Maya's heart unclenched.

"Your other friend, the bald one, he helped her after we brought you inside the walls," the girl said. "She's still asleep, but she looks better. His medicine works almost as well as the Eldest's."

Thank the fucking Chosen for Varo. More of Maya's tension left her. *Okay. We're all still alive. So where the plague are we?*

"Do you need anything?" Calla said. "Food? Abir said I was to see to you."

"I'd like to see my friend," Maya said. "And I could use some more water."

Calla nodded eagerly and waited while Maya got to her feet. The girl opened the door—really just a few planks nailed together—and led her out into a large common area. There were tables and chairs, all made from rough wood, and a few threadbare cushions. A pair of open windows looked out onto a patchwork of fields, leafy vegetables, and tall grain nearly ready for harvest.

Several other doors led off the main room. One hung open, and the small space beyond was empty except for a bedroll, where Beq lay under a blanket. Her eyes were closed, but she was breathing easily.

"It's about time for more 'quickheal.'" Calla pronounced the term carefully, as though she'd never heard it before. "I'll get that and some water for you."

"Thank you," Maya said. "Where's Varo?"

"Outside, with the others." Calla slipped out.

Maya knelt beside Beq and checked under the blanket, finding the bandages still clean and in place. Beq gave a murmur and looked up at her through heavy-lidded eyes.

"Hey," Beq mumbled.

"Hey yourself," Maya said, taking her hand and interlacing their fingers. "How do you feel?"

"Numb," Beq said. "Which I guess means the quickheal is working. How bad is it?"

"Pretty bad," Maya admitted. "But you'll be all right."

"What happened?" Beq said. "I remember running. One of them bit me." She squeezed her eyes shut a moment. "Did we make it to the Archive?"

"We've found a...village, I think," Maya said. "I just woke up myself, but it seems to be safe."

Beq's forehead creased. "I thought there was nobody left out here."

"I'm trying to figure that out," Maya said in a whisper. "You just rest for now."

"Okay." Beq smiled weakly. "I'm glad I'm not dead."

"Me too." Maya couldn't quite keep her voice steady. She bent down for a kiss. "Now sleep."

The door opened with a rattle, and Maya sat up. Calla handed her a pitcher of water and sat down with a bowl and a packet of powdered quickheal.

"I'll give this to her," Calla said. "Your other friend showed me how to do it."

"Thank you," Maya said. "For everything. We'd have died, if not for you."

"I didn't do anything," Calla said, reddening. "Just tended you overnight."

"I have some . . . questions," Maya said. "If you don't mind."

"You should talk to Abir," Calla said quickly. "She wanted to see you as soon as you were awake. I'm sure she'll tell you whatever you need to know."

"She's in charge here?"

"I suppose so." Calla gave a slight smile. "Everyone just kind of does what she says, most of the time."

"All right." Maya drank deep from the pitcher and gave a satisfied sigh. "Tell me where I can find her."

It was a clear morning, the air crisp with autumn in spite of the sun. Maya stepped outside and shaded her eyes.

The most striking thing about the village was the wall, which was at least three meters high. It was made of unmetal scraps, jagged-edged chunks of Chosen detritus fixed onto poles, with the gaps filled in with wood and stones. There was no wall walk, but small watchtowers stood at intervals.

Within the perimeter, the forest had been entirely cleared. There was a ring of fields, with some grassy meadows occupied by a herd of vulpi yearlings. Within that was a circle of buildings, of which the one Maya had just come out of was the largest. It was a two-story unmetal structure with ragged edges, as though it had been broken off from some larger construction and dragged here. The rest of the village was human-built, shacks and huts incorporating unmetal scraps. Maya could see coils of smoke rising from chimneys.

At the center of the village was a broad green surrounded by a circle of low, craggy fruit trees. Chickens ran wild here, pecking through the grass, pursued by small children with sticks. A few adults were about, and Maya got some curious stares.

I suppose I don't look my best. Her traveling clothes were sweat-stained and spattered with plaguespawn gore, and they'd left her spares behind with their packs and tents. She wore her haken on her hip, as usual, but neither Calla nor the villagers paid any particular attention to it. In the Republic, people couldn't keep their eyes off the legendary weapon. *Maybe they don't know what it is here.*

Abir was easy enough to find, a tall, heavyset woman in her thirties with a vast blue-and-green dress and a puff of orange-yellow hair. She was chatting to a pair of young men, but all three broke off their conversation when Maya came over. The boys goggled at her until Abir snapped her fingers in front of their eyes.

"Yes, she's an outsider. You've got a good look. Now go and get that frame built. Before sundown, you hear?" Abir had a deep, confident voice, used to being obeyed. *Definitely the one in charge.* To Maya she said, "Glad to see you awake. Did Calla offer you something to eat?"

"She did, thank you," Maya said. "I'm afraid my stomach's a little uncertain at the moment. But she said you wanted to see me."

"I thought we might have a little chat," Abir said, "and I'm sure there's things you'd like to know. Walk with me, would you?"

She started off across the green without waiting for a response, and Maya hurried to keep up with her. Chickens bolted out of their way.

"I'll start," Abir said. "You're not from one of the other villages, are you?"

"We didn't know there were *any* villages here," Maya said. "We're from . . . farther away."

"And it's just the three of you? No more?"

Maya nodded. "We're looking for something. A Chosen relic."

"I heard a story about outsiders coming to look for old things," Abir said. "My ma said *her* ma met one of them. Never thought to see it for myself, though."

"Your village has been here a long time, then," Maya said.

"Longer than anyone can remember, anyway."

"And there are others?"

"So the Eldest tells us," Abir said. "He's the only one who can make it from one to the next. Sometimes he brings goods, or people who need homes."

"Who is the Eldest?" Maya said. "And how does he move around if no one else can?"

Abir snorted. "You'd have to ask him yourself, and he's not likely to answer. The Eldest knows a good deal but isn't fond of sharing."

"Can I speak to him?"

"As it happens, you'll get a chance soon. We're expecting him the day after tomorrow." Abir halted under a fruit tree, some distance from any of the other villagers. "This thing you're looking for. Is it far?"

"I don't think so," Maya said. "Not more than a few kilometers up in the hills. It's a sort of cave." That was how previous expeditions had described the entrance, a tunnel into a solid hillside.

"I think I know the spot you mean. The monsters, they don't like anyone going up there. You're better off leaving it alone."

"I . . . need to talk to my friends. And the Eldest, if you don't mind us staying that long."

"I'm not going to turn you out," Abir said. "You're welcome to our food as long as you're here, and you'll be getting the best of it. Tomorrow night is feast night." She lowered her voice. "But I need a promise from you in return."

"What kind of promise?"

"The place you come from. There's no way to get there from here, not for us, is that right?"

Maya hesitated a moment. "No. It's . . . a long way."

"That's what my ma's ma was told, too." Abir sighed. "In that case, I'll ask you not to tell tales about it to any of ours. They ought not to pry, but if they do . . . just stay quiet. Stories will make them curious, and curious will get them dead. Especially the young ones."

Maya gave a slow nod. It was a reasonable enough request, though for some reason it made her a little uncomfortable. "I won't say anything."

"Good!" Abir clapped her on the back, hard enough to sting. "Then we'll get along nicely. You'll be wanting to see your bald friend, I'm guessing?"

"Yes, please," Maya said. "And then I may risk some food."

"Maybe throw in a bath beforehand," Abir said, looking Maya over. "That's what your friend is doing. Over behind the hall, there." She grinned. "Move quick, and you might catch an eyeful."

Maya chuckled weakly, and Abir slapped her on the back again. The hall was close to the outer wall, and as she walked back to it Maya heard the faint splash of running water. She edged around the jagged side of the building and rapped her knuckles against the unmetal.

"Varo?" she said. "Are you decent?"

"No," Varo said. "But I'm dressed, if that's what you mean."

Maya leaned around the corner. Varo was pulling on his jacket, his scalp fresh-shaved and gleaming. Behind him, a large boulder mounded through the soil, with a natural spring spilling out of it. The villagers had dug a large pool to catch it, lined with rocks.

"Good to see you up and about," Varo said. "You barely made it through the gate last night. Are you feeling better?"

Maya nodded. "I'm all right. I pushed harder than I should have."

"If you hadn't, they'd have eaten us all," Varo said cheerfully. "So I'm not complaining. You've seen Beq?"

"She woke up for a bit, and I told her to rest," Maya said. "Calla said you took care of her. Thank you."

"Stitching up friends is part of a scout's duty, when there's no one better around," Varo said. "And one that I've had a lot of practice with, funnily enough. She'll be on her feet by tomorrow, though it'd be better if we waited another day before moving on." He scratched the back of his head. "Speaking of which. Have you talked to Abir?"

"I have. She sent me back here to have a bath."

Varo laughed. "You'd better get to it, then."

Maya hesitated. The pool wasn't exactly out in the open, with the boulder on one side and the windowless back wall of the large building on the other, but anyone could still walk into view. It wasn't her modesty she was concerned with so much as the Thing in her chest, which was supposed to remain secret.

"I'll sit facing the other way," Varo said, catching her expression. "And we can have a little chat."

That was enough for Maya. She stripped and climbed in, wincing as the water reached her scrapes and blisters. It was warmer than she'd expected.

Varo, staring off into the distance, said, "So I assume you've noticed this place is impossible."

"Impossible?" Maya said. "Why?"

"You saw what the plaguespawn around here are like," Varo said, keeping his voice low. "Do you really think a three-meter wall is keeping them out? Or that these villagers would be able to stop them if they came over?"

Maya frowned. "Maybe the plaguespawn aren't always so dangerous. The whole reason there's only the three of us is because the larger groups attracted more attention."

"There have to be a couple of hundred people in this village, though," Varo said.

"Maybe it's not people that attract attention," Maya said with a sudden shiver. "Maybe it's centarchs." *In which case, my being here is putting the whole village at risk.*

"It's possible. But you'd think they would have climbed the walls when we came in last night, then. Instead they just sort of gave up, which doesn't sound like any plaguespawn I've ever heard of."

"Plaguespawn aren't supposed to hunt in packs, either," Maya said. "Maybe the villagers have some kind of protection."

"Maybe. They say this 'Eldest' can walk outside the wall without getting eaten."

"Abir mentioned him." Maya rolled over and scrubbed at a stubborn bloodstain. "Did you get a sense of who he is?"

"A priest, I think." Varo shook his head. "It just feels wrong. This whole area was supposed to be deserted."

"Maybe humans are tougher than you give them credit for," Maya said.

"Maybe," Varo said, and sighed. "Did I ever tell you about the time me and my friend found this little village in the woods? Everyone seemed so friendly. But that night—"

"You can skip to the end," Maya said.

"Still the best damn steak I ever tasted," Varo said without missing a beat. He clambered to his feet and stretched. "I'm going to poke around a bit more."

By that evening, Beq was sitting up without much pain, and Maya helped her into the common room for dinner. The arcanist, who'd reclaimed her spectacles, grinned at the sight of Maya, who was wearing a baggy brown dress much too large for her.

"I borrowed it from one of Abir's daughters," Maya said. "Since we dropped our packs, it was this or come to dinner smelling of plaguespawn guts."

Beq looked down at herself. "Do I smell of plaguespawn guts?"

"Only a little. But you've got a good excuse."

She laughed, then winced, putting her hand to her side.

"You okay?"

Beq nodded. "It just pulls at the stitches."

"I'll try to restrain my hilarity," Maya deadpanned, then lowered her voice. "So you're aware, Abir has requested that we not answer any direct questions about where we came from. She doesn't want any of her youths trying to follow us and getting themselves killed."

"Fair enough, I suppose."

Beq put her weight on Maya's shoulder, and together they hobbled through the open doorway. Several tables had been pushed together to make a large, uneven surface, and Abir was presiding over an extended family of at least a dozen. Varo was already sitting at one end, next to a handsome young man with dark blue hair and across from three younger children. By his gestures, he was well into a story already, and his audience seemed appropriately horrified. Calla, sitting directly across from Abir, shot to her feet and helped Maya settle Beq on a bench, then slipped in beside them.

"It's poor fare, I'm afraid," Abir said as two younger women started bringing plates to the table. "That's not a slight on Yrea and Gani here, it's just that we've been saving up the best for the feast tomorrow."

"Gani can do wonderful things with a mushroom," said the heavily pregnant Yrea. For some reason this produced general laughter, Abir slapping her knee in mirth.

The food might have been poor by Abir's standards, but after a couple of days of hardtack and dried meat it was a welcome relief to Maya. A thick stew, the kind of thing that bubbled for hours, reminded her of meals she'd eaten with Jaedia and Marn, stopping at an inn after a day on the road. There was thick crusty bread to mop it up, and a green she didn't recognize fried in vulpi fat. Everything was available in quantity, and Maya was relieved to see that Beq had a healthy appetite.

The conversation mostly proceeded as though the three outsiders weren't there. Abir asked the adults at the table—they were all her children or their spouses, apparently—about various ongoing projects, fields being cleared or fences mended, without paying attention to the new arrivals. The others went along, though Maya caught some surreptitious glances in her direction when they thought Abir wasn't looking.

The only exception was Calla. The girl kept her eyes on Maya and Beq and tried several times to turn the discussion to the outsiders, only to be firmly squelched by Abir. Maya, feeling awkward, could only smile and nod at this intrafamily conflict, and focused on polishing off another bowl of stew.

Eventually the party broke up, various families heading off to their own houses. Calla jumped up to help Maya with Beq, and together they got her back to her bed.

"We're going to have to put the three of you in here tonight," Calla said, looking around the small room apologetically. "The room you were in is really Mari's, and she's raised a fit about having to share with her brother."

"It's all right," Maya said. "We'll manage."

"I'll bring some more mats and blankets." She went out the door, narrowly missing Varo coming the other way.

"She seems like a nice girl," Varo said.

"I bet she's one of the ones Abir doesn't want us talking to," Maya said. "She kept staring at me."

"That boy Watt was staring at Varo," Beq said. "Though I think for different reasons."

"I can't help being a magnificent specimen," Varo said.

"So have you two figured out what we're doing next?" Beq lowered her voice. "Are we going to try to make it to the Archive?"

"I did my best to pin down exactly where we are on the map," Varo said, settling against the wall with a sigh. "If I've got it right, we're not far off. Call it five kilometers."

"It doesn't matter if it's five or fifty if we have to fight through all those plaguespawn," Maya said. Her hand tightened into a fist, relaxing only when Beq took it gently in one of hers. "We barely got away the last time."

"We don't know if they've dispersed or if they're waiting for us outside the walls," Varo said. "And if they *are* out there, going back to the Gate might be as hard as pressing on."

"If they're really defending the Archive, they might let us go," Beq said.

"But why would plaguespawn defend the Archive?" Maya extracted her hand from Beq's and rubbed her eyes with her palms. "We don't know what's really going on here."

"We can climb the towers on the walls," Varo said. "See if we can spot any plaguespawn waiting."

"That's worth a try." Maya sighed. "The Eldest is supposed to arrive the day after tomorrow. He might know something. Though Abir implied he's not likely to be helpful."

"We should give Beq another day to heal in any case," Varo said. "I can't see the harm."

Beq nodded, and Maya let out a breath. "All right. We'll rest here for a day, talk to the Eldest, and see what comes of it. Varo, you can look around for plaguespawn tomorrow."

"Oh, wonderful," Varo said, closing his eyes. "I can't wait."

Maya woke early the next day. Beq lay beside her, her breath whistling faintly, and Varo was curled into a ball on the other side of the room. Maya shuffled free of the sheet, quietly, and slipped out the door.

Calla was in the common room, scrubbing the tables from the night before. The girl started at the sight of Maya, then gave a shaky smile.

"Good morning," Maya said.

"Good morning." Calla took a long breath. "Sorry. I'm not used to anyone being around at this hour. The others are mostly outside working."

"Do you always get the indoor jobs, or is it just because you're taking care of us?"

"Abir keeps me close," Calla said. "She wants me to learn from her, I think. I don't know." She looked down, squaring her shoulders as though gathering her courage. "The—the place you came from. It's a long way off?"

"A very long way," Maya said carefully.

"And there are a lot of people there. More than here in the village."

"Quite a lot more," Maya said. "But Abir—"

"Told you not to tell us anything. I know." Calla's face fell. "She just wants to keep the Eldest happy."

"Happy?" Maya frowned. "The Eldest wouldn't like me talking to you?"

"Maybe. I don't know." She picked up her rag and went back to scrubbing the table. "It doesn't matter."

Hmm. Maya watched the morose girl a moment longer, her brow furrowed.

Changing back into her now-dry clothes made Maya feel more like herself again—she'd never gotten the hang of dresses—and when she looked outside she saw preparations for the feast in full swing. Tables were being carried out of every house and set up on the green, chickens shooed away, and a bonfire laid in the center. People Maya vaguely recognized from the night before waved a greeting, carrying bushels and baskets from a storehouse.

Returning to her own room, she found the others awake. Calla brought a breakfast of eggs, bread, and butter but hurried off quickly, busy with her own duties. Varo announced he was going to have a look around, waggling his eyebrows to make it clear what he meant. Maya helped Beq wash, then rebandaged her wounds, satisfied to see the stitched gashes were already closing up under the influence of quickheal. Beq pronounced herself fit to walk, and they wandered back to the green.

"No sign of plaguespawn," Varo told them over lunch. They sat on their own, away from the feast preparations. "Can't see much of anything, to be honest—the trees are thick. But if they're waiting for us, they're not being obvious about it."

"That doesn't add much, unfortunately," Maya said. She recounted what Calla had told her that morning. "It makes me even more eager to talk to the Eldest."

"He must know *something* about the plaguespawn," Beq said, "if he can travel from village to village."

"Or else the plaguespawn don't bother the villagers at all," Varo said.

They went over the same set of possibilities a few more times before admitting, again, that there was no way to know. Once lunch was finished, Maya volunteered herself and Varo to help with the preparations. Abir happily accepted and set Varo to plucking and gutting chickens, a task the scout turned out to be disturbingly adept at. After admitting she was terrible at sewing and cooking, Maya ended up chopping more wood for the bonfire, which was pleasantly monotonous.

"I'm sorry," Beq said. "I feel like I should be doing *something*."

"It's all right," Maya said. Sweat beaded on her brow, and she wiped it away with one hand, positioning another slice of log on the stump she was using as a chopping block. "I'm used to it. This was always my job when Jaedia and I were traveling."

"Jaedia never taught you to cook?"

"You want to know a secret?" Maya hefted the axe and grinned. "Centarch Jaedia Suddenstorm is a *terrible* cook. Marn and I were always for pushing on to the next inn, because otherwise Jaedia would try her hand at something."

Beq chuckled. "Sounds a bit like me."

"You don't cook?"

"I grew up in the Forge. There were always servants to cook for us." Beq shook her head. "Makes me sound like nobility, I guess."

Maya brought the axe down, splitting the log with a satisfying *thunk*. "Well. If we end up traveling the Republic together, one of us is going to have to learn."

"You seem happy," Beq said after a while.

"I'm happy we're not dead, for the moment," Maya said. She wiped her brow again and looked over her shoulder. "This place just reminds me of the little villages Jaedia and Marn and I would stop in. There were a lot of local festivals. Nothing grand, just food and wine and dancing. At the time I always wanted a little more excitement, but..." She shook her head.

"Jaedia will wake up," Beq said quietly.

"Yeah." *And if this Archive has a chance of helping her, then we have to get there. Somehow.*

The festival proper began at sundown. Plates of sweet bread and roasted vulpi were laid out on the tables, and barrels lined up nearby. Abir stood by the bonfire, holding a lit torch.

"Tomorrow's for the Eldest," she said. "So tonight's for yourselves. Enjoy it!"

Everyone shouted approval and Abir dropped the torch. The kindling flared up, flames licking higher and higher. On the edge of a crowd, someone started playing a stringed instrument, and a drum joined in. The crowd pressed toward the table, especially the barrels.

"Shall we?" Maya said.

Beq grinned and nodded, and together they fought their way through the press, giving and receiving good-natured jostling. After considerable struggle, they emerged triumphant, bearing clay mugs and rough wooden platters laden with food.

"It's a little different than the last party we were at," Beq said when they could hear one another again.

"Party?"

"In Deepfire. You danced with Tanax and I threw up in a potted plant."

"Oh yes." Maya rolled her eyes. "This is honestly more my speed."

"Agreed."

There was no silverware, and the roast vulpi left Maya's fingers slick with juice. She licked them clean and tried the drink. It was thick, almost like syrup, honey-sweet, and it burned the back of her throat like cold fire.

"Whew," Maya said, wiping away tears with a knuckle. "Remind me to take it easy with that stuff."

Beq sipped and wrinkled her nose. "You're not kidding."

Varo, Maya saw, was across the clearing, sharing a plate with the tall, handsome young man named Watt. She spotted Calla as well, alone among the chattering, excited villagers. Squadrons of younger children ran back and forth, with adults shouting at them ineffectually.

It could have been any village in the Republic. *Hard to believe we're a thousand kilometers from the edge of civilization.* It was nice to think that Varo's pessimistic vision—communities splintering ever smaller—didn't *have* to come to pass. *At least not everywhere.*

"Hey," Beq said, poking Maya's shoulder.

"Hmm?"

Beq nodded toward the bonfire. More musicians had joined the first two, some with real instruments, others with no more than a hollow gourd. Somehow, the plucking and shaking and drums joined into a song that everyone seemed to know. Circles formed up around the bonfire, arm in arm, spinning and kicking.

"You want to dance?" Maya said.

"You danced with Tanax last time. It seems only fair." Beq took a deep breath. "Besides, I've never danced with anybody before."

"Never?" Maya swallowed the rest of her mug and got to her feet. "Well, we can't have that."

Beq got up more slowly and took her hand. Maya paused a moment. "Your side is feeling okay?"

"It's mostly closed up," Beq said. "I'll tell you if it hurts."

"Good enough for me."

The circle opened to let them in, sandwiched tight between villagers, arms linked. What they were supposed to actually *do*, Maya wasn't exactly clear, but it didn't seem to matter much. Everyone was laughing, sweating in the heat of the bonfire and the warm evening, and jugs of the sticky-sweet stuff were making their way around the circle. Maya took only a small swallow, and Beq passed it on with a smile, but everyone else drank deep. They spun, laughing, kicked, and stumbled. A sudden jolt pressed Maya up against Beq, and then a quick reversal of direction nearly had her in the lap of an older man on the other side.

The sun passed below the horizon, colors draining slowly out of the western sky, and shadows spread across the green. The rest of the village was dark, the trees looming beyond the wall like black teeth. The circles broke up into groups and couples, and Maya found herself alone with Beq, arms around her, spinning in vague time with the music. Once again, there was no form to the dance, but it didn't seem to matter. Beq pressed against her, spectacles gleaming with firelight, and Maya didn't want the evening to end.

All at once, the music stopped, and everyone came to a halt. The world kept spinning for a few moments, and Maya wondered how many sips of the sweet stuff she'd had. Then Beq kissed her, and she stopped worrying about it. When they finally broke apart, Maya was short of breath, sweat trickling down her cheeks.

"I need water," Maya said.

"Me too." Beq pointed to the edge of the clearing. "Over there, I think."

There was a half-full barrel by the benches. Maya filled a mug, and they sat and passed it back and forth as the music started up again. It was different, lower and faster, an urgent, throbbing beat shot through with pulsing drums. Some people were drifting away, herding children off to bed. Maya spotted Varo and Watt, hand in hand, headed off into the darkness. The rest stayed by the fire and started a new dance.

"What are you thinking?" Maya said, leaning back on the bench.

"I'm thinking I'm getting tired," Beq said. "And tomorrow..."

"Yeah." Maya got up and held out a hand to help Beq to her feet. "I'm glad we got to dance."

"Me too."

They kissed again, lips sweet with the sticky liquor.

It took Maya a moment to get her bearings, but she spotted the irregular shape of the main hall and oriented herself. She led Beq in that direction, circling around the dancers, and a lone shape broke off and came toward them. Maya paused. It was Calla, she saw, but something seemed...wrong.

"Maya!" the girl said, weaving on her feet. "Leaving already? There's plenty of night left."

"Beq's still recovering," Maya said apologetically. "But it's been wonderful."

"It's just getting started." Calla grabbed at Maya's arm. "Come on."

When she turned to the light, Maya could see that Calla's eyes were glazed with alcohol. The top of her dress was untied, and it flapped against her waist, her small breasts spattered with drops of liquor. When Maya pulled back, abruptly, Calla overbalanced and staggered backward. Beyond her, Maya saw, the dance had changed. Some couples held each other tight, spinning and shrieking with laughter. Others had slowed, kissing and groping in the dark. The rest, on the soft grass or up against the tables, were... not dancing. Under the music, she heard breathy moans.

"Sorry," Maya said. "We're... tired. Right?" She prodded Beq, whose eyes had fixed on two girls grappling only a few meters from where they stood.

"Right," Beq said. "Tired."

"But..." Calla said.

"You might want to go to bed too," Maya said.

"Course not." The girl straightened up as best she could. "Last night. Last chance."

"Last chance?" Maya frowned, but Calla was already slipping away in the shadows.

Beq tugged at her arm, and they left the bonfire behind. Maya's skin felt steaming hot, and she was glad no one could see her flush.

"That didn't usually happen at the village festivals," Maya said.

"I was wondering," Beq said carefully. "You did say you thought they could use more excitement."

"I suppose every place has its own customs." Maya shook her head.

"Do you think Calla will be all right?" Beq said.

"Probably. She was trying to get us to join in."

Beq frowned. "She seemed... I don't know."

Scared. There had been terror in the back of her eyes, under a thin layer of alcohol and bravado. *Last night. Last chance.*

Tomorrow's for the Eldest, Abir had said. *So tonight's for yourselves.* Maya paused and looked over her shoulder at the distant fire. "I'm starting to be really interested to hear what the Eldest has to say."

In the morning, Maya's head throbbed more than she would have liked, but probably less than she deserved.

Beq was sleeping peacefully, but Varo was either up already or hadn't returned. *Most likely the latter.* He and Watt had disappeared at some point during yesterday's festivities.

There was no sign of Calla in the common room. Maya debated for a moment, then took a cloth and headed for the bath. It would be safer if there were someone to keep watch, but she'd had plenty of experience hastily covering the Thing if it came to that. *And I probably won't get another chance to clean up before the Eldest arrives.*

She undressed carefully, setting her haken on top of the pile of folded clothes. There were no villagers working in the fields. *I assume they're all sleeping it off.*

What was *that?* She'd been at festivals that had gotten rowdy. And though she'd never had the chance to participate—Jaedia was a watchful mentor—she'd certainly seen blushing couples sneak away from a dance. But they'd always seemed, well, *happy* about it. Whereas the looks she'd seen last night...

Desperate. That's how Calla had sounded. *Desperate for the night not to end.*

Something rustled, back toward the building. Maya put one hand on her cloth, folded at the edge of the pool, and said, "Hello?"

"It's just me," Calla said. She sounded miserable.

Poor girl. "It's all right," Maya said, climbing out of the bath and wrapping the cloth around her midsection. She made sure it covered the Thing, then looked over her shoulder. "Are you feeling—"

Sunlight gleamed on the blade of the knife.

Maya had only a moment of warning, thanks to habitual caution from years of hiding the Thing. Calla held the blade in both hands, low and straight, aiming to plunge it into Maya's belly. Maya grabbed the girl's wrist and twisted away, pushing the knife far enough that it drew a long, shallow cut on her hip instead. Calla's body cannoned into her, and Maya managed to bring her knee into the girl's gut, doubling her over. The breath went out of Calla, but she still struggled to bring the knife up, and it was all Maya could do to keep it away.

Her side stung, bleeding freely. Ordinarily her panoply protected her from small wounds, but her panoply was folded up with her clothes, underneath her haken two meters away. That was two meters too far to help. *Plaguing* fuck!

"Calla?" Maya gasped out. "What are you *doing*?"

"I'm sorry," Calla said, and for a moment Maya thought it had all been a *mistake*. But Calla was still trying to bring the knife to bear, forcing it centimeter by centimeter toward Maya's skin. "I'm sorry—"

Maya rocked backward, shifting her weight, and brought her leg around behind Calla's, yanking her knee out from under her. The girl went down with an *oof*, and Maya scrambled away. Unfortunately, that took her farther from her haken, and Calla got back on her feet, brandishing the blade.

It was a long carving knife, not a real weapon. And Calla had tears running down her cheeks. *What in the name of the Chosen is going on?*

"Drop it," Maya said. "I don't know what's happening, Calla, but—"

"I can't." Calla swallowed, shifting the knife to a one-handed grip. "This is my only chance, Maya, I'm so sorry."

"Only chance for *what*—"

But Calla charged again, one shoulder down, bringing the knife around in an arc. Maya, naked, her hair still dripping chill water, dropped into a crouch to meet her. She stepped out of the direct line of Calla's rush, blocking the wide swing of the knife with her forearm. But Calla twisted with wiry strength, wrapping her other hand around Maya and tangling their legs, and together they stumbled and fell.

It was not a kind of fighting Maya had much training for. Jaedia had showed her a few basic punches and grapples, but centarchs weren't supposed to be caught unarmed, where they were no more capable than an ordinary human. Maya was stronger from years of swordwork, but Calla seemed to be fueled by despair. They struggled for a moment, limbs flailing, and Maya got her hand on Calla's shoulder, pushing her up. Calla pulled the knife in, trying to drive it down, and Maya kept one hand around her wrist. The blade trembled in the space between them.

"Calla," Maya gasped, "*please.*"

"You wouldn't come last night," Calla said. "So it's on me, and I'm *sorry—*"

Calla forced the knife down nearly to Maya's collarbone, tip shivering dangerously. Desperately, Maya shifted her grip, changing directions. She twisted Calla's wrist and shoved. Calla fought back, grabbing Maya's arm with her off hand, but Maya's skin was still slippery and she couldn't get purchase. The knife twisted and bit home, and the girl gasped. All at once, the strength went out of her, and Maya sent her tumbling over.

No no no. Maya scrabbled to her feet. Calla lay on her back, arms spread, the blade buried to the hilt in her chest just below her breast. Her breath came quick and fast, flecks of crimson appearing on her lips. Her eyes found Maya.

"...sorry..." she managed, coughing up a bubble of blood.

"Maya!" Beq's voice, and rapid footsteps. "Maya, where—oh, *fuck.*"

"She tried to kill me," Maya said. "I don't know—why would she—"

"There are plaguespawn inside the walls," Beq gasped out. "Down on the green."

"*What?* Where are the villagers? Where's Varo?"

Beq shook her head frantically. "Don't know."

Focus. Maya fingered the Thing, then tore her hand away. "Get Calla inside. She needs quickheal."

"But you said she tried to kill you."

"She didn't want to. Something horrible is happening." Maya grabbed at her clothes. "We have to find Varo."

She couldn't recall ever dressing so hurriedly, though she took a moment to make sure the panoply belt was in place. Her side was still bleeding sluggishly, but there was no time to do anything about it now. Back inside the hall, Beq had dragged Calla through the door and given her a waxy tablet of quickheal to chew, pressing her mouth closed. From the opposite window, the green was visible, and Maya risked a quick peek.

A half dozen plaguespawn of the strange humanoid variety stood in front of last night's bonfire. They weren't moving, just waiting quietly, and to Maya's shock the villagers were assembling around them. Many were still in soiled clothes from the night before, or half-naked, but they came out of their buildings in an obedient mass and gathered amid the trash still strewn around from the festival. Maya looked for Abir, but she was nowhere to be seen.

"Maya," Beq said. She looked stricken. Calla's jaw hung open, a mass of frothy red running from the corner of her mouth, and she didn't move.

Fucking Chosen. Maya swallowed against a sudden block in her throat. *Why would she—*

Get out of here first. Jaedia's voice, rising from her memory. *Figure it out later.*

Movement outside. Maya turned in time to see the villagers falling to their knees, heads lowered, murmuring in low voices.

"Eldest." Another figure was coming through the crowd, wearing a hooded cloak. The villagers shuffled out of its way. "Eldest."

At the front of the crowd the new arrival stopped, facing Maya, and threw back its hood. The features underneath had once been a young woman's. Her skin was filthy and gray, and half her hair had grown down to her waist, greasy and ragged. The other half had fallen away, and her skull looked like it had *bubbled*, rising like a loaf of bread. One eye had been replaced with a weeping sore, and strange protrusions bulged beneath her torn, ragged shift. One of her legs had an extra joint, surrounded by sores and dried fluid.

On the back of her neck, half-hidden by her hair, a fat black thing hung like a satiated tick. Spidery legs reached around under her chin and across her collarbone.

Eldest. Maya felt a boiling rage. She closed her hand into a fist, and a blast of flame slashed out the window, white-hot, to obliterate the horrific thing altogether. Before the bolt struck home, though, the monster moved, grabbing the nearest villager. The man abruptly *unfolded*, his body splaying outward like an umbrella of muscles and bone while his guts splattered unneeded on the grass. The fire hit this barrier and evaporated, leaving a charred curtain of organic wreckage. The monster lowered its hand, and what was left of the villager collapsed in a smoking heap.

"Well," the creature said, its voice twisted and bubbling. "That answers *that* question. Calla failed again, did she?"

Maya ducked back out of the window, back pressed against the wall, breathing hard. Beq got to her feet by Calla's body, looking shaky.

"We have to find Varo," Maya hissed. "I'd bet he's with Watt. They were together at the dance."

"He lived one building over, I think," Beq said. "You think Watt tried to—"

"I'll hold the Eldest's attention," Maya said. "You get out the back and make sure Varo's all right."

Beq swallowed and nodded. "Then what?"

"One of these spider-things was a match for me and Tanax," Maya said. "It was Jaedia who stopped it, and we can't count on that. I'll need your help."

"Of course."

Chosen defend. Her wounds are barely healed and I'm asking her to throw herself into the fight again. Maya's fist clenched, but she kept her voice level. "Okay. When you've got Varo, fire a few shots to draw its attention, then *move*. If you can distract it, I may be able to take it out. If I can't, you'll have another chance when it turns back to me. Got it?"

Beq gave a quick nod, checked her blaster pistol in its holster, and ducked out the back door. Maya returned to the window and found the Eldest had stalked closer, flanked by its plaguespawn and a small group of cowering villagers.

"Centarch?" it said. "Is Calla still with you?"

"Calla's dead," Maya shouted back. "Because you made her try to kill me."

"I see." The villagers flinched, anticipating the Eldest's anger, but the monster's tone remained mild. "Always a risk, I suppose. Abir was grooming her to be my host, but there's no shortage of replacements. And her meat will make a fine addition to my children." The thing gave a bubbling laugh, high and insane. "Unless you've incinerated her? A waste of fine flesh, that."

"It's *you* I'm going to burn," Maya said. "I've killed one of your kind already."

"How nice for you." The thing giggled again. "But the others are not of my kind, any more than a newborn baby is of yours. I am the *Eldest*, foolish little human. The others are mere echoes of our father, but I have had centuries to transform myself into something greater. When our father returns, I will be exalted above all others!" Its voice rose, cracked, and the woman's twisted body doubled over, spitting black blood on the ground.

Out of another window, Maya caught sight of Beq, sprinting across the gap between buildings. Hurriedly, she shouted, "If your father has left you here this long, what makes you think he's coming back?"

It was a shot in the dark, but apparently she'd touched a nerve. The Eldest straightened up, teeth bared in a snarl, black fluid dripping off its chin. It reached out a hand, and the pile of charred meat rose again, reshaping itself into a long, ropy tendril of flesh, which coiled like a whip before lashing out. Maya threw herself back from the window as the tentacle slammed through, slashing itself on the edges of the unmetal.

"I will be *exalted*!" The Eldest raised its hands to the sky, and the tentacle reached farther in through the window, splitting apart into a dozen smaller tendrils that groped toward Maya like blind roots. "How many of *your* kind, centarch, do you think I have taken to pieces? I've certainly lost count. Their blood and bone are part of my children now, as yours will be. And yet you keep coming. Is the pathetic wisdom of the *Chosen* so important to you?"

Maya ignited her haken, slashing through several tendrils, and retreated toward the door. She waited for a moment, watching more pulsing flesh lever itself into the common room, ropes of bleeding muscle smashing the furniture.

Then, from outside, the *crack* of blaster bolts and the boom of explosions. Maya kicked the door open in time to see a plaguespawn shield its master from the fusillade and get blown apart. A final bolt detonated against the Eldest, sending the creature's arm spinning away in a gory pinwheel. It gave a vicious screech and pointed. Plaguespawn sprinted toward the source of the bolts. The Eldest grabbed another villager, a woman who managed an agonized scream before her flesh tore itself apart, muscles unwrapping to form more tentacles.

Maya was already throwing herself forward. Whatever the villagers had done, whatever the Eldest had made them do, they didn't deserve *that. No one does.* A pair of plaguespawn turned back to rush her as she came outside, but she sent a blast of flame that blew one into charred ashes, and slashed the other in two with her haken, ignoring the still-twitching pieces.

The Eldest saw her coming, turning back toward her and sending ropy tendrils spiraling in from all sides, laughing as black blood dripped from its severed arm. Maya planted a foot and spun, a circular blast scything outward. Pieces of tentacle fell, writhing on the ground like snakes, but the severed stumps simply exploded outward in a fresh orgy of growth. Maya pressed forward, hacking away like Varo with his machete, clearing a path.

All of a sudden the Eldest was right in front of her, tick legs twitching, its twisted body's face split in a broad grin. It reached its remaining hand into the deliquescing corpse of its latest victim and emerged holding a dripping spinal column, the vertebrae stiffening until they formed a blade in its hand. It raised this macabre weapon to parry Maya's overhead strike, solid fire slamming into fresh bone with a jolt.

"The Chosen liked to say flesh and blood are no match for *deiat*," the Eldest said, gurgling with laughter. "But I always thought they lacked vision."

Something strange was happening at the point of impact, where fire and bone met. The *deiat* blade charred its way through, but the bone-sword rippled and grew back as fast as it was destroyed. In the meantime, the tendrils began to tighten, closing in on Maya from every side. Her panoply flared under multiple impacts, the drain of power like ice water flooding her veins.

"Don't feel bad." The Eldest laughed. "As I said, you're not the first, and you won't be the last. You and the rest of your deluded Order—"

An explosion rocked the tightening cage of meat and bone, and the Eldest clucked its tongue, spraying Maya's face with black fluid.

"Your friends are persistent," it said. "Perhaps I'll weave all of you together, strand by strand. Would you like that?"

"Shut. Up." Maya leaned into her rage. She saw Beq's determined features, Calla's face slick with tears. "You've twisted these people long enough."

"People? You mean my breeding stock?" The Eldest gave another choking laugh. "They'd have died out long ago without my help. You humans are so *fragile*."

"*Shut. Up!*" *Deiat* poured into Maya, and her haken flared brighter. The Thing was flaring too, first blood-hot, then white-hot. She could hear the flesh around it sizzle, but the pain was far away. The Eldest's smile faded, and its bone-blade faltered.

"Impossible." It snarled, black-stained teeth twisted into horrible shapes. "You can't—"

Its distended eye focused on the Thing, now searing its way through Maya's shirt, and something like horror came over its face.

"One of *you*." Its tendrils pulled in tighter. "Father sent *you* here? *Now?!*" Its voice rose into a mad shriek. "*Impossible!* I was to be *exalted*!"

"I told you," Maya gasped out. "Your father's not coming back for you."

The bone-blade snapped, and her haken plunged down, carving through the black tick-thing and its twisted host in the same blow. With a wail, the Eldest detonated in a spray of black gore and bone shrapnel, and Maya felt her panoply flare bright as it absorbed the blast. The last thing she saw, before *deiat* exhaustion claimed her, was the terrified villagers running for their lives.

Chapter 7

Tell me again," Sarah muttered, "why we're not fighting our way out."

"For starters, this thing is nearly empty." Gyre gestured to the energy bottle on his hip and winced. The motion tugged against the rope wound around his wrists, scratching skin already rubbed raw by the bonds. He kept his voice low. "I'd have a couple of seconds at best. And if you haven't noticed, there are quite a lot of them."

"I could handle a few myself," Sarah said. Her artificial fingers flexed inside their leather glove.

"Even if we got clear, we still can't outrun warbirds," Gyre said. "At least they're taking us in the right direction."

In truth, it was pretty much the route Gyre would have followed on his own, although he would have much preferred riding to walking with bound hands. From the Chosen-built bridge over the Ghir, the road ran south, winding through gentle hills. The Kingdom of Ehrenvare—not that Gyre had ever heard of such a polity before today—seemed like a prosperous country, and they passed large, well-tended fields and hillside orchards.

Ichtricia's soldiers kept to the center of the road, with the wagons and the rest of the party strung out behind them. People going the other way gave them a wide berth, offering deep bows at the sight of the armored riders. In addition to the dozen lancers, they'd met up with a squad of infantry, poorer soldiers with leather caps and crossbows, accompanied by loadbirds and servants. A few of these took charge of the three hardshells, and Gyre was privately pleased when one of them nearly lost a finger to Evil Bastard's chelonian malice.

Kit's bodies were still in the wagons, closed up tight, along with what was left of their cash, Gyre's spare energy bottles, and the weapons the soldiers had relieved them of. *Along with the cargo, which is the point of the whole exercise.* Even if they could get out from under the watchful eyes of the crossbowmen, the hardshells couldn't manage more than a slow walk. *If we could swap them for teams of loadbirds, then maybe...*

Part of him was still furious at being taken unawares so easily. He glanced down at the nearly exhausted energy bottle and shook his head. *There are definitely drawbacks to this thing.*

Elariel walked beside him, shoulders slumped. Gyre made sure none of the guards were paying close attention, then leaned toward her.

"Hey. You okay?"

"Feet hurt," the ghoul muttered. "Will they kill us, do you think?"

"I doubt it. They're more likely to want our supplies."

"Which means this has all been for nothing." Her voice cracked. "Perhaps I should have let the Geraia execute me."

"I'm working on it." Gyre lowered his voice to a whisper. "You can refill the energy bottle, right? How long does it take?"

"A few hours," Elariel said. "I'd need to touch it."

Gyre grimaced. "Keep watch for a good chance. Maybe when we make camp for the night."

The ghoul gave a small nod.

He had been hoping they'd stop in a village, somewhere that offered a place to hide. When evening came, though, Ichtricia just turned off the road into the yard of the nearest farm, paying little attention to the farmer's frantic bows. The servants swarmed over the ground, erecting tents at a speed that would have done credit to Kit and her constructs and staking out the warbirds near the farmer's nyfa bushes so they could feed. One woman, wearing Ichtricia's colors and presumably her personal valet, told the sweating farmer that the lancers would require dinner. Gyre expected the man to object—feeding a dozen guests at short notice would strain the resources of any small farmer—but he only bowed deeper and hurried inside. When he reappeared, accompanied by his wife and a small swarm of children, they were carrying platters of roasted vegetables, fresh bread, and steaming vulpi.

That was only for the lancers, though. The infantry and servants—and the prisoners, of course—made do with their own supplies, the tiresomely familiar double-baked biscuit and jerky. After dinner, the three of them were escorted to a tent with the flaps tied up, and a crossbowman settled himself on a stone a few yards away. Clearly, Ichtricia had given orders that they weren't to go unobserved even for a moment. Gyre mentally kicked himself for his earlier bravado over the plaguespawn's corpse. *If she thought we were ordinary merchants, she might not be so careful.* Elariel pulled herself into the corner as far as she could and curled into a ball. Sarah watched her and frowned but said nothing.

Gyre turned his attention to the guard. The man—a boy, really, with a peach-fuzz beard, too-large cap leaning on his head—had his crossbow on his lap, not ready to fire. *I might be able to get to him before he shoots, but not before he screams.* One shout would bring the whole camp down on them.

Instead, Gyre sat with his bound hands in his lap until the boy met his eyes, then gave an exaggerated smile. The guard scowled, which he probably thought made him look fierce.

"Can I ask you something?" Gyre said.

"No tricks," the boy said, gripping the crossbow a little tighter. "Or I'll fetch Ichtricia."

"I certainly don't want that," Gyre said. "I was just hoping you could explain something to me. When we were detained, she said something about our being accused of killing a plaguespawn. Did I hear that right?"

"Gyre," Sarah murmured. "What are you doing?"

"Just gathering information," Gyre said quietly, then added at a normal tone, "I'm just trying to figure out how it can be a crime to kill plaguespawn. Surely the king wants them dead?"

"It's no crime to kill a little one," the boy said, warming a little. "Done it m'self. But the big ones are the king's pre-rog-a-tive." He pronounced the word like something he'd carefully memorized. "He grants the hunting rights to the nobles he favors."

Thus preventing anyone out of favor from building up goodwill with the commoners, I suppose. It made a certain twisted sense. *If protecting the people is the king's job, he can't have anyone else doing it for him.*

"Lady Ichtricia had the rights to the one you killed," the guard added, and lowered his voice. "That's why she's so angry. She and her lancers spent days getting ready for the hunt."

"I...see." Gyre exchanged a look with Sarah. "Any idea what the penalty for us might be?"

"That's up to the king," the boy said. "Or the Logothete, probably." He shifted a little, as though trying to restrain himself, and gave up. "How'd you do it, anyway? Everyone's dying to know. Longtooth bet Alan ten thalers you're a centarch in disguise."

"If I was a centarch in disguise," Gyre said, "why would I let myself get arrested?"

"Dunno. Maybe it's all part of the plan."

"Quiet from the prisoners!" another man shouted.

The boy shrugged helplessly. Gyre grinned at him and waggled his eyebrows, just for effect.

After a bad night's sleep on rocky ground and a hurried breakfast, they got back on the road. Ichtricia and the other lancers hadn't put their armor back on, and they might have passed for a group of nobles on a pleasure ride. The infantry were still armed and alert, though, and several crossbowmen sat atop the hardshells, enjoying the chance to rest their legs.

"Never thought I'd see Halfmask being obediently led off to prison," Sarah said as they trudged along.

"We're waiting for the right moment," Gyre growled. He checked his energy bottle and swore inwardly. *Not even close to enough.*

"When's that? After they hang us?"

"You don't actually seem worried."

"Nah. You'll come up with something."

Gyre shook his head. "What makes you so sure?"

"You always have." She glanced at her artificial arm, still concealed under the shirt and glove. "Except once."

"Yeah." Gyre looked at the ground, throat suddenly thick. "Right."

Sarah grinned. "Still, overall, it's a pretty good record."

Abruptly she lunged forward to grab the back of Elariel's shirt as the ghoul stumbled. They grappled awkwardly, hands still tied, but managed to remain upright. Several of the escorting crossbowmen raised their weapons at the sudden movement.

"Easy!" Sarah said. "Easy. Just helping her. Elariel, are you okay?"

"Feet hurt," the ghoul muttered, pressing toward Sarah and away from the guards' unfriendly stares.

"She's not used to walking," Gyre said. "She'll have blisters. Can we stop so I can tend to her?"

The sergeant, an older woman with a sour look, stared in silence for a moment before she trudged up the column to Ichtricia. They conferred, and the noblewoman shook her head sharply.

"We'll be at the city in another hour," the sergeant called back. "You can rest then."

"Gyre," Elariel whispered. Gyre bent closer to hear. "I am not in as much pain as I professed. Look over my shoulder."

Gyre blinked and scanned the side of the road. Down in a weedy ditch, difficult to spot among the tangled stems, was a many-legged black construct, hunkered down to stay out of sight. Gyre risked a tiny wave in its direction, and it bobbed briefly in return.

"Nicely done," he told Elariel as the sergeant returned. "We'll make a proper rebel of you yet."

The city, when it came into view, wasn't much to look at. Built on a low hill overlooking a small river, it was surrounded on three sides by a wall built around large unmetal fragments linked by segments of crude stone. Inside, buildings were packed as tightly as dwellings in the tunnels of Deepfire, rising three or four rickety stories over the street. A second wall circled the hilltop, where a few grander residences surrounded a single palatial building.

The road ran over a stone bridge and up to a gate, which stood wide open and jammed full of carts and wagons. People came and went in a steady stream, peasants in homespun and leather, watched by a few bored-looking guards. At the sight of Ichtricia, they perked up and began shouting in a vain attempt to impose order and clear a space for the hardshells and wagons to pass. Just on the other side of the gate, Gyre caught a glimpse of a bustling market square. He prodded Sarah with his elbow.

"This is it," he muttered. "Once we're through the gate. Run for it, stay together, and we'll lose ourselves in the crowd."

"What about the cargo?" Sarah said.

"One thing at a time. Once we're clear we can figure out how to get it back."

The artificer nodded slowly and leaned over to Elariel. Their guards' attention was focused on the upcoming traffic jam, where Ichtricia was now berating the gate sergeant for not opening a path quickly enough. Carts were shoved aside, teams squealing or squawking in protest. In all the confusion, no one but Gyre saw a small black shape scuttle through. He spotted it again, atop a hay wagon drawn by four ornery-looking loadbirds. Kit raised two limbs questioningly, and Gyre gave a vigorous nod. The spider vanished into the hay.

"Follow my lead," Gyre said to Sarah.

The hardshells plodded forward, chuffing with agitation at the sudden onslaught of sounds and smells. A narrow street led up the hill, overhung by tenements on both sides. Ichtricia's voice cracked like a whip at the head of the column, the commoners cringing as they got out of the way. They stared openly at Gyre and the others as they passed.

They were through the gate, past the outer cordon of guards, with the press of the market on all sides. Gyre kept his eyes on the hay wagon. *Anytime, Kit...*

A fast, dark shape scuttled from under the wagon. Tiny limbs reached out to stick the loadbirds in their sensitive feet—only pinpricks, but enough to spook the none-too-bright animals. Two of the four squawked and tried to bolt, vestigial wings flapping wildly. They pulled the wagon forward half a step, startling their companions, who began a vigorous squawking protest of their own. Nearby, a team of thickheads went into their threat display, rearing up to display their colored underbellies. Another of the lizard-like creatures, terrified, hunkered down with forelimbs over its eyes to wait for the danger to pass. In an instant, the slim space cleared by the guards was a mass of hissing, shoving, flapping animals.

Gyre concentrated and felt the *click* in his skull. The street slowed to a crawl, thick with the future-shadows of everyone and everything in motion. The energy bottle at his side grew warm at once. *Not much time.*

The nearest guard was turning to them, her mouth slowly opening into a shout, her crossbow coming to her shoulder. Gyre grabbed the weapon with his still-bound hands, aimed it skyward, and pulled the trigger, then gave her a shove from behind that sent her stumbling in slow motion into her nearest comrade. Behind him, Sarah burst her own bonds with a quick flex of her artificial arm and grabbed hold of Elariel, dragging the startled ghoul after her.

So far, so good. They needed an exit from the square. The nearest alley wasn't far, but the way was blocked by a row of vegetable stalls. Gyre shoved them aside, shadow-carrots tracing out parabolic arcs overhead. Sarah, sprinting but still moving slowly from Gyre's perspective, followed in his wake.

Behind them, a guard managed to level his crossbow and shout a warning. Gyre picked a hurtling cabbage from midair and slung it at him, disarming the man in an explosion of shredded leaves. Ichtricia was pointing and shouting, but she was inaudible over the general babble. The loadbirds were pecking furiously at the thickheads, who hissed in return, the two species falling easily into their eternal conflict. Gyre spotted Kit's spider following them, dodging through a forest of ankles.

They'd just cleared the entrance to the alley when the energy bottle suddenly went cold. The flow of time abruptly returned to normal, and Gyre stumbled against the plaster wall of the nearest building.

"Gyre!" Sarah pulled Elariel over. "Are you—"

"Drained it too low," Gyre gasped out. Darkness seethed at the corner of his vision. "Find somewhere to hide. Recharge—"

Too late. The ghoul augmentations pulled more energy than he had to give, and he fell forward into darkness, only just aware of Sarah's strong arm catching him around the waist.

When he woke up, he immediately regretted it. There was a deep ache in his chest, as though all the breath had been sucked out of him. It subsided only gradually as he gasped for air, giving him plenty of time to appreciate the smells that were thick in the air—overripe midden, mostly, with a heavy note of blood.

"Elariel said that would bring you around," Sarah said. She was a vague shape leaning above him as Gyre worked his gummy eyes open. "How do you feel?"

"Like I got kicked by a warbird," Gyre said. "Are we safe?"

"More or less," Sarah said. "Ichtricia's soldiers are still searching the alleys, but they haven't found us yet."

"I think they've given up," Kit said from somewhere nearby. "Or else snuck off to the pub."

Gyre sat up, the ache slowly fading. The energy bottle at his hip had the glow of a full charge. He'd been lying on a threadbare rug, folded over into a makeshift bed and crammed into a room small enough that he could touch both walls. There was a window, or at least a hole in the wall, plaster flaking at the edges. Kit's spider was perched there, overlooking the twisting streets below. The day was nearly gone, long shadows throwing the alleys into darkness.

Sarah sat on the other side of him, in the doorway to the rest of the building. A rag curtain hung in another doorway behind her, and through it he could hear the quiet murmur of voices. She offered him a canteen, and he took a long pull.

"Okay," he said. "So where are we? Where's Elariel?"

"She's just out in the main room with Lizanne," Sarah said. "We're in the middle of one of the tenement blocks, on the third floor."

"She says the guards don't come in here much," Kit said. "Not at all if they can help it."

"And who's Lizanne?" Gyre said.

"It's a long story." Sarah pursed her lips. "Well. Not that long. I was carrying you and we ran into her coming the other way—"

"Literally," Kit added. "You're lucky you didn't break anything."

"—and when she asked us where we were going, I said that you were sick and Elariel was a doctor and we needed somewhere to work on you out of sight. She agreed to let us into her place so we could get off the street."

"Kind of her," Gyre said. "She'll be in danger if the guards do find us."

Sarah nodded. "Elariel agreed to take a look at her son after we got you settled."

"Is that what she's doing now?" Gyre said.

"Sort of." The artificer looked over her shoulder. "It's . . . gotten a little bit out of control. You should probably talk to her."

"Before she tips off half the city we're here," Kit muttered.

Gyre extended a hand, and Sarah grabbed it and hauled him up, tottering only a little. "Kit, you—"

"Stay and keep watch?" Kit said peevishly. "Yeah, yeah. Just hurry up, all right?"

There was less teasing in her voice than usual, and more real anger. Gyre frowned as Sarah led him out to the curtained door.

"Is something wrong with her?" he said quietly.

"No idea," Sarah said. "Maybe she's not happy having to stay out of sight?"

On the other side of the curtain was a larger room, four or five meters square. It seemed to serve every possible purpose for its residents—there was a wobbly table and a couple of boxes to sit on, and a stack of makeshift bedrolls in the corner ready to spread out on the floor. Elariel was currently sitting on the only cushion, examining a stick-thin girl in her teens with pale, filth-crusted skin and ragged green hair. An older woman sat in the corner, with a small child in her lap looking on through wide, owlish eyes.

"That's the best I can do." Elariel leaned back from the girl. "I've cleared out the diggerworm, but it'll come back if you don't keep your feet dry. And you need..." She gave a weary sigh. "More to eat. Like the others."

The girl gave a little bow, half gratitude and half terror, edging backward out of the room through another curtain. A gangly man poked his head through as soon as she was gone.

"Is this the doctor?" he said. "I heard—"

"The doctor needs a moment to rest," Sarah said, pushing forward and putting a hand on Elariel's shoulder. "Wait for a moment, please?"

Reluctantly, the man withdrew. Gyre bowed politely to the woman in the corner, who watched him cautiously.

"You're Lizanne, I take it?" Gyre said. "Thank you for letting us use your home."

"You can thank me by getting your circus out the door," Lizanne said. She crossed her arms protectively around her son. "I'm grateful, but this can't go on. If someone blabs to the guards..."

"After Elariel helped her son," Sarah murmured, "one of her brothers brought *his* girl by. And then word got around."

Gyre nodded. "Elariel, can I talk to you?"

The ghoul nodded and clambered to her feet. Her fatigue was obvious, and there were dark bags under her eyes, but her face was a tight mask.

"There are so many of them," she whispered when they were on the other side of the curtain. "I didn't think... how many could need help?"

Gyre winced in sympathy. "Most of the people in the city probably need help with *something*."

"Diggerworm and heart-rend and vick fever and..." She trailed off, shaking her head. "I know you humans don't have *dhaka* to rely on, but I'm not sure I ever understood what that *meant*. It's... obscene. If my people saw this..."

"They'd probably say it was just what the primitive humans deserved, right?" Kit said. She scuttled up to Gyre and climbed to his shoulder.

"If someone has pain or illness, you help them," Elariel said. "Every ghoul understands that."

"But only among yourselves, safe in your hole under the mountain."

Elariel glared at the little spider. "We are trapped there, because *your* people would kill us on sight."

"Neither one of us is exactly part of our own people anymore, if you haven't noticed." Kit's legs dug a little harder into Gyre's shirt. "And healing a few orphans isn't going to get us out of here."

"Enough," Gyre said. "Elariel, you need to rest."

"I do." She swallowed. "But there are so many more."

"I know." Gyre tentatively put a hand on her shoulder. "You've done what you can."

After a moment, she gave a weary nod and pushed past him into the tiny back room. When she was gone, Gyre looked down at Kit.

"Is there some reason you're picking fights?"

It was hard for a faceless spider to look chagrined, but Kit managed it. "Sorry. It's this place."

"What about it?"

"Too familiar. I grew up in a place like this. In Grace. When I got out of it I swore I'd never go back. These people..."

"Like the tunnelborn in Deepfire," Gyre said. "Huddled up to the city for a hint of warmth."

"Stupid," Kit muttered. "Why stay? *I* didn't."

"Not everyone can be Doomseeker," Gyre said.

She gave a credible snort. "I suppose not."

"So," Gyre said after a moment of silence. "Give me the bad news. What's happened to the wagons?"

"I can't tell exactly where they are," Kit said, clearly relieved by the change of topic. "I peeked out a little, but there are guards around. Looks like a stone building with stalls for loadbirds. Too small for the hardshells—they've taken them off somewhere."

"Have they gone through the cargo?"

"Not much. I think they got spooked when they saw the alchemicals. Maybe they sent for what passes for an alchemist down here."

Gyre breathed out. *Not ideal, but better than I feared.* As long as their supplies were still aboard the wagons, stealing them back wasn't impossible.

"Do you have any way to locate your other bodies more precisely?"

"Not really," Kit said. "I'd have to break out and get somewhere with a view, and they'd definitely notice."

"Okay. So we need to figure out where they took the wagons before we can work on getting them back."

"The place looks like a stable with locks and bars. Could be a garrison or a guardhouse?"

"Hmm." Gyre glanced back out toward the main room. "Let's see if Elariel has bought us any goodwill with the locals."

*   *   *

Lizanne wasn't exactly eager to help, but she *was* eager to be rid of them. She declared that one of her cousins was the man they needed, and her son was duly dispatched to fetch him.

The cousin's name was Arman. When he arrived, he turned out to be a man in his early twenties with dark skin and long blue hair, dressed to a considerably higher standard than the threadbare homespun that seemed to be norm in the tenements. He greeted Lizanne warmly but gave Gyre a distinctly cool look.

"This is the doctor?" he said. "I've been hearing crazy stories all day."

"She's resting in the back," Lizanne said. "These are her friends, and they need a favor."

He frowned. "I don't like doing favors."

"She helped Georr, Arm." The boy was dozing beside her, and Lizanne put her arm around him and squeezed. "And your Uncle Vid's boy and a dozen others. We owe them something."

"Well. I don't like owing people, either." He gave Gyre a longer look. "I'm Arman Alleycat. You work with the doctor?"

"More or less. I'm Gyre Silvereye, and this is Sarah."

"I'll get Elariel up," Sarah said, retreating into the back.

"Silvereye." For a moment Gyre wondered if his fame had spread all the way out here, but Arman was just examining the artificial optic. "Interesting. Have you been in Ehren City long?"

"Just since the morning, and we don't intend to stay," Gyre said. "Lancer Ichtricia confiscated three wagonloads of goods from us, and we want them back. Then we'll be away from here as fast as we can manage."

"Ichtricia?" Arman's eyebrows rose. "She's spiky, that one. Not a good enemy to make." He sighed and rubbed his face. "I might be able to do something, but it'd take time and thalers. Confiscated goods get auctioned for the king's treasury, but a little grease can make sure we get them before anyone else does—"

"We haven't got time." *Or thalers.* Apart from a few bills in his pocket, their funds were still aboard the wagons. "But we have... other resources. All we need to do is find where the wagons are being kept. We know they're somewhere in the city, a stone building with a stables."

"And how do you know—" Arman blinked and looked up, suddenly all smiles. "Is this the doctor? No one mentioned she was a beauty as well."

"This is Elariel," Sarah said, bristling.

"Hello, Elariel." Arman extended a hand to the ghoul, who blinked sleepily. "You have my thanks for what you've done for my family."

"It's... You're welcome." Elariel yawned. "I'm sorry I couldn't do more."

"So." Arman looked back to Gyre. "Your wagons are probably in the stables of the Inner Gate barracks, but there's no way to get them. I have a few friends in the guards, but no one highly placed enough to pull *that* off."

"We'll manage," Gyre said. "As long as you can show us where that is."

"A plan of the building would help too," Sarah said.

Arman looked between them, not sure what to think, then shrugged.

"If that's what you want," he said. "Just promise me that when they catch you, you'll keep Aunt Liz and me out of it."

Gyre nodded agreement. They sat around the little table, and Lizanne grudgingly fetched a pencil and a bit of torn linen that Arman could sketch on. He arranged to sit beside Elariel, their shoulders touching in the tight quarters. Gyre couldn't help an inward smile at the ghoul's obvious incomprehension of the man's interest.

"Here's the inner wall and the gate," Arman said, drawing a curved line. "The barracks is on one side, and the stables is on the other. There's a door between—that's always locked and barred."

"Are there loadbirds in the stables?" Sarah said.

"Should be. Especially at night. There's a big door here for carriages and a little one on the other side." The pencil scratched over the gray sheet. "They'll both be guarded, though. Maybe four men. And if your cargo is valuable, I'd guess as many more inside."

"Thank you," Gyre said. "This is exactly what we needed."

Arman sat up from the completed sketch, shaking his head. "As soon as someone shouts, there's another forty, fifty soldiers in the barracks who are going to come running. You'll never get out of there, even if you can get in." He put his hand atop Elariel's. "Are you sure you want to do this? There are other ways."

"I'm sure," Elariel said. "We can't stay here."

"Let me borrow this for a moment." Gyre scooped up the drawing. "Sarah, get ready to head out. We've put these people in enough danger as it is."

Sarah nodded and started gathering their few possessions. Gyre, slipping into the back, spread the sheet out to show Kit.

"Yeah, that looks about right," she said. "You've got a plan, I take it?"

"Getting there," Gyre said. "Can you shadow us without being seen?"

"In this maze?" Kit snorted. "I could have done that when I had a big clunky body to worry about."

"Stay as close as you can. Just in case."

The little spider danced a quick jig of excitement and scurried out the window.

"Are you feeling any better?" Gyre said to Elariel. "I'm sorry we couldn't let you rest for longer."

"It will suffice," the ghoul said. "Thank you."

Ehren City at night was distinctly claustrophobic, the looming tenements blotting out the sky and leaving only the faintest tinge of moonlight. Neither Sarah nor Elariel seemed to mind, and Gyre reflected that they'd both grown up in underground caverns, so that was probably to be expected. With his energy bottle full again, his silver eye pierced the darkness, painting the alleys with weird washed-out colors. He'd made himself a cudgel to replace his missing sword, and wore it prominently on his belt. A pair of would-be thieves, lurking in the shadows, were sufficiently disconcerted by Gyre staring directly at them that they decided to wait for less wary prey.

"Can you pull off that go-to-sleep trick you used on Lynnia?" Gyre said. "I'd rather not kill anyone we don't have to."

"Of course," Elariel said. "It's a simple adjustment. I must touch the target, though."

"That shouldn't be hard, if we can take them by surprise," Sarah said.

"Think they'd believe her as a prostitute?" Gyre said, eyeing Elariel.

"Probably not," Sarah said.

He smiled. "Arman seemed taken with her."

Sarah rolled her eyes. "No subtlety, that one."

"I was somewhat baffled by his behavior," Elariel said. "He came into physical contact with me in ways that seemed accidental, but the pattern was too clear to be anything but deliberate. And he watched me closely but looked away when I returned his attention."

Gyre heard a muffled laugh from the shadows beside them, and Sarah was fighting a grin. Elariel looked between them, then rolled her eyes.

"I see that this is another nuance of human culture I have failed to grasp. Please explain."

"He was trying to flirt with you," Sarah said. "Pretty badly, to be honest."

"Meaning what?" Elariel said.

"That he wanted to...sleep with you, basically," Gyre said. "Or at least see if you showed any interest."

"To...sleep with?" Elariel snorted a sudden laugh. "He was express-ing a *sexual* interest?"

"More or less," Sarah said, grin widening.

"If he wished to have a sexual encounter with me, he should have simply said so," Elariel said.

"Is that how it works for ghouls?" Sarah said, fascinated. "You just... ask?"

"Of course," Elariel said. "Only humans would contrive such an absurdly inefficient means of communication. If it were a proposal for pair-bonding—"

Gyre held up a hand as they rounded a corner. "This is it."

"I'll have to take your word for it," Sarah said. "Remember I can't see in the dark like you two. All the nighteye is in the crates."

"It does seem to be the building Arman described," Elariel said. "I can see the wall behind it, and two soldiers with torches."

"There's two more by the door," Gyre said. It was odd, standing in the open and staring at a target, but to anyone without ghoul augmentation the alley would be an impenetrable void. "Looks like the other two are going back and forth. Kit?"

"Here," Kit said by his feet, scuttling out of a gutter.

"How many in the stable? And can you see the door that leads to the barracks?"

"Let me take a peek. Looks like... maybe four more? And there's only one door facing the wall, so that must be it."

"What about loadbirds?"

"You've got your pick of a dozen teams."

Two-bird teams could move their wagons, though out on the road he would miss the hardshell's ability to subsist on scrub grass. *Can't be helped. We'd never get away, even if we could find them.* A hardshell could plod along indefinitely, but any bird could leave one in the dust in the short term. *I hope Evil Bastard nips a few more fingers.*

"Okay," Gyre said. "We'll wait until the four on the outside are together. I'll get them down, and Elariel will put them out. Simple."

Elariel looked nervous but gave a determined nod.

"I'll be right behind you," Sarah said.

Gyre watched the lanterns move. There was a broad street running in front of the inner wall, and the barracks was set back from the buildings on either side. It seemed unlikely that anyone would see them, which was just as well. *The real trick is going to be when the garrison comes after us.* The gate was a hundred meters away, closed for the night, with its own cadre of guards. *If we can keep the stable door closed, they'll have to go around, get the thing open…*

It would be tight, either way. The pair of patrolling guards walked back toward their comrades at the door, waving their lantern in greeting, and Gyre gritted his teeth and concentrated. With a *click*, time slowed to a crawl.

The energy bottle at his hip was reassuringly full, thanks to Elariel, but he still wanted to keep the fight brief. Running with the great floating strides the augmentations allowed, he crossed the street in moments, leaving Elariel and Sarah behind. The pair with lanterns, a man and a woman, were just starting to turn when he arrived, swinging his cudgel into the first guard's stomach. That started him doubling over, and Gyre kicked his partner's feet out from under her and moved on before she had a chance to fall.

The pair by the door were going for their swords, shadow-hands darting ahead of the real things. One opened his mouth to yell but only managed a squeak before the cudgel slammed into his chin, sending him back against the stable wall with a *thump*. His partner managed a clumsy swing, which Gyre sidestepped casually before bringing the cudgel down on the back of his head.

Part of him wanted to automatically pivot into a killing blow, make sure the man didn't get up again, but he held back. *These aren't the Order, or even the Auxies.* They didn't deserve to die for drawing the wrong night for guard duty.

With a *click*, time returned to normal. Elariel and Sarah arrived, Kit scuttling next to them. The guard Gyre had tripped was struggling to rise, but Elariel laid a hand on her and she slumped back into peaceful unconsciousness. The other three quickly followed.

"Did they hear anything inside?" Gyre asked Kit.

"A little, I think," she said. "The four of them are getting up, but they're not sure what happened."

Plague it. Shouldn't have slammed that one against the wall. No helping it now, though. He turned to the door, which was set deep in the stone wall and secured with a heavy iron padlock. *Better and better.*

"Keys," he said. "Sarah, see if you can find keys on one of them—"

"I think I can handle it," Sarah said, coming into the doorway. "Kit, are you set?"

"Ready!"

Sarah took a deep breath, grabbed the padlock with her artificial hand, and ripped it clean out of the doorway. It took a large chunk of wood along with it, and the half-broken door shuddered open, revealing four more guards gaping with surprise. But not for long—the three wagons were parked side by side behind them, and Kit's bodies poured out of the closest, small- and midsized spiders heading for the guards while the others went for the doors. The watchmen didn't even have a chance to draw their swords before they were swarmed under, screaming.

"Elariel, put them out!" Gyre shouted over the noise. "Sarah, the inner door!"

"On it!"

Sarah sprinted for the second wagon, neatly sidestepping the guards and their construct assailants. She wrenched the door open and rummaged furiously, then came back out with two large clay spheres, which she hurled from a safe distance.

The door leading from the stables into the barracks proper was a heavy one, banded with iron and secured with a bar on the far side. The spheres broke against it, releasing a spray of thick gray goop. The stuff hardened instantly when it met the air, turning nearly as tough as stone and sealing the portal.

That'll buy us some time. The guards on the other side must have heard the screams, but they would have to either break the door down with axes or go around through the gate.

"Kit, brace the outer doors," he said. "Sarah, seal up the way we came in and then help me with the loadbirds."

"On it," Sarah said, hefting another big sphere. Its goop covered the hole she'd torn in the front door, closing it tight and leaving the carriage-sized doors at the far end of the room as the only entrance.

Kit's two large bodies planted themselves there, ready to brace them closed.

The loadbirds were in wooden stalls running along one wall of the building, sleeping with their heads tucked under one wing like big feathery balls. A few had roused themselves at the brief commotion, coming forward with curious chirps in hopes of a feeding. They were stabled in pairs, which probably meant teams trained to work together. Gyre went over to the first set, clicking his tongue reassuringly.

I wish we had Harrow with us. The boy had been part of the old group, with a gift for animals and a hopeless crush on Yora. He'd died deep under the mountains, crushed by a ghoul construct from which the rest of them had barely escaped. Gyre didn't have his skill with the beasts, but the loadbirds were accustomed to their role and suffered unfamiliar hands to fit their harnesses with only a few indignant squawks. He led them out and over to the first wagon, while Sarah readied a second pair.

The birds perked up at a heavy *chunk* of metal on wood. The main doors vibrated, and a moment later a sliver of lantern light shone through a fresh axe cut. The two heavy constructs dug their legs into the dirt, shoving back against the pressure from outside.

"Better hurry," Kit said. "Unless you fancy fighting the whole barracks."

Plaguing fuck. They're faster than I gave them credit for. Gyre ran to another stall and hurriedly got two more birds into their harnesses, ignoring their complaints. He handed them off to Sarah, who started fitting them to the third wagon.

"Question," the arcanist said as she worked. "Loadbirds won't convoy like hardshells, so we need a driver for each team. Who's driving this one?"

Gyre blinked and stifled a groan. They both looked at Elariel, who eyed the big birds with mistrust.

"It's not that hard," Gyre said. "You just pull on the reins when you want them to turn, and..."

He stopped as Elariel walked up to the loadbirds. They ruffled their wings, irritable, but went quiet when she put a hand on their flanks.

"I believe I shall manage," Elariel said. "At least for a time. This is somewhat draining."

"You're using *dhaka*?" Sarah said, fascinated.

Elariel nodded. "They are simple-minded things. But hurry, please."

"Right." Gyre swung himself up onto the box of the first wagon. "I'll take the lead. Stay as close to me as you can. Kit, get ready to clear the door, then jump aboard."

"Ready!" Kit said brightly. Her small spiders swarmed onto the third wagon, clinging to the walls. "Hit it!"

Gyre gave a sharp whistle and the loadbirds lurched into motion. The wagon accelerated slowly, but with a great deal of weight behind it. Kit's two large constructs backed up and the doors swung inward, a dozen guards stumbling against the lack of resistance. Both of the big spiders reared up, limbs splayed, and there was a chorus of screams.

"Plaguespawn!" someone shouted. "Plaguespawn in the stables!"

Most of them ran. A few tried to stand their ground, but Kit's heavy spiders slammed them aside. In moments the door was clear and the wagons were out onto the road, still picking up speed. Kit's two large constructs grabbed the open doorways of the wagon as it passed, hauling themselves aboard.

"Just follow this street!" Kit shouted. "It should be a straight shot to the west gate."

"The gate will be shut!" Gyre shouted back. "Sarah—"

"I'm on it!" the arcanist yelled.

He risked a look backward. Sarah was rummaging in a pack with one hand, eyes fixed ahead, while Elariel simply sat on the third wagon with her hands in her lap. The birds obeyed without commands. *That's a neat trick.*

They'd left the guards behind. Buildings rushed past on either side as the loadbirds reached a full gallop, wagon wheels squeaking and rattling furiously over the uneven ground. Up ahead, lanterns came alight, shining in their direction. Once the guards on the gate saw what was coming at them, though, they made no attempt to get in the way, diving aside from the speeding vehicles.

It turned out to be the right choice on their part. Another clay sphere flew over Gyre's head and hit the wooden gate in their path, detonating with a low *thump* and blowing the doors to splinters. The birds tried to shy away, but he held tight to the reins, and they passed through the cloud of smoke without slowing. A moment later and they were through the wall, Ehren City behind them and open country spreading out ahead.

"Gyre!" Sarah shouted. "I can't see a plaguing thing!"

"I can!" Gyre shouted back. With his real eye closed, his silver eye lit up the darkness. "Just stay behind me. I think we may be in the clear—"

"We are being followed!" Elariel shouted, her voice distant.

"The guards can't keep up on foot," Gyre said.

"It's not the guards—it's Ichtricia and her lancers," Kit said from Gyre's shoulder. "They're catching up!"

Another look backward showed Gyre a dozen warbirds in pursuit. He saw the long lances slung behind their saddles, and more worrying still the heavy crossbows in their hands. The first rank was already taking aim.

"Everyone *down*!" Gyre shouted as bolts *snapped* out. One of them *thrummed* as it passed overhead, and another embedded in Sarah's wagon with a *thock*. *At least they won't be able to reload without stopping. Unless one of them has a blaster...*

"Gyre?" Sarah said. "They're getting closer!"

There was no blaster fire, but the warbirds were fast, and they were quickly pulling alongside. *Plaguefire!* Gyre let his wagon drift out of line, to the side of Sarah's, and dragged on the reins to slow the birds down.

"I'll hold them off!" he shouted. "Go!"

"I still can't *see*—" Sarah protested, and then she was past him.

"Kit," Gyre said, "get a couple more bodies over here!"

"On it," Kit said, and three of the small spiders jumped across as Elariel's wagon thundered past. "What now?"

"Find my sword! It's in there somewhere!"

The first of the lancers was alongside. His weapon was three meters long and tapered to a fine point, like a giant needle. It wasn't at its best against a moving target—it was designed to spear plaguespawn or people on foot—but Gyre didn't dare let go of the reins for fear he'd never get them back. He engaged his silver eye with an internal *click* and watched the shadow of the lance extend toward him. At the critical moment he ducked, letting it go over his head. The lancer wound up for another try, and a second rider approached on the other side.

"Kit!" Gyre said.

"I've got it!" Two of the little spiders emerged from the wagon, holding his silver sword between them.

"Take the reins!"

"*What?*"

"Just hold on to them!" Gyre shoved the reins at one of the spiders and hopped up on the top of the wagon, narrowly avoiding another needle thrust.

The energy bottle at his belt was getting hot. Gyre crouched, feeling every jolt in the rough ground, and waited as the second lancer came forward. This time, he sidestepped the lance and brought his own blade around in turn. The thin metal of the rider's weapon was no match for the silver sword, and half the lance clattered away. The rider dropped back, already reaching for a replacement from the quiver behind him.

Crossbows *twanged* again. Gyre saw one bolt coming, shadows drifting in his silver eye, and he ducked as it hummed past. The second rider swung at him, hoping to use the shaft of his lance to sweep Gyre off his feet, and Gyre had to do a standing jump to avoid being tripped. He managed to slice the weapon apart as it went past. *That makes two out of . . . too many.*

"Gyre!" Ichtricia's voice, muffled by her armor. She galloped alongside. "Stop this wagon at once or face the consequences!"

"We're leaving your stupid kingdom, all right?" Gyre twirled the blade in his hand, silver glittering in the faint light. "I promise not to kill any more plaguespawn on the way!"

She snarled, closing in, eschewing her long lance in favor of a saber. Gyre met her blade to blade with a shivering hum; he expected to cut right through the steel, but too late caught the iridescent sheen of unmetal from her weapon. The two Elder blades locked, shuddering, then sprang apart. Gyre watched the shadows race ahead of her, twisted away from a strike, and slammed the flat of his blade into her elbow. She veered away, cursing, but held on to her weapon.

"Gyre!" Kit said. "Sarah says eyes closed!"

That was an instruction Gyre had heard often enough in the old days. He obeyed at once, dropping flat on the wagon's roof. A few moments later, an alchemical bomb burst not far overhead with a *whoomph* and a blast of shattered clay.

It was a stunner, the noise ineffective at this distance, but the *light* was bright enough that he saw orange through his eyelids. The lancers following, charging down the road in near darkness, were blinded at once. Gyre heard screams, curses, and the frantic squawking of warbirds. When he rolled over and blinked away flickering afterimages, the road behind them was empty.

It wasn't much longer before they entered a thick forest, the road curving in among the trees and up through some hills. Gyre guessed this marked the edge of Ehrenvare territory. As they climbed, a hundred little loggers' tracks split off, and Gyre took them down a few turns at random. Finally they came to a halt in a clearing edged with tree stumps and an abandoned lean-to.

"I doubt they'll come this far," Gyre said. "But we'll be off the main road if they do. Kit, can you make sure we didn't leave any obvious tracks?"

"Got it." One of the little spiders skittered off the way they'd come. "You want me to set up the tents?"

"May as well," he said. "We're not going anywhere without resting the birds for a while."

"I, for one, could sleep for a week," Sarah said. "If my pulse ever slows down. Chosen *fucking* defend. Next time we go for a night gallop, we need to get me some nighteye so I can see where the *fuck* I'm going."

"I can agree to that," Gyre said. He hopped down from the wagon, legs a little wobbly, and went over to where Elariel was sitting. "Are you all right?"

"What?" She blinked and looked at him. "Oh yes. I am uninjured."

"You did great with the birds."

"Thank you." She let out a long breath. "It was my first experience of this kind of mortal peril. I found it alarming but not entirely distasteful."

Kit set up the tents with her usual alacrity, constructs working together to pound stakes and tie lines. Gyre retrieved his packs from the wagons and settled down to checking them over, absently chewing through one of the ubiquitous hardtack crackers.

Elariel came in as he was stowing everything again, muttering under his breath. The ghoul raised an eyebrow.

"Something wrong?" she said.

"Just checking to see what the guards stole." He sighed. "The cargo's still there, but what's left of the money is gone. We're going to have to sell some alchemicals before we get to Khirkhaz."

"We should have sufficient for the purpose, I think?" Elariel said.

"We do. It's just a complication I'd rather avoid." He shook his head. "Sorry. Did you need something? We've only got a few hours before dawn, and I could use some sleep."

"I will be brief, then," Elariel said. "Do you wish to have a sexual encounter with me?"

Gyre blinked. "Excuse me?"

"My heart rate is elevated and my bloodstream is full of adrenaline byproducts," Elariel said. "I believe these conditions ideal for sexual activity." She started to pace in front of the tent flap. "I know you said asking would be considered rude by a human, but I do not know how to initiate an encounter in a fashion humans would consider polite, and my feelings are urgent. I apologize if I have offended."

"I'm not offended. But..." Gyre paused. "Is it *really* that simple, with ghouls?"

"Of course. A suggestion to enter a research partnership would require more consideration, but a simple sexual encounter is straightforward." She hesitated. "Do you consider me unattractive by human standards?"

"No," Gyre said. "It's not that."

"Then why do you refuse?"

"Humans are...more complicated, I guess." Gyre sighed. "Sorry. Can we talk about this tomorrow?"

"If you wish." Elariel shrugged. "But I am increasingly convinced I will never understand this aspect of your psychology."

"That's fair," Gyre said. "I don't think we do, either."

Chapter 8

Maya hung from her wrists in a brick-lined cistern, deep under Bastion. She was naked, and the manacles cut her skin cruelly. When she pointed her toes, she could barely brush the scum-encrusted floor.

"*Sha'deia.*" A voice from the darkness. Then a whole chorus. "*Sha'deia.*"

Black shapes slipped out of the shadows, fat-bodied, spider-limbed creatures, reaching toward her with quivering claws. She kicked away from them, desperate not to be touched, but they closed in from every side. She shuddered as the first spindly leg found purchase on her calf, its small claw digging into her skin.

"*Sha'deia.*" Jaedia's voice, twisted and bubbling. "Maybe you are the one…"

The spiders climbed her body, the weight of them pulling at her, leaving tiny drops of blood in their wake. There were dozens, on her thighs, her back, across her stomach, dragging at her breasts. One of them touched the Thing and yanked a limb away as if burned.

"One of *you*." The Eldest's horrible rasp. "Father sent *you* here?"

They climbed higher, claws at her neck, her cheeks. One hooked into her lower lip and pulled it down.

"Impossible. I was to be *exalted*!"

"*Sha'deia...*" It was a chant now. "*Sha'deia...*"

"Maybe you are the one..."

Maya screamed.

"Maya!" Hands on her shoulders pressing her down, and Beq's voice. "It's okay. You're okay."

"I..." Maya was gasping. "I was..."

"We're still in the village," Beq said. "Do you remember? We're safe. You killed the plaguespawn."

The village. Maya's hands clenched into fists. *The Eldest.* She remembered the despairing scream as she'd blasted the vile thing to vapor. *I killed it.*

"*Maybe you are the one...*"

"Maya?" Beq said. "Can you look at me?"

Maya took a deep, shuddering breath and blinked the world into focus. Beq, worriedly adjusting the lenses on her spectacles, leaned over her. Above, she could see an unmetal ceiling. *The village hall. The common room.*

Her limbs ached, but the worst hurt was in her chest. Maya went to touch the Thing, but Beq caught her fingers.

"It's badly swollen," Beq said. "I don't know exactly what's wrong, but you shouldn't press on it. I've given you some quickheal. That should do something for the pain." Beq lowered her voice. "I'm just glad it's not worse. When I found you, it had burned a hole through your shirt."

Maya leaned back, closing her eyes for a moment. Beq patted her cheek gently.

"Hey," she said. "Stay awake. You need water."

"I'm awake," Maya croaked. "I'm just...tired."

"I can imagine." Beq put a canteen to her lips and trickled in a little cool water.

"How long?" Maya said.

"Just a few hours," Beq said. "It's a little after noon."

Deiat exhaustion. *Nothing I haven't dealt with before.* It would be a few hours more until she could use her abilities again. *But that doesn't explain the Thing trying to roast me alive.*

"Varo?" Maya said.

"He's all right," Beq said. "He's up in one of the watchtowers."

"And the villagers?"

"Hiding, or fled into the forest," Beq said. "I tried shouting, but nobody's answering."

"Not surprising." Maya pushed herself up onto her elbows and took the canteen, drinking in great gulps. "The Eldest was...using them. Breeding stock." She shook her head. "Makes sense. You can't keep up a population of plaguespawn without large animals to make them out of."

"Varo says he hasn't seen any plaguespawn since...what happened," Beq said. "There was one left inside the walls, but it went mad when you killed the Eldest. He and I blasted it to bits."

"Just like at the ghoul ruins," Maya said. "Once I got the spider off Jaedia, all the plaguespawn in the valley went wild. Even started attacking each other. The spiders must control them with *dhaka*."

"Spiders." Beq shuddered. "I was hoping that was the only one. Some kind of...weird abomination."

"Believe me, so was I." Maya struggled to a sitting position. "But there have to be more. The Eldest said 'the others' and talked about its father."

"It talked to you?" Beq said. "What else did it say?"

Maya hesitated. "Mostly how it was going to kill me, and how it had killed other centarchs. It said it was waiting for its father to return, and that when he did it would be exalted."

"*Father sent* you *here?*"

"*Sha'deia...*"

Maya went to clutch the Thing but stopped herself with an effort.

"You think the Eldest is what's been keeping us away from the Archive all these years?" Beq said.

"I don't think there's any doubt," Maya said. "It said it's been here for centuries."

"Hopefully that means we'll have an easier time getting there, at any rate," Beq said. "You can rest up for today, and tomorrow—"

"No," Maya said. She felt like the bottom had suddenly dropped out of her thoughts. "We need to go today. Now."

"What? Why?"

"The Thing. The way it reacted..." Maya lowered her voice, though she wasn't sure who she expected to overhear. "It's done that before. When I first fought Gyre, at Raskos' warehouse in Deepfire. You remember what I was like afterward?"

"Sick," Beq said thoughtfully. "But that wasn't *deiat* exhaustion. It was worse than that."

"I don't understand either," Maya said. "All I know is that it was a week before I was good for anything. If we don't get to the Archive now—"

"Forget the Archive," Beq said. "We'll go back to the Forge until you're recovered. With the Eldest dead, we can come back whenever we need to."

"*No.*" Maya grabbed Beq's arm. "We don't know if the Eldest was the only one of those...things around here. We might only have a short time before another one takes over. It has to be now."

Before the arcanist could object further, Maya got to her feet. It took more effort than she would have liked, but once she was up she felt reasonably steady. Apart from the pulsing ache in her chest, her pain was manageable.

"Wait," Beq said. "How long do you have before...whatever it is starts?"

"It was a day or so, last time," Maya said. "That should be enough to make it to the Archive. You and Varo may have to help me on the way back."

"I still don't like it," Beq said.

"I'll be fine," Maya said. "Eventually. We just need to get the mission finished. If I need to spend a week in bed after that, so be it."

Beq's lips were tight, but she didn't argue further. With their packs abandoned somewhere in the forest, Maya didn't have a spare shirt to replace the one the Thing had burned a fist-sized hole in, so she was forced to improvise an extra wrap with some torn cloth from the common room. Beq, she noted gratefully, had covered Calla's body with a sheet.

Outside, there was no avoiding the detritus of the brief battle. Pieces of plaguespawn lay where they had fallen, attended by flies. The spot where Maya had confronted the Eldest was a blasted mess, the ground seared black. Any remains of the spider and its host were nothing but piles of gray ash.

They found Varo at the base of one of the watchtowers, tying off a leather sack.

"I borrowed this," he said. "And scrounged some food. We may need it."

"You can't just steal from the villagers," Beq said.

"They were feeding us freely," Varo said. "And then they tried to kill us. It seems fair."

"You can't blame them," Beq said. "You saw what the Eldest did."

"When we get to the Forge..." Maya shook her head. "We'll tell Basel about this place. Maybe the Council will know what to do. They could send an expedition and bring everyone back to the Republic." The fate of the villagers felt like a bigger problem than she could shoulder right now. *That's what the Council is for, isn't it?* The other two seemed inclined to keep arguing, so Maya pressed on. "Varo, how does it look outside?"

"No plaguespawn in sight, though that was true before."

"And how far to the Archive?"

"A few hours' walk, if we don't run into anything." Varo frowned. "We're leaving now?"

Maya nodded wearily. "We have to get there and get back to the Forge as soon as we can."

He looked at her for a moment, and Maya felt a touch of guilt. *Maybe I should explain.* It wasn't that she didn't trust Varo, but she'd spent her life keeping the Thing and everything about it a secret. *You never know how people will react*, Jaedia had told her. *They might call it* dhak. Her hand came up, finding the coarse fabric wrapped across her chest. *Maybe they're right.*

"Whatever you say." Varo cinched the sack closed and slung it over his shoulder. "I'm ready when you are."

Maya was glad to leave the village behind, with its smell of burnt meat and the rotting plaguespawn corpses. Not to mention poor Calla, lying under a sheet. *If we'd never come, she'd still be alive.* On the other hand, the Eldest had said it had planned to use her as a host. *I'm not sure if I should be sorry or not.*

The day was warm, at least, with only a few scattered clouds and no sign of rain. They left the village through the gate in the unmetal wall, then turned uphill, hiking between well-spaced trees under a thick canopy dappled with sunbeams. It would have been pleasant if Maya hadn't had to split her attention between keeping an eye out for plaguespawn and checking herself for signs of weakness.

Maybe I'm wrong. Just because the Thing had made her sick *once* didn't mean it always would. Somehow, though, she couldn't believe it. Her skin already felt hot, and her breath came faster. *It's still too soon*, she told herself. *You're imagining things.*

Varo led them with confidence, picking their way through a series of narrow valleys. Even with the occasional switchback, they were climbing all the way, and after a couple of hours everyone was breathing hard. Maya called a halt in the lee of a boulder and leaned against the rough, cool rock. Beq threw herself on the ground with a sigh, and Varo opened up the sack.

"Here." He handed a loaf of crusty bread to each of them. "May as well eat it now; it won't last."

Beq attacked hers happily, but the thought of food made Maya's stomach roil. She tore off a chunk and forced it down, along with some water, then handed the rest back to Varo.

He raised an eyebrow. "I had a friend once who didn't eat when he had the chance."

"Another time, please." Maya closed her eyes. "Let's just get this done."

Varo grunted agreement. They kept climbing, mostly in silence. Beq threw worried glances at Maya when she thought Maya wasn't looking. At least the plaguespawn were nowhere to be seen. *Thank the fucking Chosen for that.*

"There," Varo said as they crested yet another ridge. "That's the entrance, I think."

It took Maya a few moments to see what he was pointing at. The hill sloped up from where they stood, rising steeper and steeper, the tree cover thinning out. Halfway up, there was an irregular line of rocks. Two of them leaned against one another to make a sort of doorway, and when Maya peered at it she could convince herself that there was a deeper darkness beyond.

Thank the Chosen for Varo as well. She'd never have spotted it herself. Beq straightened up, panting, and adjusted her spectacles. Lenses clicked into place, and she gave a decisive nod.

"There's a tunnel, at least," she said.

Maya put one hand on her haken and reached out to *deiat*. Her connection still felt a little shaky, but it was there, recovered from the abuse she'd put it through that morning. She led the way up the remaining slope, legs aching abominably.

The passage between the rocks was barely large enough for a single person. Maya threaded *deiat* into her panoply and summoned a ball of light in her off hand. Beyond the cliff face, the way opened up again into a broad corridor, edges weathered by time but with the clean lines of something carved by the Chosen, like the Forge itself.

"Not much to look at," Varo commented.

Maya raised the globe of light, which illuminated only more corridor. She shrugged.

"Only one way to go," she said.

They walked, the blessedly flat ground a relief after hours of climbing. The air under the hill was cool and stagnant, but sweat still trickled out of Maya's hair and got into her eyes. Her heart felt overloud in her chest.

When they'd gone a considerable distance—enough to put them at least a few hundred meters underground, Maya guessed—the corridor dead-ended at a tall unmetal door. There were no hinges or seams, just a triangular design with a crystal outgrowth at the center. Maya stepped aside, holding up the light, and let Beq examine it.

"Looks like a power loop," she said after a moment. "A plaguing big one. Prodominus said you had to provide the Archive with energy, right?"

Maya nodded. "If I power it, the door will open?"

"That's my guess." She glanced around. "Not a lot of other options."

"I'll try it, then." Maya stepped up and touched the crystal. "Be careful."

She reached through her haken, drawing on *deiat*, and directed a thread of power into the door. It responded at once, eagerly drinking in the energy. Maya had to pull harder to feed it more and then still more. It was like activating a hundred Gates at once, and she felt chills as the power flowed out of her. She held herself ready to cut it off—*the last thing I need is to pass out again*—but before she reached her limit the thing's appetite was finally satiated. A blue glow ignited, deep in the crystal, and rapidly grew to a steady illumination. Then, with a *hiss* of escaping air, the door swung inward on silent hinges.

The room beyond was lit by more blue crystals, throwing soft-edged shadows. It was surprisingly small, a circular space perhaps ten meters across, with unmetal panels set into the native rock of the walls. Traces of metal and crystal ran everywhere, adding smaller shifting glows. In the center of the room was a dais about a meter across.

"This is the Archive?" Varo said. He stepped in cautiously, one hand on his blaster. "I was expecting...books."

"The Chosen had better ways of storing information than paper and ink," Beq said in a whisper. Her mouth hung half-open, the blue glows reflected like fireflies in her spectacles. "This place is..."

"This is the Archive Interface Chamber," another voice said. "The storage medium is embedded in the rock beneath us, for maximum security."

The dais shimmered with light. A blue glow, diffuse at first, gradually took on humanoid proportions. It was mostly a blur, hanging there like a person seen through a badly focused looking glass, but two dark spots approximated eyes.

"I am the Librarian," it said. "A guide to this instance of the Emergency Archive. Please state your query."

There was a long moment of silence.

"That's not a Chosen, is it?" Varo whispered.

"No," Beq said, looking up at it reverently. "It's not a person. *Deiat* can't create life, just—"

"A simulation," said the Librarian. "Correct. I am a device intended to facilitate access to the Emergency Archive."

"And you've just been waiting down here all this time?" Beq said.

"I am only active when supplied with energy," the Librarian said. "Please state your query."

"Can you...see?" Maya said.

"I have sensors throughout the interface chamber," the Librarian said. "Query complete. Please state your next query."

"Chosen above," Beq said. Her eyes were shining. "There's so much I want to ask it."

"Maybe if we get a chance to come back," Maya said. Her forehead was slick with sweat. "I don't know how long I can keep this place running, so let's get on with it. Varo?"

More from dumb luck than any particular planning, Maya had given Varo Prodominus' sketches to keep in his map case, so they hadn't been lost when they'd abandoned the packs. He fished them out and handed them to Beq, who spread them on the floor in front of the dais. The blurred shape didn't look down.

"These are drawings of a piece of arcana," Maya said. "It's unfamiliar to us, and we need to know what it does and if it's important."

"Term unrecognized: 'arcana,'" the Librarian said.

"A device," Beq filled in.

I suppose the Chosen wouldn't use a special term for their own work. Maya nodded. "Can you get a good look at these?"

"Resolution is sufficient. Search with imperfectly specified parameters will require additional time to complete. Please wait."

"Wait?" Maya wiped a hand across her brow. "How long—"

"Search complete," the Librarian interrupted. "Query results: with a high degree of certainty, depicted object matches no known record. No information available."

Plaguing fuck. "Nothing?" *It can't all be for* nothing. Maya's throat felt thick, and her legs were suddenly rubbery.

"Wait," Beq said, stepping in front of her. "There are some pieces here even I recognize." She tapped the drawings. "This is a power draw, and this looks like a spectrum splitter, right?"

"Subsections of depicted object do appear to be constructed from standard templates," the Librarian agreed.

"Can you guess what it might do, based on those?"

"I am incapable of speculation," the Librarian said, and paused a moment. "Analysis of probable function based on subsection matches appears possible but may yield uncertain results. Execute query?"

"Yes," Beq said. "Do that."

"Please wait."

"Thank you." Maya leaned forward and put her arm on Beq's shoulder. "I was about to start screaming."

"I've read about these things," Beq said. "They're very literal."

"I'm glad one of us knows what she's doing."

"Analysis complete," the Librarian said. "Warning: low certainty. Receive results anyway?"

"Yes, please," Beq said.

There was a brief flicker in the blue glow. "Subsection analysis suggests that device transforms received signals into visual and audio data, and records and transmits such data."

"So it's some kind of long-range communicator?" Varo said. "That doesn't seem like it would be so hard to figure out."

"We know the Chosen used devices like that," Beq agreed. "People on the skyfortresses could talk to people on the ground as though they were standing in front of them."

"Depicted device lacks any visible mechanism for transmitting and receiving data," the Librarian said. "No *deiat* resonance antenna is present, as in standard transceivers. There is a cylindrical component, fifteen centimeters in height, three centimeters in radius, purpose unknown."

"So it lets you see and talk to someone," Beq translated, "but you don't know *how*, or what it might be connected to."

"Summary imprecise but substantially correct," the Librarian said. "Query complete. Please state your next query."

"Is that going to be enough for Prodominus?" Varo said. "Just that it's something you could use to talk to someone, somehow?"

"Query parameters unclear," the Librarian said. "Please restate." Varo rolled his eyes and looked at Maya.

"It's going to have to be," Maya said. Her voice was strained. "It sounds like that's all the Archive has to give us."

"Are you all right?" Beq said. "You're flushed."

"Just straining a bit." Maya shook her head. "We're finished here. You two head back out, and I'll shut everything down."

"I'll stay—"

"Just go." Maya gritted her teeth. "I don't want you stuck on the wrong side of the door when it closes."

Beq met Maya's eyes for a moment, then nodded. She gathered up the sketches and handed them back to Varo, who returned them to the map case.

"You're sure you're all right?" Varo said.

"Fine," Maya said. "I'm just... lifting something heavy, and I'd like to put it down, but I can't until you're out from under it. All right?"

"Funny you should say that, I once—"

"Later," Beq said, grabbing Varo's arm and towing him outside.

Maya waited, counting breaths. Their footsteps gradually receded.

"The interface chamber door will close only after the power-down sequence is complete," the Librarian said. "You will have ample time to depart."

"I figured." The weight of the Archive's draw on *deiat* was heavy, but for the moment Maya could still handle it. She fumbled with the extra cloth knotted around her middle. "New query."

"Ready," the Librarian said.

Maya unwrapped the cloth, revealing the hole burned in her shirt and the Thing beneath. "What is this?"

"Object matches no known record. No information available."

Maya's teeth ground. "Can you do a... subsection analysis?"

"Yes. Analysis complete. Warning—"

"Low certainty," Maya said. "Get on with it, please."

"Device contains a high-capacity *deiat* overflow protection circuit. I cannot observe the internal structures, but it is positioned to intercept the primary medial flow."

"Can you..." Maya took a deep breath. "What does it *do*?"

"An overflow protection circuit blocks *deiat* transmission above a certain power threshold, converting excess energy to heat. It is often used to protect delicate equipment that cannot withstand a power overload."

"So the Thing... blocks *deiat*?" Maya shook her head. "That doesn't make any sense."

"Degree of certainty is low," the Librarian said. "However, the most probable usage is to prevent a flow of *deiat* above a given threshold."

"And if I tried to draw more than that, *forced* more power through it, it would get hot. Start to glow."

"Theoretically," the Librarian said. "However, the connection of a circuit to living tissue is not something that could be accomplished with any known *deiat* technique. With a high degree of certainty, *dhaka* was involved."

Dhak. The Thing, the Thing that Baselanthus had told her he'd put in to save her life, was *dhak. And it limits my power.* That, at least, made sense—it had been during the moments when she was drawing hardest on *deiat* that the Thing had started heating up. *No wonder I get sick afterward. It's cooking me from the inside out.*

It all made sense. *Except* why? *Why would Baselanthus lie? Why put it there at all? Why did he have* dhak, *and where did he find a* dhakim *to use it?*

"Power supply growing unstable," the Librarian said. "Please route additional power or shutdown sequence will begin."

"Shut down," Maya said. *It'll have to wait.* She felt hollowed out, her connection to *deiat* scraped raw.

"Shutdown sequence in progress," the Librarian said. "Please exit before seal activates."

The glow on the dais vanished, and the rest of the lights began to fade. Maya turned away and staggered back into the tunnel. The door hissed closed behind her.

The trip back to the Gate was half a nightmare.

By the time they emerged from the hillside and started down the way they'd come, Maya could no longer deny that the fever she'd feared was on her. Beq fed her quickheal, which helped a little, and took her arm as they picked their way down the forested slope. Going down was easier than coming up, but it had its own dangers, especially with night coming on. It was easy to put a foot wrong, twist an ankle, trip and roll down a rocky hillside.

When they lost the light, they made camp, if "camp" was the right word for huddling together beneath a half-rotten log. Maya drifted in and out, Beq pressed against one side of her and Varo on the other, her skin alternately damp with sweat and hot as an oven. She remembered Beq pressing more quickheal into her mouth, making her chew, forcing her to drink water. Swallowing hurt her swollen throat, but the arcanist insisted, giving her tiny sips.

As soon as there was enough light to see, they started off again. Maya walked, or thought she did, but between blinks she found herself being carried on Beq's back, her arms dangling around the arcanist's neck. Another blink and it was Varo beneath her, lowering her gently to the ground so Beq could administer more water. Maya tried to swallow, but her stomach rebelled and she vomited a thin stream of bile into the weeds. Beq let her finish, holding her shoulders gently, and then returned with the canteen.

"I'm sorry," Maya said when Beq was carrying her again. "It's... thing. Limiter. Makes me... like this. I can't. Do it."

"It's all right." Beq put her hand against Maya's cheek. It felt ice-cold. "You're going to be okay. We're almost there."

Another blink. The forest was gone. There was a plain, then a wind-swept hillside. The delicate arch of a Gate, outlined against a setting sun. Beq was pushing quickheal into her mouth, and Maya obediently chewed the waxy stuff. It numbed her throat like cool vapor as it dissolved.

"Maya." Beq's face swam in her vision. "Maya, please. We need you to do one thing. Just one, and then we're safe and you can sleep for as long as you want. But you need to save yourself."

"And the rest of us," Varo said, somewhere overhead. "It's a long walk home."

"Shh." Beq leaned closer. "Maya? Can you activate the Gate?"

"Right." Maya struggled to sit up. "The Gate." She put her hand on her haken, tried to draw on *deiat*. The power spun and crashed inside her, like waves breaking against a rocky shore. Extracting a single thread took all her concentration.

There was something else. *Coordinates.* Her mind felt like it was made of sand, falling apart as she tried to use it. But Jaedia had always made her activate the Gates, and this was the most familiar one of all, a simple pattern for the hub of the whole network. *There.* The archway filled with swirling gray fog.

"Thank you." Beq's lips pressed against Maya's forehead. "I knew you could do it. Everything's going to be fine, you'll see."

Fine. Maya tried to smile, but she was already dropping away.

Chapter 9

The old man regarded Gyre with a mix of mistrust and contempt, looking between him, the three wagons stopped on the narrow dirt track, and the stack of quickheal in Gyre's outstretched hand.

"Well," he said, stretching the single syllable out into a yawn. "I s'pose it's a fair trade."

It wasn't; even in mountaintop Deepfire, Gyre could have had sacks of nyfa seeds for a quarter of what the quickheal would bring. In the old man's defense, he supposed, it was a seller's market. The land south of Ehrenvare between the Ghir and the Absom wasn't quite as desolate as the country to the north, but farmsteads were still widely separated and carefully defended, with only occasional patrols from the nominal authorities at Cliffedge.

They'd been digging into their supplies more than Gyre would have liked, but since they'd lost the last of their funds at Ehren City there was no helping it. *At least everyone needs quickheal.* He handed the medicine to the farmer, who hiked up the track to his high-walled compound. Someone let him in, and after an interminable interval he emerged again, followed by a boy dragging a handcart full of sacks. Sarah hurried over to help, and the two of them got to work tossing the bags into the front wagon. Gyre untied one of them and took out a fistful of fat nyfa seeds. He tossed a few in the direction of each of the loadbird teams, who pecked at them eagerly.

Unlike hardshells, who could subsist on dry grass and a few handfuls of water for weeks at a time, loadbirds needed a steady supply of either grubs or seeds. Fortunately, practically every farmer maintained a small patch of the tough little nyfa bushes to provide fodder for their own animals.

Elariel, sitting on the third wagon, caught the old man staring at her and gave him a wave. They'd taught her to drive the loadbirds the conventional way, but she still looked awkward perched up there. Kit's bodies, of course, were hidden away.

"All set." Sarah grinned at the kid, who gazed back at her in awe. Gyre chuckled as he helped close up the wagon.

"You've got an admirer."

"I noticed, around the third time he dropped a bag. Probably the first woman he's seen that's not his mom."

Sarah, in point of fact, was looking considerably better than when they'd left Deepfire. Her face had filled out, and her skin had darkened a few shades from days of sun. Her hair, growing out, was gathered at her neck in a wavy mass. And, of course, she had her new arm, hidden by a glove and a long-sleeved shirt.

Gyre climbed up on the first wagon and clicked his tongue, reins held loosely. Dusk was still a few hours away, and he wanted to find a campsite far enough from the local farms that they didn't have to worry about running into anyone. He kept the loadbirds to a slow walk until they swung off the track onto the main road.

It was warmer here, and wetter. The road ran between low hills crowned with forest, the flat ground between thick with tall golden grass. Little creeks ran alongside it, lined with nettles. Gyre chose a campsite near one of these. Moments after they came to a halt, the doors of the third wagon slammed open, and constructs poured out.

"Every time the stupid birds need food I have to spend hours sitting in the dark," Kit said, one of her small spiders climbing up Gyre while the others set up the camp. "You'd better not be planning to keep me cooped up once we get to Khirkhaz."

"We shouldn't need to," Gyre said. "The whole point is to get the Commune to enter an alliance with the ghouls, so we can pass you off as ordinary ghoul constructs. They won't know any better."

"At least I'll have more people to amuse me," Kit said. "I should have left a body in Deepfire. I could have been sneaking into brothels this whole time."

"What would you do in a brothel, if you snuck into one?" Sarah said. She sounded fascinated.

"Watch. Bemoan the cruel fate that has left me without genitals." The spider ripple-shrugged. "It would be something to do."

The old farmer had thrown in a package of vulpi bacon and some fresh berries, which made a nice change from the rabbits that Kit brought down to supplement their rations. Sarah tossed seeds to the loadbirds while Gyre fried the bacon over a small fire. Elariel, already munching on berries, leaned close and inhaled the delicious scent.

"Still not ready?" the ghoul said.

"Trust me," Gyre said. "I'm not good at cooking many things, but vulpi bacon is one of them."

"But the edges have already begun to char." At a look from Gyre, Elariel sat back and sighed. "I am always hungry of late. I wonder if this body requires more food."

"I suspect you're just working a little harder out here," Gyre said. "No constructs to do all the labor."

"Hey!" Kit said, in the middle of setting up a tent. "What exactly do you think I'm doing over here?"

"You're a person, not a construct," Gyre said, holding up one hand. "But point taken. We're all very grateful." He picked up a long-handled fork and lunged, extracting dripping slices of bacon. "And *now* this is ready."

Sarah hurried back to claim her share, and for a few moments there were only ecstatic chewing noises. Gyre laid fresh slices on the pan, fat sizzling.

"Okay," Sarah said. "You *are* good at that."

"My father taught me," Gyre said. "We'd slaughter the terminals in the fall. Most of the meat went to market, but he always saved enough of the bacon so we'd have some to eat all the way through the summer. Sometimes you have to spend a night outside with the yearlings, and we'd cook it up over a fire like this."

"You sound as though you miss the pastoral life," Elariel said.

"Sometimes." Gyre shrugged. "They took Maya when I was eight, and it wasn't the same, afterward. I don't know if it's the life I miss or... just what things were like, beforehand."

There was a moment of silence. Fat *popped* in the fire.

"I have a question about humans," Elariel said. "If you don't mind."

"Go ahead," Gyre said, poking the bacon.

"In Ehren City, there was a palace full of costly things, while those in the outer city went hungry. Ichtricia used unmetal weapons, but I healed people of illnesses that would have been cured by a little clean water."

"That sounds like humans," Sarah said. "In Deepfire the Moor-cats ate off gold plate and Raskos' cronies lined their pockets while the tunnelborn died of cold every winter. I imagine it's the same everywhere."

"But why do those in the tenements stay behind the wall?" Elariel said. "The king's soldiers were few in number."

"There were still enough of them to make an example of anyone who steps out of line," Gyre said.

"Any *one*," Elariel said. "But not all, surely."

"You'd have to get everyone to agree to turn on the king, all at once," Gyre said. "That's not easy."

"We had a hard enough time convincing people in Deepfire to fight Raskos," Sarah said. "Even the tunnelborn."

"Why? Would it not be in their interest?"

"Only if we win," Sarah said. "If you try, and not enough other people get on board, you end up on a gallows."

"Besides," Gyre said, "everyone is hoping that everybody *else* will fight, and they'll just get to enjoy the results. So nobody fights, unless they're crazy enough to want to do it on their own."

"Like you," Elariel said.

"Like me, I suppose." Gyre dashed in with his fork again, extracting more bacon. "Is it that different in Refuge? No rich and poor? Nobody goes hungry?"

"There have been times when the whole city has gone hungry," Elariel said, "though not since long before my birth. As for rich and poor, most of my kind would not even understand the question. When I began working with Naumoriel, it was one of the first things he had to teach me about humans, this concept of property."

"You have *power*, though," Gyre said, gesturing with the fork. "The Geraia makes decisions and everyone obeys. They were going to sentence you to death."

Sarah sat up straighter, evidently not having heard that part. "Really?"

"Decisions must be made, of course." Elariel looked into the fire. "Leaders are chosen by acclamation. Though normally that simply means the oldest."

"There must be someone to enforce order, though," Gyre said. "What if you'd refused to go along with the Geraia's judgment? Fought back?"

"I...I honestly have no idea." Elariel cocked her head. "The Geraia represents the community. Anyone who would resist their decisions with force is by definition outside that community. I suppose they would have turned the soldier-constructs on me." She shrugged. "But no one who wasn't already mad would consider such a thing."

There was a pause. Sarah cleared her throat.

"The trouble out here," she said, "is that the world is dangerous, and we don't have constructs to protect us. That means you need people with weapons to guard against plaguespawn and bandits and so on. But someone has to pay the soldiers, or at least feed them, so now you've got taxes and all the rest. And no matter how you start off, eventually the soldiers decide that they ought to be the ones making the decisions, and they've got all the weapons.

"And the hell of it is, usually you're *still* better off with them than without them." Sarah picked up a piece of bacon with her artificial arm and popped it into her mouth. "Those peasants back in Ehrenvare are better off than the poor bastards trying to live on the plains. At least they have a hope someone will come to their aid when the plaguespawn turn up, and paying taxes to the king isn't any worse than getting robbed by some gang of marauders. You remember the tunnels in Deepfire—people *come* to the city, bad as it is, because it's better than trying to live in the mountains on your own. It's probably the same in Ehren City."

She turned to Gyre. "You were born in the Republic. Are ordinary people better off than in the Splinter Kingdoms?"

"Probably. Unless the Order decides they want your family, or your dux is a corrupt monster like Raskos, or the local Auxie commander works for a loan shark." Gyre sighed. "But we didn't have walls against plaguespawn. In the Republic this whole valley would be farms, not just a few patches."

Kit spoke up, sounding mischievous. "And this is the system you're so eager to tear down."

"The Order keeps people from being able to fend for themselves and then tells us they need to be in charge, for our own protection," Gyre said. "Everything has to be the way it's always been. It's the dead hand of the Chosen, pressing down, keeping anything from changing or getting *better*. Why can't everyone get quickheal and bone-break potion and whatever alchemicals they need without it being labeled *dhak*?

Plague, we could all learn *dhaka* ourselves and turn the Republic into Refuge."

"*Dhaka* is difficult for humans," Elariel said. "It requires years of study."

"At least anyone can try," Gyre said. "It's not just something you're born with, like *deiat*. The only reason the centarchs get to be in charge is because nobody can stop them. There has to be a better way to choose leaders than by who's the best killer."

Another pause. Sarah gave Gyre a grin across the fire, and pushed herself to her feet.

"On that note," she said. "Time to turn in. Elariel, would you mind dropping by for a moment? There are a few adjustments I want to make to this." She opened and closed her gloved hand, frowning.

"Of course." Elariel licked her fingers clean. "Thank you for indulging my questions, Gyre. And for your excellent bacon preparation."

The two of them disappeared into Sarah's tent. Gyre wrapped up the remaining bacon and doused the fire, then headed back to his own.

"You know," Kit said, her little spider body scrambling up to his shoulder. "Adjusting Sarah's arm isn't the only thing they're doing in there."

Gyre picked the construct up and set it on the floor of the tent, then sat down on his bedroll and started pulling his boots off. "Meaning what?"

Kit lifted her forelimbs and stared at them for a moment in silence.

"You know, there are certain lewd gestures that are impossible to execute without proper fingers," she said. "How am I just now discovering this? Anyway, fucking, I mean they're fucking."

"Sarah and Elariel?" Gyre finished unlacing his second boot and slid it off, sighing with relief. "Good for them, I suppose." His eyes narrowed. "Does that mean you've been spying on them?"

"I think I've found my true calling as a voyeur," Kit said, dancing happily back and forth. "But it raises a question."

"Does it," Gyre deadpanned.

"I'm going to put this as delicately as I can."

"Oh, good."

"Why is our extremely fuckable ghoul companion over *there* with Sarah's head between her thighs instead of in *here* getting railed by our moderately handsome leader?" The spider-construct raised its forelimbs inquisitively. "She *did* come to you first."

"You heard that, I suppose." Gyre sighed. "Is there any point to my telling you to stop spying on me?"

"No. Answer the question. Were you too weirded out by her being a ghoul? I wouldn't have thought that would bother you. It definitely wasn't that you didn't feel the need, because I saw what you did after she left."

"*Kit.*"

"Look, when *I* shove *you* unwillingly into a swarm of construct bodies, you can watch me jerk off if you want. I just want to know what you were thinking."

"Why?" Gyre said. "Is it important?"

"It's important if you were thinking what I *think* you were thinking, which is that you shouldn't go sleeping around out of some kind of loyalty to yours truly."

Gyre sighed and gathered his legs underneath him, hands on his knees.

"I knew it," Kit said. "Because that's *really* stupid, Gyre. What we had wasn't like that. It wasn't a loyal-unto-death thing. And even if it *was* I'm technically dead."

"I thought it was 'the kind of partners who spend time naked together,'" Gyre said.

"Right. I mean, look. I'm flattered. But let's not be impractical here. One of us ought to be getting some, and while I'd prefer that it be me I no longer have the appropriate equipment. I hereby release you of any lingering responsibility, all right?" The spider came closer, placing one limb on Gyre's knee, in what Gyre guessed was supposed to be a reassuring gesture. "It's *all right*, Gyre. I mean, I did betray you and leave you for dead."

"You said you were going to come back for me," Gyre muttered.

"I was lying, obviously. You're very gullible, you know."

Gyre snorted and managed a faint smile.

"So. Fuck freely, okay? Or don't, but either way don't make it about me." There was a brittle edge to her voice.

"Has this really been bothering you?"

"I can't have your celibacy on my conscience. I wouldn't wish that on anyone." She skittered back a few steps. "Besides, if I'm stuck as a voyeur, I need something to watch."

"I thought you wanted to watch Sarah and Elariel."

"Believe me, I am. I'm getting better at splitting my attention between bodies." She gave a respectable imitation of a sigh. "Okay. Topic finished. Message delivered. Right?"

"Message delivered."

The town of Cliffedge clung to the heights above the river Absom like a tumorous growth.

Even at its current low ebb, the Absom was vast, nearly half a kilometer of deep, swift-running water. It had carved a channel deep into the bedrock, leaving the plains towering hundreds of meters above the riverbed. On the south bank, smaller waterways had cut more gradual slopes, but the north side was a sheer face of red-and-white stone.

It was here, several hundred years previously, when some now-forgotten entrepreneur had dragged a length of salvaged unmetal girder and buried one end of it as deep as he could, leaving the far end to stretch out over the cliff. This indestructible pivot, combined with hundreds of meters of resilk cable, formed the basis for a pulley system that allowed a comfortable descent to the edge of the river far below. On the basis of this innovation, the town that came to call itself Cliffedge had grown wealthy and now exercised at least nominal authority over a sweep of territory extending well north of the river and across it to the Republic border.

Approached from the north side, as Gyre and his companions had come, there was initially nothing particularly impressive about it. A semicircular wall of mortared stone rose three meters high, defending a section of cliffside shaped like a giant bite from a slice of bread. Outside the wall were campgrounds, with clear lanes running through a motley collection of tents, wagons, and lean-tos, along with beasts of burden of every possible description. On the other side, slate-roofed stone buildings rose in neat ranks.

It was only once they were through, having paid a toll to the leather-capped guards on the gate, that they caught sight of the transports that had made the place wealthy. An open market at the center of town mirrored the semicircular shape, centered on the elevators. This was evidently the most valuable real estate around, and the cliffside was lined with buildings cantilevered out over the edge, making maximum use of available frontage by hanging their back ends over empty space. It reminded Gyre of the Smoking Wreckage and other buildings along the side of the Pit in Deepfire. *Though at least here there's no acid fog eating away at the rock.*

The elevators themselves—two more unmetal shafts had joined the original over the years, with cargoes slung between them—were flat platforms big enough to fit wagons three abreast and three deep, with flimsy rails around the edges. One was rising to the top as they arrived, with several carts, teams of loadbirds, and a small crowd of people. It locked into place at the edge of the cliff with a *clang*, and guards lowered the rail, allowing everyone to disembark. Nearby, more wagons were queued waiting for a chance to descend.

Sarah was rapt, watching the pulleys in their giant housings, the black resilk cables improbably thin to bear so much weight. She looked as though she wanted to run to the edge of the cliff to dangle over the edge.

"Steady on," Gyre said. They'd left the wagons and loadbirds outside, in the care of a young stable hand—*and Kit, of course*—and were walking on foot through the crowded square. "We'll get a chance to stare on the way down."

"What causes them to rise?" Elariel said.

"They're *counterweighted*," Sarah said. "Look, see the rocks?" She pointed to a pile of irregular white stones waiting beside the platforms. "You add rocks to the top side until it's heavier than the bottom, then let go. The top falls and pulls the bottom up. Then you unload the rocks down below, load more on up here, and do it again." She grinned broadly, eyes going distant. "Of course, you'd also have to account for the weight of the cargo, and there must be some sort of braking mechanism—"

"Constructs would be easier." Elariel sniffed. "Or simply cutting a ramp through the cliff."

"Let's stay focused," Gyre said. "The Republic isn't far once you get over the river, and we definitely don't want to run into any border checks."

"You have a plan, I take it?"

Gyre nodded. "I sent a note ahead to the Commune, by Yora's old channels. If they got it, there'll be someone here to meet us."

"And if they didn't?" Elariel inquired.

"Then we're going to have to figure something else out— Ah!" He pointed across the market. "There. The coffee shop."

"Why there?" Sarah said, peering.

"See the flag? Top-right window." It was a red square of cloth, with a black design hard to see at this distance. Gyre's silver eye let him make out seven lightning bolts in a circle, points inward. "That's for the Commune."

"I'm surprised they can be so open about it," Sarah said as they threaded their way past a team of screeching loadbirds and narrowly avoided a load of thickhead dung.

"Cliffedge is supposed to be neutral territory," Gyre said. "The merchant council that runs it is officially only interested in getting fat on their tolls. Unofficially, there's a lot of support for the Commune, but they don't want to risk Republic retribution."

"Did you get all this from Yora?" Sarah said.

"More or less." The wash of guilt and sadness at her name had faded now, but Gyre suspected it would never be gone entirely. "She used to drink with their agent in Deepfire. They bought a lot of alchemicals from us." He shook his head and glanced back at Elariel. "Are you keeping up?"

"With the conversation? Not really. But I am managing with the crowd." The ghoul grimaced. "Though I still do not enjoy it."

"It should be quieter inside." They'd reached the coffeehouse, a two-story stone building with many small windows and a cheerful man raising a mug painted on the front door. Gyre smiled immediately at the familiar aroma. "Come on."

Inside, the place was divided into dozens of small nooks separated by wooden screens, with a central bar where coffee was made and dispensed. Well-dressed men and women occupied perhaps a quarter of the tables, holding quiet conversations. This far west, coffee was expensive, so only successful merchants could afford to use a place like this for their meetings. Gyre looked around and caught a scrap of red hanging in the stairway. He beckoned to the others to follow.

Upstairs were more tables, with an even more exclusive clientele. Young men in neat uniforms circulated, taking orders. One of them looked disapprovingly at Gyre and his companions, but Gyre ignored him. In the back corner another scrap of red fabric beckoned, pinned to the edge of a screen. At the table beyond, a large, heavily bearded man was just visible, reading something.

Right. Gyre fought back a nervous rush. *We've already come all this way. This should be the easy part.*

But nothing's ever easy. The cynical voice in his mind sounded a lot like Kit.

"Hmm?" The big man at the table looked up as Gyre approached.

He was elegantly dressed in tailored pants and a buttoned shirt, with a long leather coat and three-cornered hat hanging on the wall beside him. "Sorry, can I help you?"

"I hope so," Gyre said with a polite bow. He kept his voice low. "They call me Gyre Silvereye."

"Silvereye." The man's gaze went to Gyre's face, observing the eye in question, and his brows went up. "Of course. We've been expecting you. Please sit, sit."

Gyre let out a breath and sent up a silent thanks. The nook was barely big enough for the four of them. One of the waiters started over, but the bearded man made a quick gesture, and the boy nodded and withdrew.

"My name is Anton Quivernot," he said, sitting back in his chair. "It's an honor to meet the Halfmask in person."

"I didn't know my name had spread quite so widely," Gyre said.

"Probably not in ordinary circles," Anton said. "But among those of us in the business of sticking it to the Republic, word gets around." His face went solemn. "We heard about Yora as well. My sympathies. At least that bastard Rottentooth got what he deserved."

"Some of it, anyway." Last Gyre had heard, Raskos had fled Deepfire, and no one had seen him since. *Too much to hope that he's dead in a ditch somewhere.* "You got my message, then."

"I did indeed," Anton said. "I don't mind telling you it's caused something of a stir among the brethren. Given recent upheavals in Deepfire, many of our usual routes of supply have become unreliable, so whatever you've brought will be very welcome."

"It's more than the usual alchemicals," Gyre said. "There's an opportunity here—"

"I'm sure there is," Anton said smoothly. "But this is not the place to discuss it." He was looking, past Sarah, toward the stairs. "I think you and your friends had better come with me."

"What's wrong?" Sarah broke in, looking over her shoulder.

"Not so obvious, please," Anton said, picking up his coat and hat.

"The Commune has many enemies. Follow me. We can lose them out the back."

Anton slid through the narrow gap between Elariel and the wall. Sarah leaned close to Gyre and whispered, "Do you trust this guy?"

"Not sure we have an alternative right now," Gyre said, getting up as casually as he could. "But watch our backs."

Anton crossed the coffeehouse, waiters obediently clearing a path, and made his way to an unmarked door. It opened into a dark hallway, and he beckoned Gyre and the others. At the same time, there was a shout from the stairs as a waiter with a tray laden with coffee cups collided with someone.

"The boy's really earning his tip," Anton said with a grin as he ushered them past and shut the door. "Straight on, then left."

"Who are they?" Sarah said. "Republic? Order?"

"Both possibilities," Anton said. "But not the most likely. Things around here are more... complicated. There, the barred door."

Gyre pulled the bar out of its socket and pushed the door open, finding himself on a narrow outdoor landing. A rickety set of steps led down to a small, grubby square shared by the coffeehouse and the buildings beside it, accessible only by a narrow alley. He hurried down, stairs bouncing and creaking under his weight.

"Out the alley and make a right," Anton said, shrugging into his coat. "I've got a—"

"Anton," a woman's voice said. "I thought you might put in an appearance."

A slim figure in a three-cornered hat and a neat suit came out of the alley, stepping fastidiously over a pile of manure. She had pale blue hair to her shoulders and carried a heavy crossbow, a bolt already loaded.

Gyre put one hand on his sword and glanced at Anton, who was just coming down the steps. The Commune agent smiled broadly and spread his hands.

"Maeris," he said. "Good of you to join us."

"You blackrags have a lot of guts, I'll give you that." The woman turned to Gyre. "Told you he was here to welcome you on behalf of the Commune, did he?"

"I have the authority," Anton said. "Truestrike—"

"Plaguing Truestrike doesn't speak for the Greens, as she keeps conveniently *forgetting*. Doesn't speak for anything beyond a gang of puffed-up—"

"I'm sorry," Gyre said. "What exactly is going on here?"

Maeris kept the crossbow aimed at Anton. "What's going *on* is that this tub of fish guts was planning to take everything you had 'for the Commune,' and then keep it for himself and his boss."

"Oh, like your plaguing greenbloods would share and share alike?" Anton said. He turned to Gyre. "Just a little...disagreement among the brethren. Politics, you know. I'm sure—"

"Drop it!" someone shouted from above. "Everyone on the ground!"

Three more figures, all in the tricorns that seemed de rigueur among Communards, burst out of the coffeehouse door. All three had crossbows, which they were aiming down at the fetid little square. Maeris raised her weapon to point at them, and as soon as she did Anton reached under his coat and came out with a pair of blaster pistols, splitting his aim between opponents.

"Fucking bedsheets," Maeris snarled. "You too?"

"Shut it!" said the man on the balcony. "We're just here to see we get our fair share."

"Can we—" Gyre began, but no one was paying attention to him anymore.

"You seem a little outmatched, my dear Maeris," Anton said.

"If you've got any shots left in those things, I'll eat my hat," Maeris said. "Besides, I'm not exactly alone here."

She gave a sharp whistle, and two more crossbows swung out from the coffeehouse roof, covering the men on the balcony and Anton both. Gyre grabbed Sarah and Elariel and started edging sideways, out of the line of fire.

"Now what?" Sarah mouthed at him.

"Working on it," Gyre hissed. The silver eye would let him get clear, probably, but it would be a poor start to his relationship with the Commune to kill half a dozen of its emissaries, whatever their internal disagreements. *And keeping Sarah and Elariel safe would be hard. If I only had some idea what the* sides *are...*

"Hey." Another voice, behind him, a young woman. "You're Silvereye, right? Don't look up."

They'd backed up against the wall of the square, and Gyre felt the wood of a door right behind him. Anton, Maeris, and the new arrivals were still shouting at one another, so he risked a whisper. "Would it be healthy if I was?"

"You're trying to reach the Commune, right?"

"I thought I had," Gyre said.

Sarah groaned. "Don't tell me you're on *another* side."

"More or less. I'm Nina Kotzed."

"Wait." Gyre frowned, trying to remember conversations with Yora. "Kotzed as in *Baron* Kotzed?"

"That's my older sister, Apphia," the voice said.

"You know her?" Sarah said.

"Baron Kotzed is the one who put the Commune together," Gyre muttered. "She's supposed to be the closest thing they have to a leader."

"Which isn't very close, most days," Nina said. "But I can get you to her, if that's what you want."

"Can you get us *out* of here?" Sarah asked.

"If you're ready to run," Nina said.

"If we run," Gyre said, "someone is liable to start shooting."

"I can give us some cover," Sarah said, one hand in her pocket. At Gyre's raised eyebrow, she grinned. "Always come prepared, right?"

"On three, then." Gyre glanced at Elariel, who was watching the standoff with fascination. "Ready?"

"What? Oh yes." The ghoul shook her head. "Humans."

"One. Two. *Three.*"

Sarah yanked a clay sphere out of her pocket and hurled it to the ground at Anton's feet. It exploded with a sharp *crack* and an enormous bloom of thick, acrid smoke, rapidly billowing out to fill the square. Gyre spun and yanked at the door behind him, which opened onto a narrow hallway. Sarah and Elariel followed, while behind them the air was suddenly full of the hiss of crossbow bolts. *Fortunately, I doubt anyone can aim anymore.*

Nina was halfway down the hall, waving them on. She was younger than Gyre had imagined, perhaps fifteen, with pink hair in a neat braid, bright red eyes, and a mischievous expression. She wore the same long leather coat as the rest of the Communards, and he saw the hilts of daggers on her hips.

"Bar the door," she said, "then come on. They may have backup waiting."

Sarah shoved the bar into its socket on the door behind them and gave Gyre a nod. Nina led the way through a shipping office, with rooms full of boxes and crates at the back and studies packed with surprised clerks in the front. Nina gave the office workers a wave as they passed by and headed for the front door, which let onto an adjoining street. A bell jangled as she pushed it open, and then they were outside again.

"See?" Nina said brightly. "Not so difficult. Now, I think we should make a proper introduction—"

"That's far enough!" Maeris, coughing and trailing smoke, came around the corner. She had a long blade in her hand, and a heavyset man beside her still carried a loaded crossbow, which he aimed at Nina.

"You sure you want to do that?" Nina said, still smiling. "What're you going to tell my sister if you shoot me?"

"Good point," Maeris said. "Shoot her in the leg, then."

"Okay," Gyre said. "That's about enough."

The thing in his skull went *click*, and the world slowed down around him. A moment of frenzied motion later, and Maeris was slumped against the wall, gasping for breath, while her large companion was laid out in the street with a lump growing on his head. Gyre pulled the bolt off his crossbow and tossed it to the ground.

"Oooooh." Nina's grin widened. "You and Apphia are going to get along *just* fine."

Chapter 10

For most of a week, Maya alternated between a sleep full of fevered nightmares and waking hours curled in her bed with alternating sweats and chills. She recognized the stone walls of her own dusty, barely used bedroom at the Forge. Beq was with her at intervals, and servants brought medicine and the thin soup that was all she could keep down.

Eventually, the fever broke, and Maya got her first really restful sleep in days, waking up drenched in sweat. The world no longer felt like it was in danger of spinning away from her. She lay in bed for a while, savoring the sensation, until there was a knock at the door.

"Maya?" Beq said.

"Come in," Maya croaked.

Beq carried a tray with a wax packet of medicine, the usual soup, and a plate of soft white bread. She grinned.

"They told me you were looking better last night," Beq said, "so I figured we'd try something more exciting this morning."

"Is it morning?" Maya said. "I've lost track. But I'm hungry, which is probably a good sign."

"You look like a drowned rat," Beq said, flicking one of Maya's damp locks.

"I *feel* like a drowned rat." Maya stretched toward the tray, which she couldn't quite reach without sitting up, and gave Beq a pleading look. Beq laughed and pushed it closer. "You're an angel."

"Flatterer," Beq said, but she looked pleased.

Maya gulped down the powder and most of a pitcher of water, then started on the bread and soup.

"You're definitely on the mend," Beq said. "Do you feel up to a bath after this?"

"Chosen above, yes," Maya said, swallowing hurriedly. Beq laughed again.

A few minutes later, Maya was gingerly lowering herself into the big, blood-warm bath. It was empty, as usual—the Forge was so big that it wasn't uncommon to have a whole wing to one's self. Beq sat near the doorway, ready to warn off anyone who might try to come in.

"You're not going to join me?" Maya said, settling in. Water lapped over the rim, running along channels in the floor to the drains.

"I wish I could." Beq adjusted her spectacles, then took them off and rubbed the lenses on her shirt. "Baselanthus wants me to clarify a few things in my report for the Council."

"Right." Guilt prickled in Maya's stomach. "Sorry. That should have been me."

"Please. You were seriously ill from—what was it? Saving all our lives? Again?" Beq put her spectacles back on. "Ducking out on a little paperwork seems like a reasonable exchange."

"You've talked to Basel, then? And Prodominus? What did they say?"

"Not very much, actually. I told them about the plaguespawn, the village, and what we learned from the Archive."

"I hope they didn't grill you too badly. Basel can get intense when he wants to know something."

"He was nice enough," Beq said, looking down at her hands. "I still get a little tongue-tied answering questions from Kyriliarchs."

"I'm sure you did great." Maya leaned back, letting her hair spread out on the surface of the water. "I assume Basel wants to see me, too?"

"Eventually. He and the Council are in Skyreach for the next few days, meeting with the Senate." Beq sat up straighter. "You don't think he's going to give my report to the *Senate*, do you?"

"Is that better or worse than the Council?"

"I have no idea!"

Beq looked so alarmed that Maya laughed out loud. "Relax. If they're keeping this secret from the rest of the Order, I doubt they're going to tell Republic politicians about it."

"That's true," Beq said, then sighed. "I'd better get back to work, though. Are you feeling all right? Not going to pass out?"

"I'll be fine," Maya said. "Go, write your report."

"I'll come by with dinner," Beq said.

"I think my excitement could stretch to a sausage or two."

Beq winked. "I'll see what I can do."

She left Maya alone with the drifting steam. Maya pushed herself across the bath, which was big enough for her to lie back without touching the sides. For a long moment she held her breath and floated, feeling the heat slowly unkinking sore muscles.

We made it back. It had been a near thing. *I'm alive; Beq and Varo are alive. We made it.*

That helped open the knot in her stomach, but a significant lump remained. They hadn't found out anything about Jaedia's condition, other than the fact that the black spider that had taken her over wasn't the only one of its kind. *Nothing to actually* help *her.* Maya wondered if she should have tried to take the Eldest prisoner, forced it to answer questions. *It didn't seem like it would come along quietly.*

Instead of answers, she'd only come back with more mysteries. About Jaedia and the spiders, but also about herself, and Basel. *And the Thing.*

Her toes touched the side of the bath, and she pulled herself onto the stone seat, letting her hair drain over the side. Carefully, she touched the crystal protuberance of the Thing, exploring the seam where it met her skin. The puffy, injured feeling was gone, but the familiar contours suddenly felt alien. Having the Thing be a part of her body had always seemed natural, but now it felt *wrong*, an intrusion of crystal and unmetal where there should be flesh. *Dhak.*

I still don't know anything for sure. The Archive hadn't been certain, as it had pointed out at tedious length. *Still. It seemed to think the Thing was designed to* limit *me. Why would Basel want to do that to a five-year-old?*

And, in a whisper at the back of her mind, *What could I do if he hadn't?*

Too long in the bath. Maya shook her head and hauled herself over the side, cooler air pebbling her bare skin into goose bumps. *Basel taught Jaedia, for the Chosen's sake. He's been helping me my whole life. Whatever the Thing does, I'm sure he thought using it was the right move.*

I'm going to have to ask him, aren't I? Out of everything, *that* made her heart quiver most. *What if he won't tell me? What if he lies?* Or, maybe worst of all, he could have a good reason, and be badly hurt by her suspicion. *He has to understand why I'd want to know. Doesn't he?*

Mulling over these questions got her through the rest of the day. The Forge servants, silent and efficient as ever, had changed out her bedding and left a plain lunch. Maya wolfed it down and did some light exercise, wincing at the strain in her muscles after a week of inactivity.

By dinnertime she was ravenous again. Beq had foreseen this and arrived with not only a stack of sausages but roast vegetables, potatoes, and a loaf of bread still steaming from the oven. Maya paused long enough to kiss her, and then they attacked the feast together.

"How's Varo?" Maya said between bites.

"He's fine." Beq licked juice off her fingers. "Writing a report too, I think."

"I hope they give him a break this time." After they'd gotten back from Deepfire, Varo had been off on another mission before Maya had recovered.

"I don't know," Beq said. "There's a lot of rumors going around. Problems in the south, problems in the east. They say that's why the Council is meeting with the Senate."

"There are always problems," Maya said, frowning.

"More than usual, I mean."

Maya stopped herself from asking more. *Enough.* The Republic's problems would be there tomorrow. *I deserve a break too, don't I?*

One thing led to another, and Beq ended up staying the night, the two of them making the best of Maya's narrow bed. When they were finished, Maya sprawled, naked and pleasantly exhausted, while Beq lay on her stomach beside her, head pillowed on her hands. Her green hair, unbound, cascaded over her shoulders, and Maya idly rolled it between her fingers.

"I want to ask you something," Maya said. "Speaking purely hypothetically."

"Uh-oh," Beq mumbled. "That's never a good sign."

"Honestly, it's just a question." Maya touched the Thing, running a finger along its crystals. "If I asked you to disable this, could you do it?"

"The Thing?" Beq blinked and sat up, reaching for her spectacles. "Really?"

"Just hypothetically."

"I thought it was supposed to be keeping you healthy," Beq said.

"I know," Maya said. "I don't want you to actually do it. I'm just curious if you could."

"I mean..." Beq leaned forward, adjusting her lenses. "Parts of it look pretty standard. I can see the control loop, for instance. If I reversed this part"—she touched it, gently, and Maya felt the pressure in her chest—"that would turn it into a null node, which in theory should negate any effect it was having. You'd need a little nullifier attachment."

"Would it be difficult?"

"Not really. But I wouldn't do it."

"Why not?"

"Because I don't understand it!" Beq shook her head. "It's *part* of you, Maya. It's practically touching your heart. If I just…broke it, Chosen above knows what it would do to you."

"All right! Never mind." Maya raised her hands defensively. "Like I said, I was just curious."

"Does this have something to do with what the Eldest said to you?" Beq said. "Or—"

"It was just a strange idea," Maya said. "Forget it."

"Maya…"

Maya leaned forward and kissed her, pulling her spectacles aside with one hand, the other losing itself in the mass of Beq's thick hair. Beq hesitated for a moment, then pressed in tighter, and it turned out they weren't finished after all. Whether it was the lack of fever or the proceeding activity, Maya's dreams that night were considerably more pleasant, but she awoke feeling guilty.

I should tell her. She stared at Beq's soft features, smoothed by sleep. *What I asked the Archive about the Thing. My worries about Basel.* Beq had earned her trust a hundred times over. *It's not about trust, though. I'm just worried I'm driving myself crazy over nothing.*

There was a slight rustle at the outer door. Maya rolled out of bed and found a tray waiting, with bread, jam, and bacon. Beside it was an envelope, with the Council seal in Baselanthus' colors.

"Morning." Beq yawned, stretched hugely, and sat up, fumbling her spectacles into place. "Is that breakfast?"

"And something else." Maya took the tray back to bed. Beq raised an eyebrow at the envelope, but Maya shook her head. "Food first."

Eating with Beq, naked and giggly, heedless of getting crumbs all over the sheets, somehow felt like the height of self-indulgence. Maya abruptly didn't want to face the note at all, didn't want the moment to end. It would be another complication, and for just an instant things seemed so *simple.*

But the Order needs me. Jaedia needs me. Maya licked the last of the jam off her lips and broke the wax seal with her fingernail. Beq shifted to read over her shoulder, bare breasts pressing distractingly against Maya's back.

"It's from Basel," Maya muttered. "Unless someone's faked the seal. But…"

Centarch Maya Burningblade,

First, my utmost gratitude for your efforts thus far. I am told you have recovered from your illness, for which I am thankful.

Arcanist Bequaria has conveyed to me the details of what occurred on your expedition. I have questions for you, of course, but that will have to wait. While you were away, I conducted some investigation of my own, and found that the arcana described in Prodominus' sketches appears nowhere in the Order's archives. No such thing is or has ever been in our custody, as far as the records are concerned.

And yet Prodominus seemed adamant that it was of great importance. I have striven to give him the benefit of the doubt, and provided ample time in which he could have brought the matter to the attention of the Council. He has not done so, and I must regretfully conclude that something more suspicious is afoot.

I dare not confront him and risk an open break, especially while the conference with the Senate is ongoing. I will endeavor to enlist the rest of the Council and make certain we are in a position to demand an explanation. However, I worry that this will not be quick enough to keep pace with circumstances, especially in light of my second discovery.

My agents have uncovered a private warehouse in Skyreach leased through an intermediary by Prodominus himself. Arcanist Xalen, well-known to be Prodominus' protégé, has been seen coming and going, sometimes with bulky cargo. My suspicion is that Prodominus is using this site to keep important discoveries from the Council for his own purposes.

The address is below. Once again, I cannot order you to investigate this matter. However, I hope you think, as I do, that not even the members of the Council should operate without the scrutiny of the rest of the Order. And given what you learned from the Archive, if Prodominus does possess this arcana and believes it to be important, we must know more. In particular, if it is a communication device of some kind, who or what does it communicate with?

I trust you to do as you think best, Maya. I will speak with you when my duties allow.

Kyriliarch Baselanthus Coldflame

There followed a string of numbers that meant little to Maya, which she assumed was a Skyreach address.

"Basel wants us to break into Prodominus' private safehouse?" Beq said. "Am I reading that right?"

"He won't actually say it, but I think so," Maya said. Her skin pebbled in a sudden chill. "Chosen above."

"He must really think Prodominus is a traitor," Beq said. "First Nicomidi, and now this."

"Prodominus is the oldest living Kyriliarch," Maya said. "He's been with the Order since before either of us was born. How could he be a traitor?" She shook her head. "It doesn't make sense."

"None of this has made sense since we got back from Deepfire," Beq said, flopping back on the bed. "Why should it start now?"

Maya read the note again. *In particular, if it is a communication device of some kind, who or what does it communicate with?*

"Well?" Beq said. "Are we going to do it?"

"I think I have to," Maya said slowly. "I need to know what's really going on here. But—"

"Please don't insult me by suggesting I'd let you go off on your own."

"Perish the thought." Maya grinned. "Actually, I was going to say we might need help with this one. I've never even been to Skyreach."

"I've only been a few times," Beq said. "And I've never gotten to wander around. Varo would be willing, I'm sure."

"That's a start," Maya said. "But I have another idea."

Once again, they were gathered around a table in the checkerboard-tiled atrium outside the archives and the quartermasters' office. A few other groups were present, but Maya had picked a spot well away from them, so as not to be overheard.

Unlike on previous occasions, there were four of them. Tanax sat beside Varo, reading the note from Baselanthus in fascinated silence.

"If this is true..." Tanax said when he was finished.

"Exactly," Maya said. "So that's what we have to find out."

"It's not going to be easy," Varo said. "Skyreach isn't the Forsaken Coast, or even Litnin. If you start blowing things up, people are going to notice." He shrugged. "You've got my help, of course, but I don't know how much it's worth. The big city isn't exactly my area of expertise."

"I was hoping," Maya said, "that Tanax could help with that."

"Let me be clear," Tanax said. "You're asking me to help break into private property owned by a member of the Council of Kyriliarchs."

"More or less." Maya scratched the back of her neck. "To be fair, it's *secretly* owned. He can hardly complain."

"He won't need to complain, if we get caught," Tanax said. "You realize that, don't you? Skyreach's Auxiliaries are well equipped and backed up by Legionaries. If they find us, we're not going to be able to fight our way out. Even if I were willing to use force against loyal Order soldiers, which I am not."

"Right," Maya said. "So we can't get caught."

"Easy to say," Tanax said. "Harder to achieve." He blew out a breath. "You took a big risk coming to me with this."

Maya cocked her head. "You told me I could trust you, didn't you?"

"I did." A tightening of Tanax's lips indicated that he might be regretting that now. "And I might have some ideas about how to make this work. I'll need to do a little bit of research first."

"Then you're on board?"

"Chosen protect me." Tanax shook his head. "You and your master had better be right."

Chapter 11

The descent from Cliffedge was less harrowing than Gyre had imagined. The big platforms barely swayed as they slowly dropped, meter by meter. Sarah said something about rachets and guidelines, but as far as Gyre was concerned the important thing was that they didn't end up smashed against the rocks.

He'd been anxious about interference from Anton, Maeris, or the other factions, but Nina told him not to worry.

"The Cliffedge authorities tolerate the Commune as long as we don't cause trouble," she said, swinging her legs over the platform's edge. "Nobody wants to jeopardize that, and attacking a merchant caravan in broad daylight would definitely count. We'll have to be more on guard once we're over the river, but we should be with our people by then."

"So you were alone up here?" Gyre said. "The baron's sister?"

Nina shrugged. "Apphia trusts me."

No further explanation seemed forthcoming, so Gyre turned away. Sarah was at the back of the platform, watching the machinery, and

Elariel was nowhere to be seen. A few other small parties had joined them, but it was the first descent of the day, and the platform was largely empty.

He went to the first wagon, where the pair of loadbirds were pecking enthusiastically at some nyfa seeds, and opened the door. Inside, Elariel groaned.

"Are you all right?"

"No." The ghoul had retreated to her nest of blankets. "I'm hanging in midair from nothing more than a bit of sun-lover trickery. It will fail at any moment and we'll all plunge to our deaths."

"They've done this ten times a day for years, you know."

Elariel gave another groan. "Shut the door, please. I'm trying to pretend I've been walled up in a tomb."

"As you like."

Gyre closed the door and went to the last wagon. The ghoul-made boxes occupied most of it, along with the odd, egg-like shapes of Kit's bodies in their inactive forms. One of the smaller ones popped open, limbs unfolding in a complex ballet.

"Nearly there?" she chirped.

"About halfway down," Gyre said. "But you're going to have to stay quiet until we actually get to see this Baron Kotzed and I can explain things properly."

"That's fine," Kit said in a sarcastic singsong. "Don't mind me. I'll just be sitting in the dark losing my mind, which is particularly bad in my case since my mind is really all I have left."

"Sorry," Gyre said. "You know what people will think if they see you too soon."

"Yeah, yeah." She gave an artificial sigh and waved her front limbs. "Remind me why I'm doing this again?"

"You feel bad about nearly getting me killed at Leviathan's Womb?" Gyre said.

"That doesn't sound like something I would feel bad about," Kit said.

"Then probably because you're bored and I'm the only human who won't think your bodies are plaguespawn and try to smash them."

"*That* sounds more likely." Kit did a little hopping dance, which Gyre was starting to associate with her old, mad grin. "Seriously, Gyre. Do you think this is going to work? You trust this Kotzed?"

"I think yesterday demonstrated that we shouldn't trust anyone where the Commune is concerned," Gyre said. "But at least Nina seems willing to trust *us*, and she didn't try to stick a crossbow in my face. We have to start somewhere."

"Fair enough." A dull *clunk* came through the deck, and the descent slowed. "I think that means we're at the bottom."

"Right," Gyre said, opening the door. "Now we have a river to cross."

"Make sure to check in and keep me up on all the gossip."

Getting the wagons across the river was surprisingly easy, as it turned out. The Cliffedge engineers had designed a floating dock to anchor the bottom of the elevator, to which large, flat-bottomed barges could attach. The Absom was powerful but smooth here, and the boats were driven by teams of bare-chested, sweating oarsman. Gyre reluctantly bartered a cache of quickheal and bone-break potion with one of the boatmasters, and his three wagons were taken aboard three craft and pushed out into the river.

It's a good thing we're not actually merchants. The bag of thalers was gone, along with a chunk of their cargo. *I don't know how we'd ever make a profit. I suppose that's why* dhak *costs so much in the Republic.*

Fresh moans issued from the wagon containing Elariel as the boats rocked, and Gyre guessed that floating in water was no better than hanging in midair as far as the ghoul was concerned. Nina raised an eyebrow but didn't comment. The loadbirds were also less than pleased at their circumstances and made it known with a series of irritated squawks. At least it wasn't long before the efforts of the oarsmen brought them to the quay on the other side of the river, where the barges dropped their ramps and the flustered loadbirds, ruffling their feathers, pulled the wagons back onto dry land.

From there a road led inland, climbing steadily for several kilometers as it curved away from the riverbank. Elariel emerged, looking a little green, to take her position on the third wagon, while Nina road beside Gyre on the first. It was nearly midday, and the sun shone through gaps in the shredded clouds. Snow-peaked mountains, blued by distance, lined the sky ahead and to their left.

"Those are the Worldspine Mountains," Nina said. "Follow that range north and east, and eventually you'll get all the way to Skyreach. That's Khirkhaz's northern border, more or less."

"We're not going through them, I hope," Gyre said. "I don't think the wagons would make it."

"The main road follows the coast," Nina said. "But that means going straight through Hooked Bay, and there's a Legion garrison there. We'll split off well before that. The hills are rough going, but there are paths if you know where to find them." She gave her bright smile. "Which I do, of course."

"Good to know," Gyre said. He clicked his tongue at the birds, who looked like they wanted to stop and peck at something. "So what can you tell me about your sister?"

"Apphia?" Nina put on a thoughtful expression. "She's...not as scary as everyone says, I guess. Most of the time."

"She leads the Commune?"

"Nobody really *leads* the Commune, as you may have noticed," Nina said. "Everyone supposedly agrees that Apphia's in charge, but the banners all do what they like unless she really pushes them." Nina idly flipped the end of her braid back and forth. "The banners are...factions, I guess you'd say? They each have a different color version of the flag. Black, Green, and White. Also known as blackrags, grass-stains, and bedsheets, depending on who you ask. They're the ones who ambushed you in Cliffedge."

"Charming," Gyre said.

"What about you, Master Silvereye?" She bent her head back to look at him upside down. "Is it true you found that thing in a dead ghoul's skull and cut your own eye out so you could use it?"

"Is *that* what they're saying about me?" Gyre said.

"Among other things. Well?"

"I bought it, if you must know, from a scavenger who found it in the deep tunnels." Gyre had settled on a cover story that was at least vaguely plausible. "And obviously I didn't cut my own eye out. A cent-arch did that for me."

"In battle?" Nina said, excited.

"Not much of a battle," Gyre muttered. "I was eight years old."

"Oh." She leaned back against the seat. "Still. You're the only person I've heard of with a working ghoul part. Did you bring along any more eyes in those boxes?"

"Why?" Gyre said. "Do you need one?"

"Not at the moment." Nina curled her fingers in front of her face. "But you never know, right?"

As promised, when the road turned south and east toward the coast, Nina directed them up a small track that carried on due eastward. At first the way was still flat, but gradually the ground grew rougher, and small stands of forest merged into a single blanket of trees covering the rolling landscape. At Nina's direction, Gyre brought the wagons to a halt in a clearing dotted with stumps.

"Not lost, I hope," he said.

"Of course not," Nina said. "But this is where we pick up our escort. With me along, the banners *probably* wouldn't ambush you outright, but it's best not to tempt them."

She shoved her fingers in her mouth and whistled, so loud that the loadbirds startled and fluffed out their feathers. A dozen figures emerged from the trees on the other side of the clearing. They wore the leather coats and three-cornered hats of Communards and carried swords and crossbows, but at least for the moment none of the weapons were actually pointed in Gyre's direction.

"Milady," one man said. He was tall and broad-shouldered, with a thick, graying mustache. "I'm glad to see you returned safe."

"Good to see you too, Bren," Nina said. She hopped down from the box and beckoned to Gyre to follow. "Gyre, this is Lancer Brennard. His family has been sworn to mine for four generations. Bren, this is Gyre Silvereye."

"Then the message was genuine." Brennard gave Gyre a long look. "We were uncertain. It has been some time since we received anything from Deepfire."

"Things have been . . . difficult," Gyre said. "There's more Republic presence than usual."

"Gyre needs to see Apphia as soon as possible," Nina said. "Is she still up at Blacktree Crossing?"

"I have not heard otherwise," Brennard said. "But may I ask why the hurry?"

"Word has got around." Nina waved at the wagons. "The banners are eager to keep all this for themselves. Somebody might take it into their head to make a play for it, peace of the Commune or no."

Brennard grimaced. "I wish I thought that was less likely. But they'll not catch us unawares." He made a sharp gesture, and several of his men vanished back into the brush. "We'll take the Southcrest road. You know the way?"

Nina nodded. "I'll stay with Gyre, then."

They set out again in short order. Brennard and one of his soldiers rode ahead of the wagons on warbirds, and another brought up the rear. The rest, Gyre surmised, were ranging ahead and to their flanks keeping watch.

"They seem very professional," Gyre said when Nina was back on the box beside him. "Not what I was expecting of Communards, if I'm being honest."

"Bren commands what's left of my sister's guard, the ones who stayed loyal." Nina pursed her lips in irritation. "I wish she'd keep him close instead of sending him to babysit me, though."

"I imagine she's just concerned for your safety."

"She should—" Nina stopped and bit her lip. "Never mind. She can explain things when we get there."

The wagons rumbled on. As Nina had promised, while the tracks grew rough at times, they were never so bad that the vehicles couldn't get through, winding through gullies and sloping up the broad shoulders of the hills. This was deep, old forest, with few signs of human habitation. Every so often, Gyre spotted a log cabin amid the trees, with a curl of smoke rising from a chimney. Once they had to take a crude bridge over a steep ravine, roped-together logs creaking ominously as the wagons crossed one at a time.

Near sunset, Bren announced that they'd reached a good campsite and they'd make their destination the next day. The road here ran along a ridge, with a steep slope down on one side and a rocky hill on the other. Gyre nodded with approval as the soldier guided them off into a small clearing between two boulders. *Out of sight, and no way for anyone to sneak up without coming along the road. He knows his business.*

The presence of outsiders meant that Kit couldn't help erect their tents, unfortunately. Gyre felt foolish struggling with the things while Bren and his soldiers set up their camp in half the time, efficiently laying out two large tents, making a campfire, and producing rations from their saddlebags. At least Gyre could contribute some fresh meat and bread they'd stocked in Cliffedge, which the hard-bitten foresters appreciated. Elariel, after dinner, retreated from the presence of so many strangers and holed up in her wagon, but Sarah made up for it by being her usual ebullient self. Before long she was telling a long, involved joke so dirty it had Bren's soldiers blushing as they hooted and slapped their knees.

"I like her," Nina said. Gyre had taken a seat on a stump, and she'd wedged herself in beside him. "Is she your girl?"

"My girl?" Gyre blinked and shook his head. "No. She's an arcanist, a plaguing good one. We'll need her to make use of what I've brought."

"Ah yes. The sealed boxes nobody is allowed to discuss, in the mysterious third wagon." Nina grinned at Gyre's discomposure. "Relax. You need to negotiate with Apphia first, I understand."

"It's not that I don't trust you—"

"It's just that you don't trust us." She grinned and looked up at the sky. "Come with me, I want to show you something."

Nina bounced to her feet and walked away from the camp. Gyre shrugged, caught Sarah's eye for a moment, and then followed. The girl led him along the narrow path back out to the main road, exchanging a wave with one of Bren's soldiers standing sentry.

On the other side of the road, the ground fell away steeply, providing a good view. Only the western horizon retained a hint of color, and stars were already visible in the east. The moon was close to full, and there was enough light to make out the rise and fall of the land. It looked like a sea of trees, waves frozen in time.

"What do you think of my country?" Nina said. She stood on the edge of the cliff, hands clasped behind her back.

"It's...different," Gyre said. "There's nothing like this anywhere near Deepfire. It's all rocks and scrub grass."

"Is that where you grew up? Deepfire?"

Gyre chuckled. "I grew up in the Republic, on a little vulpi farm. There wasn't anything like this there either. What we called 'the woods' was just a pile of sticks by comparison."

"Farther south, toward the coast, there's more open country," Nina said. "But the forest has always felt like the heart of Khirkhaz to me. That's where most of the people who fight for the Commune come from. Loggers, hunters, herders, and farmers from the little valleys. They're the ones who got fed up with the Lightning Barons." She shrugged. "Apphia can explain the history better than I can. I just wanted you to see this."

"It's a nice view," Gyre said. "Though I might be able to see more in the morning."

"Some things are easier to miss during the day." She pressed close to him, extending a hand. "See the little black box up there?"

Gyre didn't, at first, but he closed his real eye and let the silver one cut through the darkness. On the crown of a hill some distance away, there was a blocky tower. Long, spiky *things* protruded from it at intervals, like feathers or leaves curling off the stem of a fern, stretching out and then upward. There were so many of them that the top of the tower was nearly obscured in a forest of curving quills.

"I see it," Gyre said. "What am I looking at?"

"That's Spire Kotzed," Nina said. "Apphia's birthright. It's bigger than it looks from here. All you can see is the outer wall and the tower, but there's practically a whole town around the base."

"I'm sure it's beautiful," Gyre said diplomatically.

"Just watch," Nina said.

All at once, a jagged line of pure brilliance connected the spire to the sky. The rest of the scene went dark as Gyre's silver eye cut in filters, leaving that single twisted arc as the only light in the world. Before it faded, the lightning bolt was joined by another and another, writhing as though in agony. A few moments later, a continuous growl of thunder reached them, rising and falling.

"That's home," Nina said. When Gyre glanced down at her, he could see the strobes of lightning reflected in her eyes.

The next day, at Gyre's prompting, she explained a little. There were seven spires in all, spread in a circle through most of northwest Khirkhaz. The original buildings were Chosen constructions, with unmetal walls and rooms full of arcana no one understood. Twice a day, at dawn and dusk, storms of lightning slashed down from the sky and crackled across their towers. Even so, their value as fortifications had been obvious, and after the Plague War and the collapse of the empire Nina's ancestors had moved in and turned them into fortresses. That had been the beginning of the Lightning Barons, the seven families who had ruled Khirkhaz for more than three hundred years.

"The thing is," Nina said, "by the time the Republic got itself sorted out and started appointing duxes and so on, here in Khirkhaz we'd already been more or less shifting for ourselves for almost a century. There were already wars with the Splinter Kingdoms going on, and some people thought that we should declare ourselves independent and be done with it. The barons met and had a vote, and decided four to three to stay with the Republic, as long as they agreed to let us manage our own affairs. Which they did, at least at the time."

"So what changed?"

"Ask Apphia." Nina sighed. "I was only a girl. I grew up out here in the forest with nothing but tents and Bren's stories about the good old days."

Once the track veered away from the edge of the cliff, they were deep in the forest again. The first sign that they had reached their destination was a rising whistle from the trees ahead, to which Nina gave an answering two-tone sound. More Communards appeared, as if from nowhere, and Brennard rode forward, answering greetings and shouting orders.

Blacktree Crossing, it turned out, wasn't a town or even a village, but literally what the name implied. The track they'd been following met with several others beside a small hillock topped with the blackened corpse of a massive, long-dead tree. There was a small encampment there, laid out with military discipline. Rows of tents, heavily patched and faded, stood beside some open farm carts loaded with supplies. Several dozen loadbirds were staked out in neat lines. Gyre estimated there were forty or fifty people living here. By the accumulation of bird shit, they'd been in place for some time, but the impression was of a group ready to pack up and leave at a moment's notice.

Only a dozen soldiers were in camp at the moment, joining those from Nina's escort. Brennard barked orders, and men ran to help Gyre and his companions pull their wagons up and get the birds unharnessed.

"Come on." Nina jumped down. "Apphia will be eager to talk to you. One of Bren's soldiers went ahead by swiftbird, so she's waiting for us."

"Give me one moment," Gyre said.

He got down himself and stepped between the other two wagons, beckoning Sarah and Elariel. They climbed down as well. Pressed in between the two vehicles, it was as private as they were likely to get, but Gyre still kept his voice low.

"I'm going to go talk to the baron," he said. "With any luck, this is our way in. But stay together, and don't get too far from the wagons. If things go wrong, get to Kit and head into the woods."

Sarah frowned. "What about you?"

"I can get away just fine, but I'm not going to be able to fight this whole camp," Gyre said. "We'll meet up after dark and figure out... something." He sighed. "Hopefully it won't be necessary."

"Plan B?" Sarah said.

Gyre grimaced at the memory of Raskos' raid on their hideout. "Exactly." He turned to Elariel. "How are you holding up?"

"I am managing," the ghoul said stiffly, "for the moment." She looked around and deflated a little. "This is... a lot of humans. But I must grow accustomed to such things."

"I'll stay with her," Sarah said, putting a hand on Elariel's shoulder. The ghoul startled slightly but didn't pull away. "Go, negotiate. That's what we came here for."

Gyre nodded and slipped out from between the wagons, where Nina and Brennard were waiting for him. The lancer gave an apologetic bow.

"I must request your weapon, Master Silvereye," he said. "I promise it will be well cared for."

"Of course," Gyre said, trying not to let it jangle his nerves. He unslung the silver sword and handed it over. "Please ask your soldiers to keep out of the wagons. Some of what's inside could be dangerous."

"Certainly." Brennard bowed again, and Nina tugged impatiently at Gyre's sleeve.

They went to the largest tent, which had once been a rich royal purple. Some color survived, but most had faded into a dull gray and been patched repeatedly. Nina scratched at the tent flap.

"Come in."

She ducked inside, and Gyre followed. The small space was laid with threadbare rugs and held only a bedroll and a low folding table. Nina ran forward, arms spread, and embraced the single inhabitant.

"Apph!" She wrapped her arms around her sister. "I found him. I found Silvereye!"

"I see that," Apphia Kotzed said. "Good work, little sister. And it's good to see you safe." She shifted her attention to Gyre. "I hope that Nina has been making herself useful."

"Extremely." Gyre bowed. "Greetings, Baron Kotzed. My name is Gyre Silvereye."

"Your fame precedes you." Apphia disengaged herself from her sister. "Nina, I should speak to Gyre alone. Go and make sure his companions are cared for."

"Brennard is looking after them," Nina said. Apphia merely set her jaw, and her younger sister gave a theatrical sigh and left the tent.

Apphia did not look like the sort of person who lost many arguments. She was as tall as Gyre, and he guessed her to be a few years older than himself, in her midtwenties. Her most striking feature was a scar all along her left side, from her collarbone up across her face and onto her scalp. It was made of many thin lines of shiny white flesh, tightly packed and twisted like a pile of worms, but never crossing or intersecting. She had no hair from her squashed, shriveled left ear to the top of her head. What was left, a purple a few shades darker than her sister's, was cut at the nape of her neck and pinned behind her good ear. Her eye on that side looked intact, but the eyebrow was gone, giving her expression a lopsided look.

"Lightning," she said into the silence that followed.

"Excuse me?"

"This." She touched her left cheek. "A lightning strike, when I was a girl. Always a danger, living as we do. You've seen the Spire?"

"From a distance." Gyre raised his eyebrows. "I'm surprised your family lived there if it was so risky."

"It's safe enough on the ground," she said with a dismissive wave. "I was playing somewhere I shouldn't have been." She shrugged. "People are usually desperate to ask, but they try to be polite, so I find it best to dispense with the whole issue. Please sit."

"I suppose," Gyre said, settling behind the table, "that I owe you as much in return." He touched the scar across his own left eye. "I got this from a centarch when I was eight."

"A centarch?" Apphia settled cross-legged. She wore much the same thing as the rest of the Communards, though there were ragged edges of embroidery around the buttonholes of her shirt. "No wonder you wound up a rebel."

"It wasn't *quite* that simple," Gyre said, although in truth it probably was. *But it wasn't just the eye they took. It was Maya.* "I suppose that *is* the gist, though."

"And stories of your work with Yora have reached us even in the south, along with your excellent alchemicals," Apphia said. "Are you here on her behalf?"

"Not exactly." Gyre looked down at the empty table. "Yora's dead. She was killed by a centarch in an Order ambush, along with most of the rest of her team."

"You escaped?"

"I was... elsewhere."

"I see." She studied his expression. "Would you like a drink, Gyre Silvereye?"

He nodded. Apphia leaned over and flipped open a heavy trunk, pulling out a bottle of something amber and a pair of battered silver cups. She poured a finger into each, then tossed hers back in one go, slamming the cup down hard enough that the table rattled.

"It's local *eviske*," she said. "Made from apples and honey."

Gyre cautiously sniffed and found his eyes watering. There might have been apples and honey involved in the process, but what was left was strong enough to strip paint. He tossed it back, imitating his host, and managed to swallow without coughing. The alcohol burned its way down his throat and settled into his stomach.

"Very good," the baron said. "I like a man who can handle his *eviske.* So." She put her hands flat on the table, either side of the bottle. "Yora is dead. Your team is broken by the Order. How does that end with you here, offering three wagonloads of goods to the cause?"

Gyre took a deep breath, his tongue still numbed. He'd thought about how to play this and had never quite come to a conclusion. Now it was time to roll the dice.

"Fighting the Republic in Deepfire is hopeless," he said. "At least for the moment. The people, even the tunnelborn, aren't with us, and without them we'll never have the strength to do more than annoy the Auxies. Even if we get the upper hand for a moment, as soon as the Order sends in a centarch, everything falls to pieces. Yora...taught me that."

Apphia nodded, silent, sharp gray eyes attentive.

"I went into the mountains to look for another way. Something that would give us an edge over the Legion, even the centarchs. I think I've found it. But weapons take skilled hands to wield them, and the support of a population that wants the Republic gone. Deepfire doesn't offer either anymore."

"But Khirkhaz does," Apphia said. "You knew we were fighting the Republic."

"And that you have the support of your people," Gyre said. "I still had Yora's smuggler contacts, so I sent a message and gathered up whatever I could."

"And then traveled for hundreds of kilometers with no guarantee of repayment?" The baron smiled like a knife. "Such charity."

"I'm not in it for the money, if that's what you mean," Gyre said. "I'm offering my services to the Commune, along with connections in the north. If you and I can play this right, we can build an army here that will force the Republic and the Order out of Khirkhaz forever."

"What do you care about Khirkhaz?"

Gyre hesitated for a moment. "It's not my home, that's true. But if we're ever going to be rid of the Order and the Republic, people are going to have to believe that they *can* be beaten. That has to start somewhere, and this seems like the best chance."

"Get rid of the Order!" Her smile widened. "Well, Gyre Silvereye, no one can fault you for lack of ambition."

Gyre forced a grin of his own. "Nothing wrong with ambition."

"Indeed." Her smile faded. "Unfortunately, matters here are more complicated than you know."

"I got a taste of that in Cliffedge," Gyre said. "But the banners all want the Republic gone, don't they?"

"Theoretically." Apphia sighed, leaning back on her elbows. "But that always seems far away, while feuding with one another over recruits and supplies is a more pressing problem. They'll happily take your cargo, but they'll fight one another to get hold of it. They like to *call* me leader of this rebellion, but the only people I can count on are Brennard's guards and a few lancers who owed fealty to my father."

"I get the feeling you have a suggestion."

"I do." She sat up again, picking up the *eviske* bottle, and poured another finger into each cup. "A demonstration, let's say, of what you can offer."

"What kind of demonstration?"

"There's an Auxiliary transport route not far from here, bringing supplies to the garrison on Three Ridge Point. We've hit it before, so it's well guarded. Part of my grand strategy, such as it is." She slid one of the cups from one hand to the other, amber liquid sloshing gently. "Spread them out, make them cover as much ground as possible. But after the last time, they started sending Legionaries with the convoys. That would usually be my signal to pull out and find another target. I don't have enough soldiers that I can afford to waste them against blaster rifles and unmetal armor."

"How many Legionaries are we talking about?"

"Two to four," she said. "Plus two dozen Auxies and some drivers."

"If I lead the attack," Gyre said, "and take out the Legionaries…"

"Then the banners will know that we really have something new." Apphia's smile returned. "They'll clamor to be a part of it, if only to get their share. If you were then to make it clear that you stand behind me, I might be able to assert some real authority."

"Which serves both our interests," Gyre said. "Very neat."

"I thought so." She pushed one of the cups toward him, then abruptly put her hand flat over the top. "*If* you can do what you claim. If you can't, then my people are going to get killed for nothing."

Gyre met her cool-eyed gaze. "I can handle four Legionaries."

"Interesting." She stared back at him for a long moment, then raised her hand, offering him the cup. "Well, then. Shall we drink to a fruitful partnership?"

Gyre picked up the cup and raised it in salute.

The supply route was another forest trail, this one switchbacking up a steep slope toward the crest of a ridge. A few kilometers farther on, the Auxiliaries maintained a garrison on the heights, part of a string of small forts intended to try to lock down the Communards' movements.

"It doesn't work, of course," Apphia said as they settled into the underbrush. "We know the forest and they don't. And they haven't got nearly enough men to block every path. But they can certainly make the hunters and loggers miserable."

"It doesn't sound like the local dux has much idea what he's doing."

Apphia snorted. "Baron Rashtun has the command, and he couldn't find his arse with both hands and detailed instructions. Tourmarch Gorga, the Legionary commander, has more sense. Thank the Chosen he outranks her."

The ambush party was two dozen strong, armed with swords and crossbows. Half lurked on the steep, heavily overgrown slope between two of the switchbacks. The other half, including Brennard and another lancer on warbirds, waited in the forest below, ready to charge up the path and take the Auxies in the rear.

It was a good plan, simple and direct, but against Legionaries it wouldn't be enough. Crossbows were worthless against their armor, and while it was possible to slip a blade in, their blaster rifles made it hard to get close enough to try. *Which means it's up to me.*

Sarah, lying on Gyre's other side, peered at the track, gauging the distance. They'd left Elariel with Kit and the rest of Apphia's soldiers.

"Can you make the throw?" Gyre said quietly.

"Easy," Sarah said. "You want stunners or smoke?"

"Stunners." Smoke would last longer, but it would keep the rest of the Communards from finding their targets. "Pass the word to everyone to keep their eyes shut until they go off."

Sarah nodded, and whispered to the next man in line.

"Stunners won't stop a Legionary for long," Apphia said.

"Just needs to be for long enough."

"Hmm." The baron gave him an inquisitive look, then shook her head. A low whistle echoed through the forest, and she abruptly went still. "Scout coming. Heads down."

Gyre froze. He felt absurdly exposed, with nothing in front of him but leaves and narrow branches, though he knew it would be difficult to make anything out from the road. The scouts, when they came into view, weren't particularly notable, just a pair of Auxies in leather vests and steel caps, carrying short spears and chatting to one another as they wearily climbed the ridge. By contrast, Gyre was again impressed with the discipline of Brennard's soldiers. None of them so much as twitched as the two Auxies trudged by only a few meters away, climbing up to the switchback.

Behind the scouts came the convoy proper. Five lizard-like thickheads plodded along the rutted path, tied together nose to tail and heavily laden with packs. Several drivers walked beside them carrying long crops, and six Auxies took the lead, with six more bringing up the rear. In between, on either side of the beasts, were four Legionaries.

Four. Gyre had been hoping it would only be two. Two was the most he'd ever fought at once, during their escape from the Spike with the Core Analytica. He was considerably better at handling the ghoul augmentations now, but...

There's four of them, he told himself, *and that's what you're going to have to deal with. Too late to back out now.*

"Wait until they're just below us," Apphia whispered.

Sweat tricked down Gyre's brow, tickling his nose, and he fought a terrific urge to scratch. The first group of Auxies went past, then the thickheads. Someone said something, and there was a chorus of laughter. One of the drivers swatted a thickhead briefly distracted by an interesting grub.

"Sarah," Gyre said. "Now." He squeezed his eyes shut.

There was a rustle in the brush, a moment's pause, and then a *whuff* like indrawn breath and light that turned the insides of his eyelids orange. Gyre was already gathering himself, giving the stunner a count of three to fade. He opened his eyes in time to see glowing sparks still cascading down on the soldiers below, who were shouting in alarm and clutching at their faces.

Go. In spite of flickering afterimages, he pushed himself free of the underbrush and skidded down the slope. The thing in his skull went *click*, and the world slowed and filled with shadows. The rocks he'd kicked free bounced and stretched ahead of themselves in neat parabolas. Where the slope leveled out, directly ahead, the two closest Legionaries were going for their blaster rifles.

He reached the first before the soldier had recovered. Gyre drew his silver sword and used the momentum of his downhill rush to drive it up and under the Legionary's breastplate. The off-white unmetal scales there were thinner, but they were still proof against any merely human weapon. Gyre's ghoul-made sword punched through easily, slicing flesh and bone until the tip met the unmetal backplate. He pulled the weapon free as the Legionary started to collapse, moving toward the next opponent before the first had hit the ground.

The faceless, insectoid helmets of the Legionaries weren't immune to stunners, but they mitigated their effects, and the second soldier saw Gyre coming. She tossed her rifle aside and wrenched her sword out to meet his charge. Gyre, drifting through the slow, shadowy world, watched her parry his first stroke, unmetal shivering and screeching against the silver sword, then pull back for a riposte. It was fast, for a human, but he saw the shadow of the blade extending through his chest and stepped neatly aside. As she thrust, he grabbed her wrist and yanked her forward, the tip of his sword punching into her throat. He whipped the blade free, spraying blood in the dirt.

Crossbow bolts were hissing down, the sound stretched to something closer to the roar of surf in the shadow world. The Communards were concentrating on the Auxies at either end of the column, and several had already fallen. A high whistle from Apphia brought the ambushers below out of hiding, caped men sprinting up the slope with swords in hand, followed by Brennard and his companion on warbirds.

Gyre's attention was on the two remaining Legionaries, on the other side of the line of thickheads. They were both backing away, raising their blaster rifles. Thickheads, thankfully, tended to hunker down in a panic rather than run wild, so the beasts were frozen in place. Gyre grabbed the nearest and pulled himself over. One of the Legionaries fired, aiming up the slope, the bolt tracing a leisurely course through the air to explode with a roar against a tree.

The other soldier aimed at Gyre, shadow-bolts zipping out as his finger tightened on the trigger. The shot would be on the mark; rather than dodge, Gyre just gritted his teeth and waited. *I hope Apphia's paying attention.*

The rifle *cracked* and the bolt of concentrated *deiat* power lanced out. Instead of exploding when it reached Gyre, it *splashed*, like water against stone, the energy crackling and fading in a shower of sparks. This was another one of Naumoriel's augmentations, a shield that blocked most *deiat* projections. It wouldn't stop a haken, and the old ghoul had warned him that concentrated power could overwhelm it. But shock was visible in the Legionary's stance, and before he could get off another shot Gyre was on top of him, silver sword finding the thin armor under his arm to punch into his heart.

The last Legionary turned to run. *Sensible, under the circumstances.* Unfortunately, this brought her directly into the path of Brennard's charging warbird. She managed to avoid the point of his long lance, but the bird itself lashed out as she passed, beak slamming into the side of her helmet and knocking her into the underbrush. Then Brennard was past, leveling his lance to skewer a hapless Auxie, and Gyre caught up. He put his boot on the Legionary's chest as she tried to rise and drove the silver sword into her throat.

Four, he thought, as her struggles ceased. The energy bottle at his hip was getting warm. Plenty of power remained, but he could see that he wasn't going to need it. All the Auxies were down, most in the first volley, while those that escaped had been finished off by Communards charging from both directions. He concentrated, breathing out, and felt the *click* in his skull.

Apphia vaulted the still-cowering thickheads, advancing on Gyre with a determined expression. Gyre sheathed his silver sword and raised his hands as she drew to a halt, looking him carefully up and down.

"You're not even fucking *singed*," she snapped. "How?"

"I told you I could handle them."

"You didn't tell me you could take a blaster bolt to the face!" She stared at the scabbard on his hip. "And that weapon can cut through unmetal?"

"If you hit it in the right spot," Gyre said. He tapped the chestplate of the dead woman at his feet. "The thick armor will still turn it."

"I thought—" The baron shook her head, then turned, looking for Brennard. "Any of ours hurt?"

"Falise has a nick from some flying splinters, but she'll be all right," the lancer said. "Otherwise, none at all, my lady."

"Chosen above." Apphia looked back to Gyre. "And this is what you've brought us?"

He nodded.

"Then," she said, "we have a great deal to discuss."

First, though, the Communards stripped the caravan clean.

It was an efficient, purposeful operation, not mere looting of the dead, but it still made Gyre squirm. The thickheads, once they'd recovered from the stunner, were led away, their supplies now destined for a Commune camp instead of the Republic garrison. The Auxie corpses were relieved of spears, swords, and vests, then hauled into the forest.

The Legionaries, of course, were the greatest treasure trove of all. Communards carefully unstrapped their armor, piece by piece, cutting straps when they wouldn't come loose. Something about the process turned Gyre's stomach, especially when they pulled the helmets free. Abruptly, the faceless *things* he'd been fighting were transformed into *people*, an older man with a salt-and-pepper beard, a girl Gyre's age with a neat red-brown ponytail and vacant sky-blue eyes.

They work for the Order. He wanted to turn away and forced himself not to. He'd always made himself look at the aftermath back in Deepfire, too. *They chose to work for the system. They can't escape the consequences.* It had been his mantra, back then, but somehow now the certainty wouldn't come. When the corpses were down to their gray undershirts, the Communards carried them off to pile with the others.

"We'll send people out later to bury them," Apphia said.

"I would have thought you'd leave them for the next group," Gyre said. "A warning."

She gave him a sidelong look, eyes narrowed, then sighed. "Some of the men in the banners would like that, I imagine. But it's counterproductive. Leaving a bunch of bodies out would make the rest *angry*, and they can take that out on the civilians. What we want is for them to just . . . disappear. That makes the rest *scared*, and that we can use."

"Ah." He forced a smile. "Here I was thinking you weren't completely ruthless."

"I am not often accused of insufficient ruthlessness." Apphia clapped him on the shoulder. "Come on. Back to camp. There's a bottle of *eviske* waiting for us, I'd say."

The column of fighters threaded its way through the woods. Sarah caught up to Gyre, flecked with grime but otherwise unhurt, and burst into a passionate monologue about the properties of his silver sword and how it compared to unmetal. Gyre, feeling suddenly exhausted, could only manage to nod at appropriate intervals and promise to let her run tests later on.

The farther they got from the ambush site, the more the rest of the soldiers adopted Sarah's excited attitude. They slapped one another on the back, roared with laughter, and recounted the best parts of the brief battle over and over. Gyre noticed a lot of looks in his direction, but no one seemed eager to include him in the camaraderie. *Thank the Chosen.* His mood was darkening by the moment.

The camp had the same air of celebration. Shouts and cheers greeted the returning ambushers, and a number of bottles appeared as if from nowhere. Brennard interrupted the festivities only briefly, ordering a few of those who hadn't fought to take up sentry duty, to a chorus of groans. Once they'd gone, though, he picked up a bottle himself and took a generous swig while the rest cheered him on.

"He's good, isn't he?" Apphia said. "Brennard."

"They seem to like him," Gyre said.

He was leaning against one of the wagons, some distance from the fire. The baron looked over her shoulder for a while, then shook her head.

"It's more than *liking* him," she said. "He has the knack for maintaining the right distance, not quite one of them but not fully apart from them either. Authority and empathy." She sighed. "He's half the reason this lot didn't go to pieces years ago."

"You lead them," Gyre said.

"I tell them what to do," Apphia said. "*He* leads them. I'm ... too distant, whatever I do. If I went over there it'd be all 'yes, my lady,' and 'no, my lady,' and nobody would have any fun."

Gyre wasn't sure what to say to that, so he said nothing. After a few moments of uncomfortable silence, Apphia shifted and pulled a slim flask from her belt. "Drink?"

Gyre nodded. He was ready for the bite of *eviske* this time, and kept his swallow shallow. It still burned going down his throat. He passed it back, and Apphia took a pull herself.

"You didn't look happy with what we did today," she said.

"I ..." Gyre hesitated, choosing his words carefully. "I'm happy to strike at the Republic and the Order."

"But?"

"But I'm reminded, sometimes, that the Republic and the Order are made up of people who don't always have a choice." He shifted uncomfortably. "Legionary positions are hereditary, often as not. Some girl was raised to go off and do her duty, defend the Republic, protect the innocent, all that bird shit, just like her parents did. And then she put on the helmet and came out here and now she's dead."

And is that going to be Maya, someday? He tried to force the thought down. *Is she going to be the next corpse at my feet?*

"The Republic taught her all that. The Republic sent her here." Apphia's voice was calm. "The Republic is to blame."

"I know," Gyre said. "It doesn't mean I'm not sorry about it."

She grunted and passed the flask back over. The second swallow burned less than the first, and its warmth felt good in his stomach.

"I know why I hate them," Gyre said, touching his scar. "What about you?"

"It's not any great secret." Apphia settled against the wagon. "My father, the old Baron Kotzed, was always at odds with the rest of the Lightning Barons. He used to say the Republic had seduced them, or just plain bought them like a bunch of whores. Some of the barons barely visit their spires anymore. They just collect the rents and spend their time in Skyreach with the rest of the upper crust. When the Senate asked for more control, my father was the only one who would push back.

"The Rashtuns have been our rivals for generations, and Baron Rashtun saw his chance. He had my father accused of working with smugglers bringing *dhak* into the Republic. The trial was a joke. Father came back and hunkered down in the Spire, told Rashtun and the Senate they'd have to come dig him out. I don't think he expected them to call his bluff, but they did. Rashtun led an army to Spire Kotzed, with the Republic behind him and the other barons cheering him on. My father sent me and Nina away, with Brennard and some of the guards. He stayed to fight, and they killed him. My mother too."

"This is the same Baron Rashtun serving as dux now?"

"The same." Apphia took another swig of *eviske*.

"How old were you?"

"Fourteen. Nina was seven." She passed the flask back. "I'm going to hang the plaguing bastard from a tree, or die trying."

"It's important to have goals," Gyre said, and took another drink.

Apphia chuckled and pushed herself away from the wagon. The shiny trace of her lightning scar gleamed in the firelight.

"I think I like you, Gyre Silvereye. I much prefer a man who'll think twice before killing than one who gets a thrill from it."

"So what now?" Gyre straightened up, or tried to. He found his head spinning a little. Apphia's smile widened.

"I'll send messengers to the banners," she said. "After news of our raid tonight has had time to spread, they'll come, if only out of curiosity, and you can make your pitch. If what you've brought us is as good as you say, they may get on board."

"And then?"

"And then," Apphia said, "we might have a chance at taking Spire Kotzed back."

Chapter 12

They met at the boat dock, not long after sunrise. Maya had dug up some of her traveling clothes, simple canvas trousers and a loose shirt. She was surprised at how odd it felt putting them back on. On the road with Jaedia, her Order uniform had stayed at the bottom of her pack for months at a time, but in her time at the Forge she'd grown used to its tighter tailoring.

Perhaps more of a shock was seeing Beq in a long dress. It was pale green, accenting her hair and her dark skin, and showed off her figure to considerably better effect than her uniform did. Maya raised an appreciative eyebrow as the arcanist walked down the pier, a pack slung over one shoulder.

"Good morning," Maya said.

"Morning," Beq said. She looked down at herself, touching the dials on her spectacles. "I hope this is all right. I haven't had much occasion to wear it."

"It's perfect," Maya said, though in truth she had no idea what would help them blend in on the streets of Skyreach.

Varo turned up last, wearing a dark leather vest and trailed by a couple of burly Forge servants in their gray uniforms. They went to the end of the pier without a word and started readying one of several small boats waiting there, while Varo wandered over to his two companions.

"I feel like I'm sneaking out of the dormitory after dark," he said. "Not that I have any experience with such things. But a friend of mine once did it, back when we were first in training. Got all the way to Skyreach, I'm told, but on the way back he tripped and went over the side of the boat."

"Let me guess," Beq said. "He couldn't swim?"

"He could swim," Varo said, "but it's a big lake. Once the boat left him behind..." He shrugged.

"Charming," Maya muttered. "But we're not sneaking anywhere."

"Yet," Varo said.

Maya threw a warning look at the two servants. "I have a perfect right to go to Skyreach, in whatever clothes I please, and to bring my team with me."

One of the servants coughed, and bowed deep to Maya, while the other held the boat. It was wide enough for two people to sit side by side, with three rows of benches. Oars were strapped to the sides, but at the back was a chunky arcana, dipping angled crystal rods into the water.

"Do you require assistance?" the servant said.

"We'll be all right," Varo said. He gestured to Maya. "Climb aboard."

She did, gingerly. Boats had not featured heavily in her life to date, and the way it swayed alarmingly when she shifted her weight caught her briefly off guard. She quickly sat on the last set of benches, near the arcana, and Beq took the place beside her. Varo moved easily to the front, arcana compass in one hand.

"We probably won't need this," he said, "but the clouds may stick around. Here we go." He pushed them back from the pier with one foot, waving the two servants away.

It was, indeed, a cloudy day, with the sun a mere gray presence overhead and a heavy layer of fog clinging to the lake. The mountain that housed the Forge was mostly invisible behind them, and in the other direction there was only water.

"Get us going," Varo said, "but take it slow, if you please. It *is* an awfully big lake."

Maya nodded and touched her haken, pulling a thread of *deiat* to feed into the arcana propulsor. It came to life with a *whirr*, pushing the boat gently across the water, a bubbling froth forming around its crystals. It took her a moment to get the hang of controlling their direction, but before long they were lined up with Varo's compass, heading due east.

The lake was several hundred kilometers long, but considerably narrower, and fortunately the Forge and Skyreach were positioned nearly opposite one another. Still, the trip took more than an hour, even with the propulsor driving the little boat along far faster than any oarsman could have managed. The sun rose higher, sending fingers of light through the shredding clouds, and the fog retreated under its glare. By the time Varo announced they were halfway there, it was clear enough that Maya could see the towers of Skyreach ahead.

She'd caught glimpses of them from the balconies of the Forge. They'd had the look of distant mountains, so far off that their size didn't register. Now, though, as she watched them grow taller and taller, the city took her breath away. Spires rose in uneven ranks, each different from the next, their surfaces vast sheets of angled, curving glass that threw shimmering planes of light onto the lake. Even the smallest was higher than the tallest stone tower ever built by humans. The biggest—the Senate building, which housed not only the actual Senate chamber but most of the apparatus of government—was supposed to be close to three kilometers high, topped by a vast spike twisted like a ram's horn. Tall spikes were a feature of many of Skyreach's buildings, and the reason became obvious as they came closer. Tiny black specks moved through the air, speeding from the crown of one tower to the next.

"Flitters!" Beq leaned against the rail so abruptly the boat rocked, lenses shifting and whirring in her spectacles. "There's so many of them!"

"The things are a plaguing menace," Varo muttered.

"Why?" Beq said. "It's not like they run people over."

"Rich idiots drop things over the side," Varo said. "Not their fault if it cracks someone's skull five hundred meters down, right?"

Varo had grown up in Skyreach, Maya recalled, but in what he'd termed the "bad part." Looking at the shining city, it was hard to imagine what part that might be.

"When I was a kid, Jaedia told me about Skyreach, and I said I wanted us to get a flitter to fly around the Republic," she said. "Then we wouldn't have to put up with smelly loadbirds."

"Flitters aren't true skyships," Beq said. "They're linked to a repulsion grid buried under the streets, so they don't work outside the city."

That's what Jaedia had said, too. And the little flyers were prodigiously expensive to operate, draining a sunsplinter in less than an hour. Only in Skyreach could anyone afford such an extravagance.

The boat rocked underneath them. Maya looked up and realized they were cutting across the wake of a larger vessel, a high-sided fishing ship heavy with sails.

"Careful," Varo said. "It's getting a little crowded."

He pointed her toward the river docks, a seemingly endless stretch of piers and jetties hosting vessels of every description, from leaky barges to sleek pleasure yachts. Fishing boats and other humble vessels moved by sails or oars, while the transports of the rich used *deiat*-powered propulsors. Colored buoys marked out lanes, a bit of order amid the chaos. Fortunately, there was a pier reserved for Order use, guarded by a pair of Legionaries. Maya aimed for it and brought the little boat up alongside, and the armored soldier tossed Varo a line. Spotting Maya's haken, he bowed.

"Greetings, Centarch. Do you require assistance?"

Maya shook her head, then paused. "Varo? How are we getting to this meeting?"

"We'll take an auto," the scout said, tying off the line. "Don't worry about it."

Beq gave an excited squeak.

An auto was a grounded version of a flitter. It was oval-shaped, narrowing at the front and rounded on the bottom, a bit like a mussel shell made of unmetal. The top was open, and two pairs of cushioned seats faced one another in the back while a driver sat in front. The whole thing hovered half a meter off the ground, driven by sunsplinters and the same repulsion grid that powered the flitters.

Behind the docks was a long, busy street, full of vehicles of every description. This section was mostly fishing craft, so there were carts being loaded with the catch, and others delivering stocks of food and bait to waiting vessels, pulled by loadbirds, thickheads, or occasionally small, curly-haired ponies. Farther out from the dock, traffic ground slowly forward, and the transport carts were joined by carriages and autos. The latter mostly bore fluttering green flags at their sterns, which Varo explained meant they were for hire. He secured one by stepping fearlessly in front of an offended loadbird and flagging down the driver, who obligingly stopped his strange craft and waited for them to climb aboard.

"Blueglass Restaurant," Varo said. "Over on Seventeenth."

The driver nodded amiably and named a fare that made Maya's eyes pop. Fortunately, the travel funds they'd been given were ample. She counted out the bills. Varo slid another dekathaler from the stack and added it to the total, which the driver acknowledged with a cheerful smile.

"If you don't throw in a little extra," Varo explained quietly, "he might get 'lost' and demand more anyway. Auto drivers are all crooked."

"Really?" Beq said. "He looks nice enough."

"Trust me," Varo said darkly.

"I'm glad you came along," Maya said. "I would have been lost already."

Varo gave a grunt, looking uncharacteristically sour. He settled back in his seat as the auto turned off the dock street and accelerated, traffic opening out. The buildings they were passing were of normal size, Maya was somewhat disappointed to see. The spires of the city core rose off to her left, but this area reminded her a bit of Deepfire, block after neatly laid-out block of well-trimmed stone and brick buildings with slate roofs and glassed windows.

If Beq was disappointed too, it didn't show. She lurched from one side of the auto to the other, staring at everything they passed. Every squeak she made seemed to irritate Varo, but Maya found her energy infectious.

"It almost feels like we're back in Elder times," Beq said as they rounded a corner. A long street led all the way to the Senate building, spires rising beside it like a glassed-in canyon. "Can you imagine?"

"Not sure there would have been quite as much bird shit on the road in Elder times," Varo said. "Can't see the Chosen putting up with it."

"Is this close to where you grew up?" Maya said.

He blinked, then laughed. "This? This is for *respectable* people." He gestured to their right. "Head that way, and things get...less respectable. The slums go on for kilometers. Not that I could find the street where I lived, even if I wanted to. Every couple of years there's a fire and half of it gets rebuilt."

"Ah," Maya said. It didn't feel like enough.

"Sorry." The scout sighed and shook his head. "I haven't been back here since I joined the Order. It just brings up a lot of...bad memories. There's no place quite like Skyreach, for better or for worse."

Maya understood what he meant. If you squinted, you almost *could* believe you were back before the Plague, when the Chosen had ruled an empire stretching across the continent and no one had ever heard of plaguespawn. Back then, skyships and skyfortresses had drifted through the air like solid clouds, and Gates had linked the far-flung cities and outposts together.

And then it all came crashing down. There were stories about the collapse in the *Inheritance*. The ghouls had broken some Chosen cities with strange and horrible creations, and the Chosen's own weapons had wreaked terrible destruction in the fighting, but most of the damage had been done when the Chosen themselves began to die out from the Plague. So many of their structures required a steady supply of *deiat* to maintain themselves. A small matter normally, since every Chosen was more powerful than any centarch, but as the Plague worsened, their human servants had only been able to look on in horror as the great cities crumbled. Only Skyreach, maintained by the centarchs of the newly born Order, had survived.

The auto turned again, taking them down a narrower street, and stopped in front of a building whose windows were tinted a deep blue. A heavy wooden door stood open, embellished with delicate wrought-iron curlicues, and a man inside watched them suspiciously as they climbed out of the auto. He wore a sharp suit with black tails, and the patrons Maya could see behind him also looked on the formal side.

"Can I help you?" he said doubtfully, then stopped as his eyes found Maya's haken. His face rearranged itself into smooth obsequiousness. Being a centarch, apparently, trumped not being dressed for the occasion.

"We're here to see Centarch Tanax," Maya said with a certain satisfaction. "He should be waiting for us."

"Of course," the man said. "Follow me."

Maya did her best not to gawk as he led them inside. She hadn't really been *expecting* the common room of a country inn, but this place looked more like the dux's palace in Deepfire than any restaurant she'd ever dined at. Small, intimate tables were tucked into corners amid hanging curtains, and well-dressed people chatted and laughed behind filmy screens of gauze. Waiters in black moved back and forth in efficient, dignified silence.

Their host led them up a flight of carpeted stairs to a long hall lined with private dining rooms. Portraits hung on the walls, alternating with sunstones in brass fittings. The man stopped in front of a closed door and knocked, gently, then opened it and bowed.

"Thank you," Tanax said. He was sitting on the other side of a polished table, wearing his dress uniform and looking well turned out. "See that we're not disturbed until we send for something."

"Of course, Centarch." The host bowed and ghosted away.

"If I'd known we were dining in style," Varo said, "I would have dressed up a little."

"The Blueglass specializes in discretion," Tanax said. "Close the door. I hope they didn't give you any trouble downstairs."

"A few nasty looks," Maya said, shutting the door behind her.

"I apologize." He frowned. "Unfortunately, in my current position, it can be difficult for me to get away from scrutiny."

"What exactly is your current position?" Maya said, taking the chair opposite him. Varo followed, while Beq was briefly distracted by a massive portrait.

"I've been assigned to assist the Council in their meetings with the Senate," Tanax said. "I stand guard over their deliberations, drive flitters on occasion, that sort of thing."

"Sounds dull," Varo said.

"Unbelievably." Tanax sighed. "But I suppose it does put me in a position to help you."

"This is Tyrio Goldtouch," Beq said, pointing at the portrait. "He was one of the founders of the Moorcat Combine, and—" She abruptly noticed everyone looking at her, and turned her eyes down, nervously adjusting her spectacles. "It's... it's a very old painting. Sorry. It's my first time in Skyreach."

"Mine, too," Maya said. "I'm starting to understand why the people who live here talk like the rest of the Republic doesn't matter. It feels like another world."

"That's half the problem," Varo muttered.

"The Senate would be happy to ignore anything that happens outside its tower," Tanax said. "When I left, the Council was trying to persuade them to do something about the situation in Khirkhaz. The rebels have grown bold, but the Senate would rather pinch centithalers than act. They ask why the centarchs can't handle it, and Baselanthus has to explain that there aren't enough centarchs to be everywhere at once." He stopped himself with an effort. "That's neither here nor there, of course. But this assignment has been... revealing."

"Right now it's Prodominus I'm worried about, not the Senate," Maya agreed. "Have you found anything on this bolt-hole of his?"

"Quite a bit, as it turns out." Tanax took a folder full of loose pages from his pack. "One thing about Skyreach is that everyone keeps records of everything. I copied these from the land tax office." He riffled through some slightly blurry sketches and arranged them on the table. Beq, twisting the dial on her spectacles, came to sit beside Maya. "This is the building we're looking for."

"Two stories," Varo said. "Nice big grounds. This must be in the outer city."

Tanax nodded. "Forty-Seventh Street, on the east side."

"If I'm reading this right, someone is serious about people not getting in." Beq touched one of the drawings. "Screamer wire and watch charms on the windows and stairs."

"And a half dozen guards on the first floor," Tanax said. "I walked past last night. Hired muscle, not Order people."

"The storeroom is upstairs," Beq said. "Nothing here about what's actually inside it, but it's a good bet it'll be some sort of arcana protection."

"Which is why we brought you along," Maya said, trying to sound encouraging. "If it's arcana, you can crack it."

Beq colored, looking down at the table. After an awkward moment of silence, Varo coughed.

"That still leaves us the problem of getting into the storeroom in the first place," he said. "We can't just fight our way in—the guards would call for backup from the Auxies."

"What about the roof?" Maya said.

"It's reinforced iron under the slate," Varo said, examining the plans. "It'd be hard to get in without making a racket—"

"For anyone who wasn't a centarch," Beq said, looking at Maya's haken. "That's our edge here. No one expects a centarch to be doing something like this."

"That's because most centarchs would know better," Tanax said under his breath. "But you're right. Maya could make a hole."

"If we can get her up there in the first place," Varo said. "The watch charms will cover the walls."

Another moment of silence.

"Tanax," Beq said slowly. "What happens to the flitters at night?"

"I would have thought there'd at least be a guard," Varo said.

"No point," Tanax said. "They remove the power sources and keep them in vaults. Without that, the flitter is just some bits of arcana in an unmetal shell."

"Unless you're a centarch with a good arcanist," Beq said.

Maya smiled.

It was some hours later. After a meal at the Bluegrass—tasty, Maya had to admit, though the portions felt scanty—Tanax had reported back to his post in the Senate building. He'd reappeared close to sunset, rendezvousing with the rest of them outside this small, grassy park, tucked in behind a row of stately manor houses running along the riverbank. This, it turned out, was one of several places where the city's flitters parked at night, when flying was prohibited.

"Not that that actually stops people," Varo said. "Rich idiots use *dhak* to see in the dark and go joyriding."

"At least that means nobody will go running for the Legion if they do spot us," Maya said.

A small copse of trees provided a covered spot to keep watch on the place. They'd taken up position there and waited while one flitter after another had landed, the drivers carefully detaching the blocky power arcana from the back of the craft before leaving. Now the field was nearly full and the sun was vanishing, though fires and sunstones all over the city provided a dirty yellow glow.

"You're sure you're ready for this?" Maya said to Beq.

"No." Beq twisted the dials on her spectacles, flipping new lenses into place. "But I'm going to do it anyway."

Maya caught her hand and squeezed, and Beq gave a shaky grin.

"I think we're clear," Varo said. "That was the last of them."

They gave it another few minutes for safety. Then the scout crept slowly out of the trees and toward the rows of flitters. Grounded, the vehicles looked similar to the auto, half-rounded shells with seats and a driver's perch at the front. Long, spiky protrusions extended from the bottom of the shell, providing pointed legs for the thing to sit on when inactive. Varo reached the nearest and pulled himself over the side, then waved the rest of them forward.

"Let's go," Tanax said. He'd changed out of his dress uniform into civilian garb, though he still looked considerably more formal than Maya in her traveling clothes.

"You're sure you want to come?" she said. "You've done plenty already, and if we get caught—"

"I told you that you could trust me and that I would help," Tanax said. "I meant it."

Maya nodded and followed him across the dry grass, with Beq behind her. Tanax climbed into the flitter with Varo, while Maya and the arcanist examined the rear, where the power source had been removed. Beq—whose spectacles let her see in the dark—peered into the gap left behind and frowned.

"This may be harder than we thought," she said.

"How so?"

"There's no separate steering mechanism." She fished a small pick tipped with crystal from the pocket of her dress. "That must be part of the power system—these are just control circuits. I can tweak it so you can provide power, but…"

"But?" Maya said.

Beq raised her head. "You'll have to steer, er, manually. By feeding power directly to the repulsors." At Maya's expression, she hastily added, "It doesn't look that complicated! There's only a couple of control circuits."

"I can give it a shot," Maya said.

"You'll be fine." Beq clambered aboard. "I'll tell you which way to go."

"I had a friend who could see in the dark," Varo said from farther forward. "He kept telling us there were monsters prowling around our cabin. The rest of us just laughed at him, but one morning we came outside, and all that was left was his boots."

"Brilliant," Maya said, scrambling over the side herself. "Exactly the right time for that."

"Just trying to give the benefit of my years of experience."

"Maya," Beq said, "there should be three repulsors, one on each side and one in the back. Left and right keep us airborne and stable, and the back one pushes us forward. Try to activate the side ones, as evenly as you can."

"Okay. Here goes nothing."

Maya closed her eyes and reached for her haken. Feeding power to multiple arcana was no great trick—she did that every time she used her panoply belt. But doing it *simultaneously* wasn't something she'd practiced. *No one ever told me I'd need to.* She tried readying one thread of *deiat* and holding it while reaching for another, but that just let both dissolve, slipping through her mental grip. Frustrated, Maya switched to another approach, unspooling the thinnest possible thread and feeding it into the repulsor. *It's easier to adjust the flow once I'm connected, so…*

The flitter rocked like they were back in the boat and a storm was kicking up. Beq gave a startled squeak, and Tanax tumbled sideways against a cushion. Hurriedly, Maya connected another thread to the opposite repulsor, which sent the little craft lurching back the other way. Varo grunted, and she heard Tanax swearing. Beq, scrambling to the front, looked around wildly and shouted, "Up! Maya, take us up!"

The world spun sickeningly. With both repulsors active, the flitter raised itself a few inches from the grass, and now drifted in circles on the breeze as it rocked back and forth. Before Maya could react, the neighboring flitter loomed out of the darkness, and the two unmetal hulls slammed together with a screech, sending everyone stumbling. Maya forced herself to close her eyes and concentrate, feeding in more power and keeping the levels as steady as possible. The bottom dropped out of her stomach.

"Better!" Beq said with a note of terror in her voice. "That's ... better. Now maybe a *touch* of drive, and we can stop spinning?"

Someone was noisily sick. Even with her eyes closed, Maya could feel them whirling round like a demented top. She sent another stream of power to the third repulsor, as gently as she could, and felt the kick of acceleration. The spin turned into an expanding spiral.

"You should be able to steer by letting one side drop a little," Beq said. Her tone was still that of someone inching along a ledge above a bottomless abyss. "Just ... not enough to flip us over."

Easy for you to say. Maya gritted her teeth and gently, *gently* eased off on the left repulsor. That side of the flitter dipped alarmingly, but she flattened it out and felt their turn easing.

"Yes. Yes!" Beq said. She laughed giddily. "You're doing it!"

"You ..." Tanax gasped for breath. "You are *really* bad at this."

"I'm sorry," Maya grated. "Would *you* like to try?"

"He's just bitter because he couldn't hang on to his expensive lunch," Varo said.

"How high up are we?" Maya said.

"Not too far above the rooftops," Beq said. "Keep it there. Let me just get oriented—okay, come to the right."

"*Gently,*" Tanax moaned.

Maya let one side of the flitter dip, bringing it around in a wide turn. She risked opening her eyes and saw the lights of the city spinning around them in a stately dance, the steady firefly glow of sunstones and the flickering of torches. The great spires were alive with brilliance, blue, red, and green patterns of illumination that shifted and changed from moment to moment.

"That's enough," Beq said. "Straighten out. Maya, *Maya*!"

"Sorry!" Maya squeaked, tearing her eyes away from the colossal towers and returning her attention to the task at hand. A few moments later, they were on the right course, gliding across the city a few meters above the chimneys.

"I'm beginning to see why nobody worries about a centarch stealing a flitter," Tanax said, leaning against the rail and breathing hard. "You'd have to be crazy to try it."

"Good thing we didn't know that in advance, eh?" Varo said.

"Would Maya have really let that stop her?" Tanax said.

Maya grinned, her crimson hair streaming in the wind of their passage. "Probably not."

Landing was the tricky part, of course.

Or at least *a* tricky part. Locating the building they were looking for was tricky enough, in a long stretch of warehouses and commercial buildings that all looked more or less the same, with no street signs to guide them. In the end, Maya hovered the flitter silently over likely candidates, while Tanax felt for the *deiat* powering Prodominus' defenses. After two buildings that were guarded only by mundane locks and sentries, the third made Tanax's eyes go wide.

"This is it," he said. "Unless somebody else has a dozen sunsplinters powering arcana defenses."

"Seems unlikely," Varo said. "Guards are a lot cheaper."

"Okay." Beq peered over the edge of the flitter. "The roof is pretty flat, and we're right above it. Maya, can you bring us down quietly?"

That was easier said than done. The flitter was only really stable when it was moving forward—if there was a way to hover without starting to spin, Maya hadn't figured it out. She managed to halt the movement whenever it started by dipping the appropriate repulsor, but the constant back-and-forth was doing bad things to her gut. Tanax wasn't the only one in danger of losing their last meal. Beq called out the distance, occasionally swallowing hard.

"Four meters left…three…two and half…" She gulped as Maya wiggled the flitter to kill another spin. "One and a half. One meter. Half a meter. Slowly…cut it!"

Maya pulled all her threads, and the flitter dropped a couple of centimeters onto its spiny underside. Slate clattered beneath it, and then they were still.

"We did it!" Beq said, then slapped her hands over her mouth as Tanax violently shook his head.

"Plenty of guards down there, remember?" he hissed.

"Sorry!" Beq squeaked.

"It's okay." Maya worked her way forward, stomach still churning, and threw an arm around Beq's shoulders. "You did great."

"So did you!" Beq's throat worked. "It was only a little bit…spinny."

"I've had worse rides," Varo said, then cocked his head. "Not *much* worse, though."

"Let's get on with it," Tanax said. "If we're not off this roof before dawn, someone is going to start asking questions."

Maya couldn't argue with that. This section of the city was very dark, only a few lights glowing around each property, and the sliver of moonlight was barely enough for her to see where she was putting her feet. She climbed over the edge of the flitter and found herself on a slate-tiled roof, barely sloped. The others followed, and Beq, the only one who could see what she was doing, consulted one of Tanax's sketches.

"Over here," she said, pointing, then turned in a slow circle and shook her head. "No, sorry. Over *there*."

"You're sure?" Tanax said.

"Pretty sure." Beq frowned at the page. "These drawings could be clearer."

"I'm going to grab your elbow," Maya said. "Walk me there."

Beq let her clamp on, and they shuffled across the roof together. A few meters from the edge, Beq stopped and stamped on the tile.

"Okay. If you cut through here, we should be right in the inner storeroom."

Maya nodded. "Everyone, stand back a little."

"Try not to let too much light show," Tanax hissed.

"Obviously," Maya shot back.

She drew her haken and pressed it against the tiles. It ignited at her mental command, white-hot blade slicing effortlessly through the slate and the wood beneath. Sparks spat up at her for a moment, then faded. Slowly, Maya pulled the weapon around in a broad circle, wincing every time a tile *cracked* audibly. Halfway through, the section she was cutting started to sag.

"Get hold of it," she told Varo, reaching out with *deiat* to press down the residual heat.

The slate tiles had fused together along where the haken had cut them to form a nearly solid mass. Varo grabbed it, and Beq shuffled in beside him as Maya finished the cut. When she was done, she set her haken aside and joined them, and together they lifted a plug of fused stone and sliced boards up onto the roof. A few pieces fell away, clattering.

"That worked better than I thought it would," Tanax muttered.

Maya had thought the same thing, but she wasn't about to admit it now. "You stay with the flitter and keep watch. I'm going in."

She threaded *deiat* into her panoply, in case the drop was more than she anticipated, and grabbed hold of the edge of the hole to lower herself into the dark beyond. When her arms were fully extended, she took a deep breath and let go. Fortunately, the sketches had been accurate, and it was only three meters to the floor. Maya absorbed the fall with a crouch, then touched her haken and conjured a small light.

The room was smaller than she'd expected, only a few meters square, its walls lined with empty shelves. Squatting against one wall was the vault they'd come for, an unmetal cube about a meter and a half to a side, with a crystal-and-wire panel on the front. A door leading to the stairs was closed, and Maya listened for a moment before calling up to the others.

"I think we're clear," she said. "Come on, Beq, I've got you."

Beq slipped over the rim, dress billowing slightly, and Maya caught her smoothly under the arms. The arcanist grinned and touched her spectacles. Lenses whirred. Varo hopped down beside her.

"Not much around," he said. "No sign of the guards?"

"Not yet." Maya brought her ball of light to hover beside the vault. "What we're looking for has to be in here."

"It's an arcana lock, obviously." Beq was already kneeling in front of the panel, examining it through a stack of lenses. "You have to feed it power to open, so only a centarch could get in. But there's more. Prodominus isn't taking any chances." She tapped one of the crystals with a jewel-headed pick. "There's a command sequence you have to send it, or it sounds the alarm."

"Any chance you can get around it?" Maya said.

"Possibly." Beq prodded the thing a little further, then swore under her breath. "I can't get a good look at it without power."

"That's easy enough." Maya reached for her haken, and Beq's hand shot out and grabbed her wrist.

"Once you power it, if you don't send the code within a minute, the alarm starts," Beq said.

"Ah." Maya lowered her hand. "So you'd have to crack it in that time."

"Yeah." Beq looked at the floor. "I don't think I can. Not that fast."

"Counterpoint," Varo said. "Maya just carves the plaguing thing open."

"That will *definitely* sound the alarm," Beq said.

"Right." He shook his head. "Sorry."

Maya put her hand on Beq's shoulder and pulled her close. "You can do this."

"You don't know that." Beq pressed her forehead into Maya's arm. "You don't know arcana."

"I know *you*," Maya said quietly. "Or I like to think I do. And I can tell when you actually think something's impossible, and when you're just not giving yourself enough credit."

"I just..." Beq looked up and swallowed. "If we get caught, I have no idea what they'll do to us."

"Nothing good," Maya admitted. "But if we give up, we'll never know what Prodominus is up to, and whether he was working with Nicomidi, or...*any* of this." *And Jaedia will waste away in that hospital bed until she dies.*

"Right." Beq took a steadying breath. "Right. Okay. I'll try."

"I'll be right with you." Maya kissed her forehead. "Just tell me what to do."

"Give me a minute," Beq said. She pulled out a leather wallet and unfolded it to reveal all manner of small, spiky tools. "When I tell you, push some power into that thing. I'll take care of the rest."

"Got it."

For a short interval, Beq stared at the lock, frowning and adjusting her lenses. Then she looked up, one eye weirdly magnified, and gave a quick nod.

"Do it."

Maya touched her haken, pulling a thread of *deiat* through it and feeding it into the lock. She felt it activate, the mechanism drawing in only a trickle of power. An interrogative quiver came back along the link, like a Gate asking for coordinates. It wanted the code, and she didn't have it.

Beq was already moving, tapping one of her picks gently against the crystals of the lock, then scraping a thin-edged blade across one of the circuits. She moved quickly and precisely, pulling odd-looking tools from the wallet one after another, pausing only to click a new lens into place.

"Someone's coming," Varo hissed. "I hear footsteps on the stairs."

"Fucking plague it," Maya muttered. She shifted, and Beq hissed.

"Keep the power steady. Otherwise I can't..." She trailed off, a pick in each hand, tongue poking out of the corner of her mouth.

Half the minute had to have passed already. Maya heard the footsteps too, a dull clack of boots getting closer. *If the alarm goes off now—*

She'd have the choice between the cold-blooded murder of a guard who was only doing his job or being found out breaking into a civilian property for no reason she could explain.

Come on, Beq. Maya didn't dare move. A bead of sweat rolled down her face, lingering on the tip of her nose. Beq set one pick aside, picked up a tiny hammer, and tapped one of the crystals.

Fifteen seconds. The footsteps paused outside the door. *Ten.* The drop fell from Maya's nose, tumbling until it splashed on the floor.

"Got it," Beq said, twisting the loosened crystal in its socket. Maya felt the arcana's insistent presence disappear, and something in the mechanism went *clank.* The whole front of the vault swung outward a few centimeters. Beq reached for it, and Maya grabbed her shoulder and squeezed, hissing in warning. Outside, the door rattled as the guard checked it, and then the footsteps began to recede.

Maya breathed out.

"Well," Varo said. "That was easy enough, wasn't it?"

When the sounds from outside had vanished, Maya swung the vault door open. Inside, sitting on a padded shelf, was the arcana Prodominus had so wanted to hide.

It looked exactly as his sketches had described it, half a sphere about the size of a man's head, with a circular depression in the flat top filled with tiny crystals and three curved, fang-like spikes converging above it. It was light in Maya's hands as she lifted it, and to her surprise something inside *shifted* as it tipped, as though it were half-full of water.

"It certainly looks like the right thing to me," Maya said. "Beq?"

"Definitely." Beq pointed with her small pick. "This part is an image projector. I've worked on those back at the Forge. The Archive said it's connected to . . . something, but it didn't know what."

"So what do we do with it?" Varo said. "Take it with us?"

"That would definitely tip Prodominus off," Maya said.

"We may not have a choice," Beq said. "If it needs another code, or there are any tricks to activating it, I might have to take it apart to figure it out."

"I can at least try turning it on," Maya said. "Maybe it's obvious."

"I suppose it can't hurt." Beq adjusted her spectacles. "It's supposed to be a communicator, not a weapon."

"Unless it does something loud," Varo said.

"Point," Maya said. "Be ready to get out of here in a hurry."

She touched her haken again, extending another slender thread of *deiat*. The arcana took it in eagerly, pulling more power down the link. Light flickered in the array of crystals.

"I think," Maya said, "it's working—"

She nearly dropped the thing when a *head* appeared, life-sized, above the device. It was the image of a handsome young man with bright red eyes, dark skin, and golden hair, slicked back smooth. His neck faded out where it touched the arcana, centered between the three spikes.

An image projector. She'd never seen one functioning—though the Archive probably worked on similar principles—but she ought to have known what to expect, and she felt a little embarrassed by her shock. The face was staring at her, expression turning from surprise into a smile. *If it's a communicator, can he see me? He must be able to.*

"Uh," she said. "Hello?"

"Hello," the young man said.

"Who are you?" Maya said. "What is this thing?"

"As you have probably guessed, this is a device for communication across long distances," the young man said. "We call it a resonator. And I am Nial-Est-Ashok, one of the Chosen."

One of the Chosen. Maya stiffened her fingers, or she really *would* have dropped the thing. "That's ... not possible."

"It must be a recorded image from before the war," Beq said, coming close to Maya's shoulder. "Or a construct like the Archive."

"I am neither," Ashok said. "And I know you, Maya Burningblade. It is fortunate indeed that you have discovered the resonator now."

"You *know* me?" Maya's mind felt like a sandcastle someone had started kicking to pieces, all whirling clouds of grit where there once was order. "How can you possibly—"

"There's no time," Ashok said. "You cannot risk being found here, and there is still much to be done. You must follow my instructions to the letter. Do you understand?"

"No!" Maya said. "I mean, no, I don't understand. How am I supposed to—"

"*Listen,*" the image interrupted again. "I can explain everything, but not now. You need to get away from here before anyone notices what you've done."

"If we leave," Beq said, "how are we supposed to speak with you again?"

"That is what I am trying to tell you." Ashok glanced at Beq. "You are an arcanist?"

"Y ... yeah." Beq shrank, abruptly self-conscious. "Are you really a—"

"I will instruct you on how to dismantle the resonator," Ashok said, talking over her. "At the core you will find the communication medium, a vial of black liquid. You must pour off half of this and take it with you. When you return to the Forge, you can construct the rest of a new resonator from standard parts. I will explain the process. Then we can speak where no one can overhear, and I can tell you what you need to know. But you must *hurry*. Please." His expression was urgent. "We cannot waste this chance."

Beq glanced at Maya, questioning. Maya wanted to scream, or throw up her hands. *How am I supposed to know what to do?* But if there *were* answers to be had, then doing as Ashok asked seemed to be the only way to get them. So Maya nodded, and Beq turned back to the projected image.

"I'll do it," she said. "Tell me what to do."

"Start by removing the fasteners along the axial seam—"

There followed a couple of minutes of jargon that made little sense to Maya but seemed perfectly comprehensible to Beq, who was rapidly scribbling notes. When Ashok was done, she blinked and nodded again.

"I think I've got all that. But I still don't understand how this communication medium works. If it's connected with—"

"You don't need to understand that," Ashok said. "Not yet. I promise you, it will function. Now I must go. If all goes well, we will speak again, and at greater length."

The device went dark and the Chosen's face vanished. Maya stared at Beq, who just looked back at her with wide eyes.

"I know we're all a little stunned," Varo said, "but remember we're in someone else's vault. We need to get moving sooner rather than later."

"Right," Beq said. "Give me that."

She took the thing—the *resonator*—from Maya and set it on the floor, then attacked it with one of the tools from her kit. Within moments it split apart like a melon, revealing a complex mess of internal workings. Beq poked through, using another tool to pull a crystal mesh aside, revealing a clear tube mostly full of something black and viscous.

"Once you do this," Maya said, "this one will still work?"

"That's the idea, at least," Beq said, gently working the tube out of its socket. "I don't pretend to understand *how*. But if...Ashok is right, then nobody should know any better." She paused. "I need something to carry this stuff in."

"Here." Varo tossed her a small silver flask. At Maya's raised eyebrow, he grinned. "For emergencies."

"It's empty?" Beq said.

"There have been a lot of emergencies lately."

Beq tipped the flask out, just to be sure, and unscrewed a metal cap on the top of the cylinder. The stuff inside was thick and heavy, dribbling in a smooth stream, and she managed to transfer half of it to the flask without spilling a drop. Carefully, she tipped the cylinder back, recapped it, and started reassembling the device.

Maya went back to the hole and cupped her hands to her mouth. "Tanax?"

"Here." His face appeared over the edge. "We've been here too long."

"Nearly done. Drop the rope."

Tanax nodded and pushed a coil of rope over the side. Varo scrambled up it, nimble as a squirrel. Maya knelt beside Beq, who was reattaching the last of the fasteners on the resonator.

"Time to go," she said.

"Yeah." Beq tucked the silver flask into her pocket and put the resonator back in the vault. She closed the door, then carefully twisted one of the crystals on the arcana lock. Her spectacles clicked as she looked up at Maya. "That should do it. Do you think...was that really..."

"Later," Maya said, as much to her herself as to anyone. She guided Beq to the rope and helped lift her. A few moments later, they were all on the roof again, and Maya and Tanax levered the circular plug back in.

Maya touched her haken, and bright fire bloomed around the edges of the slate, fusing it into place. It wouldn't stand up to any actual scrutiny, but at least the roof wouldn't collapse. *Hopefully people don't come up here very often.*

"What happened?" Tanax said quietly. "Did you find what you were looking for?"

"You wouldn't believe me if I told you," Maya said, half-dazed. "I'm not sure *I* believe it."

"But—"

She clapped him on the shoulder. "Let's get out of here first. Then we can try to figure it out."

Chapter 13

The leadership of the Khirkhaz Commune assembled in the shadow of a rocky crag. It was a good site, protected on two sides by screens of boulders, with plenty of gullies between them to allow for a quick escape if necessary. Gyre watched the tents going up and tried not to feel a sense of foreboding.

They were in the deep woods now, and getting the wagons over the last few kilometers had been difficult. It was necessary, Apphia had explained, because none of the three banners would meet in the territory of either of the others. Neutral ground, far from the normal paths through the forest, was required.

Brennard's people had broken camp with the professionalism Gyre had come to expect of them, and they'd arrived at the crag before anyone else, taking the position closest to the rocks. Over the course of the rest of the day, the representatives of the banners had arrived, and immediately started bickering with one another over where they would pitch their tents. Gyre watched from the box of his wagon, with Elariel sitting beside him, while Nina lay behind them on the roof, chin in her hands.

"I admit I do not understand," Elariel said. "They are all part of your Commune, are they not?"

"Theoretically," Nina said, lazily kicking her feet.

"And they all want the Republic expelled from these lands," the ghoul went on.

"Oh, absolutely."

"Then why does it matter whose flag is erected first?"

That was the subject of the current argument. A group of ragged-looking men had attempted to plant a version of the Commune flag with a white background, only to be physically tackled by a large, angry fellow carrying a green variant. A party of better-dressed Communards with a black flag stood by, watching the brawl with superior expressions, while Apphia and Brennard tried to impose order.

"It's about pride, I guess," Gyre said.

"It seems counterproductive. They all have the same goal."

Nina yawned. "My sister says that the banners all share the same goal: a Khirkhaz free of the Republic, with themselves in charge of it."

Gyre snorted. "That sounds about right."

"You did not encounter such tensions in Deepfire?" Elariel said.

"I guess we never got close enough to succeeding to think about what would come after," Gyre said.

At Apphia's direction, a representative of each faction took hold of their flag, and they all plunged the stakes into the earth at the same moment. Gyre laughed out loud.

"At least that's settled," he said.

"Give them a minute," Nina said. "Something else will come along."

"How did this rivalry begin?" Elariel said.

"It's always been a problem, I guess," Nina said. "Apphia helped put a bunch of smaller rebel groups together into the Commune proper after Rashtun took over. They've never liked working together much. The Blacks are mostly lesser nobility who want the Republic to butt out and let them run their lands as they want. The Greens are the foresters, who say they just want to be left alone. And the Whites are the groups that have fled up into the woods from the coast and want the Republic gone so they can go home. Before Apphia started talking to them, they were fighting each other as much as the Auxies."

"And now?" Gyre said.

"Now they're arguing about flags," Elariel said. "I suppose that is an improvement."

"It looks like they might actually be ready before nightfall," Gyre said, watching Apphia and the others. "I'd better check on Sarah."

He swung down off the box and went to the third wagon, whose doors were tightly shut. Gyre rapped, and they opened wide enough to let him in. The small space inside was lit by a blue-tinged glowstone, throwing long shadows as Sarah moved around. Several of Kit's constructs were active as well, scuttling back and forth poking through the crates.

"How's it going out there?" Sarah said, not looking up.

"About as we predicted," Gyre said. "Arguing about flags."

"They sound like lovely people," Kit said. One of her spider-bodies crawled up onto Gyre's shoulder. "Glad we're about to give them a bunch of really powerful weapons."

"I'm going to talk to them first," Gyre said. "Hopefully I can get everything pointed in the right direction."

"Have you thought about how much you're going to tell them?" Sarah said. "About where this comes from, I mean."

"I'll keep it vague for now," Gyre said. "Let them get used to the idea."

"Which means you're still keeping me cooped up?" Kit said. "This is getting really tiresome, Gyre."

"Sorry."

"That's what you always say."

"We're almost there." He shook his head. "Apphia's on board. If we can convince the others, we might have a real shot at this. She's already drawing up plans to take back her Spire, which is more than they've managed in the last five years."

"Gyre?" Apphia's voice said from outside.

"Speak of the ghoul," Kit said, hopping off his shoulder.

"You'll be ready to show these things off?" Gyre said to Sarah.

"Give me another half an hour," Sarah said.

Gyre nodded. Any negotiation with the banners was going to take at least that long. He slid out the door again, keeping it mostly closed to shield against prying eyes, and hopped down to earth. Apphia stood with her hands on her hips, watching him curiously.

"For someone who says they brought equipment to share, you're very secretive," she said.

"Just for the moment," Gyre said. "Sarah's arranging a demonstration."

"Ah." Apphia smiled. "So you're just a showman at heart."

"Something like that." Gyre nodded at the clearing between the four sets of tents, where they'd been wrangling over flags. "Have they worked things out?"

"They're sitting in the same place without trying to kill each other, which I suspect is the best we're going to get," she said.

"And they've all heard what happened at the convoy?"

"Oh yes. Rumors will have gotten everywhere now, in addition to the notes I sent. Curiosity is definitely rampant."

"Right." Gyre took a deep breath, fighting down nerves. "Let's see what we can do, then."

Apphia followed him out into the clearing. Nina hopped down to join them, while Elariel remained perched atop the wagon, watching with the wary attitude of a suspicious cat.

The representatives of the banners were waiting, each under their respective flag. Gyre guessed they'd each brought about a dozen people to the meeting, but only two per side were waiting in the clearing, a compromise presumably arrived at after laborious argument.

Somewhat to his surprise, Gyre recognized one of the faces— the woman named Maeris stood beside another man under the green banner, still sporting a bruise from where he'd knocked her unconscious back in Cliffedge. *Well. That could be awkward.* She and her companion had traded their hats and cloaks for sturdier forest gear.

Beside them, under the white flag, a younger man and a stout older woman still had their three-cornered hats, though they looked a little the worse for wear. In spite of being on the same side, the pair didn't seem fond of each other, and frequently exchanged angry looks when they thought the other wasn't watching. Across from them, beneath the black banner, was a slender young man in good hunting clothes, with dark, well-coiffed hair and a superior expression. An old woman wrapped in a black veil leaned heavily on his arm.

"Hello, my friends," Apphia said. "Thank you for coming—"

"We're not friends," the old woman snapped in a surprisingly loud voice. "And I hear the grave calling me louder every minute, so skip the pleasantries. We all know why we're here." She focused on Gyre, eyes bright beneath the veil. "You're the northerner who's got everyone riled up?"

"Great-Grandmother," the young man beside her said.

"Don't 'Great-Grandmother' me," she snapped. "I don't recall asking for your opinion."

"This is Gyre Silvereye," Apphia said. "Also known as Halfmask. Gyre, this is Vaela Racent Truestrike and Fillow Racent, for the Black. Geston Squirrelfinder and Maeris for the Green—"

"We've met, actually," Maeris said, touching the bruise. Her expression looked more mischievous than angry.

Apphia raised her eyebrows but went on, "And I don't believe I know the representatives of the White."

"Ira Ironfist," the woman said.

"Nobody calls you that," her companion objected. "She's just Ira, and I'm Gatz, of the First Irregulars, representing Legate Villier."

"He's not a plaguing legate, he's just a bandit with delusions of grandeur," Ira said. "And what would you know about what people call me? Your lot spent the summer on a fucking *fishing trip*."

"We were performing vital reconnaissance," Gatz said stiffly.

"This is why the leadership of those born to the role is required," said Fillow, to his great-grandmother's evident approval. "The alternative is simply chaos."

"So we should all swear allegiance to the crazy old bat?" rumbled Geston Squirrelfinder. He was a big, broad-shouldered man, with muscles that spoke of long hours cutting wood.

"That *would* be preferable," Vaela said. "And I'll thank you to show some respect."

"*Friends*," Apphia said, a little too loud. "Please. We're here for a purpose, and we all want the Republic expelled from our lands. Gyre has come a long way to offer us his aid."

"I haven't heard him offer anything," Vaela said. "Can he speak for himself?"

"I can," Gyre said, stepping forward. "And Apphia is right. I want to do what I can to help."

"So what's in it for you?" the old woman snapped, fast as a viper.

"It's a fair question," Maeris said. "How much will this aid of yours cost us?"

"I'm not worried about money—" Gyre began.

"—said every swindler ever born—" Ira muttered.

"—because I share your goals. As Halfmask, I worked with Yora, the daughter of Kaidan Hiddenedge. You've heard of Hiddenedge's rebellion, I assume?"

There was a moment of silence.

"Course we've heard of it," Vaela said. "But he went and got himself killed, and what good is that to us?"

"That is what I have…come to understand," Gyre said. "Yora was killed in an Order ambush, and everything we'd tried to do in Deepfire was crushed. It made me realize that while we have resources in the mountains that are lacking in the south, you have the most critical piece of all—a *people* willing to resist Republic domination."

"Some of us are, anyway," Ira said. "Some would rather go fishing."

"Or just squat in the forest eating squirrels," Fillow said, and then: "Ow!" as his great-grandmother rapped his knuckle.

"Quiet," she said. "I'd like to get out of here before my bones are dust. Get to the point, northman."

"I want to unite the strengths of our groups," Gyre said. "We have the weapons. You have the people to wield them. Together we can push the Republic back and show people across the continent that it *can* be done."

"That simple, eh?" Maeris said.

"That simple," Gyre said.

"So what have you brought us?" Ira said eagerly.

"Alchemicals, to start with. Quickheal and other medicine, bombs, stunners—"

Vaela snorted dismissively. "That doesn't explain how you took out a Legionary patrol."

"There are other weapons," Gyre said. "Things from the deep tunnels."

"I didn't believe a word of it at first," Apphia said. "But I watched him take a blaster bolt without flinching, and that sword at his side can cut through unmetal armor."

"That would be a wonder," Vaela said. "But what's the price?"

"The only price," Gyre said, "is that you have to work together. When I heard about the Commune, back in the north, I thought that people here had the right idea. Not just fighting the Republic and the Order, but *building* something to take their place when they're gone." He glanced at Apphia. "I want to help, but only if we're going to be pulling together, not fighting one another."

There was a long silence.

"It's all very well to say 'work together,'" Geston said. "But under whose leadership? And to what end?"

"You all swore, once, to help me regain my seat," Apphia said. "To take back Spire Kotzed. Or have you forgotten?"

"Nobody's forgotten," Vaela said. "And I for one would be pleased to see your family restored, provided we receive certain guarantees."

"We all grieve for your father," Geston said. "But..."

"The legate would attack the Spire tomorrow, if we had the strength," Gatz said. "But the garrison is too strong."

"He's right," Ira said. "Unfortunately."

"If we were strong enough," Gyre said. "If what I've brought is enough, then would you join us to retake the Spire?"

"That's an awfully big 'if,'" Maeris said. "A couple of Legionaries are one thing. Anyone can get lucky. But if we move on the Spire..."

"The Order would intervene," Vaela said. "Have you brought us some magic to keep the centarchs away?"

"No," Gyre said. "But even centarchs can be beaten."

Another silence. Maeris and Ira exchanged knowing smiles. Fillow chuckled to himself behind his hand. Gyre gritted his teeth and heard Apphia sigh.

"They don't care about Father anymore," Apphia said, pacing the length of the tent and back again. "They don't even care about whether we can beat the Republic, just what might give them an advantage against *each other*. Plaguing useless *idiots*."

"You knew that already," Nina said, sitting cross-legged in front of the fire.

"Knowing it is one thing, having it rubbed in my face is another." The baron spun on her heel again, fists clenched. "This is the best opportunity we've had since the Spire fell, and if it were up to them we'd just let it sail by."

Gyre, sitting opposite Nina, shook his head dully. The past couple of hours had been an exercise in mounting frustration, as his every effort to get the banners to commit to a united front devolved into poisonous sniping. They'd eventually retreated, ostensibly for dinner, but in his own case because he couldn't stand another minute among that company.

"The Greens seem like the best of the lot," Nina said. "They were at least listening."

"They're not as petty as that old harridan," Apphia said. "But they're cautious to a fault. They'll nod and smile and agree with you and then not *do* anything. Believe me, I've tried every way I can think of to push them."

"Who's this legate the Whites were talking about?" Gyre said.

"Oh, there's always someone calling themselves legate or comes or even dux with them," Nina said. "There are a hundred little bands, and each one has a leader who fancies themself the leader of a grand army to overthrow the Senate. About all they agree on is not liking the Greens and Blacks."

"Maybe we have the wrong approach here," Apphia said. "Maybe we should pick one of them and be done. If this legate is willing to fight, we could use Gyre's weapons and his numbers to bring the others to heel—"

"*No*," Gyre said, a little too sharply. "I didn't do all this just to set up my own Splinter Kingdom. Things here were supposed to be different."

"Sorry to disappoint you," Apphia said bitterly, sitting down between him and Nina. "People in Khirkhaz are the same selfish plaguing assholes they are everywhere else."

"It suits us, when we send agents to Deepfire and so on, to pretend that the Commune is a united front," Nina said. "And it suits the Republic to pretend that we are, too, because it makes us sound scarier to their own people."

Gyre stared at the fire, trying to think. Unfortunately, he was having difficulty tearing himself away from the growing worry that all of this had been a mistake. After Leviathan's Womb, he'd been reeling, punch-drunk, eager to throw himself into some new adventure to take his mind off how badly the last one had failed. *And now here I am, with three wagonloads of weapons, surrounded by an army of bickering rebels who can't even agree on the color of a flag.*

But there has to be a way. Doesn't there?

"I'm going to check on dinner," Nina said. She exchanged a

look with her sister, who scowled. Nina grinned and skipped out through the tent flap, leaving them alone. For long moments, the only sounds were the crackle of the fire and the murmur of the camp outside.

"You believe it, don't you," Apphia said.

Gyre blinked, realizing he'd been staring into nothing. "Believe what?"

"What you told them. What you told me earlier. That we could really throw the Republic out and rule ourselves."

"I have to believe it," Gyre said. "Otherwise humans are...children, who can only get along by following our parents' rules even after we've grown up. The Republic puts on a show of democracy, but it's the Order that props them up, and that means whether you've got *deiat* in your blood matters more than anything else."

"You've been over the border," Apphia said, shuffling closer. "Is it any different in the Splinter Kingdoms?"

"Not really," Gyre said. "But at least being a king is a...a *human* thing. You're only a king because people agree that you are, not because you've had the power to flatten cities from birth. And if people want to try to figure things out, make things better, there's no Order to come and throw them in prison for being *dhakim*."

"You've thought more about this than most of us, I suspect," Apphia said. "The people out there joined up because they were angry, or because their friends did, or because they were hungry and had nowhere else to go. Brennard and the others are here because *I'm* here."

"And you?" Gyre turned to face her. "If the Senate forced Baron Rashtun to give you your Spire back, would you give all this up? Go back to being a Lightning Baron instead of leading the Commune?"

"I don't know." Apphia shook her head. "Once I would have said no. If the Spire is *given* to me it's only mine on sufferance, hostage to my good behavior. How could I stand up for my people, like my father did, knowing that? But..."

Gyre said nothing. Apphia poked at a spark flung from the fire with her boot until it faded out.

"Nina's fifteen," she said very quietly. "She shouldn't be living like this. She should be...I don't know, studying the *Inheritance* or sneaking out to kiss boys. Whatever it is normal girls do. Not helping us strip rations from dead Auxies so we might have enough food to get through the winter."

"Nina seems happy," Gyre said.

"Sooner or later, something's going to go badly wrong." Apphia's jaw was set, her face a mask. "I have to be here. I owe it to Father, to Brennard, to all the gallant fools who believe in me. But for her..." She sighed. "It's a moot point, I suppose. There's no sign the Republic is planning to let bygones be bygones—"

There was a *boom* from outside, a low rumble followed by a clatter of stone and rising screams. Apphia jumped to her feet, her lassitude instantly gone, and Gyre was close behind.

"One of those *plaguing* idiots must have started something," she said. "Stay here, better if I sort it out—"

"No!" Gyre grabbed her wrist. "Listen. Those are blasters."

Another *boom*, louder, and beneath it the unmistakable *crack* of blaster bolts detonating. Gyre had seen a few of the arcana weapons among the rebels, but nothing like enough to produce this volume of fire. Apphia apparently reached the same conclusion.

"The Legions," she said. "They've found us."

Gyre nodded. "I'll try to distract them. Get your people organized and get away from here."

"Right."

She stepped aside to let him pass, and Gyre pushed through the tent flap and into pandemonium. People were running in every direction, each shouting at all the others. The blaster fire was coming from the far side of the clearing, among the tents of the banners. A few rebels were shooting back with crossbows, and bodies lay strewn beside the evening's cook fires.

Standing in the center of the clearing, ignoring the blaster bolts crashing all around her, was a tall woman with short pale blue hair. She wore no uniform, just traveler's clothes and a pack, and carried no weapons but one—a bladeless sword hilt, adorned with a single gemstone. Where the blade of a sword would have been, the air rippled and roiled.

Centarch.

As though in confirmation, she filled her lungs and shouted. "I am Centarch Niassa Featherbreak. You are all detained in the name of the Twilight Order. Come quietly, and you will have the opportunity to present a defense."

Her haken snapped up, intercepting a blaster bolt from the rebels' side of the clearing, and she laughed out loud.

"Well," she said. "I suppose there wasn't much chance of that."

"The gullies are blocked!" Apphia hurried up. "We're surrounded. Something collapsed half the hillside—"

"Her."

The baron focused on the centarch and went pale. "Oh, plaguing *fuck*. We have to surrender."

"They'll kill you," Gyre said.

"They'll kill *Nina*," Apphia said. "She's still out there!"

Among the debris of dinner, a small pile of boxes and sacks had become a makeshift barricade. A half dozen rebels crouched behind it, including Maeris, who was firing back at the Legionaries in the woods with her twin blaster pistols. Nina was with her, bent low. At first Gyre thought she was cowering, but then she straightened, and he realized she was loading a crossbow. She handed it to one of Brennard's men, who leaned out and fired, only to catch a blaster bolt in return and flop backward, horribly charred. Nina snatched the crossbow from his smoldering hand and started loading again.

Not a dozen meters away, the centarch parried another blaster bolt, then stalked forward.

"I'll take the centarch," Gyre said.

"Don't be an idiot," Apphia said. "I'll give myself up. You can take Nina and get her *out* of here."

"I said I'll take her," Gyre said, drawing his silver sword. "I need you to trust me."

"I..." Apphia gritted her teeth. "If you get my sister killed, I will carve your balls into scrimshaw."

"Noted," Gyre said. "Find Sarah back at our wagons. Tell her to let Kit out. Understand?"

"Who is—"

"Go!"

Gyre concentrated and felt the *click* in his skull as his augmentations activated. The world slowed and split into shadows, blaster bolts racing along straight paths, people blurring into manifold possibilities. The energy bottle at his side was full—he'd taken the precaution of swapping in a fresh one before the meeting—but all his replacements were in the wagons. *Better take care of this quickly, then.*

Behind the barricade, Maeris' companion Geston Squirrelfinder threw himself forward, rolling into a crouch and narrowly avoiding a volley of blaster fire. He was a big man, and he had a weapon to match, a two-handed, single-edged axe that looked like it could fell a tree in one stroke. He swung it in a wide arc at the centarch Niassa, who dodged and backed away. The axe whistled past her, and she reached out with her free hand and squeezed. Geston froze in place, pinioned by invisible force; then he *burst*, blood splashing into a neat sphere as it painted the inside of an unseen barrier. The centarch lowered her hand, and blood and ruined meat cascaded to the dirt, along with the twisted remains of the axe.

At that point, Gyre had covered half the distance between them. He kept his approach quick and silent, hoping to end the fight with a single strike—he'd lost any scruples about stabbing an enemy in the back long ago. Unfortunately, Niassa saw him coming and spun to meet his blade with her haken. His thrust slid by, missing her side by inches, and she grinned at him as she clenched her fist.

Deiat flared, a sphere of force materializing around him, and Gyre's ears popped. Just as quickly, though, the constricting bubble shredded and faded away, leaving behind nothing more than a faint breeze. Niassa's eyes went wide, and she jumped backward, skidding out of range of Gyre's crossing cut.

"Now, *that* is interesting," she said, squaring off. "And who exactly are you supposed to be?"

"Take your soldiers and get out of here," Gyre said. "Now."

Niassa laughed. "It might have escaped your attention, but I'm a centarch of the Twilight Order. We don't take kindly to threats."

"I figured." Gyre shrugged, and for a moment saw a red-haired figure in front of him in Niassa's place. "But I thought I'd give you a chance."

"*Very* interesting." Her smile widened. "*You* are coming back to answer a few questions, I think."

She attacked, her rippling haken slashing from side to side in horizontal arcs. Gyre saw each coming, watching the shadows of her swordplay, giving just enough ground that he avoided the blade without revealing his true speed. Confusion and frustration played on Niassa's face, and she drove at him harder.

Poor technique. This woman was half a decade older than Maya, but Gyre was willing to bet his sister was the better sword. *Then again, what's the incentive for a centarch to be a decent swordsman?* Apart from one another, there was no one for them to fight; even a Legionary with unmetal armor and weapons would provide only a moment's sport.

Niassa's swing grew wider. That left her open to a riposte, but perhaps that was the point. *What does she care, with her invincible panoply protecting her?*

Gyre struck.

The centarch had just committed to a swing, shadows racing ahead of her blade to show where it might fall. Gyre twisted lightly past them, his silver blade slipping through in a textbook-perfect lunge that caught her in the center of her chest. Her panoply didn't even spark as cloth, flesh, and bone parted easily, her momentum carrying her forward until the hilt slammed into her stomach. Gyre planted his foot, and Niassa stumbled into him, the two of them standing for a moment in a frozen tableau.

"That's... not possible." Her voice was a wheeze, and blood drooled from her lips, painting her teeth crimson. Her haken slipped from suddenly nerveless fingers.

"I warned you," Gyre said.

The centarch's eyes were distant. "He told me... if I came here... I... would be..." She slumped against him, her final word a whisper. "... exalted..."

She shuddered again and went still. The battlefield around him had gone similarly quiet, Gyre noticed, as though everyone had stopped what they were doing to watch. Gyre stepped back, withdrawing his blade, and let Niassa's body flop into the dirt. In the woods opposite, he saw white-armored figures approaching, blaster rifles raised.

Then, behind him, screams, and the clatter of many feet.

Kit's constructs raced into the clearing, the two largest in the lead, the smaller ones following behind like chicks hurrying after a mother hen. Their arrival stunned even the Legionaries, who took a moment too long to open fire. By the time blaster bolts *cracked* out, the multi-legged constructs were already among them, the larger ones bowling them over while the smallest pried at their armor. Gyre saw one of the little spiders blow apart as a bolt caught it, and another bolt cut a gouge out of a large construct's carapace; Kit's bodies, not truly designed for war, lacked the shields of ghoul soldier-constructs. Given time, the Legionaries might recover.

Better not give them time, then. Gyre bent and scooped up the dead centarch's haken, holding it aloft where everyone could see. He pointed his silver sword at the beleaguered soldiers and shouted at the top of his lungs.

"Finish them! Then on to the Spire!"

"*On to the Spire!*" The first voice to join him was Nina's, as she vaulted the makeshift barricade. A moment later, he heard Apphia's deeper yell. "*On to the Spire!*"

The rebels rose from where they'd hidden, among the tents and wagons, and charged.

Chapter 14

Maya had never been inside the Forge's storerooms before. They seemed to go on forever, row after row after row of ancient shelves. She suddenly half believed Varo's story about the quartermasters who'd discovered the skeletons of novices who'd gotten lost centuries before. The rows were numbered according to some scheme she didn't understand, but Beq seemed to know where she was going.

The quartermasters' clerk hadn't been happy about letting them back here, into a domain that was supposed to be private even from curious centarchs. But the permissions Baselanthus and Prodominus had written Maya were still valid, so ultimately the man didn't have much choice, as much as he'd huffed and complained. He'd grown even more acerbic when Maya made it clear she and Beq wanted to be alone, but ultimately he'd heaved a sigh and retreated to his office, no doubt hoping they ended up like those mythical novices.

"This should be the right section," Beq said, looking down at the notes she'd copied out of the master catalog. "Wreckage of the skyship *Second Flowering*, taken from where it crashed near Bastion to keep it out of the hands of scavengers. They put the entire control ring here—there has to be something we can use."

"If you say so." Maya touched her haken, brightening the ball of light hovering over her head. The shelves on either side varied in height, some sections close-packed with dozens of tiny boxes full of crystals or shredded wire, others sporting great hunks of twisted material. The only constant was the dense layer of dust that covered everything, puffing into the air at the slightest breeze. Maya guessed they were the first to disturb this particular row in decades.

"Here." Beq knelt, waving a hand and coughing. Dust glittered and sparked in Maya's light. "Look at these."

The shelf held a row of curved chunks of arcana, each about as long as Maya's arm, which looked like they might once have fit together into a circle. Their surfaces were covered in wire and twisted patterns, but she saw a few pits layered in crystal that reminded her of the one on the resonator, complete with the fang-like protrusions.

"Image projectors," Beq said happily. "Look, there's half a dozen. We should be able to cobble together at least one that works from the pieces."

"Maybe we should have brought a cart," Maya said, eyeing the hefty arcana.

"I should be able to extract what we need," Beq said. She unfolded her leather wallet full of tools, then looked up and down the aisle. "This . . . this is all right, isn't it? Taking these parts."

"We do have permission from the Council," Maya said, patting her pocket.

"I suppose."

Maya waved dust away from her face. "And it's not like anyone else is doing anything with them."

"That's true," Beq said, brightening. "I just . . . what that . . . person, Ashok, said. Is it *possible*?"

"I don't know," Maya said uncomfortably. "But we have to find out."

"Yeah." Beq looked down at her hands.

"I know that look." Maya bent over, putting a finger under Beq's chin to turn it upward, and kissed her. "You did *brilliantly* in the vault. Don't give me that 'I'm not sure if I can do this' expression." Maya's grin widened. "I'm onto you."

Beq laughed out loud. She bent to her task, clicking her lenses into place. In a few minutes, she had the arcana open and their guts splayed out in front of her, pulling them apart with the precision of a master butcher with a freshly killed vulpi. She muttered to herself as she worked, filling a bag with detached pieces.

Maya shook her head at the complexity. "I wish I could actually help."

"I may need you to melt some bits of unmetal, actually," Beq said. "But we can do that back in your room. I've got just about everything I need."

"Tomorrow," Maya said firmly. "Neither of us got much sleep last night."

In fact, between the vault break-in and the trip back to the Forge by boat, Maya hadn't managed to close her eyes for more than an hour. Beq had to be exhausted as well, but she grumbled nonetheless, putting a few more components into her bag and replacing the gutted arcana on their shelves. By the time they'd extracted themselves from the quartermasters' labyrinth, even Beq was wobbling on her feet. They went back to Maya's room, where Forge servants had left a tray of sandwiches. Maya bolted a couple and collapsed into bed, Beq snug against her.

She woke to the sound of quiet swearing and raised her head blearily. It was impossible to tell what time of day it was—a constant problem in the depths of the Forge—but it couldn't be *that* late, unless she'd slept through the servants bringing breakfast. The sunstone in her room gave off a dim glow, and Beq's side of the bed was cold. Maya sat up and found the arcanist on the floor, staring through her multilensed spectacles at the thing she was assembling. It looked half-completed already.

"You've been making progress, I see," Maya said blearily, shuffling until she was lying chin in hand at the foot of the bed. "How long have you been up?"

"A while," Beq said vaguely. "Hope I didn't wake you. I got up to use the toilet and then I couldn't stop thinking, so I figured I might as well do something about it."

"I'm not sure a thickhead could have woken me." Maya yawned. "And how's it going?"

"Getting there." She indicated the body of the thing she was building, which was centered on a crystal-lined pit like the one on the resonator. "I got the image projector basically whole, and I've only had to replace a few pieces. The tricky part is replicating the connection to the... fluid medium, I think he called it. But I pulled out a few other components that will help."

"So it'll work?"

"Maybe not as well as the real thing," Beq said. "But I think so."

"You are a genius." Maya grabbed her shoulders and pulled her back, kissing the top of her head. "Geniuses deserve breakfast. Anything you want in particular?"

"Eggs and bacon," Beq said, her attention already drifting back to the project.

"Coming up," Maya said.

She rolled out of bed, tiptoed past the mess of discarded pieces, and hurriedly dressed and headed to the nearest kitchen. A quarter of an hour later, she returned with a tray piled high with eggs and bacon, plus vulpi ham, toast, and juice.

"Perfect," Beq said when she came in.

"I mean, I didn't cook it," Maya said, "but I'll accept praise."

"Not that. I need you to melt something."

"Ah." Maya set the tray down carefully and picked up her haken. "Where?"

Beq pointed, and Maya focused a tiny but intense stream of *deiat* on the spot, powerful enough to weaken even unmetal. At the same time, she pulled in the heat from the surrounding components and the air, a useful trick Jaedia had taught her to keep from starting a fire. Beq poked at the join with a tool, nodded, and pointed to another spot, and then another. Finally she sat back, satisfied.

"That's about it, I think," she said. "The only thing left is to plug the black stuff in and see if it works."

"Breakfast first," Maya said. "I'm not sure I can face this on an empty stomach."

"Definitely."

Beq attacked the eggs and bacon with nearly the same enthusiasm she'd showed for working on the arcana, and between the two of them they managed to finish most of the tray. When that was finished, Beq extracted Varo's silver flask and carefully tipped it into a glass jar she'd scrounged. The black stuff flowed smoothly, leaving no residue at all behind. Beq tipped it back and forth, then shrugged and screwed on the top of the jar, thick with wire connecting it to the rest of the device.

After that, it was just a matter of assembling the thing. As Beq had promised, it didn't have the elegance of the original—it was awkwardly shaped, half-boxy and half-smooth, and some of the crystals lining the imaging pit were uneven. But Beq seemed satisfied, and she set the completed resonator on the floor in front of Maya.

"Now what?" Maya said. "Any special controls?"

"Just run power to it," Beq said. "Same as before. As best I understand things, that should be enough." She hesitated. "Should we wait for Varo? Or Tanax?"

"Tanax is still stuck in Skyreach, and we don't know when Varo will be available." The scout had been called to duty the morning they'd returned to the Forge. "The...Ashok seemed to think something was urgent."

"And we shouldn't..." Beq swallowed. "Bring this to the Council?"

"Prodominus is on the Council. *Nicomidi* was on the Council." *And Basel is, too.* Maya touched the Thing, now both a familiar gesture and a reminder of its hard-edged alien presence. "Apart from the four of us—and Jaedia, if she were awake—I don't know who I trust anymore."

"Okay," Beq said, wiping her palms on her trousers. She clicked the dials on her spectacles, lenses whirring. "Okay. Do it."

Maya touched her haken, drew a thin stream of *deiat*, and fed it into the makeshift resonator. For a moment, the thing didn't respond, and she had a spike of worry that they'd fouled it up somehow. Then the thread caught and power flowed through her. The space above the crystal pit flickered, and the image of Ashok's head appeared. It wasn't *quite* the same—the edges were fuzzy, and in the light of the sunstone it was translucent—but it was still startling. Maya pushed the resonator back a little. Ashok beamed at them.

"Maya Burningblade," he said. "You have succeeded. I was beginning to worry."

"Beq built the thing," Maya said. "I really just watched."

"Ah yes. Arcanist Bequaria, was it? Fine work." Ashok glanced at Maya. "You trust her, I take it?"

"Of course." Maya grabbed Beq's hand and squeezed.

"I cannot force you to keep this a secret," Ashok said. "But I beg you to tell no one you do not absolutely need to about our communication. The enemy has infiltrated the Order, and if word of this gets to the wrong ears, you could both be in danger, not to mention everything we are trying to accomplish."

"The *enemy*? I..." Maya shook her head. "Okay. Look. I want to believe you're...what you say you are." Who *hadn't* fantasized, at one time or another, about the Chosen swooping in and putting the world to rights? *But...* "And I don't want to be disrespectful. But..."

"You're not certain," Ashok said mildly. "I understand."

"You do?"

His image nodded. "Of course. From your perspective, it's quite an extraordinary claim. Little wonder you'd ask for some proof."

"Then..." Maya trailed off. *How can he* prove *anything?*

"Can you reach the bottom level of the Forge without anyone noticing?"

Maya blinked, then glanced at Beq. The arcanist gave a cautious nod.

"There's another couple of floors below the deep testing rooms," she said. "I'm not sure I've seen anyone go down there."

"Good," Ashok said. "Take the resonator and follow the north hall to the end, then turn left. After three sunstones, examine the wall on your right hand. Feed *deiat* into it, and a door will open. Activate the resonator again when you're inside."

"A secret door?" Beq's eyes were wide. "But how do you—"

"Because I was there when it was built, of course." Ashok's smile broadened, and then his image winked out.

Down they went, past the residential levels, past the quartermasters, past the vast storerooms packed full of supplies against a siege that had never come. Beq carried the resonator, wrapped in a canvas sack, while Maya wore her formal uniform and tried to walk as though she knew exactly where they were going.

The arcanists' workshops were close to the bottom, and they hurried past, not wanting Beq to run into someone she recognized. The great stairs finally ended in a four-way junction like all the ones above it, and Maya led the way down the north corridor.

She was certain no one had come this way in some time. It had the feel of a place not *abandoned* but at least uninhabited. There was only a thin film of dust, and the sunstones on the walls cast their usual glow, so servants certainly walked these halls to clean and replenish. But door after door stood open, looking on to big, empty stone rooms.

"Old storerooms, I guess," Beq said, looking into one of them. "From back when there were more of us."

Maya nodded. Up ahead, the corridor dead-ended in a junction, and she took the left turn, counting the sunstones in their brackets. When they'd passed three, she stopped. The wall was ordinary stone, no different from anywhere else in the Forge, but—

"I can feel it," she told Beq, one hand on her haken. "There's something in there. Arcana." She took a deep breath. "Here goes."

Beq stepped a little closer to her. Maya drew a thin thread of *deiat* and attached it to whatever device was waiting, bracing against a sudden drain of power. Instead there was only a light chill, like a breeze in a closed room. Without any fuss, a section of rock she would have *sworn* was solid slid into the ceiling, revealing a room beyond. A sunstone came on inside.

"Secret door." Beq leaned forward, lenses clicking as she examined the edges of the rock. "It's so perfect. It has to be part of the original Chosen construction."

"Do you think anyone else knows about it?"

Beq shook her head. "No footprints in the dust, at least."

No servants had come in *here* to sweep up, and the floor was thick with the dust of centuries. Maya stepped forward cautiously, but every footfall raised a slowly rolling curtain. The room wasn't large, a round space four meters across with a domed ceiling. The walls were a flat, polished white, unlike the rougher stone of the rest of the Forge. But there was nothing else to see, and no other exits.

"Is this his proof?" Beq said, standing in the center and looking around. "Just that the door exists?"

"It means he knows something that nobody *here* knows." Maya held out her hand for the resonator. "Let's ask him."

She threaded more *deiat* into the jury-rigged device. It caught, drawing power, but Ashok did not immediately appear. Instead the secret door slid closed and the sunstone winked out, leaving them in total darkness. Beq squeaked in surprise. Before Maya could call flame from her haken, the light came back on, but...different.

They were outdoors in broad daylight, the bright blaze of a summer day. A brilliant blue sky streaked with fluffy wisps of cloud stretched overhead. Underfoot was an off-white unmetal deck, grooved so as not to be slippery in the rain, shimmering with iridescent patterns. Directly in front of Maya a tapering spire rose thirty meters into the air, coming to an impossibly fine point like an enormous needle.

Ashok stood there with them, not as a blurry projected face but in the flesh. He was a tall, handsome man, golden hair gleaming in the sun, wearing a brilliant white robe that left one shoulder bare and was fastened at the other with a silver clasp. His smile was the same, broad and welcoming, and he clapped his hands in delight.

"Wonderful," he said. "Welcome, both of you."

"Where are we?" Beq said, turning in a circle, the lenses of her spectacles flipping frantically in and out. "How did you—"

"We are atop the Sunward Tower," Ashok said. "The highest spot in Skyreach. The tallest building in the world, so far as we know." He gestured at the horizon, where hulking mountains, blued by distance, rose over the lake. "The Forge is over there. Or will be."

"*Will* be?" Maya hesitated, putting a hand to her cheek. The clouds were scudding across the sky, but she felt no wind. She ran her boot across the deck, but it didn't catch in the grooves, and very faintly she could see a rising plume of dust. "This is a projection."

"Oh!" Beq said. "Like the resonator, on a larger scale."

"You are unfortunately correct," Ashok said. "Specifically, it's a recording from the day the skyfortress *Pride-in-Power* first docked at Skyreach. A historic occasion, only a short time before the Plague and the beginning of the end. It seemed a fitting moment to mark the apex of our civilization." He pointed outward. "There."

The skyfortress was approaching. It was shaped like a flattened teardrop, blunt at the back and tapering to a sharp point at the bow. Maya had seen one at Grace, half-buried in the ground, but it was no comparison to this magnificent thing, gleaming and iridescent. It hung in the air with no effort at all, as though gravity simply didn't apply. For a moment she didn't grasp the true scale of it, but abruptly she realized the tiny dots visible around it were *flitters*, vehicles like the one she'd flown in Skyreach, as tiny beside the vast ship as minnows next to a whale.

"Half the city turned out," Ashok said wistfully. "It takes a great deal to bring my people out of their salons and sanctums, but everyone wanted to see the *Pride*. It was the greatest of our creations, and building it strained our resources even at the height of our empire. At the time people said it would never be surpassed." His smile faded. "They didn't know how right they were."

"Why can you show us this *now*?" Maya looked around at the stunning vista.

"The room must be an image projector," Beq said, looking to Ashok. "Right? And the resonator links up to it."

"Correct," Ashok said, which made the arcanist beam with pride. "Don't walk too far, or you'll bump into a wall. I thought it might help you understand to provide a...demonstration."

"Right." Maya closed her eyes, trying to calm her breathing. "I have questions."

"I'm sure," Ashok said mildly.

"You're one of the Chosen," she said. "As far as I know—as *anyone* knows—all the Chosen are dead."

"Only *nearly* all of us." A shadow passed over Ashok's handsome features. "A pitiful few of us remain. I am the only one awake, for now. The rest are asleep in stasis webs."

"*Where* are you?"

"The specific location does not matter. We are in a research facility, deep underground, accessible only via Gate. This place was designed to be completely self-sufficient, not even mingling its air with the outside world. That is the only reason we have survived this long."

"The Plague," Beq said. "You were protected from it there?"

"Correct."

"Then you can come out now, can't you?" Maya said. "The Plague only affects the Chosen, and all the other Chosen are dead. You'd be safe."

Ashok shook his head. "Unfortunately, it's not that simple. The Plague *kills* only Chosen, yes, but it infects humans as well, and those humans can spread it to others. It is in the air, the water, the food. Once you contract it, it remains with you for life. To stand this close to you, in reality, would be a death sentence for me. We are trapped in our tiny safe haven, today just as much as when we entered it four centuries ago."

"That's..." Maya tried to imagine spending years—*centuries*—imprisoned under the earth, able to step outside at any time but knowing it would mean her death. *I think I would go mad. No wonder they sleep when they can.*

"But we have not been idle," Ashok continued. "There is a *way*. We can annihilate the Plague for good and take back the world. We have waited so long for someone like *you*, Maya."

"Me?" Maya blinked. "Why me?"

"Not all centarchs are equal," Ashok said. "You have the potential to be more powerful than any born in centuries—perhaps any since the last of us left your world. Unfortunately, the enemy got to you before I was able to influence events."

"What do you mean, the enemy?" Maya said. "What enemy?"

"*Them*, of course. The ghouls, and the *dhakim* who serve them." Ashok's lips twisted with distaste. "They bound you with a device that limits your power."

"The Thing?" Maya touched the arcana, fingers tracing its familiar outline, and looked at Beq. "But it was Basel who gave me the Thing. He's...I trust him." *I have to. Otherwise...* "He's certainly no servant of the *ghouls*."

"The enemy has long since infiltrated the Order. I believe you've encountered their servants already."

"Those...things," Beq said. "The black spiders."

"Yes." Ashok nodded gravely. "Intelligent constructs, capable of overwhelming the will of any human."

Not any human, Maya thought, fiercely proud. *Not Jaedia.*

"And they are not alone," Ashok went on. "The ghouls are masters of corruption, and they have many tools. Power, wealth, luxury, and all that *dhaka* can provide—a cure for an illness, or fresh vitality. Most of the Order's centarchs are true to their oaths, but enough have fallen to *dhak* for the ghouls' purpose, and those can deceive the others. It may be that this Baselanthus did not know the true nature of the device, but it remains true that the melding of flesh and arcana can only be accomplished with *dhaka*."

"What about Prodominus?" Maya said. "He's the leader of the Revivalists, but he's the one who sent me to the Archive. Is he..."

"He is foremost among the ghouls' servants." Ashok looked pained. "For some time, I have used the resonator to speak with a few members of the Order. Unfortunately, one of them trusted the wrong person, and it fell into Prodominus' hands. I won't communicate with him, of course, so he remains unaware of my presence, but he knows something is working against him. He sent you to the Archive in an effort to understand exactly what."

Prodominus. Maya stood for a moment in silence. It was hard to picture the bluff, bearded old Kyriliarch as a traitor to the Order. *But I would have said any traitor was impossible, before Nicomidi.* The black spider had even turned Jaedia against them, until she'd confronted Maya herself. *Anything is possible.* She touched the Thing. *I can't trust any of them, can I?*

"So what is this *way*?" Beq blurted out. "How do we destroy the Plague?"

"We must be careful," Ashok said. "Very, very careful. If the ghouls and their servants learn of what we intend, all will be lost." He raised his hands and the scene faded into darkness, leaving the three of them standing in an empty black void. "Listen closely. Baselanthus and Prodominus will ask you to go to Khirkhaz, to fight the rebels there."

"Khirkhaz?" Maya frowned. "Now? Why? They've been fighting rebels there for a decade."

"Because I have taken pains to arrange it," Ashok said with a hint of irritation. "*Listen.* The rebels are only an excuse. You must go to Khirkhaz because the Purifier is there."

"The—"

Maya's question froze in her throat as ground and sky appeared. They were hanging in midair, miles up, over a vast forest lumpy with tree-covered hills. The soles of her feet tingled—she was certain she was about to fall—and she surreptitiously shifted to feel the solid stone still beneath her. *It's only an image.*

Beq turned in place, giddy with excitement, lenses snapping into place. "It's Khirkhaz!" she said. She pointed north at a range of mountains. "Those are the Worldspines. We're over the interior, the old Lightning Baron territories."

"Indeed." A spotlight shone down from the heavens, illuminating a long mountain in the middle of the forest, its rocky peak breaking free of the tree line like a whale breaching the surf. "The Purifier is here, safe underground." More lights came on, seven of them, equally spaced around a circle surrounding the mountain. "These are its power stations, what you call the Spires."

"It's an arcana device," Maya said, feeling a bit left behind by the conversation. "Like the Archive. What does it do?"

"It destroys the Plague," Ashok said.

"What?" Beq said. "How?"

"The details are…complex, and irrelevant. What is important is that a great deal of *deiat* is required to begin the chain reaction. Once that is provided, and the device is active, it will spread on its own." White light gathered at the Purifier, then burst outward in a vast ring, rippling through the hills and forests and passing out of sight of the horizon. "Wherever it finds the Plague, it will destroy it and spread outward again. Our final weapon."

"Why haven't you turned it on already, then?" Maya said.

Ashok's lips twisted bitterly. "It came too late. By the time our human servants finished the construction, those who had given them their orders were dead. The only Chosen left were me and my pathetic few, and we would not survive long enough to use it. There has never been a centarch with enough power." His voice went soft. "Until now."

"You..." Maya put her hand on the Thing. "You really believe *I'm* strong enough?"

"I am certain of it." Ashok stepped closer, as though he wanted to put a hand on her shoulder. "Maya, please believe me. I have watched you all your life. I would not ask this of you if I thought it was impossible. It will be very dangerous, make no mistake—if the ghouls discover your purpose, they will stop at nothing to destroy you. But if you *succeed*..."

He spread his hands, and they were suddenly standing atop the tower in Skyreach again. The skyfortress hovered almost directly overhead, and flitters darted all around them, full of beautiful, colorfully dressed people. Music played from somewhere, and crowds cheered.

"We will set things to rights," Ashok said, voice rising. "Our world, *this* world, will come again. A world where no human need live in fear. We will destroy the ghouls and their plaguespawn. Rebuild what has been lost. And you, Maya, will have a place of highest honor. All of you in the Order will, as those who held humanity together in its darkest hours, when we who should have been guiding it were gone."

He made a glorious image, intangible wind whipping his robe around him, sun shining in his golden hair, the colossal skyship hanging in the sky behind him. Maya swallowed.

"And Jaedia?" she said quietly. "She won't wake up. Can you..."

"Of course." Ashok lowered his hands and gave her a warm smile. "As I said, we will set everything to rights. We are the *Chosen*, Maya. You understand what that means." He shook his head. "But you *must* succeed. We are betting everything on you. Our last chance. Will you help us?"

Maya glanced at Beq, then back to Ashok. Very slowly, she gave a nod.

"Thank you." Ashok shook his head. "Our communication window is closing. Contact me again when you reach Khirkhaz, but wait as long as you can. Our power is very limited and replenishes only slowly. You must find a way to reach the mountain without attracting any notice." He bowed to her, deep and solemn. "We are in your hands."

The image flickered and vanished. The sunstone came back on, illuminating the small, white-walled room behind the secret door, with no hints remaining of the vistas it had contained. She and Beq stared at one another in stunned silence for a long time.

"Chosen above," Beq finally muttered, then gave a half-hysterical laugh. "Or should it be Chosen below?"

Maya stared at the resonator, her thoughts a mad whirl. "I have no idea."

"I'm sorry to bring this to you," Maya said. "But I figured you wouldn't mind."

Jaedia lay in her hospital bed, as always, her eyes closed, her chest gently rising and falling. The doctors took good care of her, keeping her washed and dressed, moving her regularly to prevent sores. She was in good health, as far as anyone could tell. But she wouldn't wake up.

Half a day of contemplation had not clarified matters much in Maya's mind. She and Beq had gone around in circles, until they'd agreed to separate and try to think on their own. Varo would be back soon, and he might have something to add. In the meantime, she was here, talking to the only person apart from Beq she truly, implicitly, believed in.

Of course, the "walls" of their little nook were only curtains and there was no way to tell whether a doctor or servant was hovering outside, so she had to keep things vague. But Maya figured Jaedia wouldn't mind that either.

"There's someone who's telling me that I have the chance to do... something incredible." Maya put one hand through her hair, shaking her head. "So incredible that I'm not sure I believe it. He could be lying, or just... mistaken. About me. I don't know.

"I'm just so worried I'll get it wrong." She swallowed. "I can take the chance, or ignore it, or bring it to the Council, but... whatever I do, whatever choice I make, it could be the *wrong* choice. It could screw things up for *everyone*. The whole world. That can't be *my* decision to make, can it? There has to be... someone else."

Maya reached out for Jaedia's hand. Her mentor's fingers were cool against her skin, and Maya gripped them tightly, as though to press some warmth back into them.

"I wish you were awake," she said very quietly. "I want to talk to you so badly. I want you to tell me whether this is the right thing to do, or whether I've got things backward. To threaten to strip the hide off me if I even think of doing something so stupid again." She sniffed. "Plague, I even miss Marn sometimes. They tell me he's recovering, I guess. They've got him out in the country somewhere." Maya shook her head. "Chosen. I'm babbling. I just wish..."

She shut her eyes, brimming with tears, and bowed her head.

You have to do better, Maya. Jaedia's voice in her memory, after rescuing her from the cistern in Bastion. *When you get your cognomen, I'm not going to be here to pull you out of the fire. You have the heart of a proper centarch. I just need to knock a little more sense into your head.*

That was what being a centarch *meant*, in the end. *Responsibility. We are given access to the fires of creation to wield on behalf of humanity.* All their training, everything Maya had learned from the *Inheritance* and at Jaedia's side, had been to prepare her for that. *Not* how *to use* deiat, *but* why *to use it.*

I think I understand. Maya squeezed Jaedia's hand, then let go, sitting back. She stayed there for a long while, staring into nothing.

"Centarch?" came a soft voice from beyond the curtain.

"Yes?" Maya said.

"Apologies for disturbing you. Kyriliarch Baselanthus has returned to the Forge and requested your presence."

"Now?"

"Yes, Centarch. In the Council chamber."

"All right." Maya stood up and stretched. She felt lighter, somehow, as she looked down at her mentor. "I'll be back soon," she whispered. *And you'll be awake to greet me.*

* * *

The Council chamber was usually crowded, not just with the twelve Kyril-iarchs sitting on one side of a great oval table, but with their servants and faction members crammed in along the back wall or sitting in the corners. Now the huge space felt abandoned. Only two of the Kyriliarchs' seats were occupied—Baselanthus sat, hands folded in front of him, while Prodomi-nus leaned back in his chair and ran his fingers through a tangle of beard. On the other side of the table, Maya stood at attention beside a tall, thin man with short purple-black hair. His uniform was edged in black-blue-red, and the lists Jaedia had drilled into Maya automatically supplied his name—Centarch Va'aht Thousandcuts—though she couldn't recall that they'd ever met. He had aristocratic features, schooled to a carefully neutral expression. Apart from the four of them, the great chamber was empty.

"Thank you for joining us," Baselanthus said. "The rest of the Council is still in Skyreach, but we have become aware of an ... urgent difficulty."

"Meaning things have gone to shit," Prodominus said. "And some-thing's got to be done."

Maya suppressed a smile. *Is he really a ghoul agent?* There was certainly no black spider clinging to his neck, but Ashok had said that wasn't the only kind of servant the "enemy" had access to. *He's definitely hiding the res-onator from the Council*, she reminded herself. *That has to mean* something.

"Colorfully put," Baselanthus said, "but essentially correct. I assume you're both aware of the situation in Khirkhaz?"

Maya nodded. "Rebels, right?"

"The Commune," Va'aht said, crisp and precise. "A group led by a former noble, seeking to establish their own Splinter Kingdom outside of Republic control. Due to the rough, forested nature of most of the area, they've proven difficult to eliminate."

"Indeed," Basel said. "But, it must be said, neither have they been particularly effective. While the Legion presence in Khirkhaz is larger than usual, for the most part the local dux, one Baron Rashtun, has been able to handle the Commune with his own resources. Recently, however, that seems to have changed."

"Rumor is there's someone new in the area," Prodominus said. "Someone with arcana weapons that can defeat Legionaries with ease. That kind of rumor is common enough, but there happened to be a centarch nearby, so the Council sent a messenger to ask her to investigate. Niassa Featherbreak."

"I know her," Va'aht said. "A good woman. What did she discover?"

"She's dead," Basel said quietly. "One of our scouts tracked her haken and found her in the forest, buried in a shallow grave. She'd been killed by a single sword thrust to the chest."

"Ambushed?" Va'aht said, without apparent emotion.

"It's our best guess," Prodominus said. "Seems unlikely that she would be so foolish, but what else are we to think?"

"It is...at least possible," Baselanthus said, "that some weapon has been unearthed, some piece of arcana that enabled her to be taken unawares."

Or worse. For a moment, Maya felt the cold, biting pain of metal sliding through her flesh. Gyre's friend Kit had run her through from behind with a blade that passed through her panoply as though it weren't there. She'd survived, thanks to luck and quickheal, but...

"Either way," Va'aht said, "this obviously demands a response. Order blood has been spilled, and that cannot go unanswered."

"Indeed." Prodominus glanced at Basel. "Which is why I am going to Khirkhaz personally."

"I thought it might be better to proceed in a more...measured fashion," Basel said, a little peevishly. "I was overruled. Prodominus will take a detachment of scouts and Legionaries to Khirkhaz, along with a pair of centarchs. We would like that to be the two of you." He peered at Maya. "However, in light of your recent service, if you need more time to recover—"

"I'm at your command, Kyriliarch," Va'aht said immediately.

"So am I," Maya said hastily. "I mean, yes, I'm fully recovered." She hesitated. "Can I bring my team along?"

Basel glanced at Prodominus, who shrugged. "I don't have a problem with it."

"This is not just a matter of reasserting the Order's authority," Basel said. "It's also an opportunity. Our scouts report that this victory has encouraged the rebels, and they may be preparing a major offensive. If that's true, it will bring them into the open, where they can be crushed once and for all. Removing this thorn from our side would go a long way toward easing the demand on our resources." He folded his hands. "However, you are to exercise all appropriate caution, in case there *is* some kind of new weapon. Needless to say, if you find it, it should be captured and brought back here for study."

"Of course, Kyriliarch." Va'aht saluted. "With your permission, I will prepare at once."

"Granted." Basel's eyes flicked to Prodominus, then back to Maya. "You're certain you're ready for this?"

"Certain," Maya said. *Ashok was right about what they'd ask me to do. That has to mean something too.*

"Very well." Baselanthus gave a tired sigh. "As I said, be careful."

"Don't worry," Prodominus said with a huge grin. "I'll make sure they keep their eyes open."

Chapter 15

Y ou're sure you're okay with this?" Gyre said in Elariel's ear.

"Of course." The ghoul gave him a cold smile. "I have faith in my people's engineering."

It was Tyraves, the hostile ghoul they'd dealt with at Refuge, that Gyre didn't have much faith in. But he held his tongue and finished securing the harness around Elariel. It consisted of a belt, plus leather straps that crossed over the chest and went over the shoulders, all layered with wire and metal. According to Elariel, it provided a shield against *deiat* manifestations like the one in his augmentations.

"Check it," Gyre said. "Just in case."

Elariel nodded, tracing the belts with her hands before giving him a thumbs-up. He led her back out from behind the wagon, into the glade where the Communards were waiting.

After the attack, the entire camp had been packed up and moved with impressive speed, the Republic dead stripped and hastily buried in the forest nearby. Some of the rebels had been eager to keep Niassa's haken, if only as a trophy, but Gyre and Sarah had managed to convince them to leave it with the body. The Order could *track* haken, over long distances, and keeping one was as good as guaranteeing yourself a visit from a centarch later on.

There had followed three days of trundling down forest paths, extracting the clumsy wagons when they got stuck and taking the long way around every hill and ridge to reach a new meeting site, closer to Spire Kotzed and well concealed under a heavy canopy. This time, representatives of the banners were already there when they arrived, their mutual animosity suppressed by excitement. The stories of Gyre's victory over the centarch during the ambush were already spreading.

Not that it was much of a victory. She hadn't thought he could hurt her, and he'd taken her by surprise. *Maya put up a lot more of a fight.* He couldn't help but think about his sister, as much as he tried not to. *Someday, it'll be her they send after me.*

Now, the morning after the banners had gathered, he and Sarah had opened the crates in the wagons at last, unpacking the ghoul-made equipment in front of the curious rebels. No one got *too* close, however, because Kit's constructs were waiting nearby. One of the large ones had been damaged in the fight, and several of the medium and small models destroyed, but there were still almost two dozen of the spider-like things, and they made the Communards nervous. Every time one of them moved, people flinched and reached for their weapons. Kit had obviously noticed this and made a game of twitching their legs at odd moments.

Gyre was still keeping her—and the fact that the constructs could talk—secret. *One thing at a time.*

When he and Elariel emerged, the rebels crowded a little closer. Vaela and Fillow were there for the Blacks, attended by several well-armed guards, and Maeris still represented the Greens after Geston's death in the ambush. The two Whites had been replaced by a dozen, all arguing with one another incessantly and insisting on their authority to represent the whole. Sarah, who had been demonstrating a few of their alchemicals, turned eagerly to Gyre as he came up.

"Finally," Vaela said. "Bombs are all very well, but that's not how you beat the centarch. What do you really have for us?"

"Let me demonstrate." Gyre gestured for Elariel to take a few steps back. "The harness my companion is wearing is designed to block most manifestations of *deiat*. It has its limit—it won't stop the blade of a haken, for example—but it can protect the wearer against most long-range attacks, including blasters."

Sarah held out a blaster rifle, and Gyre took it up and put it to his shoulder. Elariel squared off, unsmiling, and Gyre silently hoped that Tyraves hadn't stiffed them. He fought the urge to aim wide, and pulled the trigger.

The bolt *cracked*, flashed across the intervening space, and splashed like water around Elariel instead of exploding. The gathered crowd gasped, and Gyre let out a relieved breath.

"This sword," Gyre went on, drawing his weapon, "is of ghoul manufacture. Where an ordinary weapon would break against unmetal, it will hold." Sarah, on cue, swung lightly at Gyre with an unmetal blade looted from a dead Legionary. Gyre parried, drawing a fat spark, and the two blades scraped against each other. "It will also penetrate unmetal armor, if you have the strength and aim for the weaker sections."

"What about your monsters?" someone yelled from the Whites.

"They're not monsters," Gyre said, raising his voice to drown out a rising hubbub. "They're constructs. They may resemble plaguespawn, but I assure you they are quite different, and firmly under my control." He beckoned, and one of the medium constructs trotted over. "Roll over," he told it, and pictured Kit laughing as the thing flipped awkwardly on its back.

"Can anyone command them?" Vaela said. "Or just you?"

Depends what kind of a mood she's in. "Me, or those who I designate," Gyre said.

"And how many of these weapons have you brought us?" Maeris said, eyeing the wagons. "Not enough for an army, I take it."

"No," Gyre said. "Three dozen blades, as many shields, and the constructs you see here. Plus the alchemicals, medicines, and other sup-plies. But this is only the beginning." He spread his hands, feeling a little bit like a carnival barker or dubious loadbird salesman. "I have sources in the north that can assure us a steady supply, once we prove that we can take the fight to the Republic."

"In exchange for what?" Vaela said.

"In exchange for us using these weapons *to* fight the Republic. Our cause has allies. They can't speak openly, but they want to help none-theless." It wasn't *too* bald a lie. *Just don't mention that those allies have fur and fangs.*

"And what about the dangers?" A young man stepped forward from the ranks of the Whites, ignoring the angry muttering of his neighbors.

"The dangers?" Gyre said. "To whom?"

"To all of us!" He spread his hands. "You can dance around the sub-ject as much as you like, but we all know where these weapons came from. You didn't dig them up from some cave." He turned to face the assembled rebels. "These are *dhak*, and Gyre is a *dhakim*."

There was a moment of quiet muttering. The young man turned again to point at Gyre.

"We all know the dangers of *dhak*," he said. "It attracts plaguespawn and turns men into monsters."

Gyre, who had been expecting something like this, opened his mouth to reply, but Elariel beat him to it. She stomped over, thrusting her finger in the young man's face, her expression so thunderous that he flinched backward.

"*Dhaka* is not responsible for the plaguespawn," she snapped. "Nor does it create monsters, when under the control of a responsible practi-tioner. The people you call *dhakim* are meddlers and fools."

The man rallied. "And Silvereye is better than that?"

"Of course not." Elariel snorted. "*I* am."

Another, more fragile silence. Very carefully, Vaela said, "You are . . . a *dhakim*?"

In answer, the ghoul snatched a handful of long-stemmed grass from the forest floor. She gave it a long look, and it started to writhe on its own, stalks weaving deftly around one another and curling back on themselves. In a few seconds, a small bird made of braided grass stood in her hand, hopping stiffly and ruffling its wings. Elariel held it out toward the White, who recoiled as though she'd offered him a poisonous snake. She snorted and let the thing fall to the ground.

"Call it what you like," she said. "But the ones you call *dhakim*, who sell poison and create monsters, are as much like a true practitioner as an ape with a carving knife is a butcher."

"This..." Vaela shook her head and looked at Gyre. The old woman seemed genuinely shaken. "*These* are the allies who want to join us?"

"And why not?" Gyre raised his voice. "*Dhak* is what the Order calls things they don't think we can be trusted with, because they want to keep us under their control. Yes, it can be dangerous. So can a sword, if you don't know how to use it. That danger doesn't mean the Order gets to treat the entire rest of humanity like children, while conveniently keeping anything that might be a threat to their dominance out of our hands. If *dhak* is what it takes to overthrow the Republic—and to protect ourselves afterward, from plaguespawn or anything else—then so be it."

More muttering, and a few scattered cheers. Vaela was frowning, and the young man from the Whites looked unconvinced, but at least nobody was actually running away.

For now.

"You might have told *me*, at least," Apphia said.

"Why?" Gyre folded up the sketched map. "Would you have turned me in to the Order as a *dhakim*?"

"You know I wouldn't." Apphia sighed. "I could have given you a little bit of warning, that's all."

"I was hoping to take a little longer to get everyone used to the idea," Gyre said. "The ambush forced my hand."

"I know." Apphia hesitated, then shook her head. "You really think this plan will work? These . . . constructs are smart enough to obey such complex orders?"

"They'll manage," Gyre said. "I'm more worried about the banners, to be honest."

Apphia barked a laugh. "Fair enough. I'll make it clear to them that if they're not willing to fall in line, we don't want their help. None of them want to be left out of the glorious victory."

Gyre held out the folded map. "You're sure you don't want my help explaining things?"

"I think it's better if it comes from me," Apphia says. "Brennard will back me up, if I need it. You and Sarah have preparations to make."

Gyre nodded. "Good luck, then."

"Thanks. Where Vaela's involved, I'll take all the luck I can get." She smiled, clapped him lightly on the shoulder, and left the tent.

It was getting on toward evening, and the light coming through the canvas was turning crimson. Gyre slipped outside himself and found the camp painted with long shadows. Dinner was in progress around a dozen cook fires, and loadbirds pecked happily at handfuls of nyfa seeds.

The rebel leaders—to the extent anyone actually agreed who those were—convened to discuss the plan that Apphia and Gyre had spent most of the day working out. Gyre suspected they'd go along in the end, though he was learning not to count on anything where the banners were concerned. *But it's a good plan. And we're the ones who take on most of the risk, regardless.*

Sarah, Kit, and Elariel were working on one of their wagons, making the adjustments the plan required. Gyre headed in that direction, stomach rumbling to remind him that he hadn't eaten since breakfast. He was just contemplating a detour to the nearest bubbling soup pot when Nina Kotzed stepped from the shadowed side of a tent to stand in front of him.

"Silvereye," she said with a bow.

"Nina."

"Do you have a moment?"

"I suppose I do," Gyre said. "Is there a problem?"

"Not exactly." She looked down at her hands. "I just wanted to... thank you, I suppose."

"Thank me?"

"For saving my life, when the centarch attacked us." She swallowed. "I know you saved... all of us, really. But I heard what you said to Apphia, that you'd come and get me."

"Ah." Gyre felt obscurely embarrassed. "I could hardly have just stood by."

"You could have run away," Nina said. "Everyone else was. *I* would have, if I thought I'd had a chance." She looked up at him. "You've done that before? Fought a centarch?"

"Once," Gyre said.

"It was the first time I'd ever even seen one. The way she killed Geston... it wasn't even a fight. More like squashing an ant."

"That's what we are to them," Gyre muttered. "Or they like to think so."

"I wasn't even scared, you know?" Nina said. "Not really. I remember thinking, 'Well, fuck. This is where I die, then.' But I wasn't *scared*. I'd always wondered if, when the time came, I would be."

"I saw you shooting back," Gyre said.

"There didn't seem like much else I could do," she said. "Anyway. I just thought I should thank you properly. I know you didn't do it for my sake, but it still means I'm alive instead of dead, and that counts for something, right?"

"Of course it does," Gyre said. "And I'm glad you're okay."

"Right." Nina hesitated a moment. "You should tell my sister you're interested in her."

"I'm... that is, I'm not..."

The girl rolled her eyes. "For what it's worth, I think she likes you, too. Just... be kind to her, would you? She's not as hard as she sometimes pretends to be."

"I don't think—"

"Shhh," Nina said, putting a finger to his lips. "Go finish your plans. Big day tomorrow, right?"

Not long after first light the following morning, Gyre was on the box of one of his wagons, sitting beside Apphia while Sarah rode on the roof behind them. The pair of loadbirds pulled them down the rutted track, the wagon's springs creaking with every rock and hole in the road. It was considerably lighter than it had been the night before, and they made good time, crossing through a belt of semiwild grassland as they climbed the hill on which the Spire stood.

The ancestral home of the Kotzeds was more impressive up close. The central tower was enormous, nearly as high as the Spike in Deepfire if you counted the multipronged protrusions that caught the descending lightning. Around its base, an unmetal wall rose five meters high, with the second stories of some buildings within visible over the top. The path they were following led directly to a rectangular gate, big enough that two carts could pass through it side by side. Three Legionaries stood outside, checking incoming traffic, and Gyre could see more Auxies on guard within.

The gate lacked a conventional door, as Apphia had explained the night before. Instead, the Spire's gates were still controlled by a Chosen-built system. An unmetal barrier was held in place above the gateway, and at a signal from a control room inside the Spire it would fall straight down, blocking any access to the fortress. Raising it again required a winch and a team of draft animals.

"Which means," Apphia had said, "if we want to get in there without having to lay siege to the place or scale the walls, we need to get someone in that control room before they figure out what's going on."

Not impossible. In theory. But theory, in Gyre's experience, was a poor guide once the swords came out. He checked his own equipment, one more time, as the guards came into view. His silver sword was at his side, and the energy bottle hung from his hip, looking like an innocuous canteen. Two more were in his small pack, along with a selection of alchemicals. Sarah, sitting behind him, had a larger pack full of bombs and a concealed blaster pistol.

Apphia, for her part, wore one of the ghoul swords and carried herself like she knew how to use it. She also had a pistol, tucked out of casual view, and more importantly she and Sarah both wore the ghouls' protective harness under their clothes.

And then, of course, there were the contents of the wagon. *Hopefully it'll be enough.*

"They won't recognize you?" Gyre said as they pulled up behind a hay wagon at the gate. The Legionaries were checking papers with a show of diligence.

"Probably not." She pulled her three-cornered hat down to shade her face. "You'd better talk to them, though, just in case."

Gyre took the rolled papers from her and put on his best bored smile. The hay wagon rumbled in, and he clicked his tongue to get the loadbirds to amble forward a few steps. The white-armored Legionary came up beside the vehicle, expression invisible beneath the eyeless, insectoid helmet.

"What've you got here?" the man said.

"Some post and orders for the Spire," Gyre said. Rather than trying to conceal his accent, they'd agreed he should pose as a traveling merchant. "Northern cloth and silverwork for the market."

"Market day isn't until tomorrow," the soldier said. "You've got a receipt for those orders?"

"Thought I'd spend the night off the road," Gyre said, handing one of the papers over. "Been on this thing so long my arse is full of splinters."

The Legionary looked over the paper. It had been prepared for them by one of the Whites, who'd had experience in the service of the Lightning Barons and was confident he could forge the necessary signatures.

Gyre was less sure, and he suppressed a sigh of relief when the soldier rolled the bundle up and handed it back to him.

"Try Longbeard's, if you're looking for an inn," the man said. "The wine at the Barrelhead is swill."

"I shall, and thank you kindly for the tip," Gyre said with a grin. He clicked his tongue again, and the birds slowly ambled on, the wagon groaning a little. Sarah waved cheekily to the guard as they went past, but he was already looking for the next traveler in line.

"See?" Apphia said. "Easy."

"We're not there yet," Gyre said.

Inside the wall, the Spire itself was surrounded by a large dirt yard, which probably doubled as a market square. A large wooden stable adjoined the unmetal building, with several warbirds poking their heads out through narrow slots to watch passing traffic. Around the edge of the yard, up against the inside of the outer wall, there was a ring of timber-and-plaster buildings, including the two inns the guard had mentioned. A number of other merchants had apparently arrived early for market day and sold goods either out of their carts or from folding stalls.

"That's good," Sarah said. "Pull us up by that girl selling rugs."

Gyre twitched the reins. The rug merchant gave them an irritated look as their wagon rumbled to a halt but didn't otherwise make trouble. Apphia hopped down and started scattering seeds for the birds, while Gyre hurried around to the back of the wagon. He opened the rear door, carefully, and climbed inside. The air was dark and close and smelled of alchemy.

"You have no idea how much I'm looking forward to this," Kit said.

"So you've mentioned," Gyre said, picking up a wrapped bundle from the floor. "Several times."

"Well, it's not like I have much else to do," Kit said. "And Sarah's a genius. I never would have thought of this."

"Try not to get carried away," Gyre said. "We're not here to burn the place down or kill any civilians."

"Auxies and Legionaries are fair game, right?"

"Unless they're running away."

"You and your rules." Limbs clicked as Kit's little spider danced in excitement. "How long do you need to get inside?"

Gyre estimated the distance to the Spire and made a mental calculation. "Give us five minutes."

"Got it," Kit said. "Do you know that I'm now capable of keeping time down to ten-thousandths of a second?"

"Just make sure it's *five minutes'* worth of... micro-pico-seconds or whatever."

"Does that start from the moment you turn around, or after you get clear of the door, or—"

"*Kit.*"

"I'm just excited!"

Gyre hoisted the bundle onto his shoulder and headed outside, trying not to visibly hurry his steps. *Because the ten-thousandths of a second are undoubtedly ticking away.* He gestured for Sarah and Apphia to join him, and together they cut across the yard toward the open door at the base of the Spire. Two more Legionaries stood guard here, and the only people coming in or out were Auxies in steel caps.

"Greetings," Gyre said as they came close. He held up the bundle. "Orders to deliver for the Spire."

"Papers?"

"Here you are." Gyre handed over the bundle, and the soldier peered at it.

"For Decarch Trillus?" she said. "He's not here anymore. Transferred back to Skyreach last week."

"That's... a shame," Gyre said, acutely aware of the wagon behind him and time hissing away. "Perhaps his replacement would be interested in these fine hunting weapons?"

The second guard snorted. "I don't think Vanat would know a hunting weapon from a poker, or care."

"That's the truth," the first guard said. "You may be out of luck. Maybe someone at the market tomorrow will be interested."

"I would like to at least speak to the decarch," Gyre said, not having to feign nervousness. "You never know."

"Fair enough." The Legionary handed his papers back. "Bottom floor, toward the back. He should be at his desk."

"Thank you." Gyre sketched a bow and pushed forward, a bit hurriedly. *Five minutes has to be nearly up—*

No sooner had they passed through the arched doorway than there was a terrific *boom* from out in the yard. Glancing over his shoulder, Gyre saw that their wagon had blown apart, as they had carefully rigged it to do. The bomb didn't actually carry much force, but it made a great deal of noise and smoke, throwing the wooden sides of the wagon into the unfortunate rug seller's stall and sending out an expanding cloud of oily black vapor. The loadbirds bolted, running to the ends of their tethers and squawking for all they were worth.

It wasn't until the smoke started to churn with movement that people began screaming. Kit's constructs leapt from the wreckage of the wagon, two dozen tiny black spiders skittering in every direction across the square. Each wore a leather strap with a couple of alchemical bombs attached; Sarah and Kit had worked hard last night coming up with a fuse her limbs could easily manipulate. One of the spiders darted in among a line of loadbirds at a water trough and pulled its fuse. A moment later, the stunner went off with a blinding light and a roar, sending the terrified birds stampeding in all directions.

"Something's loose!" One of the Legionaries outside began shouting commands. "Seal the door, round up second and third squads. You two, with me!" She ran off, a half dozen Auxies at her heels, and her companion hurried in the opposite direction.

Gyre, Sarah, and Apphia, meanwhile, were standing in an anteroom with another two dozen Auxies. The Spire's layout was a square, with two opposite corners occupied by tightly curled spiral staircases, and wooden partitions dividing the original unmetal structure into smaller rooms. The first floor housed a guardroom and steel-capped soldiers were boiling out of it. Four of them shut the heavy doors and lowered a bar. None of the Auxies seemed to have noticed their uninvited guests.

"Lead the way," Gyre hissed as more *booms* echoed through the unmetal from outside. Apphia nodded and started walking toward the closest staircase.

They nearly made it. A large Auxie sergeant coming down the stairs emerged immediately in front of them and blinked.

"Who are *you* supposed to be?" He raised his voice, one hand going to his sword. "What in the name of the Chosen is going—"

Sarah's ghoul-made arm shot out, grabbing him by the collar. In one smooth motion she hurled him over her shoulder, his helmet striking the stone-flagged floor with a gong-like *clang*. At the same time, Gyre reached into his pack with both hands and came up with a pair of stunners, which he hurled to the ground on either side of the sergeant. As every eye in the room focused on the flailing man, the bombs went off, their searing light provoking a chorus of swearing and confused shouts. A crossbow went off, the bolt sticking in the plaster ceiling with a crunch.

"Follow me!" Apphia said, sprinting up the stairs.

Gyre pounded after her, Sarah close behind. The stairway was awkwardly close, coiled to fit inside an unmetal tube that Gyre suspected had once contained something like the lifters he'd seen in Refuge. His head was spinning as they passed the second floor, where more Auxies were too surprised to do anything but shout as they went past. Sarah pulled a sparker from her pack and tossed it behind them, where it began to fizz and throw off fat white motes that sizzled as they burned.

Another floor, and another, the stairway opening onto corridors lined with closed doors. Gyre's legs were burning, and Sarah was breathing hard. Apphia, up ahead, didn't even seem out of breath when she shouted back, "Next level!"

Here we go. Gyre concentrated on his augmentations and felt the *click* in his skull. Suddenly running was effortless, power drawn from the energy bottle supporting his merely human muscles. Apphia was nearly at the next doorway, and Gyre had to slow down to avoid crashing into her. She ducked into the room beyond, shadow-selves darting ahead of her. Behind him, Sarah was lighting another sparker in slow motion. Once the doorway was clear, Gyre leapt, floating lazily up the stairs, then grabbed the top of the doorway with both hands and pulled himself through.

This floor—the fifth, if he was counting correctly—was largely open. They were well above the outer wall by now, and broad windows gave a view out across the surrounding countryside. Each side had a spyglass on a swiveling stand, so guards here could scan the forests and hills. A large table in the center of the room bore a map with scraps of paper pinned all over it.

Apphia was headed for one out-of-the-way corner where an unmetal pedestal topped by three faceted crystals was positioned. A large iron lever was attached to the central crystal, human metalwork crude in contrast to the Chosen device, but the purpose was clear—if the lever was pulled, the crystal would be yanked from its socket. This, presumably, would release the gates outside, causing them to slam down over the four gateways in the outer wall and transforming the Spire into a near-impregnable fortress.

No one had gone for it yet, since the explosions and confusion were *inside* the walls. The three of them were there to make sure no one had a chance. There were eight or nine Auxies in the room, staring at the map or peering through the spyglasses. Gyre drew his silver sword and stepped forward as the shadow-Auxies started, slowly, to turn in his direction.

There was a moment of blurred motion.

"Chosen *fucking* defend," Apphia said.

She'd drawn her own blade but only managed a few steps into the room before it was over. Gyre yanked his sword free of the throat of the last Auxie, a green-haired woman who'd barely had time to look up from her spyglass. She fell, blood gouting between her fingers as she futilely clutched at the wound. A portly older man with an officer's insignia, slumped against the map table, gave a gurgle as he subsided onto the floor. The air was suddenly thick with the scent of blood and death.

Gyre let the shadow-world fade away, flicking blood off his sword. He tried to suppress the roil in his stomach. Auxies served the Republic, they were as guilty as anyone, but this felt like winning a fistfight with a toddler. He averted his eyes from the man who was noisily dying under the table and pointed to the arcana device in the corner.

"That's the gate control?" he said.

"Y...yeah." Apphia shook her head, regaining her composure.

"Any chance we can disable it?"

She shook her head. "It's designed as a deadman's switch. Break the alignment of the crystals and the gates fall. Besides, if this works, we're going to need it later."

"Okay." Gyre looked around the corpse-strewn room. It had two entrances at opposite corners, leading to the twin stairwells. "Then we have to hold out here until this is over. Sarah?"

"Here!" Sarah ducked out of the stairway. "The Auxies are still stuck at the sparkers, but that won't last. I saw Legionaries."

"Signal the others," Gyre said.

"Right!" The arcanist dashed to the south window. She pulled another bomb from her pack, adjusted the fuse, and reached out through the iron grating to toss it upward. At the apex of its flight, it burst with a *whoomph*, expanding into a rising column of bright blue smoke.

"That's going to tip off every soldier outside," Gyre said. "We have to hold the doors."

Apphia nodded grimly, sheathing her sword and drawing her blaster pistol. Sarah took up a position near the door they'd entered by, and Gyre went to the other, peeking out to look down the spiral. He heard booted feet on the stone flags and caught a glimpse of white armor.

"Legionaries coming!" Sarah shouted.

Gyre checked his energy bottle—three-quarters full—and engaged his augments again, letting time slow to a crawl. On the other side of the room, Sarah tossed a bomb down the center of the stairwell. It detonated with a low roar a few moments later. Apphia leaned out into the smoke and fired, blaster *cracking*. She pulled her head back as more blasters answered, rifle bolts blowing chunks out of the stone and raining splinters.

On Gyre's side, three Legionaries broke into a sprint, coming around the last spiral. Gyre waited until they'd reached the landing, then spun out into the doorway, much faster than they'd expected. The first tried to get his blaster up, but the hilt of Gyre's sword slammed into the side of his helmet, knocking him off-balance and tipping him over the edge of the spiral. He hit the next level down with a clatter of unmetal on stone. The soldiers behind him drew swords, but in the tight confines of the stairwell they were stuck coming on single file. Gyre parried the first man's thrust, feinted low, and jammed the tip of his silver sword into the Legionary's throat, through the thin armor there. He staggered back, forcing his companion to back up with him, and Gyre yanked a stunner from his belt and tossed it right in their faces, ducking back through the doorway before it went off with a thunderclap.

"You two all right?" he shouted.

"So far," Sarah said with an excitement that reminded him of Kit. She had a bomb in either hand, watching the figures struggling up the steps through the smoke. When they reached the point just below her on the stairway she tossed both down after them. "Going to run out of surprises pretty quick at this rate."

"Kit should be keeping them busy outside," Gyre said. "And we don't have to hold for long."

Hopefully. He badly wanted to use one of the spyglasses to see if the others were coming, but he had no time. There was shouting below, a filiarch issuing orders, and more boots on stone. Peering out, he caught a glimpse of white-armored forms ascending, before a volley of blaster fire slammed past. He ducked back hastily, but the hammering fusillade continued, forcing him to stay out of the doorway while the soldiers ascended.

Too plaguing smart by half. He grimaced, flattening himself beside the doorway, and waited. It was only moments before the first Legionary plunged through, crouching behind a wide unmetal shield. Gyre's strike, aimed at her throat, rebounded, and he swore again. She danced away from him, and another Legionary filled the doorway, sword in hand.

Not good. If he was surrounded, they'd get to him eventually, ghoul-granted speed or no. Gyre charged the man in the doorway, waiting for him to parry a high thrust and then switching to a low rush that planted his silver blade under the edge of the soldier's cuirass. It bit through and the man gasped and staggered, but the woman who'd been first into the room had already drawn her sword and was coming at him from behind. Gyre spun free, his off hand grabbing a bomb from his pack and tossing it into the stairwell over the stricken Legionary's head. It went off with a roar, but the soldiers kept coming, two more pulling their wounded comrade back and rushing through.

On the other side of the room, Apphia and Sarah had been forced back from the doorway by another shield-bearing Legionary. Apphia tossed her pistol aside and drew her sword, meeting the soldier's descending unmetal blade with a horrible squeal. The next Legionary through the door shot Sarah in the chest at point-blank range, but the blaster bolt fizzled into nothing, and she punched him hard enough to send him crashing into the man behind him and out onto the stairs.

How many of the plaguing bastards are there? Gyre was faster than any of them, but he was trying to watch three directions at once. He darted in, letting the blade of the Legionary in the doorway slip over his head, and jabbed his sword through the back of the man's thigh. The soldier started to fall, fouling the one behind him, and Gyre spun away to deal with the woman who'd gotten past him. She was already charging across the room toward Apphia, ready to spit the rebel leader from behind. Gyre pushed off to follow, running with great leaping strides, sword extended to thrust into the small of the Legionary's back. Before he got there, though, she half turned, raising her shield in time. Gyre spun past her, getting back-to-back with Apphia.

"Sarah!" he shouted. "Keep them off the switch!"

Sarah, tossing yet another Legionary down the stairs, gave a nod and dug in her pack for a pair of bombs. She hurled them at the flagstones just in front of the door controls. A slick of liquid fire spilled out, turning that quarter of the room into a sea of flame.

Apphia parried another blow, and her riposte scored under her opponent's armpit, sending him reeling backward with a curse. Another Legionary came forward, while Gyre battered unsuccessfully at his opponent's shield. He couldn't get around her without leaving Apphia vulnerable—

"Roll left on three!" Gyre said, hoping the Legionaries wouldn't hear over the screech and clang of ghoul blades on unmetal. He thought he saw a nod. His own opponent bulled forward, trying to slam her shield into him, and Gyre backed as far as he could against Apphia. He felt her tense. At the same moment, they both ducked and rolled sideways, leaving the two Legionaries suddenly confronting one another. Before the one with the shield could turn, Gyre slashed hard across the light armor of her inner thigh, opening the artery there in a welter of blood. Apphia, skidding to a halt, pivoted on her back foot and thrust into her opponent's side, sending him groaning to the stones.

That was two down, and too many to go. There were a half dozen Legionaries in the room, and more coming in. Sarah was backing toward the corner she'd set afire, feinting at two men with a bomb in either hand. Apphia, hair drenched with sweat and breathing hard, stood beside Gyre, the point of her sword unwavering. Gyre's energy bottle was growing hot to the touch, nearly empty. And outside—

Gyre let himself grin and straightened out of his fighting crouch. He raised his voice.

"*Stop!*"

For a moment, they did, perhaps because it was so unexpected. Three Legionaries faced them, swords drawn, while another moved to help one of their wounded comrades.

"Drop your weapons, and you'll live until the dux hangs you," a woman growled at him.

"I have a counterproposal," Gyre said. "Take a look outside."

They hesitated, expecting a trick, but Gyre didn't move. One by one, the armored soldiers risked a quick look out the window.

Down below, everything was chaos. A dozen lancers on warbirds were in the yard, riding down Auxies, while rebels armed with spears and crossbows fanned out from the gates. The flags of the Khirkhaz Commune—white, black, green, but red above all—were everywhere. A few Legionaries were still fighting around the northern gate, holding a perimeter with blaster fire while Auxies fled past them.

"It's over," Gyre said. In the corner, the flames crackled. "Spire Kotzed has fallen. You can either take your wounded and try to get away with your friends down there, or try to kill us and end up rebel prisoners no matter what happens." His grin widened. "I suggest you choose quickly."

"*Bastard*," the woman hissed.

Gyre gave a modest shrug. He tried not to show the tension in every limb and the rapid beating of his heart, or the relief that ran through him when the Legionaries, after a moment of silent consultation, began to retreat. Three blades stayed aimed at Gyre and Apphia while the rest gathered their limp, bleeding comrades, and only then did they retreat down the stairs.

"Want me to drop something on them?" Sarah said, rising from her crouch.

It would probably be the wise choice, since every dead Legionary was one fewer they'd have to face when the Republic launched a counterattack. But Gyre shook his head, flicking the blood from his blade and letting himself drop out of the shadow-world.

"I think," he said, "we've done enough for one day. Don't you?"

"Glorious!" Fillow said. "A charge of lancers, just like all the songs! Glorious!" He climbed to his feet and raised a wooden tankard. "To Brennard of the Commune and his brave companions!"

The rest of the table gave him a cheer. This was no great feat, since the feast was several hours old, and most of those doing the cheering were already well into their cups. Fillow himself was flushed a furious red, and his great-grandmother, several tables down, wasn't far behind.

Spire Kotzed had, indeed, fallen. The Auxies and Legionaries in the fortress hadn't had time to organize a defense of the gates when the doors didn't come down, distracted as they were by Kit's rampant spider-constructs. Brennard's lancers—what was left of the chivalry of the old barony—had been equipped with *deiat* shields, and when a volley of blaster bolts failed to stop them the Republic soldiers had broken before their charge.

Fewer than a dozen rebels had fallen, and at least a hundred Auxies and even a few Legionaries had surrendered. It was quite a victory, by any standard, but Gyre was getting a little tired of listening to some of the grandiose talk. He got up from his spot at the table, grabbing a piping hot roll from a passing tray, and stuffed it into his mouth as he went in search of Apphia.

Tables had been set up all the way around the yard outside the Spire, and filled with food and drink dragged up from the fortress's stores. Sarah was already well ensconced at one of them, drinking with a circle of rebel soldiers in the midst of huge cheers and laughter. To Gyre's surprise, Elariel was with her, pressed against her side and flinching at every shout, but not yet in flight to the safety of her wagon. One of Kit's small constructs skittered nearby, adding to the commotion.

Another one found its way to Gyre as he circled the yard, climbing up to his shoulder.

"Congratulations," Kit said. "We won!"

"For the moment," Gyre said. "Is anyone on watch?"

"You mean besides me?" Kit said. "Apphia put some of Brennard's people on it. And I've got one of my bodies up by the gate switch."

"Good," Gyre said. "Have you seen Apphia?"

"She's over at the north gate," Kit said. The spider poked him in the side of the head, which he guessed was supposed to be the equivalent of an elbow in the ribs. "Time for a rendezvous, eh? Eh?"

"I just want to check that she's all right," Gyre said. "It's not— *Ow,* that was my *ear.*"

"Oops." Kit gave a squawk as he grabbed the little spider and set it gently but firmly on the ground. "Hey!"

"No passengers needed," Gyre said. "Sorry."

"I call that rude," Kit said. "Let a girl see a little skin."

"It's not—never mind." Gyre shook his head. "I'll see you in the morning."

It's not like that. Is it? It wasn't that he hadn't *noticed* Apphia, of course. She was very different from Kit, tall and well-built where Kit was slender, reserved instead of wild. There was something about her that reminded Gyre of Yora, a little. *Maybe just the distance she keeps from everyone. Part of being in command, I suppose.*

Nina had said... *Well. It's not important.*

He rounded the corner of the Spire and nearly ran into her, stalking away from a chastened-looking group of rebels guarding the northern gate. She pulled up short at the sight of him, and Gyre gave her an awkward wave.

"Trouble?" he said.

"Not really," she said. "Just a few on watch who needed a reminder that they need to *be* on watch and not sneaking off to have a drink."

"Ah."

After a moment, she started back toward the Spire, and Gyre fell in beside her.

"It will probably take some time for the Republicans to reorganize," he ventured. "We caught them out pretty badly."

"That's my hope," Apphia said. She beckoned him closer and lowered her voice. "But this was too easy. They must have known we were going to try *something.* They could have reinforced this place, been on high guard. But they didn't."

"Maybe they didn't think we'd dare try for it."

"Maybe. I just hope we haven't played into their hands. I just..." She stopped, looking down.

"Hey," Gyre said. "Are you all right?"

"I've been working for this for a decade," she said. "This is my home. Nina's home. But now that I've got it, it feels like it won't be enough. The Republic will come back, and..." She let out a sigh. "I don't know. I can't stop thinking about their next move."

"A victory is a victory," Gyre said. "And I doubt their next move will come before morning. You can afford to relax for one evening, can't you?"

"Maybe. Probably." Apphia let out a long breath, and some of the tension went out of her shoulders. "You're not getting drunk with the rest of them?"

"I thought about it," Gyre said. "Maybe I'm having trouble not thinking about the next move, too."

She cocked her head. "If you're at loose ends, there's something I'd like to show you. Up in the spire."

Gyre raised an eyebrow. "Oh?"

Some of Brennard's soldiers were on duty at the base of the building, resolutely ignoring the antics of their drunken companions, and Gyre was glad to see another detail in place on the fifth floor around the gateway switch. Two of Kit's spider-constructs were there, too, watching out the windows as the last of the autumn sun disappeared and the stars came out over the forest one by one. Apphia waved but kept climbing, round and round the tiny spiral staircase. Gyre surreptitiously rubbed his burning thighs when she paused at a landing.

"Where are we going?"

"My old room," she said. "I wanted to see what they'd left of it. It doesn't look like they used the upper part of the tower."

"I can see why," Gyre said, peering down the apparently endless stairway. "Your room was all the way up here?"

"Another two levels up, actually," she said. "And my father and mother were the level above that."

"Your family must have been in *terrific* shape."

Apphia snorted a laugh. "You get used to it after a while."

They ascended, winding two more times around the open hole at the center of the staircase.

"Father experimented with a bucket on a rope, to get food and laundry up and down faster," Apphia said.

"How'd that go?"

"Poorly. It would start swinging and knock people off the stairs. A footman was nearly killed."

It was Gyre's turn to laugh. Apphia stopped at a dusty landing and gestured.

"Here we are. My room on the left, Nina's on the right."

A corridor led diagonally across the floor from one staircase to another, dividing it in half, with a door leading into each side. Apphia moved carefully to the one on the left, every step raising a haze of dust, and tried the latch. It swung inward with a creak.

"Feels like *nobody* has been up here since I left," she muttered. "Chosen above."

The triangular room was cozy, in spite of being covered in dust. At least some effort had at one point been made to preserve it, because the furniture was covered in dingy cloth. Tall bookshelves set into the far wall stood empty, and a hearth by the door was dead and cold.

Apphia started yanking on the dust cloths, exposing a threadbare sofa with a blue flower pattern and a massive wooden desk topped with a leather blotter. Gyre tried to imagine hauling either up all those steps and shuddered. Billows of dust filled the room, and Apphia coughed and went to the window. Glass shutters, now streaked with grime, had been installed into the gaps in the unmetal. She swung them wide open and leaned out.

"Here," she said. "Come look at this."

Gyre crossed the room and stood beside her. The window was a large one, with no iron bars blocking it like the lower levels. This high up the wind whipped and whistled, and the air was bracingly cold. Just outside was a narrow buttress, curving away from the square wall of the tower to support an intricate set of tall rods, part of the spiny crown of the Spire. Even as Gyre watched, blue-white auras flickered around them, building in preparation for the nightly display of arcing power.

After a moment steeling himself, Gyre looked down. His stomach gave an unpleasant lurch, and the soles of his feet tingled. While he'd undoubtedly *been* higher up—Deepfire was at the top of a mountain, after all—there was something about being able to look *straight* down that was unsettling, especially when his silver eye could resolve all the tiny wagons and miniature feasting people down below.

"I used to climb out there," Apphia said, a little dreamily. "It's not difficult, actually. The spines make for good handholds, and you can swing from buttress to buttress if you know what you're doing. One time I made it all the way around to Nina's window. Father was furious whenever I tried it, of course."

"I admit I can understand his point of view." Gyre pulled his head back in, watching the glow getting slowly brighter, then looked over his shoulder. "Is that where you got..." He touched his face, where Apphia's scar marked her, and she nodded.

"I stayed out too late," she said. "Silly, but when you live with lightning like we did, you can lose respect for it. I had my head out the window, watching, and..." She shrugged. "I don't even really remember it hurting much. But they tell me it was days before I could talk, so maybe my memory isn't to be trusted."

Gyre looked back out the window. Far overhead, lightning flickered from cloud to cloud, and there was a faint rumble like a shiver in the air. There was something hypnotic about the burgeoning aura, like watching the last embers of a fire, flaring and dying away but never quite going out. Behind him, he heard a rustle of cloth, and he turned to find Apphia had pulled her shirt over her head and started unwinding her chest wrap.

"Oh." Gyre blinked. "Are you—"

"I'm sorry." She paused. "Around here, when a woman invites you to her bedroom, the meaning is generally considered clear. Is it different in the north?"

"Not . . . exactly. But I didn't want to assume."

"Well. We should probably avoid the actual bed, since that sheet hasn't been changed in a decade, but the sofa seems all right." She finished removing her wrap, exposing her breasts. Gyre was fascinated with how her scar continued down her neck and across her well-muscled body, intricate, feathery marks of lightning curving to embrace one nipple and reaching almost to her belly button. "Or are you not interested after all? I've never been good with men, but I thought . . ."

There was a faint flush in her cheeks. Gyre shifted awkwardly.

"It's not that I'm . . . not interested," he said. "I just . . . you barely know me."

"We fought together. That's something." Apphia took a step forward and tugged his shirt up out of his trousers, then went to work on the buttons. "And you saved my sister's life, back at the camp."

"Apphia." Gyre put one hand on her shoulder and tilted her head up with the other to look in her eyes. "You don't owe me anything, not for that. You understand?"

"It's not about *owing*," she said with a snort. "It's about you being a person willing to risk his own life for someone who, as you say, you hardly know. Someone that *I* care about more than anyone in the world." She finished opening his shirt and put a palm against his bare chest. "It speaks . . . well of you."

"And you know I may not stay in Khirkhaz forever," he said. "If I have to go back north, to get more supplies, it might—"

"Chosen above, Gyre Silvereye," Apphia said, laughing. "I'm trying to get your pants off, not offering to marry you. Now, are you going to kiss me or not?"

For a moment, he saw Kit in his mind's eye, her rakish grin, the odd sweetness that came over her face when she was asleep beside him.

And then her voice. *"Fuck freely, okay? Or don't, but either way don't make it about me."*

Fair enough. He leaned in to kiss Apphia, his hands snaking around the small of her back to pull her close.

Outside the window, lightning flashed, close and bright, simultaneous with a *crack* and a long roll of thunder. The air suddenly smelled of ozone.

"When I was a girl," Apphia whispered between kisses, "I used to lie on this sofa and touch myself during the storm. Pretend it was my doing, like I was a centarch or a god. Ironic, I suppose, with how things turned out." She pressed herself tight against him. "I always wondered what it would be like, to bring a boy up here, but I never got the chance."

Gyre kissed her harder, running one hand alone the length of her intricate, twisted scar. Another deafening blast of thunder blotted out whatever he was going to say, but neither of them seemed to mind.

In the end, they'd pulled the soiled sheets off the bed and slept directly on the feather mattress, which hadn't weathered the years too badly. Gyre was exhausted enough that he fell asleep almost immediately, in spite of the rolling thunder that continued well into the night.

When he woke, it was past dawn, the sun lighting up dancing motes of dust like tiny fireflies. Gyre yawned and rolled over to face Apphia, who lay with her hands behind her head, staring absently at the ceiling.

"Does it bother you?" he said, after watching her for a long moment.

"Hmm?"

"This." He ran his fingers up the length of her scar, from her hip past her breast. "Would you get rid of it, if you could?"

"I've never really thought about it." Apphia touched his face, the overlapping marks around his silver eye. "I could ask you the same question."

"Fair." Gyre smiled. "It's certainly a pain when I need a disguise."

"I never even tried," Apphia said. "Mine is . . . a connection, in a way. My father had one, too, just on the back of his arm. A lot of the Lightning Barons get bitten by our homes, sooner or later."

"Some people might take that as a cue to stop living underneath a permanent thunderstorm."

"Oh, but what would be the fun in that?"

Apphia sat up and kissed him thoroughly. Gyre leaned into her, felt her fingers tighten on his arms as he ran his hands down her flanks. They were both sweaty and disheveled, but that might not have mattered; unfortunately, at that moment there came the sound of boots running down the hall and a hurried pounding on the door.

"Gyre!" Sarah's voice. "Baron!"

Apphia separated her lips from Gyre's and mouthed a silent oath. Gyre suppressed a chuckle and called out, "I'm here. What's wrong?"

"Trouble," Sarah said. "Republic scouts at the edge of the forest to the north. Legionaries and some of the dux's soldiers."

"You're sure it's not what's left of the garrison?"

"These are fresh," Sarah said. "Lots of warbirds. And ... I think I saw a centarch leading them."

Gyre's stomach contracted. Apphia was already rolling out of bed, picking up her scattered clothing.

"Are they getting any closer?" she said.

"Not so far," Sarah said. "It looks like they're making camp, a few kilometers out. Probably still waiting for the rest of their column to come up."

"We've got a little time, then. Get Brennard and the banner leaders. Gyre and I will be down soon." She raised an eyebrow at Gyre. "The next move appears to have arrived."

"It seems like it." Gyre frowned. *I thought we had more time.*

"Well, this time *we're* the ones with a fortress," Apphia said, shrugging into her shirt. "Let's see what we can do."

Chapter 16

Maya had passed through the Gate at the Forge a number of times, but never as part of such a large expedition. At most it had been her, Jaedia, Marn, and a wagon with a single loadbird, or more recently on foot with Beq, Varo, and Tanax. Now, though, the big stone chamber was crowded with a half dozen two-bird carts piled high with tents and supplies. Squeezed around them was a full company of Legionaries, more than a hundred soldiers and officers, standing in neat rows by squads. At the front, near the Gate itself, Prodominus conferred with a pair of scouts, a man and a woman, both with the look of veterans. Va'aht stood nearby in full armor, with an unmetal helmet tucked under his arm and the reins of his warbird in hand.

Maya didn't own a suit of armor and wasn't sure how she would go about getting one. She'd never felt the lack—with a panoply for protection, she'd always figured a centarch's armor was more for intimidation than actual effect. Her stomach prickled, though, and she thought back uncomfortably to her fight with Gyre. *A little armor might have come in handy there.* Prodominus didn't seem to have any, though, wearing a traveling outfit under a long cloak lined with dark fur. His wild hair and beard, nearly obscuring his face, looked more suited among preparations for war than they ever had sitting behind his desk.

Servant of the enemy. That's what Ashok had called him. As Maya watched, he laughed hugely and slapped the woman scout on the back. *Basel doesn't trust him either. But Ashok doesn't trust Basel.* She closed her eyes. *My head hurts.*

"Good morning," Varo said, slipping in beside her. "This is already my favorite kind of expedition."

"What's that?" Maya said.

"The kind where I don't have to carry my own pack," Varo said, indicating the heavy carts. "And I have you to thank."

"You may not be thanking me by the end," Maya said in a low voice. They'd explained everything they'd heard from Ashok to Varo the night before, when Maya had asked him if he was willing to come along. He'd agreed at once, but she wasn't sure he'd absorbed the full import of what she'd told him. "We could easily be walking into some sort of trap."

"Oh, of course. But what else is new? When you travel with Varo Plagueluck, you're always walking into *some* sort of trap, even if it's only a stray wasp's nest."

"You know nobody actually calls you that, right?"

Varo grinned. "Sometimes it's hard to make a good cognomen stick."

Maya turned at a touch on her other arm and found Beq there, green hair tightly braided and looking nervous behind her spectacles. She managed a quick smile.

"Hey."

"Hey," Maya said. She grabbed Beq's hand and squeezed, then impulsively leaned forward and kissed her. Beq gave a small squeak. "Are you all right?"

"Just...startled." Beq quickly kissed Maya back, then glanced around not very subtly to see if anyone was watching.

"We don't need to sneak about, you know," Maya said.

"I know." Beq made a face. "Bad habits are hard to shake."

"I had a friend who got in the habit of going for a little walk after dinner, to settle his stomach," Varo said. "One time, when we were camped in a swamp, he waved to everybody and off he went, and none of us thought twice about it. It wasn't until next morning that we figured out he'd stepped into a sinkhole. All we ever found was his hat."

"That's awful," Beq said.

"I don't know," Varo said. "It was a pretty nice hat."

"Fortunately," Maya said, "I don't think there are swamps in this part of Khirkhaz."

"Just forests," Varo confirmed. "Big, dark forests with lots of places for rebels to hide. Or plaguespawn, for that matter, or maybe—"

"I take it back," Maya said. "Plagueluck is perfect."

"All right!" Prodominus bellowed, his voice improbably loud in the confined space. "We're going through to Oak Fork Gate. The dux, Baron Rashtun, is meeting us there with Auxiliaries and his own forces, so let's not get too trigger-happy, all right? I'll take the lead with Centarchs Va'aht and Maya. Tourmarch Zinni, bring your soldiers through by squads afterward, and leave one behind the wagons as a rear guard. Understood?"

"Yes, Kyriliarch!" A diminutive Legionary with a colored insignia on her shoulder saluted. "First Squad, ready to march!"

Prodominus turned his attention to the Gate. Maya felt him send the coordinates as he fed it a stream of *deiat*, and the slender archway filled with milky white fog. The Kyriliarch strode through without hesitation, one hand on his haken. Va'aht followed, leading his warbird, and then the two old scouts. Maya tried not to feel a prickle of apprehension.

You never worried about going through a Gate with Jaedia. But that hadn't been on an expedition led by a possible traitor to the Order. She gritted her teeth and stepped through, Beq and Varo just behind her.

The other side of the Gate opened onto a pleasant morning by a bend in a small river. The arch stood against a rocky hillside, facing a stretch of clear ground along the bank. Forest spread in every direction, the first colors of autumn creeping in amid the green.

A small group of soldiers were waiting for them, facing the gate. In the center was a tall, hatchet-faced man, old enough that his dark purple hair was going gray at the temple, wearing intricate enameled armor. A younger woman, enough like him that Maya guessed she was his daughter, stood next to him, similarly clad, with another rank of armored figures a respectful half step back. Behind them, servants in red and gray livery held the reins of a line of warbirds.

"Honored Kyriliarch," the man said, his voice deep and gravelly. "Welcome to Khirkhaz. I have the honor to be Baron Gille Rashtun, dux by the appointment of our gracious Senate. This is my daughter, Lancer Fina Rashtun Tigereye."

The girl bowed. She did have yellow eyes, Maya noted, which were almost as bright as a cat's, and hair of nearly the same color.

"Thank you, Baron Rashtun," Prodominus said. "This is Centarch Va'aht Thousandcuts, Centarch Maya Burningblade, and Decarch Zinni."

"An honor," the baron said, bowing slightly. "With your help, I'm sure we will bring the campaign to a quick conclusion and avenge Centarch Niassa."

"I expect we will." Prodominus looked over his shoulder at the Gate, where the first ranks of Legionaries were coming through. "For the moment, if you would direct us to your camp? I'd like to get my soldiers settled before we go over the latest intelligence."

"Of course," the baron said. "Follow me."

The camp was far and away the largest Maya had ever seen. The caravan they'd followed north to Grace had sprawled over a considerable area with its various tents and wagons, but it hadn't been anywhere near this size, nor half as well organized. Neat rows of identical tents stretched under the trees, with stone firepits at regular intervals, flanked by staked-out rows of birds and teams of thickheads. Wagons parked in neat rows bulged with food and fodder. Men and women in Auxiliary uniform were everywhere, cooking breakfast, doing laundry, or sharpening weapons.

"Always wanted to see a proper army," Varo said as they followed the baron around the edge of the neat array. "Now I guess I have."

"There must be thousands," Maya said. She knew that duxes commanded large forces—Raskos Rottentooth had had more than a thousand soldiers just to administer Deepfire—but seeing so many soldiers in one place was still a shock.

"About two thousand, I think," Varo said. "A few more if you count the lancers."

Lancers? Maya noted that they'd passed the main camp and moved on to a separate, smaller section, where the tents were considerably larger and less severely organized. Liveried servants were everywhere, wearing an endless variety of colors, tending to warbirds and fetching food and water. Maya heard *music* from somewhere, a guitar accompanied by a woman's voice, and there was a ring of hammer on steel from a portable smithy.

"I'm proud to say that the chivalry of Khirkhaz has answered the call to arms," the baron said over his shoulder, leading them toward the largest of the tents. "We have two hundred lancers here, at least, and I expect more to join us on the march."

"Reassuring," Prodominus said. "Tourmarch, establish our camp nearby, if you would, and assign some of your people to support the dux's sentries."

"Yes, Kyriliarch." Zinni saluted and started shouting orders of her own. The column of soldiers broke apart, sorting itself out like a well-oiled machine. Va'aht had vanished somewhere, Maya noted, and Prodominus and his scouts were going off with the baron. She stood in the middle of the chaos, feeling lost.

"I suppose we should..." Maya looked over her shoulder at Varo and Beq. "Honestly, I have no idea what we should do."

"Prodominus doesn't seem to want your opinion," Varo said.

"We could help with the camp?" Beq said.

Tourmarch Zinni, however, seemed offended at the very sugges-tion and assured Maya that her Legionaries were more than capable of pitching tents and starting fires on their own. Maya watched them at it long enough to understand that she would only get in the way, then wandered back toward the lancers' camp. Varo excused himself, head-ing out in search of breakfast, but Beq stayed close on Maya's heels.

"Maya, wasn't it?"

Maya pulled up short and turned to find Fina Tigereye waiting beside her, still in armor, arms folded. A half dozen other young people were with her, all nobles by the cut of their expensive clothing. Some of their glares were distinctly unfriendly, and Maya found herself reach-ing for her haken. She refrained, straightening up instead.

"Centarch Maya Burningblade," she said. "Can I help you?"

"I didn't know centarchs came so young," said a boy at Fina's shoul-der, himself not much older than Maya.

"I am one of the youngest," Maya said. "I won my title in a duel with Centarch Tanax Brokenedge."

"Very glorious, I'm sure." Fina came closer. Unlike her companions, she was smiling. "Tell me, has your Kyriliarch said anything about who we'll be facing?"

Maya hesitated, taken aback. "The Commune, isn't it?"

Another girl snorted. "The Commune couldn't find its collective ass with a trained guide. You think they're the ones who killed a *centarch*?"

"Maybe they caught her while she was having a shit," one of the other boys said. "Or got her into bed and stuck a knife in her."

"Don't be an ass, Lian," Fina said. "Maya might have known this Niassa." She shook her head. "I apologize for my friends. They think this is all a great deal of trouble over nothing."

"And you don't?" Maya said.

"I think it's better to be safe than sorry," Fina said. She leaned closer. "And I think something strange is afoot. There've been rumors. That's why I thought you might know something more."

"Sorry," Maya said. "The Kyriliarch hasn't filled me in."

"Neither has Father." Fina sighed. "Well, I'm sure we'll get the news in due course. You just have to promise to leave some rebels for the rest of us, when it comes to that."

"That's right," one of the girls said. "It's been ages since we had a real dustup. Make sure not to ruin the fun by just..." She waved vaguely. "Blowing everybody away."

"I'll...do my best." Maya bowed. "If you'll excuse me.

She took Beq by the arm and led her back into the Legionary camp, where tents were also going up in neat rows, a mirror to the Auxiliaries'. "That was odd," she said to Beq when they were out of earshot.

"Was it?" Beq said. "I've never spent much time with nobles."

"Neither have I." She frowned in distaste. "They think this is some kind of game."

"Maybe it is, to them." Beq leaned closer. "Have you thought about how we're going to get to the Purifier without Prodominus finding out?"

Maya's frown deepened, and she shook her head. "Still working on it."

She'd hoped to consult with Varo about the problem that night but didn't get the chance. The Baron was throwing a feast, which Maya was apparently obligated to attend, and she spent the evening sitting beside Prodominus watching various lancers give impassioned toasts to the Republic and the Order. When she returned to the small tent she shared with Beq, wine and exhaustion put her to sleep immediately. This turned out to be for the best, because the soldiers began breaking camp before dawn the following morning, determined to use every hour of daylight available. Their first objective was Spire Kotzed, where Prodominus planned to establish a base and begin the hunt for the rebels.

For the most part, they walked, even the lancers. The army could travel no faster than its supply carts in any case, which trundled down the rocky forest trails slow enough that Maya could outpace them on foot. She kept to the front of the column, since no one seemed to need her for anything in particular, and at least that way she was out of the cloud of dust and bird shit that built up around the rear.

She caught sight of Prodominus, talking to Zinni and his scouts, and her chest tightened. Maya slowed her pace, intending to drop back out of sight, but the Kyriliarch dismissed the others with a wave and beckoned to her. She swallowed hard and walked over to him.

A servant of the ghouls. Ashok hadn't been sure about Baselanthus, but when it came to Prodominus he'd been adamant. *He can't be onto us yet, though.* If he knew about their plan to reach the Purifier, he wouldn't have brought Maya on the expedition in the first place. *Just stay calm.*

"Yes, Kyriliarch?" she said, and bowed.

"Maya," he said. "Walk with me."

She had little choice but to obey. The ordinary soldiers gave them a wide berth, leaving a broad clear space around them.

"Did you need something from me, Kyriliarch?" Maya said politely after a few moments of silence. She had to work to keep the anxiety out of her voice.

"We haven't had the chance to talk properly since you returned from the Archive, is all," Prodominus said. "I wanted to ask you for your impressions."

Plaguefire. "I noted everything I thought was relevant in my report, Ky—"

"I read it," he interrupted. "And you don't need the formality, not out here. We're all centarchs together until the mission is done."

Maya gave a noncommittal nod. "As you say. But if you've read my report..."

"Forget about the Archive for a minute. What did you think of the Forsaken Coast?"

"We...didn't see much of it, really," Maya said carefully. "Mostly it just seemed empty. The village we found—"

"I read about that too," Prodominus said. "Plaguing strange, that 'Eldest' creature. Some *dhakim* abomination."

"Probably," Maya said.

"Other expeditions reported no humans at all," he said. "Just plaguespawn, faster and deadlier than anything around here. That's what we encountered on my trip, certainly."

"You were on one of the expeditions?" Maya glanced over at him. "It wasn't mentioned in the reports."

"This was a long time ago. In my youth. I know it's hard for you young ones to believe I *had* a youth, but it's true." He gave a deep chuckle. "I was the most junior centarch on a team of six. We made it to the Archive, but only four of us came back."

"I'm...sorry."

He waved a hand. "That wound is decades old. My own master, Vindus Windborne, led the expedition. You've heard of him?"

"Only in passing," Maya said carefully. "I know he was a famous Revivalist."

"He was indeed. The doomed cause didn't feel quite so doomed, back then." He flashed a grin. "Vindus used to say that every centarch should have to travel the Forsaken Coast as part of their training."

Maya blinked. "Why?"

"Because it shows us what we're fighting for." He gestured around at the column. "Too many in the Order take all of *this* for granted. The Republic, the Legions, everything. But the coast was once just as much part of the Chosen Empire as Skyreach. When *we* pulled out, though, things just started downhill, until—well. You saw what was left. Either nothing at all, or poor bastards living under the thumb of some monster."

Maya thought about Calla, the fear in her eyes as they'd fought for the knife. The Eldest's bubbling voice. "*I will be exalted.*"

Prodominus was staring into the distance. Over the rumble of hundreds of boots, Maya could hear distant shouts, the scouts of the vanguard calling to one another.

The black spiders are servants of the ghouls, too. They had to be, didn't they? *Who else is there that could create such things?* But if Prodominus had recognized anything in her description of the creature, he didn't show it.

"That was what convinced me that Vindus was right, you know," the Kyriliarch said quietly. "About the revival, I mean. That trip. He said... it wasn't a matter of whether we *could* get the Chosen back. We *had* to. We in the Order are all that's holding humanity together, all that's keeping us from *that*, and there are fewer of us every year. We manage, with the Gates and the Legions, but... not forever. If the Chosen aren't waiting for us somewhere, we might as well pack the whole thing in."

He must know something. There was a gleam in his eyes, a faraway look. Maya's mind whirled. *Is he fishing? Trying to see if I'll make a mistake?*

She couldn't think of anything safe to say, so she said nothing. After a moment Prodominus grinned at her, scratching his wild red beard.

"Apologies. Just an old man's ramblings."

Maya let out a breath. "It's quite all right, Kyr—"

He held up a hand to stop her. At first she thought he was objecting to her formality, but then she heard the rapid footsteps. A couple of swiftbirds went past, each carrying a heavily bandaged passenger behind the rider. Not far behind them was a party of Auxiliaries and Legionaries on foot, considerably the worse for wear and escorted by several of Zinni's soldiers. The Tourmarch herself hurried over to Prodominus and spoke quietly for a moment before following them.

"Well," he said. "That changes our plans a little."

"What's happened?" Maya said.

"That's what's left of the Spire Kotzed garrison." He nodded at the knot of battered soldiers. "The rebels took the place this morning."

"This is an outrage," Baron Rashtun said, almost as soon as they sat down. "It cannot be allowed to stand."

It was early evening. The army had made camp some twenty kilometers from the Spire, close enough that Varo, from the top of a tree, could see the nightly lightning show. Prodominus had called a conference, summoning Maya and Va'aht along with the baron, his daughter, the decarch, and one of the Kyriliarch's scouts, who was spreading out an intricately painted leather map.

"I think it may be an opportunity," Prodominus said mildly.

"I am worried, Kyriliarch, that you do not understand...local feelings." The baron's tone was clipped. "The Commune may claim to be for 'the people,' but in truth their core is the old retainers of Baron Kotzed. After the old baron was executed for betraying the Republic, his daughters escaped with their loyalists, and regaining their Spire has always been their dream. If they are allowed to hold it for any length of time, it will be seen throughout Khirkhaz as a black eye for those who support the Republic. Kotzed's support may spread." He looked down at the map, jaw working. "They must be driven out. As soon as possible."

"Peace, Baron." Prodominus held up his hands. "I agree with you. All I meant is that the rebels have obligingly put themselves into a position where we'll have an easier time crushing them."

"Perhaps." Baron Rashtun subsided a little. "I still don't understand how they took the Spire to begin with. There was a sizable garrison of Legionaries, in addition to some of my own troops."

Prodominus looked at the decarch, who nodded and leaned forward. "It appears," she said, "the rebels have new allies. *Dhakim.*"

The baron snorted. "*Dhakim* are—" He glanced around at the centarchs. "Not a *myth*, as such, but...we do not have problems with them in Khirkhaz. I understand things are different in the north, but..."

"I spoke to the Legionaries who escaped," Tourmarch Zinni said. "They described a man who moved with superhuman speed, wielding a sword that could penetrate unmetal armor."

"An unmetal blade, surely," the baron said.

"A man," the decarch went on, "who seemed impervious to blaster fire. He was described with dark skin, black hair, and a scar around his left eye. The eye itself seemed functional, but... odd. Perhaps glowing. There was some confusion."

Maya grew stiff in her seat. She forced herself to breathe, hoping none of the others had noticed.

"Silvereye," Prodominus said.

Va'aht, silent until now, stirred. "I thought he was in Deepfire."

"He was," Prodominus said. "But it's been months since he was spotted. Some rumors, but..." He grimaced. "I didn't expect to find him throwing in his lot with the Commune."

"I'm not familiar with this Silvereye," Fina said. "Is he famous?"

"Notorious," Va'aht said primly.

"He's a scavenger from the Shattered Peaks," Prodominus said. "Supposedly he found a cache of ghoul weapons, including a replacement for one of his eyes. All we really know is he broke into the fortress in Deepfire with alchemical explosives, killed several Legionaries, and escaped with unknown arcana. There's been some suggestion that he's the thief who used to go by Halfmask, who worked with the tunnelborn rebels until we crushed that group."

Until I *crushed it, you mean.* Maya swallowed hard, fists clenching. Raskos Rottentooth, the corrupt dux, had used her and Tanax as assassins, goading the "rebels" into a fight and then relying on the centarchs to slaughter them, all to protect his own smuggling and extortion. That she'd found proof of that and toppled Raskos afterward was small consolation for the blood on her hands.

"Even so," the baron said doubtfully. "Do you think this one man, this Silvereye, would be enough for rabble like the Commune to take the Spire?"

"According to the survivors," Zinni said, "they snuck into the fortress and attacked by surprise." She hesitated. "They may have had the help of plaguespawn, as well. That seemed difficult to believe, but..."

"Hardly impossible," Prodominus said. "Not for a *dhakim*."

"Hardly," Maya murmured.

"Let's not get ahead of ourselves," the baron said. "Whether or not Silver-eye is here, our task remains the same. We must reclaim the Spire as soon as possible, or the Republic's prestige in Khirkhaz will be fatally damaged."

"I agree," Va'aht said. "What does it matter if a *dhakim* is assisting the rebels? That is, after all, why the three of us are here. Otherwise the dux could doubtless handle this on his own."

"Indeed." Prodominus scratched his chin through his beard. "The longer we give them to fortify, the nastier it's going to be when we get there. Decarch?"

"If we leave the supply train and proceed by torchlight, we can be in front of the Spire shortly after dawn," she said. "With some time for reorganization, we should be able to attack before midday."

Baron Rashtun looked a little taken aback. "A night march? The soldiers will be exhausted."

"Legionaries are accustomed to hardship," Zinni said, deadpan. "If the Auxiliaries cannot keep up, they can bring up the rear."

"I trust that your lancers won't mind missing a night's sleep," Prodominus said. "I'll want them surrounding the Spire to chase down any rebels who try to escape."

"What?" Fina looked offended. "We didn't gather the chivalry of Khirkhaz to harass stragglers. We should be leading the assault."

"No doubt the *Kyriliarch* has his reasons," the baron said, glaring at his bristling daughter. "The walls of the Spire are high, and made of unmetal. We'll need scaling ladders, or—"

"Not if we can keep the gates open," Prodominus said briskly.

"That seems...optimistic," Rashtun said, looking around the table.

"The rebels seem to have managed it," the Kyriliarch said. "Leave the gates to me. Tell your soldiers to get as much rest as they can, and prepare to march at midnight."

"I...ah...as you say, of course." The baron inclined his head and got to his feet. "If you'll excuse me, I have preparations to make."

"The same goes for you two," Prodominus said, looking at Va'aht and Maya. "You'll be leading the attack tomorrow, so be ready."

"Yes, Kyriliarch." Va'aht saluted with a cold smile. Maya straightened up, struggling to match him.

Leading the assault. She stared at Prodominus, but his expression was unreadable under the unruly tangle of hair and beard. *If he really is working for the ghouls ... and if Gyre is there ...*

We need to talk to Ashok. Now. Maya pushed herself to her feet, abruptly, and ducked out of the tent, feeling the Kyriliarch's stare on her back.

Beq poked the fire idly, stirring up swirling embers. Varo, sitting on a root, stared upward, lost in thought.

Maya had grabbed the two of them as soon as she could, pulling them away into the shelter of a small boulder. She'd repeated what had been said at the council of war, while Varo had sparked a small fire to ward off the increasing chill.

"You believe it?" Beq said softly, dancing embers reflected in her spectacles. She reached out and gently took Maya's hand. "About Gyre being with the rebels?"

"I mean, I don't know for certain," Maya said. "All I have to go on is what Zinni reported. But it certainly *sounds* like him. And ... the Commune is the sort of cause he would believe in, isn't it?"

"You must have expected to have to face him again," Varo said.

"I suppose." Maya felt Beq squeeze her hand. "I was hoping he'd ... I don't know, retire to a life of crime or something." She pursed her lips. "I guess that doesn't really sound like Gyre."

"If he's anything like you, he won't give up," Beq said. "Not if he believes in what he's doing."

"No," Maya said, thinking of distant memories of Gyre's small, determined face. "He won't."

There was a long silence. The fire gave a *pop*, and Varo shook his head.

"So what do we do now?" he said. "I understand you don't want to fight your brother, but ..."

"It's not about Gyre." Maya took a deep breath and forced herself to be honest. "Not *just* about him, I mean. We were hoping that there'd be time to find the Purifier once we settled in to hunt the rebels. But if Prodominus is right and we crush them in a single battle, then we may not get another chance. *This* might be the best opportunity we have."

"Meaning *now*?" Beq said, looking up suddenly. "Tonight?"

"We could certainly get away from the army," Varo mused. "But we'd never make it back by morning."

"I know," Maya said, keeping her expression neutral. *We'd be declared traitors to the Order. But...* "We'd have a head start, at least."

"And you wouldn't have to face Gyre," Beq said quietly.

"That, too." Maya sighed. "We need to try to speak to Ashok. Tomorrow could be too late. Prodominus might turn us around and march straight back to the Gate."

"I think I agree," Varo said. "At least that will give us a better idea of what we're dealing with."

Beq nodded and dug in her pack for the resonator. Maya looked over her shoulder but saw only a few campfires flickering through the trees. She touched the Thing, out of habit. When Beq had the little arcana ready, Maya pulled a stream of *deiat* into it and waited. Blue light flickered, and Ashok's face took shape once again.

"Maya?" The Chosen looked alarmed. "I warned you to wait. Our power is—"

"Limited," Maya said. "I know, so I'll make this as quick as I can." She laid out the situation—the rebels, the Spire, and Prodominus' plan. Ashok's eyes widened as she spoke. *Good to know even the Chosen can be surprised, I guess.*

"If we're going after the Purifier," Maya concluded, "this may be our best chance. Prodominus might come after us, but he'd be a long way behind, at least."

"You cannot," Ashok said. "Not yet. The Spires—" His image flickered, then returned. "The Spires are a *part* of the Purifier. Its power source. They must be protected. If they are disrupted during the process, we could lose our only chance."

"I don't think a gang of rebels is going to know how to sabotage a power source that's survived four hundred years," Beq said doubtfully.

"No," Ashok said. "But an ally of the ghouls might."

"Gyre," Maya said. "You think *that's* why he's here?"

"Or else Prodominus himself, once he gets inside." Ashok shook his head. "My time grows short. I will divert emergency"—he flickered again—"contact you afterward, but you must protect—"

The image vanished, and the three of them stared into darkness.

"Plaguing *fuck*," Maya said eventually.

"Maya…" Beq said.

"It's all right." Maya got to her feet, stomach roiling. "I'm going to get some rest."

Because tomorrow morning, I may have to kill my brother.

Chapter 17

Gyre

It was a sad procession that wound its way out of Spire Kotzed's southern gate. Townsfolk, bundled in all the clothing they could wear, carrying heavy packs or leading loadbirds laden with saddlebags. The day was cool and cloudy, with an intermittent spitting rain, and the road was quickly being churned into a black mud by so many passing feet. Rebels from the banners stood guard by the gateway, attracting black looks from the refugees as they trudged past.

"They're not happy," Gyre said.

"I'm not surprised," Apphia said. She stood beside him in her long coat and three-cornered hat, one of the ghoul-made swords at her hip. "But what choice do we have? We'll probably be under siege by nightfall."

Gyre pursed his lips and nodded. They were standing in the yard by the base of the Spire, where more Communards were busy putting up barricades to make a fallback line, in case they were driven off the walls. Wagons and overturned carts had been lined up end to end, with furniture and even doors and window shutters piled around them for cover.

The Spire's outer wall, a single thin sheet of unmetal, didn't have a proper wall walk, but one of Apphia's ancestors had built a series a platforms accessible by ladders. Brennard, who'd take overall command of the defense, had put the majority of the rebel forces there or at the windows of the Spire itself, ready to pepper the enemy with crossbow fire and alchemical bombs. He and his lancers, no more than a dozen, waited in the inner yard with their warbirds, while another contingent of rebels was assigned to run ammunition to the walls or barricades. An elite few were equipped with captured Legionary gear: unmetal breastplates, swords, and blaster rifles.

That left the smallest group, twenty-some of the Commune's best fighters, which Apphia had assigned to Gyre. Apart from the lancers, they were the only ones with *deiat* shields and ghoul-made swords, which meant they would have the best chance in a fight against Legionaries or centarchs. Each of the three banners had insisted on equal representation, of course, so there was a contingent from the Blacks led by Vaela's great-grandson Fillow, a set of taciturn Greens with Maeris in command, and a bickering council of Whites. There hadn't been time to practice as a group, and Gyre wasn't hoping for them to obey many commands beyond "Follow me!" *Hopefully, that will be enough.*

"Where's Nina?" Gyre said.

"Up in the tower." Apphia sighed. "She insists on fighting, but I can at least keep her out of the front line."

"I might say the same about you," Gyre said quietly.

"You know I can handle myself."

"That's not what I'm worried about. If you—" Gyre paused.

"If I get myself killed, it'll be a disaster," Apphia said. "I got that speech from Brennard already. It's a risk we're just going to have to take. I'm not going to hide while people are out here dying in my name." She flashed a sly grin. "You'll just have to make sure I come back okay."

If only it were that easy. A lot of people were about to get hurt or killed, whatever he did. *Speaking of which.* "I should check on Sarah and Elariel. Send for me if there's any movement."

Apphia nodded and strode off toward the northern gate, still open for the moment. Several rebels, as well as one of Kit's bodies, were stationed up in the control room ready to close it, but Gyre's nerves remained tight. *The Republic troops probably thought they were safe too.*

He went to the main doors of the Spire, waiting for a moment while a troop of rebels rushed out. Inside, the wooden partitions had been torn out to add to the barricades, leaving an open square with stairwells at two corners. The chests of alchemicals they'd brought from Deepfire were lined up down the center. On one side, Sarah and a few volunteers were organizing the bombs by type, ready to be rushed out to the soldiers on the walls. On the other, a group recruited from anyone with medical training was doing the same with the quickheal and other medicines under Elariel's direction. The ghoul was assisted by Vaela Truestrike, who sat in the only remaining chair and shouted orders at a volume that made up for Elariel's lack of assertiveness.

"Hey," Sarah said as Gyre entered. "Are they coming?"

"Not yet," Gyre said. "We've nearly got all the civilians outside the walls, so they won't get caught in the crossfire. Hopefully they'll give us at least another hour."

"We'll be ready here, too." She waved at the piles of alchemicals. "I think this is more firepower than I've ever seen in one place."

"Make sure nobody drops one in here," Gyre said.

"Believe me, I'm doing my best." Sarah scratched the back of her head with her prosthetic arm, wrapped in a bandage and glove. "Where do you want me once I'm done with this?"

"Let's see how things develop." Sarah could fight, especially now that she could crack stone with a punch, but her skills as an arcanist were more valuable than one more body in the line. "If it *does* come to a siege, then we'll need every clever engineer we can get."

"You don't think it will?" Sarah said.

Gyre glanced over his shoulder to see if anyone else was nearby, then shook his head. "There's supposed to be a centarch with the Republic forces. I can't see a centarch sitting around waiting for us to starve, or trying to dig under the walls."

"The walls are unmetal, but they're not that tall," Sarah said. "If they built ladders, they could try storming them. But they'd lose a plaguing lot of people doing it."

"Maybe they don't care," Gyre said. "Or maybe they've got another trick they're counting on."

"Sarah?" a woman said, waving a small clay jug. "What's this one?"

"*That* is an extremely powerful acid, Krenna," Sarah said, hurrying over. "Please don't spill it on the explosives."

Gyre smiled, crossing the line of chests to stand beside Elariel. This side of the room had been set up as a makeshift hospital, with bedding stripped from the tower laid out in rows. People were cutting sheets into bandages, and big kettles of clean water stood against one wall. Elariel was going over the piles of alchemicals, grimacing to herself.

"Something wrong?" Gyre said.

"No." The ghoul sighed. "These are just so... primitive."

"I asked Tyraves for some ghoul-made medicine," Gyre said. "She looked at me like I was crazy."

"When you have *dhaka*, 'medicine' is superfluous," Elariel said stiffly. "If a particular substance is required, you simply create it."

"Then it's a good thing we have a *dhaka* practitioner, isn't it?"

Elariel's face fell. Gyre could almost see the droop of the long ears she no longer had.

"I am... not ideal for the task," she said. "My specialty is the creation and maintenance of constructs, not healing." She looked at the carefully arranged beds. "And I will not be able to help so many. You understand that, don't you? My strength will give out before long."

"I know," Gyre said. "No one is expecting miracles, Elariel."

"I am afraid there are some who will," she said quietly. "After my... show, back at the camp."

"Do the best you can. And use the quickheal. It's better than nothing."

"Of course. I just cannot help but think of what devices were ground up to make it. It is like using works of art for firewood."

"You can tell Lynnia that, next time we're in Deepfire."

Elariel snorted a laugh. "I have only met her once, but I believe that would not be wise."

She's changed, Gyre thought as the ghoul turned away to answer one of Vaela's shouts. *Adapted, I suppose. Like all of us.* He felt a sudden surge of guilt, for bringing her into this, and fought it down. *She and Kit recruited me, after all. And it was this or the Geraia's executioners.*

He left the hospital and went to the stairs, ascending five tiresomely steep flights to reach the gate control room where they'd spilled so much blood. The bodies had been cleared away, but some of the stains were still on the flagstones. A dozen rebels with crossbows waited at the barred windows, turning nervously at the sound of Gyre ascending. A small spider-construct, sitting beside the gate lever, unfolded its limbs and scuttled over to him, nimbly ascending to his shoulder.

"Good morning," Gyre muttered. "How does it look?"

"Some movement in the trees," Kit said. "But they're not attacking yet." Several of her small bodies were clinging to the top of the wall, keeping watch from all sides. The larger constructs were waiting in the yard below. "You and Apphia probably have time for a quickie if you duck into a closet."

"What did I tell you about spying on me?"

"You're not denying it, then?"

"Kit—"

"I'm not criticizing! She's perfect if you like them tall and well muscled. If I still had a body I might have tried my luck myself. She reminds me of that blacksmith, from that little inn in Deepfire. You remember, right? Chosen above, the thighs on that girl—"

"I really hope you can keep watch and have lewd fantasies at the same time."

"Gyre, I could do that *before* I got killed." The construct did a little dance on his shoulder, legs pricking through his shirt. "Speaking of which. Check the window. I think they're coming."

"Plaguing *fuck*," Gyre said, his calm evaporating. He rushed to the north side of the room, Kit's construct digging its legs into his shirt to hold on. The rebels there stepped aside nervously, muttering to one another. One of them offered Gyre a place at the spyglass.

He didn't need it. With his silver eye, it was easy enough to see the edge of the forest had abruptly begun to boil with soldiers. At least two groups of Legionaries broke from the tree line, with armored riders on warbirds on their flanks.

"Drop the gates," Gyre said. Some of the civilians might get stuck on the wrong side, but there was no helping it. "Now!"

The closest Communard ran to the pedestal in the corner and threw the ugly iron switch that wrenched the arcana there apart. Gyre watched the northern gate as a wide unmetal panel was released, sliding rapidly downward—

—and stopping dead, still two meters off the ground.

"What's going on?" Gyre growled.

"I don't know!" the rebel wailed. She threw the switch, forward and backward, to no effect. Gyre ran to another window and found the gate there stuck in the same position. Then, slowly but inexorably, it started to *rise*.

The gates are controlled by an arcana circuit, Apphia had told him. *Cut the circuit, and they fall. But raising them is difficult, because there's no . . .*

Power.

He turned back to the north window. At the edge of the forest, between the emerging columns of soldiers, a single tall figure held aloft a blade of coruscating lightning.

Centarchs. Of course.

"Sarah!" Gyre cupped his hands to his lips as he dashed for the stairs. "We have problems!"

Maya

The sky was gray and overcast, and drops of mist flecked Maya's face. She looked up at the Spire, glowering at them from the top of the hill. For a moment she wondered if Gyre was looking back through that weird glowing eye, picking her out on the edge of the forest.

It might not even be him. Or the rebels could have fled. Either would leave the Spire safe from mischief. But if Gyre *was* there, and he stayed to fight...

We can't afford the risk. It might be that Gyre didn't know anything about the Purifier or the Spire's real purpose. But if they only had one shot at saving the world, Maya couldn't take the chance. *Of course, even if we win, we'll have to worry about Prodominus.* But that was a problem for later.

The Kyriliarch stood in front of her and Va'aht, one hand on his haken. He looked up at the fortress, too, and gave a satisfied grunt.

"Spire Kotzed's gates are operated by an arcana mechanism," he said with a modest grin. "One which I happen to know the details of. When they attempt to close them, I'll interfere. That's going to take all my concentration, so after that it's up to the two of you. Take your columns around the eastern and western sides and break through. The baron's lancers will be waiting to mop up anyone who flees. I want every rebel in there dead or in our custody by sundown. Understood?"

This was a darker, grimmer Prodominus than Maya had seen before. She gave a nod, and Va'aht offered a crisp salute. The Kyriliarch turned away and waved a hand.

"Get moving."

Maya touched the Thing and jogged back to where "her" troops were waiting. She wasn't really in command, since Tourmarch Zinni was staying with her column. Under other circumstances, that might have been a slight, but Maya was frankly glad to have the assistance. The white-armored soldiers, broken into twelve-person squads, waited quietly while the tourmarch gave them final instructions.

Varo and Beq were waiting, too. Maya went over to them, shaking her head.

"Maya—" Beq said.

"Not this time," Maya said. "I know you can both take care of yourselves, but this isn't an expedition to some ruin, it's a *battle*. You're staying back with the second wave, the Auxiliaries—"

"We know," Varo said. "I'm a scout; I know I'm not supposed to be in the front line of an assault."

"I just wanted to tell you to be careful," Beq said. She stepped closer, pulling Maya into a hug, and whispered in her ear. "Remember it doesn't have to be *you* who deals with Gyre. He's not your responsibility, Maya."

"I..." Maya's voice stuck in her throat. *He* is *my responsibility.* "I'll be careful."

They kissed for a long time. Varo cleared his throat, and Maya pulled away.

"I have to go," she said. "Be ready. For this, and...whatever we have to do afterward."

Beq gave a nod, her eyes shimmering. Maya swallowed and turned away.

"Centarch," Zinni said, saluting. "Everything is ready for your order."

"Thank you," Maya said, in the gravest voice she could manage. It felt ridiculous, and she stepped closer to Zinni's diminutive figure and lowered her voice. "Sorry. I've never actually led anyone into battle before."

"I guessed that," the tourmarch said, and Maya could hear the smile in her voice. "Just tell us which way to go, and I'll handle the rest."

"Thank you." Maya took a deep breath and pointed. "We're circling around to attack the east gate."

"Ready!" Zinni shouted. "March!"

They left the cover of the forest, moving out onto the gentle upward slope of the hill. The ground was spongy with grass and damp from the rain, flecks of mud clinging to Maya's boots and spattering the spot-less white armor of the Legionaries. The fortress, which had seemed so close moments before, now looked impossibly far away. Behind them, Va'aht's column was moving too, as were several groups of Auxiliaries. Warbirds squawked and chirped as the baron's lancers fanned out. Maya saw Fina, fully armored but not yet wearing her helmet, waving eagerly to a pack of her friends.

"When we get there," Maya said to Zinni, "then what?"

"I'm hoping you can get us through the gate itself," Zinni said. "After that, leave anyone without arcana weapons to us. Crossbows and steel swords aren't much good against our armor. If you see a blaster, take it out."

Maya nodded. They were circling wide around the fortress, hoping to come at it from east and west simultaneously, while the advancing Auxiliaries filed in behind. Abruptly, she felt a shiver through *deiat*, and the gate ahead of her started to close. An answering wave of energy came from the edge of the forest, where Prodominus had positioned himself. The intensity of it made Maya's eyes widen—she'd never felt so much raw power, not even from Jaedia or Nicomidi. Slowly but surely, the gate started to open wider.

"That'll have them rattled," Zinni said, with dark humor. "First squad, third squad, quickstep! Second and fourth, cover!"

The Legionaries broke into a jog. Maya drew her haken, not igniting the blade but threading *deiat* into her panoply, which bloomed around her as a nearly invisible blue aura. Up ahead, she could see soldiers mill-ing behind the still-open gate. Others, on a platform at the top of the wall, were already taking aim. Zinni, estimating the distance with a practiced eye, shouted, "First, third, at the run! Open fire!"

For a moment, Maya thought the rebels had heard the command too. A flight of crossbow bolts lifted from the battlements in a high arc, rattling down among the charging Legionaries. Most missed, stick-ing in the turf, but a few glanced off unmetal plates. The forward two squads of soldiers went on at a dead run, while the rear squads halted to loose a volley of their own. Blaster rifles *cracked*, the bolts sizzling over Maya's head. The rebels ducked for cover, and the energy blasts detonated against the wall.

"Move!" Zinni shouted. "Keep their heads down! Centarch, with me!"

Maya realized she'd come to a halt. She forced herself back into a run, pounding up the slope after Zinni and her soldiers. Blaster fire continued to spatter and crackle against the battlements, while the rebels popped up to loose their bolts before ducking back to reload. One of them wasn't fast enough and caught a blast to the chest, flopping backward off the wall and out of sight.

"Can you clear them off there?" Zinni said, shouting to be heard over the constant *cracks*.

Maya nodded, narrowing her eyes and sucking in a breath. It was farther than she usually reached out, but she pulled a stream of *deiat* through her haken and sent it boiling up under the feet of the soldiers on the wall. Flames erupted from the platform they were standing on, a sheet of fire that spread quickly in both directions. Men and women screamed, burning, or dove off in desperation and vanished behind the wall.

The decarch crowed and waved to her men. "To the gate!"

It's not like fighting the thieves in Deepfire, Maya told herself. *It's not. They chose this when they attacked the Spire.* But the sight of the figures collapsing in leaping flames made her stomach churn. *Centarchs are supposed to save people* and *defend the Republic. But...*

The gate was fully open again. Beyond, Maya saw a central yard surrounding the Spire itself, crisscrossed with hasty barricades. The first of Zinni's Legionaries were just reaching the gate when blasters *cracked* and energy bolts slammed out through the doorway. One of the soldiers was hit, knocking him off his feet and sending him rolling down the hill, trailing smoke. Maya ignited her haken, letting the pull of *deiat* to *deiat* draw it into the path of the oncoming fire, bolts impacting on the flaming blade and vanishing. Crossbows were firing as well, and she felt a quarrel rebound from her panoply as a cold pinprick.

"Cover!" Zinni yelled, and her soldiers threw themselves to the ground or ducked to the side of the gate, firing back at the rebels. A storm of blaster fire crisscrossed the entryway in both directions, detonating bolts tearing chunks out of the turf and sending flying splinters from the wooden barricade. Only Maya remained upright, advancing slowly but implacably, her haken weaving an impenetrable defense as it drank in every shot.

"Stay behind me!" she called to Zinni, and got a nod in return. She raised her off hand and sent a wash of brilliant fire through the gate, rolling forward over the barricade. It wasn't hot enough to sear, but it spoiled the gunner's aim, and in its wake Maya ran forward. She made it through the outer wall and past the two buildings flanking it, breaking out into the main yard. More rebels to either side released a volley of crossbow bolts, and a half dozen bounced away from her panoply with a wash of cold. Maya swept her hand in a half circle and a wall of raging yellow and orange flames rose around her.

Seeing the opportunity, Zinni led her Legionaries forward, taking up fresh positions. When they were crouched and ready, Maya closed her fist, the wall of fire blowing outward in a wave of destruction. There were more screams, audible even over the crackling roar of the flames. Parts of the barricade were ablaze, but some rebels still crouched behind it, and blaster bolts slammed back and forth at close range.

Something big clambered over the twisted, burning wood. It had a square, black body with a dozen insectoid limbs, dark ropy muscles clinging to a metal skeleton. The design was different, but it put Maya in mind of the strange plaguespawn or ghoul-made monstrosities she'd faced in Leviathan's Womb.

Here, at least, was an opponent who troubled her conscience not at all. Maya leveled her haken and charged with a shout, while behind her blaster rifles *cracked* and spat. The black spider-thing surged to meet her.

Gyre

"They're getting closer," Kit said.

"I *know*," Sarah said, bent over the exposed guts of the gate switch.

"She knows," Gyre said, stalking back and forth in front of the window.

"They're coming from both sides," Kit said, her little construct darting across the room. "Nearly at the gates."

"*We know*," Sarah and Gyre said together.

Gyre gripped his sword hilt hard enough that his knuckles went white, forced his breathing to be calm, and knelt beside Sarah.

"I don't want to put pressure on you," he said quietly. "But if you can't get those gates closed in the next few minutes, we're all dead."

"Oh, thanks," Sarah muttered. "I had no idea. That makes it much easier—*ow*." Something sizzled in the mess of crystal and wire, and she shook her hand. "You were right, it's the centarch. He's pumping a ton of power through the circuit, enough that it's arcing whenever I try to break it."

"So what can we do?"

"Wait until he gets tired and stops?" Sarah shook her head and slammed her left fist against a flagstone, not noticing the cracks that shot through it. "I know, I *know*. Maybe if I reroute, try to isolate the circuits one at a time?"

"How long?"

"Five minutes? Ten? Or never." She started yanking more tools from her pack.

"I'll try to get you as long as I can."

"Crossbows firing!" Kit said. Her tiny body scuttled over to Gyre and climbed to his shoulder. "It's starting."

"I can see that," Gyre said.

He was looking to the west, where one column of Legionaries, broken into four squads, advanced at a run as quarrels came down around them like hail. A tall man in white armor jogged in front of them. He ignored the missiles, and blue sparks sprayed from him now and then when one came close to striking. *That's a panoply field. A centarch?*

A moment later, the man removed all doubt by igniting his haken. Another step closer, and he made a crosswise gesture. Men and women on the wall above the gate *erupted* in fountains of blood, falling to pieces as though an enormous scythe blade had passed through at waist height. A girl who'd happened to duck at the right moment was screaming, most of one arm gone, while a crouching man had been neatly decapitated, his corpse flopping in a sea of blood. Gyre's gorge rose.

"I'm going out," he said. "Sarah, get those doors closed."

"I'm"—*crackle*—"*ah*, fucking *trying*!"

Gyre pounded down the stairs, Kit still on his shoulder. When he reached the first floor, panic was already setting in. Blaster fire *cracked* and rumbled outside.

"Apphia!" Gyre grabbed her and pulled her away from shouting into the face of a hapless White. "There's a centarch to the west!"

"*And* to the east," she said.

Two of them. Plaguing fuck. Gyre's heart sank, but he refused to let himself despair. "Sarah's working on getting the gates down, but she needs time."

"I know. I'll take Brennard and half the troops with *deiat* shields to the east. You take the other half west."

"I—"

"*Please* don't be an idiot now, Gyre."

"Right." He smiled, and she leaned in and kissed him. Gyre ignored Kit's cheer. When they broke apart, he raised his voice. "Maeris! Fillow! Bring your people with me *now*!"

His fighters—the ones with *deiat* shields and ghoul-made weapons— started to converge. Gyre leaned closer to Kit.

"Where are your bodies?"

"The big ones are heading out to try to hold the gates," she said. "Smaller ones mostly on lookout. Why?"

"Get as many little ones as you can back here and have them grab smokers," he said. "Just start spreading them around. That might slow the centarchs down."

"Got it!"

Kit's tiny body jumped off his shoulder and dashed toward the piles of alchemicals. Maeris and Fillow had gathered at least a dozen soldiers, which was all Gyre was prepared to wait for. He shouted at them to follow and burst out the door.

Outside, everything was chaos. Blaster fire strobed everywhere, a storm of it coming in from the east and west gates, rebels firing with captured weapons from the remaining wall platforms and the windows of the Spire itself. Blasts and flames rocked the courtyard on both sides, but Gyre turned west, beckoning his troops to follow. The barricade there had been torn to shreds, chopped through as though by enormous blades, and the bodies strewn throughout the wreckage had been given a similar treatment.

Maeris skidded to a halt at Gyre's side, one hand over her mouth. "Chosen fucking defend," she muttered over the noise of someone behind her being sick.

"We have the *deiat* shields," Gyre said. "We have to stop the centarchs. Come on!"

The cheer that followed him sounded half-hearted, but at least they *did* follow. Legionaries were advancing from the gate, moving forward in small groups while others fired over their heads. Blaster bolts slammed into the outer wall of the Spire, scorching the unmetal. One of Kit's medium-sized constructs leapt over the ruined barricade, dodging a bolt and bearing an armored soldier to the ground. The centarch stepped forward to meet it with his shimmering blue-white haken, slashing two legs off in gouts of black blood before carving the thing in half.

Gyre pointed with his sword and concentrated, his augmentations coming alive with a *click*. The world slowed to a crawl, shadows darting ahead to trace out possible paths. Blaster bolts swished by at an easy walking pace. Gyre surged forward, leaving his surprised followers behind, and leapt at the centarch. The man saw him coming and drew a line in the air with his off hand. Gyre felt the wave of *deiat* sweep past him, slashing the wooden debris, but it washed over him and his shielded followers without effect.

If the man was surprised by this, he didn't let it slow him down, bringing his haken up to parry Gyre's descending strike. The blades met with a *screech*, then Gyre twisted away, spinning to evade the centarch's counterstroke. His own riposte met the man's breastplate with a *clang* but failed to penetrate the thick unmetal. The centarch, abruptly realizing his panoply was no protection, gave ground, but Gyre pressed him, slamming his haken aside and aiming a cut at his neck. At the last moment, the centarch threw his head back, and Gyre's blade impacted the edge of his helmet and tore it away.

Before he could push his advantage home, Legionaries closed in from both sides. Gyre dodged one, parried the other, and sent the soldier toppling with a kick to the back of the knee. The second Legionary attacked again, and Gyre sidestepped, planting his blade in her armpit, where the armor was thin. She collapsed with a clatter of armor, and he took a moment to look around.

His followers had engaged the Legionaries, but it was an unequal contest. Even the ghoul blades couldn't pierce the thickest parts of their unmetal armor, and the Legionaries were confident soldiers, used to battle. Maeris was holding her own, blasting a white-armored trooper with her pistol and driving another back with her sword, but Fillow was down, clutching at a wound in his thigh, and the rest of the Black and Green fighters weren't faring much better. Columns of smoke were starting to blossom across the battlefield, thanks to Kit.

The centarch. That was what mattered. No one else stood a chance against him. Gyre pushed off again in a high, slow leap, kneeing a Legionary in the face as he went and sending the man stumbling backward. He crunched to the ground in front of the centarch, blocking a cut from his haken, then driving him back with a sweep. The man's face was visible now—thin, with high cheekbones, and purple-black hair—

Gyre stopped dead, his sword extended. The centarch backed away a half step, cautious, but for a moment it was all Gyre could do to fight his way out from under a swirl of memories. Maya, screaming, the horrified eyes of his parents, the shiver as his knife bit into flesh, and then the *pain*. The horrible *squish* as he touched the ruin where his eye had been.

"You..." His voice quivered, and he swallowed, speaking louder. "You're Va'aht Thousandcuts."

The centarch straightened slightly, brushing a smudge of blood from his cheek with his free hand. "I didn't think my fame had spread so far. Unless I'm very much mistaken, you're Gyre Silvereye."

"We've met," Gyre said. "A long time ago."

"A long..." Va'aht's eyes narrowed, then went wide, staring at Gyre's scar. "You're... *that* boy? *Really?*"

"Really." Gyre settled back into a fighting stance.

"Chosen defend." Va'aht was laughing. "Fate really does make fools of us, doesn't it?"

"You took my eye," Gyre said. "You took my *sister*."

"And now you're back for revenge? Brooded about it all these years?" Va'aht smiled coldly. "You seem to have done all right as far as the eye is concerned. Shouldn't you be thanking me, for setting you on your course?"

"Any other day, I'd draw this out," Gyre said. "But seeing as we're a little *busy*, I'm just going to kill you and move on."

"As you like."

Va'aht thrust. It was *fast*—he was not a centarch who'd neglected his swordsmanship—but Gyre saw it coming, silver eye drawing shadows in the air. He stepped gracefully aside, countering with a cut that the centarch only barely dodged. Before Va'aht could recover, Gyre pressed closer, locking their blades and delivering a kick to his armored stomach that sent him staggering backward. He swiped wildly with his haken to keep Gyre away as he recovered his footing.

"You took my eye for spilling Order blood," Gyre said, advancing. "The blood of the Chosen, you called it. It was worth every drop in my veins."

"And still is," Va'aht growled. "More, now that you've polluted yourself with ghoul *dhak*."

"My blood is right here," Gyre said. "If you can reach it."

Va'aht attacked again. This time Gyre let him come, and aimed his cut at the centarch's wrist. Va'aht twisted his arm, taking the blow on his unmetal bracer, but the impact still threw him off-balance. Gyre sidestepped, slamming another stroke into his backplate to send him stumbling forward. As the centarch went past, Gyre slashed downward, the silver sword cutting deep into the back of his calf. Blood bloomed and Va'aht went down on one knee with a shout. Gyre drew his sword back again, aiming for the man's neck.

"Centarch!"

A squad of Legionaries, seeing their leader in trouble, charged. There were four of them, and abruptly it was Gyre who was backpedaling, silver eye barely keeping him ahead of four unmetal blades. He hopped up onto a ruined chunk of barricade, slapping several attacks away, and managed a strike that found a weak spot and opened a man's throat. A moment later, Maeris arrived, engaging another of the soldiers. Gyre danced between the blades of the remaining pair. The closer one slashed desperately, and he got inside her guard and drove his silver sword under her breastplate and into her belly. Blood gushed over his hand, and she crumpled.

The remaining Legionaries were falling back, forming a cordon. Gyre saw Va'aht limping behind them, his arm around a soldier's neck, haken still in hand. There were only a half dozen blades separating him from the centarch, a few meters of burning ground. A quick rush, and he would have—

"*Gyre!*" Nina's voice, a piercing shriek that cut through the chaos of battle. Gyre looked around and saw her leaning out a window of the Spire, two rebels at her shoulders barely restraining her. "The east gate! Help Apphia! *Please!*"

Plaguing fuck. Va'aht was *right there*, the revenge he'd dreamed of, but—

It's not revenge I'm after. That's what he'd told himself, all these years. *It's not about me, or Va'aht, or even Maya. It's about the system the Order maintains, and bringing it down.*

Still, he hesitated, balanced on a knife-edge. What tipped him over was another memory, standing in Lynnia's house when he heard what had happened at the ambush. *I was off with Kit, chasing the Tomb, chasing* revenge, *when Yora and the others died.*

Plague it. Gyre turned on his heel and ran.

Chapter 18

Maya

The big construct staggered backward, flames licking from several cuts. It grabbed for Maya with its two front limbs, and she severed one of them at the base, feeling the other grate against her panoply. She pressed in closer, concentrating her power. Her haken blazed pure white, and she brought it down in a single stroke that slashed the square body of the thing cleanly in half. Black blood gouted, vaporizing in the flames.

Around her, the battlefield was dissolving into chaos. Columns of smoke rose everywhere, merging into a fog of gray and black that obscured the interior of the courtyard. Blaster bolts were brief sparks of light, bolts slamming down from the windows of the tower or zipping up to detonate against the unmetal walls. The Auxiliaries had arrived, assaulting the north gate, but they'd gotten bogged down under fire from rebels with captured Legionary weapons. Alchemical bombs detonated in a staccato chorus, sending up belches of flame. Maya even thought she saw Fina and her lancers attempting a charge, banners flapping from the back of their warbirds.

In spite of everything, her column of Legionaries had crossed the barricade. Maya extinguished it with a wave, and Zinni directed half her soldiers to take cover, while the rest climbed over and made for the central tower with Maya. Blaster fire and crossbow quarrels continued to rain down, and a bolt caught one of the Legionaries and knocked her to the dirt, blackened armor smoking. More rebels emerged from the main doors, a ragtag group in long coats and three-cornered hats, swords drawn. Maya swept her free hand across them, and a wall of fire sprang up, engulfing the band.

A moment later, she skidded to a halt in a spray of dirt as the charging rebels emerged from the flames unscathed. By then it was too late for her Legionaries to do anything but draw swords and attack, and Maya joined them. The two sides met in a confused melee, unmetal swords scraping and screeching against strange, equally unbreakable blades.

A man and a woman attacked Maya together, shifting to either side of her with an ease that indicated they'd fought together before. A moment earlier, Maya might have accepted a strike on her panoply from one in order to overwhelm the other quickly, but now she checked herself, suddenly cautious. *Gyre shrugged off my fire, back in Leviathan's Womb, and his sword went through my panoply like it wasn't there.* Her stomach throbbed in memory.

Instead, she forced herself to fight as if both blades were haken and she was back in the dueling ring with Tanax, or sparring with Jaedia. The two rebels came on, and Maya danced backward, parrying the man's blade, feinting at him, then reversing and slipping inside the woman's guard. She gave ground, blocking Maya's attack, and Maya spotted her partner closing in from behind. She ducked and spun, haken flashing, and his strike went wide while hers carved his chest open in a spray of blood and flame. The woman shouted, furious, and tried to press the attack, but Maya sidestepped and caught her descending arm at the wrist, severing her sword hand. Her next strike found the rebel's neck.

Beside her, a Legionary patiently battered a big rebel into submission, slamming blows against his parries until he lost his grip on his sword and fell to his knees. In the other direction, another soldier was getting the worst of it against a rebel woman with a half-shaved head of purple hair and an intricate scar across her scalp and face. The Legionary tripped as she backpedaled, and the rebel made a lightning-fast lunge that slipped her blade in under the soldier's breastplate. Maya descended on the rebel, snarling, and the woman turned just in time to block her descending cut.

Even caught off guard, the rebel didn't hesitate, twisting her weapon free of Maya's flaming blade and sending a cut at her face. Maya jerked backward, slamming the hilt of her haken into the woman's hand. The tip of the rebel's sword whipped past her nose, and she felt a sting like a wasp near her hairline. Maya slapped her hand to the wound and it came away bloody. Her panoply hadn't responded. *Just what I was afraid of.*

The rebel pivoted into her next attack, and Maya gritted her teeth and powered into it, meeting her blade to blade. For a moment they shoved against each other, and Maya closed her fist, summoning a column of flame that engulfed them both. It didn't harm either of them, but it was enough to break the rebel's concentration, and Maya slammed a kick into her knee that sent her stumbling backward. Maya would have finished her then and there, but another spider-thing, this one barely the size of a chicken, scuttled across the yard and leapt for her. Startled, Maya ducked, letting the thing sail past, and incinerated it with a gesture when it landed.

She turned back to the rebel, who had regained her footing. She still moved with a slight limp, and when their eyes met, Maya saw resignation on her opponent's face.

"Surrender," she said, leveling her haken. "All of you. Now. Your lives will be spared; I guarantee it."

"This is my home." The rebel woman's lips quirked into a sad smile. "It was taken from me once. I won't let it happen again."

She came forward, pushing off her injured leg, feinting at a lunge that she turned into an upward cut. Maya saw it coming, countered, and the woman only stopped her riposte by a hairsbreadth. Maya shoved, and the rebel's leg gave way, crumpling underneath her. Maya started a downward cut—

—then spun aside, warned by nothing more than a flicker of motion out of the corner of her eye. Something *blurred* toward her with inhuman speed. Maya made the parry by a fraction of a second, the strength and speed of his blade jarring her arm. He twisted into another attack, and another, her parries growing more and more frantic, and she backed away just to get time to think—

And her attacker stopped, resolving into a young man with dark skin and black hair, a silver sword in one hand. He had a horrific scar across his left eye, and something *glowed* in the depths of the socket with an eerie green light. This time, at least, she didn't have any trouble recognizing him.

"Gyre." Her throat was thick.

"Maya." His eyes went to the rebel woman, who was slowly regaining her feet. "Apphia, are you all right?"

"I'll live." Apphia raised her sword. "Do you want me on your right or left?"

"Get back in the tower. Take the rest of them with you."

"But—" Apphia glanced at Maya, then gave a shaky nod and stepped backward. "Right."

She hobbled off. The sound of fighting surrounded them, but amid the billowing smoke, they might as well have been alone. Gyre began to circle, slowly, and Maya matched him. Her breath came fast, and her chest was tight.

"I should have known," he said. "I should have known you'd come here. Anytime people try to build something for themselves, here you are to kick it down."

"They said you might be here," Maya said. "I hoped they were wrong. Fucking *plague*, Gyre. I thought that maybe after what happened..."

"I'd seen sense?" Gyre's smile was savage. "Sorry to disappoint you."

"This isn't a fucking *game*," Maya said, waving at the destruction around them, the corpses sprawled across the yard. "People are *dying*."

"And who's fault is that, exactly?" Gyre said. "Apphia and her people just want to be left in peace. You're the ones with blood on your hands."

"They don't want *peace*. They want to break away from the Republic, set up their own Splinter Kingdom, just like all the rest. Another step backward for civilization, one more province lost. How long until there's no Republic left?"

"Not fucking long enough," Gyre said.

Maya blinked, blood from her scalp wound running into her eye. She wiped it with her free hand, shaking off the drops. "So why didn't you destroy it, then? You *helped* me, back in the caves. You stopped that... thing, the ghoul weapon. Why do that if you're just going to do their dirty work now?"

"Who told you I was doing anyone's dirty work?" Gyre continued to circle with slow, careful steps. "I realized that it was no good to just *destroy* the Republic if that lets the plaguespawn grind humanity down to nothing. We have to build something better."

Maya thought of the Forsaken Coast, the villagers, and the Eldest. Her blade twitched. "And this is your answer, then? The fucking Commune? You think they're *better*?"

"At least here being in charge isn't just about who has magic in their blood. The ghouls can *help* us, if you centarchs weren't so plaguing set on destroying them. We don't need *deiat*, or the Chosen's leftovers. We can learn to defend ourselves, rule ourselves."

"I've seen what letting *dhakim* 'help' brings." Children in cages, under Litnin. A vile pit of deliquescing flesh beneath Grace. The black spider, gripping the back of Jaedia's neck. The Eldest, and the villagers bowing to it. "Your *friends* are lying to you. They don't want to help humanity. They want to rule it themselves."

Gyre sneered. "You don't know anything except what the Chosen told you four hundred years ago."

"And you do?" Maya's voice was hoarse, desperate. *I have to make him understand.* "Please, Gyre. *Listen to me.* This isn't just about the Commune and the Lightning Barons—there's more at stake. Take your rebel friends and get *out* of here."

Gyre's grip tightened on his sword. "And if I don't, what then?"

Maya stopped circling. "I don't want to hurt you."

"But you're happy cremating my friends alive, is that it?"

"They didn't leave me a choice."

"Everyone has a choice," Gyre said. "Including me."

He came at her, faster than she could follow, faster than human, the green glow in his eye leaving a streak in her vision. Maya parried blindly, falling back on her instincts, the forms Jaedia had drilled into her. Her haken slammed against the silver sword with a burst of flame. Gyre spun away, almost dancing, and came at her from the other side. She barely made the parry in time, and the force of the blow drove her back a step.

He's too fast. Maya wanted to scream. She clenched her fist, and flame bloomed around her, blindingly white. But Gyre seemed immune to that, too, parting the fire like a curtain, sword flicking toward her face. She jerked her haken up in a desperate block, and he deftly disengaged and slashed low, drawing a line of blood along her thigh. Maya swung a horizontal cut, trying for distance, but he dodged to one side and slammed the hilt of his blade into the back of her head. She stumbled forward, stars spotting her vision, before turning with a scream and a wild slash. He was nowhere close, perched on a chunk of burning wreckage several meters away, blade lowered.

Playing with me. The realization was a dull throb that matched the spiking pain in her skull. *He could have killed me there, if he'd wanted.* It had been Gyre, she realized, who had killed Niassa. Baselanthus might not believe there was a power in the world that could defeat a centarch head-on, but she knew better. *Ashok is right. This can't be relics from some dusty cave. Someone did this to him.*

Unhurriedly, Gyre removed a small object from his belt and stowed it in his pack, replacing it with another. The glow in his eye faded for a moment, then returned, brighter than ever.

"See?" he said. "I learn from my mistakes."

"Gyre." Maya's breath came in ragged gasps, her thigh felt like it was burning, and blood was smeared across her face. "Please."

He was looking past her, and now his smile was genuine. He gestured with his sword. "Sarah's done it. You've lost."

Maya followed his gesture, peering through the smoke. The gate behind them was closing, the unmetal barrier descending, slowly but surely. Seeing their avenue of retreat disappearing, the Legionaries were falling back. Maya saw Zinni gesturing frantically.

"I'll go." She lowered her haken, letting the blade gutter out. "But—"

Gyre blurred forward, and between blinks his sword was at her throat. "Who said I was going to let you?"

"If you're going to kill me, go ahead." Maya swallowed. "I can't stop you. But I don't think you will."

"I . . ." The blade trembled, then fell away. "Plague it. Go."

Maya's eyes swam with tears, and she blinked them away. Gritting her teeth and limping on her wounded leg, she headed for Zinni, and the slowly closing gate.

Gyre

It was only gradually that the defenders of Spire Kotzed realized that, at least for the moment, they'd won. The Republican troops had retreated through the closing gates and back down the hill, out of blaster range. The men and women on the walls cheered and shouted mockery as they went, but their voices were muted when they turned around and saw the scale of the devastation.

Half the buildings in the yard were wrecked, and several were still on fire. Where the barricades had been, there was only burning, shredded rubble, strewn with bodies. Some corpses were nothing but blackened mummies, while others were intact but carved in two, their eyes wide in stunned surprise, vast slicks of blood from severed trunks soaking into the earth. The air was thick with the stench of gore and shit. Many of the Republic dead had been left behind, too, the still-smoking corpses of Legionaries struck by blaster fire, Auxiliaries pincushioned with crossbow quarrels. A warbird lay on its back, legs twisted in death, stinking of burning feathers.

As soon as the fighting had ceased, the wounded started calling for help, or just screaming in their agony. As Gyre staggered back to the tower, he saw unarmed rebels fanning out, encouraged by Vaela's sharp screeching. A girl Nina's age ran over to where a badly burned rebel waved feebly for assistance. She took one look at him, vomited briskly into the dirt, then wiped her mouth and bent down to help him up.

The first floor of the tower was as chaotic as the battlefield outside. The beds laid out for the injured were already full, and more screaming casualties were being laid out wherever there was space, stacks of pyrotechnics shoved aside. Dazed-looking people worked among them, applying bandages and quickheal, calling out when they found one who'd succumbed to their wounds.

"Get her outside, then!" Vaela answered one of the latter shouts. "We'll need the bed soon enough. Just grab her, you lunk. She's gone over, she's beyond worrying about you cracking her head against the door."

"Vaela," Gyre said, stepping beside the old woman.

"Eh?" She looked at him. "Still alive, are you? You need help?"

"Where's Apphia?"

Vaela jerked her head upward. "Nina's with her."

"And Elariel?"

"I haven't seen her for a bit. Upstairs too, I imagine."

Gyre nodded and headed, wearily, for the stairs. The second level was full of the walking wounded, those able to make it this far under their own power. Looking for Apphia, Gyre saw Sarah first, wrapping a bandage around a man's burnt leg and offering him a quickheal tablet. She didn't look up until Gyre put a hand on her shoulder.

"Hey," he said.

"Gyre." She blinked, slowly, then shot to her feet. "You're okay! Apphia said you went to fight the centarch—"

"I did." Gyre's stomach was so full of acid it felt like a jagged bone stabbing at his innards. "She ran when she saw the gates coming down. You saved us all, Sarah."

"Well." She ran her artificial fingers through her hair. "Yeah. Maybe a little." Looking around at the injured, her smile faded. "Some of us, anyway."

"Where's Elariel?"

"Resting." Sarah sounded defensive. "She did everything she could. Some people I thought were dead for sure, she brought round. I could see what it was doing to her, but she wouldn't stop until she collapsed."

"She's all right, though?"

"She says she'll just sleep for a while," Sarah said. "I'll take care of her."

"Thank you," Gyre said. "Where's Apphia?"

"Up in the control room, I think," Sarah said.

That meant more flights of stairs. By the time he reached the fifth floor, Gyre's limbs were screaming, augmentations or no. On the way, he passed several grim-faced people from the banners, hurrying down the steps with papers in hand. When he arrived, he found Apphia slumped in a chair beside the rickety table, with Nina standing beside her. The baron stirred as he came in, and tried to rise, but Nina pushed her shoulders down.

"Gyre!" Apphia glanced up at her sister. "Let go of me. I'm not a cripple yet."

"Not until you faint and crack your skull on the flagstones," Nina said. "Gyre, get over here and sit down before she hurts herself."

"Gladly." Gyre lowered himself into a chair with a groan. "What are the Republicans doing?"

"They've pulled back to the edge of the forest," Nina said, gesturing at the window. "For the moment, they're not making any attempt to encircle us, but that may not last. We saw more Auxiliaries coming up, enough for a real siege."

"I'm sending messengers out while we have the chance," Apphia said. "I want every Commune cell and every town in Khirkhaz to know what happened here. *Two* centarchs, and we're still standing." She met Gyre's eye. "Thanks to you."

Gyre nodded uncomfortably. An awkward silence stretched.

Nina gave a delicate cough. "I'm going to go make sure those messages get delivered," she said.

When her footsteps had faded, Gyre cleared his throat. "You're really all right?"

"She kicked my knee, but I don't think it's broken," Apphia said. Her voice was quiet. "I'd be dead, though, if you hadn't come when you did."

"Nina told me you needed help."

"She's mentioned that. Several times." The ghost of a smile crossed Apphia's face. "I'm not sure I'll ever live it down."

Another silence. This time, it was Apphia who shifted uncomfortably and said, "That centarch."

Gyre's acid stomach jolted. "Yeah."

"You knew her."

"She's my sister." He closed his eyes. "The Order took her when she was five, along with my eye."

"Oh, Chosen above," Apphia whispered. She swallowed. "Did . . . did you . . ."

"She left with the rest of them," Gyre said. "She's out there in the woods now, trying to figure out how to get in here and kill us."

"That sounds . . . complicated."

"I try not think about it," Gyre said. He pushed his chair back from the table abruptly. "I need to sleep. We don't know how soon they'll try again. Is there a room I can use?"

"Of course. Any of the bedrooms on the next few levels, I don't think anyone is going to bother you."

More stairs. "Send someone for me if anything happens."

"I will." Apphia tried to get up, wincing as she straightened her leg. Gyre hesitated, then went around the table to her. She reached for his shoulder and pulled him down into a kiss.

"Thank you," she said quietly. "For my life, and Nina's, and... everything else. Whatever happens next."

He lay on a dusty bed in his undershirt, crusted with sweat and singed in places. Gray light filtered in through the single window. It felt as though it should be evening already, but in fact the battle had occupied barely an hour. Gyre felt unutterably weary, the ache in his muscles overlaid with a tighter, sharper pain. This was the longest he'd ever used his augmentation, burning through almost two full energy bottles, and he suspected he was feeling the aftereffects. His real eye was watery and blurred. Sleep ought to have been the easiest thing in the world, but his mind was still whirling at full speed, and every few minutes his heart gave a sudden lurch and began slamming at his ribs.

It's over, he told himself. *For now, anyway.* Maya and Va'aht would both need time to recover from the wounds he'd given them, and without the centarchs he doubted the Republic forces would assault the walls. *They'll give us a few days while they tighten the noose.*

And then...

His sword at Maya's throat. *She's a* centarch. He'd seen the charred corpses she'd left in her wake, men and women who'd done nothing but stand up to the Republic, ordinary people who were helpless as children in the face of her power. One twitch, and her blood would have sprayed over his blade. *My sister.* Little Maya, who used to run in the vulpi pens and ruin her socks, who would crawl into his bed at night when a thunderstorm rolled over. He could have ended her story forever.

I couldn't have, and she knew it. The thought of it—of watching her,

349 BLOOD OF THE CHOSEN

choking on her own blood, the light going out of her eyes as he'd seen it go out of so many others—made his heart beat fast all over again, tightening horribly in his chest. *I can't do it.* It was a fact, sinking indelibly into his mind. No matter what he told himself, the justifications he invented, he wasn't going to be able to kill his baby sister. *Even if the Order has turned her into one of their arrogant monsters.*

So now what? Sooner or later, they would attack again. And when they did, he would have to face Maya—even with the *deiat* shields and ghoul-made swords, the centarchs were too dangerous to leave to anyone else. *And if I can't kill her, and she knows it...*

Fuck. Tears welled, unbidden, and he let them roll down his cheeks onto the grimy pillow. *Fuck, fuck,* fuck. *What am I supposed to do now?*

Things were simpler, back when I was Halfmask. Before I met Maya again. Before I ruined my quest for the Tomb by actually finding the plaguing thing. He missed Yora, and Ibb, and even Harrow. He missed Kit, the moments when she let her endless needling drop, and let him beneath her mask, just for a moment. *That night, in the mountains...*

"Someone's having good dreams," Kit said.

Gyre blinked and raised his head, for a moment still feeling her body warm and soft against him. Reality found him alone, except for a tiny spider-construct currently engaged in an up-close study of his erection.

"You want to take care of that?" she said. "I can wait a few minutes. I'll be quiet—you won't even know I'm here."

"Kit," Gyre said, trying to come up with a pithy comeback. After a moment, he gave up. His brain felt like it had been dipped in glue. By the light from the window, it was getting on toward evening. *I guess I managed to sleep after all.* His mouth was dry and foul, as though something had died on his tongue. "Has something happened?"

"Nothing dramatic," Kit said, sauntering away from his privates and hopping up on the bedpost. "We're not under attack."

"That's something," Gyre muttered. He groped for his overshirt, found it liberally stained with gore, and tossed it to the floor with a sigh. "Then what's going on?"

"Dinner, mostly," she said. "Though of course not for me. I'm helping dig graves, which let me tell you is just *fascinating* work, really rich and rewarding."

"How many of you are left?"

"Leaving aside the philosophical implications of that question, not all that many. Two medium constructs, one of them short a leg, and five of the bitty ones. I would have brought more bodies if I'd known how fast I'd run through them."

"You did well, in the battle," Gyre said.

"Aww," Kit said. "I'd blush if I still had skin."

"I don't know if I . . . thank you enough. For everything you've done for me. I know you don't have to."

"Okay, now I'm getting worried," Kit said. "Did you find out you have some kind of incurable disease just now? Because if so I *might* have some relevant experience. I'll come up with some nice aphorisms, like, 'Don't worry too much about your bad heart, because what really gets you is going to be when the shredded remains of your intestines slide out through the hole in your belly.'"

"Maybe not *universally* applicable," Gyre said, smiling slightly.

"I'll work on it." She hopped to the other bedpost, balancing on two opposing legs. "Seriously. What's the problem?'

"I'm just . . . thinking about Maya." Gyre sighed. "I'll be all right."

"*Speaking* of Maya." Kit's body jumped back onto the bed, raising a cloud of dust. "There's someone outside who wants to talk to you."

"She's here?" Gyre sat bolt upright.

"Not in person," Kit said. "But the gentleman came with a white flag, asking to speak to you personally. His message was, quote, tell him I haven't got time to send a note all the way to Deepfire."

That was Maya, for certain. When they'd parted, after Leviathan's Womb, she'd told him he could get in touch through the Order outpost there.

"You could have told me sooner," Gyre growled, rolling to his feet.

"He seemed content to wait. And you looked . . . busy."

"*Kit.*"

"What? A girl can hope, can't she?"

A few minutes later, with a replacement shirt and a borrowed cloak, Gyre stepped cautiously through the north gate. Sarah had wrecked the arcana circuit controlling the unmetal doors, so the only way to open and close them now was by manually hauling them up in their tracks. For now the gate had been propped on some loose timber, easy to kick away if danger threatened.

Kit's tiny construct rode on his shoulder. It seemed best to have her along. *At the very least, if this is a trap, she can get word of it to Apphia.* But Gyre had to admit it didn't *look* like a trap. There were no centarchs or Legionaries waiting for him, just a young man with light brown skin and a shaved head in woodsman's clothes. He carried a sword and a blaster pistol, but also bore a small white flag, which he waved back and forth as Gyre approached.

"I see it," Gyre said.

"Just making sure," the young man said. "I had a friend once who went up to a strange town with a white flag, trying to buy some water. The guards were so lazy he managed to sneak up on them by accident, and they didn't notice the flag until after they'd shot him."

"I hope," Gyre said, "that we're not quite *that* lazy here."

"Apparently not." The young man put the flag away and made a slight bow. "My name is Varo Plagueluck. Are you Silvereye?"

Gyre nodded. "Maya sent you?"

"She did," Varo said. "Apparently the two of you began a conversation yesterday, and she felt like she didn't have enough time to really make her point. She would like to continue under less... urgent circumstances."

"She couldn't come herself?" Gyre said. Then, hating the slight weakness in his voice: "Is she all right?"

"She's not hurt badly," Varo said. "But she thought that a centarch strolling up to your walls might be cause for alarm." He raised his eyebrows. "Also, this little parley is not exactly *authorized*, and her absence might be noticed."

Interesting. Gyre nodded again. "So where does she want to meet?"

"On the edge of the forest, past our sentries," Varo said. "Once it gets dark, come out past the walls and show a light. I'll find you and take you to her."

"Fine." Gyre glanced at the sun, which was getting close to the horizon. "Until then."

Varo smiled agreeably and ambled away. Gyre stared after him for a moment, lost in thought.

"It could be a trap," Kit said.

Gyre shook his head. "Not Maya."

"You don't think she'd hurt you?"

"Oh, she would. But she'd do it head-on." His jaw tightened. "After all, she's the hero."

Chapter 19

Maya

Baron Rashtun's neat army camp had disintegrated into chaos.

Some disorder had crept in even before the assault had collapsed. Fina, annoyed at being left out, had apparently led a number of lancers in an attack on the northern gate that had both failed badly and disorganized the Auxiliaries who were supposed to be storming that entrance. But it was the retreat of the centarchs and their Legionaries that had spread panic. The common soldiers had assumed, reasonably, that if the rebels were too much for the Order's elites to handle, then they weren't going to be defeated by ordinary people with spears and leather armor. They'd broken and scattered, reeling back from the fortress, and what reliable troops Prodominus and the Baron could still call on were occupied rounding them up.

No one seemed to want anything from Maya, which was welcome. One look at the hospital tent had been enough to convince her she was better off letting Beq look after her injuries, which in any case weren't terrible. The cut to her leg needed stitching and quickheal, while the one on her scalp was just a nick, though it had bled profusely. Va'aht was in worse shape from his confrontation with Gyre, though he would live. The same could not be said of many of the Legionaries who'd met her brother. Even unmetal armor was a poor defense against his speed and ghoul-made weapon.

Every time she swallowed, Maya felt the ghost of that sword at her throat, and her fingers brushed the Thing for reassurance. It had been a long time since she'd felt quite so helpless. *Hanging in a cistern beneath Bastion, with Hollis Plaguetouch running his fingers across my cheek.* She had been *nearly* sure Gyre wouldn't do it, but a tiny part of her had been screaming that this wasn't the Gyre she knew. This was a Gyre who worked with ghouls—*he didn't even deny it*—and replaced parts of his own body with *dhak*. Even hours later, the memory made her heart race.

She was sitting at the edge of camp on a rock beside a fallen tree. Behind her, men and women shouted, birds squawked and flapped, and Baron Rashtun's army did its best to sort itself out again. Ahead, as the last of the color drained from the sky, the Spire came alive with light—first torches all along the walls, then great ripping blasts of lightning, tearing down from the heavens to earth themselves in the array of metal struts at the top of the tower. Thunder rolled, low and continuous. Maya's teeth buzzed.

"It's beautiful," Beq said, coming up beside her. Her lenses flickered, painted white by the flashes.

"I keep wondering what it's like to live in there," Maya said. "It must be hard to sleep."

"I suppose you'd get used to it." Beq sat on the rock beside her. "No sign of Varo?"

"Not yet."

"How's the leg?"

Maya shifted slightly and grimaced. "Hurts a bit. Your stitching is clean, though. I'll be all right."

"I'm always happy to patch you up," Beq said. "Just as long as you keep coming back."

Her tone was light, but something caught in her voice. Maya took her hand, and their fingers intertwined.

"There's Varo," Beq said, twisting the dials on her spectacles. Lenses shifted and clicked. "He's waving."

"Can't have gone that badly, then."

The light show was fading away by the time the scout reached them, a few final bolts producing drawn-out growls of thunder. Varo flopped cheerfully on the tree trunk opposite them and yawned. Maya touched her haken and conjured a dim, hovering light.

"He agreed to meet," Varo said.

"That's something," Maya said, blowing out a breath. She hadn't been sure he would. The Gyre she'd seen that afternoon didn't seem like the brother who'd hugged her goodbye after leaving Leviathan's Womb.

"Are we sure this is a good idea?" Beq said.

"Not really," Maya said. "But if he wanted to kill me, he could have done it this afternoon."

"I don't mean it's a trap," Beq said. "But do you really think he'll listen?"

"It's the only thing I can think of," Maya said. "Either Prodominus and the baron will back off, or they'll settle in for a siege. Either leaves Gyre in the Spire for the foreseeable future, and while he's there we can't afford to try to activate the Purifier."

"We don't *know* he's planning to sabotage the Spire," Varo pointed out.

"I don't think he's *planning* on it," Maya said. "I doubt he even knows its real purpose. But the ghouls must, and they sent him here. We have to assume they won't pass up the chance to keep the Chosen shut away for good. At the same time, if Gyre really doesn't know, we have a chance to make him a better offer."

"That makes sense," Varo said, "as far as it goes. But Gyre doesn't want the Chosen back any more than the ghouls do, right? So what are you going to say?"

"Oh, that's easy," Maya said. "I'm going to lie to him."

It wasn't easy.

Maya was not, by nature, deceptive. Jaedia had taught her the value of staying quiet, concealing herself, letting others' assumptions do her work, but it had never sat well with her. She'd never been able to shake the feeling that, if the world worked as it was *supposed* to, she ought to be able to carry her haken proudly at her belt; hiding it felt *wrong*. And this, tricking her brother, was even worse. Her palms were damp with sweat, a greasy film she couldn't wipe off.

But there's no choice. They couldn't leave Gyre in the fortress. He wasn't likely to leave it on his own. The only *possible* other place he could be was *with her*, if she could convince him that she needed his help. *Plague it.* Her fingers brushed the Thing, and she pulled them away. *Think about Jaedia.*

The small light drew closer, resolving into two shadowed figures. The gleam off Varo's shaved head was instantly recognizable, while behind him Gyre remained shrouded in darkness. Maya sat up straighter as they came to a halt across from her.

"Thank you, Varo," she said.

The scout nodded and slipped away, fading into the shadows. She'd told him and Beq to head back to the camp and cover for her if Prodominus came looking. That didn't seem likely, but at least they wouldn't be around if things went wrong.

"And thank you," she said to Gyre. "For coming. I wasn't...sure you would."

His eyes were shadowed, with none of that unnatural green glow. For a moment he stood silent, and Maya's throat grew tight. Finally he gave an embarrassed cough.

"You're...all right?" he said very quietly.

Maya let out a breath and nodded.

"Well?" He looked down at her. "You wanted to talk."

"Why don't you sit down?" Maya said, indicating the log.

Gyre looked at it suspiciously and finally took a seat. His hand brushed the hilt of the silver sword at his side, then jerked away.

"I don't have long," Gyre said. "And from what your friend said, neither do you. Your commander doesn't know I'm here, does he?"

"He's not my commander, exactly," Maya said. "But no. That's... sort of the issue."

"When we were..." He stopped, cleared his throat. "This afternoon. You said that this wasn't about the Commune or the Republic."

She nodded, hesitant to trust her voice.

"Then what are you doing here? Is it—" He hesitated, then forced himself to finish. "Did you know *I* was here? Is all of this for my benefit?"

"No," Maya said. "We only found out you were here yesterday. It's... hard to explain."

He gritted his teeth. "Try."

"The *Order* is here because the Commune killed a centarch and then took Spire Kotzed from the duly appointed dux."

"But not you?"

"I have... another mission. One that's secret from almost everyone, even among the Order."

"Which is why you're hiding from your superiors?"

"Exactly."

"And are you going to share this secret with me?"

"I don't have any other choice," Maya said. "Just listen. There's a... device, a powerful arcana, buried near here. Something the Chosen built toward the very end of the war, when there were only a few of them left. They never got the chance to turn it on."

"What is it supposed to do?"

"Liberate humanity," Maya said. "Destroy the plaguespawn. All of them, everywhere."

It's not a lie, it's not exactly a lie. Ashok had said the Purifier would

destroy the *Plague*, not the plaguespawn, but it made sense that elimi-
nating one would get rid of the other, didn't it? *And anyway, he did say*
there were enough Chosen to set the world to rights, which has to mean
wiping out the plaguespawn. So it's almost *true. Just not… directly.*

"It…" Gyre shook his head slowly. "That can't be possible."

"It's certainly impossible for the Order," Maya said. "But for the
Chosen? At the height of their power?"

"And you want to, what, just turn this thing on?"

"It's a little more complicated than that. But essentially yes."

"If that's true…" His eyes narrowed. "Why would you be hiding
from the rest of the Order? Destroying plaguespawn is what centarchs
are *for*. Why wouldn't they be behind this?"

If you know what someone wants *to believe,* Jaedia had once told her,
you're already halfway to fooling them. She's been talking about how to
dress so city guards wouldn't take any interest, but the principle was the
same. *Gyre wants to think the worst of the Order.*

"Because if we wipe out the plaguespawn," she said, "then who
would need centarchs?"

Gyre froze in place, staring.

"I thought about what you said." Maya looked down at her boots.
"In Leviathan's Womb, about the Order trying to protect the world
by making them *dependent*. I still think it's… more complicated than
that. Most of the centarchs I know are just and honorable, and would
give their lives to defend the innocent. But… not all of them. And
especially on the Council… our leaders…"

"Of course." Gyre's voice was soft and bitter. "The more power you
have, the harder it is to give it up."

"Exactly. Prodominus, the Kyriarch in charge here, is on the Council. You can see why I don't dare tell him what we know."

"Who is *we*?" Gyre said.

"Only my own team. We… discovered this, along with some evidence of how far they'll go to make sure it… doesn't happen." She took
a deep breath. "That's why I need your help."

"*My* help?" He raised his eyebrows. "After . . . today?"

"We were hoping the army would occupy Spire Kotzed, and we'd get sent out on patrols looking for you. Then we could have gone after the Purifier easily. Instead . . . well." She shrugged uncomfortably. "You know what happened. Now if I leave camp to go looking, Prodominus won't be far behind us. We may not find it right away. I need—"

"Someone who can help you fight another centarch," Gyre finished.

"Exactly." Maya let herself smile slightly. "Believe me, I appreciate the irony."

"And what's in it for me?"

"Apart from rescuing humankind from a scourge it has fought for four centuries?"

Gyre put on his own smile. "Apart from that."

Maya took a deep breath. "If we succeed, if this works . . . I can't tell you how much chaos it will cause, up and down the Order hierarchy and in the Republic. Prodominus will certainly have to return to the Forge to see the Council. In all probability, the siege here will be called off, and your rebel friends will have the chance to negotiate. At the very least, it buys them time to dig in."

"Interesting."

And that's not a lie, either, not quite. If the Chosen returned, certainly the siege of some minor fortress in Khirkhaz would drop to the bottom of everyone's priority list.

"Well?" Maya said, a little too eagerly. She cursed herself and paused. "Will you help us?"

"I need to . . . talk to a few people," he said. "If I . . . if we were going, when would you want to leave?"

"As soon as possible," Maya said. "The army is still in chaos."

"I'll be back outside the gate an hour before dawn," Gyre said. He got up, brushing the dirt from his pants. "If I'm coming, I'll be ready. If not, at least I can give you an answer."

Maya rose herself, working hard to keep from shaking. *Chosen fucking defend. He'll do it.* He might need some time to talk himself into it, but he'd be there. *It plaguing worked.*

Gyre

He walked back to the fortress in the dark, mind wobbling like a top given a particularly violent spin.

The hillside between the fortress and the Republican army was strewn with the detritus of war, discarded spears and shields, the corpse of a warbird no one had gotten around to butchering. Gyre picked his way through it in the dark, his silver eye turning night into day. At the gate, the guard who'd let him out was waiting, blaster rifle in hand as he squinted into the darkness. Gyre slowed and spread his hands, and the boy heaved a sigh of relief, standing aside to let him back into the fortress.

"Thanks," Gyre said. "And remember. Not a word to anyone."

The young rebel nodded vigorously. He probably wouldn't keep his promise for long, Gyre reflected, but he only needed a little while. *For better or worse, I've only got until dawn to decide.*

"I can't believe you went without me," Kit said, scrambling out of the shadows and swarming up to his shoulder. "What if they'd tried to capture you? What if—"

"You can't believe I shut you out of the gossip, you mean."

"*Yes,*" Kit said. "Did you see your sister?"

"I did."

"And?"

"I'd like to only tell it once," he said. "Let's find the others."

"You wouldn't have to tell it at all if you'd let me come," Kit grumbled, but she waited patiently while he went back to the tower and climbed to the room Sarah and Elariel were sharing. There was no light inside, and he knocked heavily at the door several times before he heard shuffling feet.

"Are we under attack?" Sarah said blearily. "Because if we are tell them to fuck off and try again tomorrow."

"We're not under attack," Gyre said. "But I need to talk to the two of you."

The door creaked open an inch, and Sarah's suspicious eye appeared in the crack. "It can't wait?"

Gyre shook his head.

"Fine." She shut the door again. "Elariel, put some pants on."

The ghoul's mumbled reply was lost. A few minutes later, the door opened again, revealing a sleepy-looking Sarah in a long nightgown, while Elariel sat cross-legged on the bed in loose trousers and an ill-fitting shirt. The rest of the room was empty of furniture, but Gyre noted it had at least been dusted.

"Sorry to wake you," Gyre said, slipping in and shutting the door behind him. Kit jumped off his shoulder and skittered across the floor. "Hello, Elariel. How are you feeling?"

"Better," the ghoul said. "I am sorry if I frightened anyone. I used... more energy than I should have."

"You don't have to apologize," Sarah said, putting her arm around Elariel's shoulders. "You helped people."

"Not enough." She glanced up at the arcanist. "I should not have maligned your 'quickheal.' It is... crude, but I could never have touched so many. If I ever return to Refuge, I will..." She shook her head, and Sarah pulled her in a little tighter.

"Gyre had a meeting," Kit announced. "With *Maya*."

Elariel froze, and Sarah's eyes widened. Gyre glared at Kit.

"I did," he said. "She sent a messenger this afternoon." He hesitated. "She wants my help."

"Your *help*?" Sarah snorted a laugh. "That doesn't seem likely."

"It's complicated."

Gyre laid out what Maya had told him, the chance to destroy the plaguespawn and the division among the Order. Sarah's smile faded, and she grew very quiet, while Elariel drew in on herself and hugged her knees. Even Kit stopped her skittering.

"That's..." Sarah whistled. "I don't know."

"Do you believe her?" Kit said.

"She believes that this is important, I could see that much," Gyre said slowly. "But she may not be telling us everything." He turned to Elariel. "Have you ever heard of such a thing?"

"No," Elariel said. "But that means little. The truth of what happened in the war is held closely by those who lived through it. I am too young to be trusted with such secrets. My master, perhaps, could have told us more."

"Though I doubt he would have," Kit said. "We tried talking to him on the way to Leviathan's Womb, and he wasn't exactly forthcoming."

"You mentioned the legends," Gyre said. "That the plaguespawn are—what was it? The Corruptor's children?"

Elariel shrugged uncomfortably. "They may just be legends."

"Either way, it's at least *plausible* that the Chosen would have constructed such a device," Sarah said. Her eyes were gleaming at the prospect. "Isn't it?"

"I don't know." The ghoul hugged her knees tighter. "I know little of how *deiat* functions. I suppose they would have *wanted* to, at least."

"Why not turn it on, though?" Sarah said.

"Maybe it was missing an important piece," Kit said. "Like the Leviathan."

"Maya didn't say anything about that," Gyre said.

"She'd hardly tell you before you agree to help," Kit said. "You *did* steal the Core Analytica from under the Order's nose."

"Fair." He took a deep breath. "So it's at least possible that she's telling the truth, and she really needs our help. If so..." He hesitated, looking between them.

"Seems obvious to me," Sarah said. "The tunnelborn lose dozens of people a year to plaguespawn. Chosen know how many more in the rest of the Splinter Kingdoms. If we have a chance to change that, how can we not take it?"

"Besides," Kit said, "I think the people Maya's afraid of in the Order have a point. If there weren't monsters waiting in the dark, they would have a lot less reason to run everything."

"That's what I keep coming back to," Gyre said. "What we saw on the way to Khirkhaz. All that territory just...empty. Little farmsteads built like fortresses. And the people in the slums in Ehren City, because they have nowhere else to go." He shook his head. "Maybe it's too optimistic to say getting rid of the plaguespawn would change everything. But at least people would have more of a chance to build without having it all torn down."

"And you really think Maya would be willing to do it?" Kit said. "If it means the Order losing control?"

"I do," Gyre said. "Order or not, she's still Maya. She wants to help people, not rule them."

Elariel shifted uncomfortably, not meeting Gyre's eye. Sarah put a hand on her shoulder gently.

"What's wrong?" she said quietly.

"I do not trust them," the ghoul said quietly. "The Order. The Chosen. This *device* of theirs...we have nothing but their word that it does what they say."

"Maya wouldn't lie to me," Gyre said.

"Someone could have lied to her," the ghoul shot back.

"Either way, we need to go with her," Kit cut in. "It sounds like she's getting ready to try this with or without our help. We can either be there and be ready to stop her or sit here and not know anything."

"If you saw the device," Gyre said to Sarah, "would you be able to tell what it was for?"

"Oof." The arcanist sucked her teeth. "Maaaaaybe. No way to know. If I could, I'd have to be right up close."

"And if we get there, and your sister is...mistaken?" Elariel said. "If the device is not what she promised? What then?"

"Then I stop her." Gyre put his hand on his silver sword. "I think yesterday proved which of us is stronger, if it comes to that."

"If we're voting," Kit said, capering in place, "I say we do it."

"We're not voting," Sarah said. "It's Gyre's decision."

"I'm going with her." Gyre's chest felt tight, but he swallowed the feeling of unease. "I've been assuming Kit will come—"

"—obviously, I'm already *so bored*—"

"—but the two of you don't have to."

"I'm not going to pass up the chance to poke into a Chosen ruin no one has ever seen before," Sarah said. Then, looking down at Elariel, she hesitated. "But...El..."

"I will go," the ghoul said.

"Hey," Kit said, "you used to yell at me for calling you El."

"Not the time," Gyre hissed. "Elariel, are you sure?"

She raised her head and nodded. "I was directed to accompany you."

"I don't get to demand that of you," Gyre said. "If you want to stay, I'm sure Apphia would be glad to have you."

"No." Elariel sniffed and wiped her eyes. "You are right. It is better to be there, and have some chance of affecting the outcome, than to hide myself away." She hesitated, then set her jaw. "Even if it means traveling with a centarch."

"I don't think Maya would hurt you," Gyre said. "But I won't let her, whatever happens."

Elariel nodded again, leaning into Sarah. Kit, bouncing in place, said, "So when do we head out?"

"I told Maya I'd meet her an hour before dawn." Gyre glanced at the window, which was still dark. "Start getting some supplies together. There's someone else I need to talk to."

The stairs up to Apphia's room were as long and steep as ever. Puffing slightly, Gyre stopped outside her door, finding it slightly open. He rapped and heard a yawn.

"Come in."

Gyre pushed the door open. Apphia was sitting up in the ancient bed—now, mercifully, provided with clean sheets. A loose shirt slipped halfway down one shoulder, showing more of her intricate, branching scar.

"Sorry," Gyre said. "Were you waiting up for me?"

"Chosen defend, no," Apphia said. "It's just been hard getting to sleep, after everything."

"Yeah." Gyre felt weary down to his bones, but he doubted he'd be able to sleep either. He sat down gingerly on the sofa. "How do you feel?"

"My leg's a bit better." Apphia yawned and tugged her shirt up, though it fell back again immediately. "It's all right, Gyre. You don't have to beat around the bush."

He froze for a moment. "You heard?"

"I can make an educated guess. You were seen leaving the fortress, first to meet a messenger with a white flag, the second time going out of sight, presumably to the enemy camp."

"I can explain." *Sort of.* "I should have told you."

"Probably." Apphia smiled at his obvious discomfiture. "It's *all right.* If you were going to betray us, you've had a thousand chances better than this one. You went to see your sister, didn't you?"

Gyre nodded.

"I can't imagine what that's like," Apphia said. "I try to imagine, what if Nina joined up with Baron Rashtun and came after me? Could I fight her? I honestly don't think so."

"It's . . . not easy," Gyre said.

"And, since you're knocking on my door in the middle of the night, I'm assuming something came of this meeting. Did you talk her into leaving the Order?"

"Not exactly," Gyre said. "But there's something we need to do together. Something important. If it works, it might even get the Republic to back off. At the very least, we're hoping the other centarchs come after us, which should keep you safe here."

Apphia nodded calmly. "When are you leaving?"

"Right away."

"Ah." Her expression flickered, just for a moment. "And are you coming back?"

"I don't know." Gyre's throat felt raw. "I hope so."

"I see." Apphia got to her feet and stretched.

"I'm...sorry."

"Gyre." Her smile was a little forced. "I told you I was trying to get your pants off, not offering to marry you. Remember?"

"I remember."

"Then give me a kiss and get out of here."

She stepped forward, and his arms wound around her, her body pressing tight against his as their lips met. It felt like a very long time before Apphia finally pulled away, one hand cupping his cheek.

"Good luck, Silvereye."

Gyre gave a lopsided grin. "Thank you, Baron Kotzed."

Chapter 20

Gyre

They left the fortress as the first tendrils of gray began to infiltrate the eastern sky. Gyre gave a knowing nod to the same young rebel he'd passed twice before. The boy drew himself up, eyes wide, and gave only a slight squeak at the sight of Kit's construct bodies scuttling along in their wake.

With the supplies from Deepfire distributed to the rebels, there was no more need for the bulky wagons. They still carried heavy packs: tents, bedrolls, food and water, quickheal and a small selection of alchemicals. Sarah had jury-rigged a satchel for Kit's remaining medium-sized body, ignoring Kit's protests that she hadn't gone to all the trouble of dying just to be a pack bird. Once they were outside, that construct brought up the rear, while another of Kit's tiny bodies rode on Gyre's shoulder and four more scuttled through the grass ahead.

Gyre shook a glowstone to life and waved it over his head. An answering light bloomed, down on the edge of the forest. *We need to be well away from here before sunrise.* Fortunately, the forest all around the Spire would make it easy to stay out of sight. They were already under its branches when they found Maya, waiting out of view of the Republic camp.

She wasn't alone. One of her companions was the scout who'd come with the white flag, bald-headed and cheery-looking. The other Gyre remembered vaguely from Leviathan's Womb, though his mind had been on other things at the time. She had light brown skin, a dusting of freckles, dark green hair drawn into a complicated braid, and arcana spectacles with elaborate multipart lenses.

Maya hadn't said anything about bringing people along, but then neither had Gyre. They looked at one another uncertainly for a few moments. Gyre cleared his throat.

"I suppose I should make introductions." He waved a hand. "Everyone, this is Maya. This is Elariel, and this is—"

"Sarah," Maya said.

"We've met," Sarah said. "That time when I lost my arm."

Of course. Gyre hadn't thought about that. He glanced between the two of them, trying to think how to dispel the tension.

"You appear to have gotten it back," Maya's green-haired companion said. "Is it a prosthetic?"

"Of a sort." Sarah grinned and flexed her artificial fingers. "But it's better than the original."

"I would love to have a look—"

"Later," Maya said. "Gyre, you've met Varo, our scout. And this is Beq, my . . . my girlfriend. And our arcanist."

Ah. Beq shot a look at Maya that was hard for Gyre to interpret, and Maya took hold of her hand.

"I suppose I'll be the one to bring it up," Varo said, pointing at one of Kit's bodies. "Those . . . things are under your control?"

Gyre nodded. *As much as Kit is ever under control, anyway.*

"Fair enough." He peered at the large one with its pack. "Useful to have along, I suppose."

"We should get moving," Maya said. "It'll be light before long."

"Where, exactly, are we going?" Sarah said.

Maya pointed southeast. "There's a mountain over that way. We're looking for a tunnel entrance along the eastern flank."

"I hope you have more detailed directions than *that*," Gyre said, "or we're going to be looking for a while."

"We should be able to...narrow it down." Maya exchanged a look with Varo. "First we've got some ground to cover."

After a couple of hours Gyre was ready to scream.

Not from the walking, which was pleasant. The others had stumbled a bit in the predawn darkness—except for Beq, who seemed to see in the dark as well as Gyre did—but once the sun came up, their pace rapidly improved.

The problem was the *silence*, which had grown awkwardly around the little column until it sat on everyone's shoulders like a palpable thing. There'd been long stretches of quiet on the ride south, but that had been a more amiable sort of mood, broken by lazy observations about the countryside sliding quietly by. This felt oppressive, with only scattered grunts and muttered warnings about mud or slippery rocks to interrupt it.

Somewhat to his surprise, it was Sarah who finally broke it, when they paused at midmorning to refill canteens in a stream. Kneeling, the arcanist splashed water over her face, then guzzled what was left in her canteen before putting it underwater to bubble as it filled.

"So you're Gyre's little sister," she said, screwing the cap back on. "I can see the resemblance, actually."

"Oh?" Maya raised her eyebrows, clearly half expecting a trap.

"I can too, actually," Beq said. "It's the nose."

"And the eyes," Sarah said.

"Everyone used to say Maya took after our mother," Gyre volunteered. "She had the same hair."

"He never talked about you, back in Deepfire," Sarah confided to Maya. "Very much the man of mystery, our Gyre."

She snorted a laugh. "Is that why he came up with that mask?"

"It's not like the rest of you talked about yourselves," Gyre said. "We were a gang of thieves, not a social club."

"You never asked!" Sarah said. "Yora, at least, knew how many siblings I had."

There was a brief hesitation, a hiccup of awkwardness at the name. But Sarah took a deep breath and charged over it, apparently as sick of the awkward quiet as Gyre was.

"So." She tucked her canteen back in her pack. "What was Gyre like as a kid?"

"Gyre?" Maya looked at him, eyes narrowed. "That was a long time ago. I think he was a little boring, maybe? Dutiful. Did his chores."

"I *had* to be dutiful," Gyre said, "because you were a brat. Always charging into places where you weren't supposed to be."

Beq laughed out loud. "*That* hasn't changed, obviously."

"Obviously." Maya drew herself up proudly and got a round of chuckles.

They went on from there, a conversation that felt like a fragile bridge thrown over a bottomless gorge. There were any number of things that could tear it apart, but by mutual agreement they steered around them, preserving at least the facade of small talk. Gyre decided he would happily take the facade. Sarah and Varo ended up doing most of the chatting; the latter had a seemingly inexhaustible fund of stories about his travels, all of which ended catastrophically, and Sarah laughed every time and demanded another. Varo was grinning ear to ear, excited at such a receptive audience.

As the day wore on, the terrain got steadily rougher. The stream they followed disappeared into a rocky hillside, forcing Varo to lead them cross-country, hacking undergrowth aside as they went. The mountain was visible now through gaps in the canopy, an ancient, weathered dome covered with trees nearly all the way to the peak. The hills surrounding it presented plenty of opportunity to get turned around, but Varo kept them on track with admirable skill, and they only occasionally had to backtrack out of rocky dead ends. Once, faced with a huge fallen tree blocking a gorge, Gyre was ready to look for a way around, but Maya simply drew her haken and blasted the wooden barrier to pieces.

"That must come in handy," he muttered to Kit, walking near the end of the column as they picked their way carefully through the smoking wreckage.

"Think she can use it to cook?" Kit said. "Or would the food just end up spread all over the landscape?"

"We'll find out," Gyre said, looking to the sun. "If that mountain's where we're headed, we won't get there before dark." He glanced over his shoulder. "Where's Elariel?"

"A bit behind," Kit said. "One of my bodies is with her."

Gyre waited, resting his aching legs until she caught up. The ghoul looked miserable, shifting her pack every few steps, her eyes fixed on the forest floor. She didn't even notice when Gyre fell in beside her.

"Hey," he said. "Are you all right?"

"No," Elariel muttered. "My legs hurt and my shoulders ache and this *stupid* body doesn't have fur so I have to wear *clothes* and they chafe in places I am apparently forbidden to mention." She looked up at him, jaw set. "And I must listen to the rest of you joke with a servant of those who hunted my people like vermin."

"Ah." Gyre walked in silence for a moment.

"Do not concern yourself," Elariel said, raising her chin. "I will be fine."

"For what it's worth," Gyre said, "I don't think Maya wants to hunt anyone."

"No." Elariel seemed to deflate a little. "I admit she is...not what I expected. At home, they talk about the centarchs as extensions of the Chosen, with all of their arrogance. Maya seems...more human."

"Humans are bad enough." Gyre rubbed the scar across his silver eye.

"Give anyone that kind of power, and some of them will go bad. But Maya…" He shook his head. "If she was the only centarch I'd met, I might actually believe that stuff about the Order being defenders of the innocent."

"And yet you fought against her," Elariel said.

"I did. But she's also my sister. That makes it…complicated." He glanced at her. "Do you have any siblings?"

"Probably." Elariel waved vaguely. "It's not something we keep track of."

"Not at all?"

"It's different for us," Elariel said. "We live with our parents for only a few years. After that we're brought up in the general creche. And most women will have a child only one or twice every century. Any siblings I might have were adults long before I was born."

"What about the ones you grew up with, then?" Gyre said. "In the creche, I guess."

"We don't associate with them after we come of age," she said. "It's not considered…healthy. As an adult, one should make new associations, based on adult rationality." Elariel's calm tone slipped a little. "I have never been…very good at it."

There was a long silence. Brush cracked and crunched underfoot.

"What do you think Maya would do, if she knew…what I am?" Elariel's voice was small.

"I really don't know," Gyre said. "But let's try not to find out."

For a while after, the silence returned.

Maya

They made camp halfway up the side of the mountain, where the dense blanket of lowland forest gave way to sparse stands of pine. Varo found them a sheltered spot beside a tiny trickle of a stream, with enough clear ground to pitch tents and make a fire. The sun was already fading as their little party settled in, exhausted, and gave a collective groan as they shrugged off their packs. Beq erected the tent she and Maya shared, then watched in fascination as the tiny constructs that accompanied Gyre extracted a tent from his pack and set it up, working in concert to manipulate poles and fabric.

Varo, meanwhile, gathered wood for a campfire, which Maya lit with a tiny spark of *deiat*. Touching her haken, she thought she felt a sudden tug, as though another centarch were drawing on power nearby. She froze in place, scanning the rapidly darkening forest, but the brief sensation was not repeated. *It could be Prodominus, following us and being cagey. Or I could be seeing things. Feeling things. Whatever.* Either way, there was not much to be done about it.

Dinner was the familiar hardtack and soup, with some slices of overripe summerfruit. Elariel, the strange young woman who thus far had barely said a word, retreated to her tent as soon as she'd shoved the meal into her mouth, leaving the rest of them sitting around the fire.

"The last time we met," Sarah said to Beq, "you promised me a look at your spectacles."

"I did?" Beq frowned, thinking back. "I guess I did!"

"Can I hold you to that?"

"Of course." Beq's hands twisted in her lap, a little anxiously. "Can I..."

"Hmm?"

"Can I have a look at your arm?" she blurted. "The artificial one. Obviously."

Sarah raised her eyebrows. "Are you sure? Isn't it *dhak*?"

"I mean. Probably." Beq glanced at Maya. "But we have to deal with *dhak*, too, so knowing more about it might help. I think."

Sarah grinned. "Well, I'm always happy to show a little skin when a girl asks nicely." Beq started, blushing furiously, and she laughed. "Not that there's much actual skin to show, in this case."

The two of them shuffled together, Sarah peeling off her glove and rolling up the sleeve of her shirt. Varo, on the other side of the fire, coughed and got to his feet.

"I'm going to check on some things," he said vaguely, and vanished into the darkness.

Which left Maya sitting, more or less alone, beside Gyre. *Right.* She glanced at him and tried to control her nerves.

"Thank you," she said. "For coming with me. I'm not sure I ever actually said it."

Gyre shrugged. "So far, it looks like you'd have been fine on your own."

"We'll see," she said. "I thought I felt...something. Prodominus and Va'aht may be following."

"I would be surprised if Va'aht was on his feet just yet," Gyre said.

He smiled darkly, staring into the fire, and Maya wasn't certain what to say to that. There was a long silence.

"It's nice," she ventured. "Traveling like this. Together."

Gyre shifted his legs and sighed.

"Have you ever thought about what your life would have been like if they'd never come for you?" Gyre looked at her out of the corner of his eye. "This could have been our life. Instead of...everything else that's happened."

"It wouldn't have been, though." Maya shook her head. "If they'd never come for me, we would have stayed home and raised vulpi. You'd probably have married some local girl and had kids of your own by now."

Gyre's eyes flicked to Beq, and he smiled slightly. "You might have, too."

"I don't think I'd be settling down *quite* yet." Maya's cheeks colored a little. Then her fingers came up, unconsciously, to brush the Thing, and she sobered. "Or I might be dead."

"That's really positive thinking, there."

"You remember how sick I would get. The Order helped with that." There was something there, the ghost of a thought, but before she could settle on it Gyre changed the subject.

"So. How long have you been with Beq?"

"Um." Maya glanced across the fire, where Beq was still engrossed in a study of Sarah's artificial arm. "Not... all that long? But it feels like forever."

"She seems... nice. Kind."

"She is." Maya fought down a furious blush. She'd never really felt like a younger sister before, but now it was hard to avoid. "And funny. And just incredibly smart."

"Is she your first?"

"Are you really asking about the details of your sister's sex life?" *Though the answer's yes.*

"Not *that*," Gyre said, grinning. "I mean is this the first time you've fallen in love."

"Oh." Maya had never thought about it in quite those terms. "I... think so. If that's what this is." She watched Beq demonstrate something about her spectacles to Sarah, then laugh at something the other woman said, outlined in the flickering firelight. "I think that's what this is."

Another pause.

"What was it like?" Gyre said. "Growing up in the Order? Were they good to you?"

"Yes," Maya said. "My master, Jaedia, was... everything you could hope for. She loved me. *Loves* me," she corrected fiercely.

"And she taught you to fight?"

"Among other things," Maya said. "It's not all fighting."

Gyre gave a suspicious grunt, and Maya set her jaw.

"It's *not*. What we did..." She paused, trying to put it into words. "After I wasn't sick so often, we were always traveling. Just me and Jaedia, and later another apprentice named Marn, in a little one-bird cart. We'd stay in village inns, or barter for a place in someone's barn—"

"A centarch?" Gyre said skeptically. "Sleeping in barns?"

"Jaedia didn't tell anyone she was a centarch. Not unless she had to. She always said there was no point in scaring people."

Gyre chuckled. "Because even in the Republic, everyone is scared of centarchs."

"All we did was help people," Maya said. "We'd hear rumors of plaguespawn and track them down, or bring medicine where there was disease or some disaster. I told Jaedia it wasn't fair that we had to hide."

"What did she say?"

"She asked me if it was fair some peasant boy had to fight off plaguespawn with a stick, while I could turn his village to ash with a wave of my hand."

"Do you think it's fair?"

"No! That's why it's *my* duty to defend *him*."

"But not everyone in the Order thinks that way," Gyre said. "That's why we're up here alone."

"It's—" Maya paused. "It's not that simple." She shook her head. "Anyway. What about you? What was it like for you, after you left the farm?"

There was a long silence. The fire *popped*.

"Trust me," Gyre said eventually, "you don't want to know."

"Sorry." Maya took a deep breath. "I—"

"I'm going to bed." He got to his feet. "Good night, Maya."

" 'You don't want to know,' " Beq said, and snorted. "What drama. He thinks he's a character from a bad centi-opera. Like Sarah was saying, the man of mystery."

Maya laughed, lying back on their shared bedroll, while Beq carefully unbound her hair by the light of a sunstone. This process had always fascinated Maya, the dexterous, effortless precision of something practiced into unconscious memory, and how different Beq looked when it finally hung long and loose, shimmering green. Maya had set the watch charm before extinguishing the fire, though Sarah had promised the little constructs would keep watch as well.

"You and Sarah seem to be getting along," Maya said. "Do I need to get myself an artificial arm to keep up your interest?"

"What?" Beq looked around. "No, of course not!"

"Beq. That was a joke."

"Oh." She blinked and adjusted her spectacles. "Of course it was. I was just playing along."

"Right."

"Anyway, it's not just the arm," Beq said. "Sarah knows things they never taught us at the Forge. She's weak on theory, obviously, but there's all this stuff about ghoul arcana—"

"*Dhak*," Maya said.

"Right. But she uses it, and it works." Beq finished her unbraiding and ran her fingers through her hair. "Mostly works, anyway. Sometimes it explodes."

"That sounds like a drawback."

"Sometimes it's *supposed* to explode. I should show you the little bombs she brought along."

"I've seen some of them," Maya said.

"Right." Beq shook her head. "Sorry. It's just...interesting. That's all."

"Is she a *dhakim*?"

"Sarah? I don't think so. She certainly doesn't *sound* like she actually uses *dhaka*. Just puts new things together from old pieces."

"But she didn't get her arm like that."

"No." Beq hesitated. "She just said they found it somewhere. But you can't just stick something like that on and expect it to work."

"Any more than you can replace a missing eye, I should think," Maya said. "What about Elariel?"

Beq frowned. "I don't think I spoke more than a couple of words to her. You think *she's* a *dhakim*?"

"It would explain why Gyre brought her along. She doesn't seem like a fighter."

"I suppose not. And someone is controlling those constructs. That has to be *dhaka*, doesn't it?"

Maya nodded hesitantly. The constructs weren't plaguespawn, clearly, but they seemed to function on the same basic principle. And only *dhakim* could command plaguespawn.

"But we knew that already," Beq said after a moment. "Ashok warned us that Gyre was working for the ghouls."

"I'd hoped they were...using him," Maya said. "But if he has an actual *dhakim* with him, then...I don't know. We have to be careful."

Beq nodded.

"Speaking of things we need to be careful with," Maya said. "Did you finish the nullifier?"

"I...think so." Beq glanced at her pack. "I wish I could test it. It might not work. Or it could do something I don't expect, and you could—"

"Unfortunately, I don't think we can afford to try it before we actually need it." Maya's fingers brushed the Thing, and she reached across and squeezed Beq's shoulder. "It'll work. You haven't let me down yet."

"Yet." Beq blew out a breath and leaned sideways, letting her head rest against Maya's. Maya let her hand run through Beq's unbound hair, feeling its slight curl sliding along her fingers. "Maya?"

"Mmm?"

"Can I ask you something?"

"Of course."

"When we first met up with Gyre," Beq said. "You said I was your girlfriend. But..."

Maya closed her eyes. "Is that not true?"

"You...didn't sound sure." Beq's voice was soft, fragile. "Is that what we are?"

"It just didn't sound...right," Maya said. Then, hastily, "It didn't sound like *enough*."

"Enough?"

"A girlfriend is...I don't know. Someone who you have your first kiss with at a town fair. Sneak into a barn with to fool around. Go to a dance with, and put flowers in each other's hair." She sighed. "It just doesn't seem like any of that will ever apply to us."

"I guess," Beq said quietly.

"I'm sorry," Maya said. "I don't know the right word. I need something that means the girl who fights monsters with me and thinks of brilliant plans when I'm in trouble." She swallowed. "Who I love, and who I never, ever want to be apart from."

"Oh."

There was a long silence.

"Beq?" Maya said. Her throat was thick.

"Mmm?"

"Please tell me I haven't ruined everything."

"Of course not." Beq turned to face her, smiling broadly, her eyes wet with tears. "Whatever the word is, I have one too."

She kissed Maya, pushing her down onto the bedroll, and her hair fell across both of them like a mossy curtain.

Chapter 21

Gyre

"That's it," Maya said. "I think."

"You think?" Gyre said, peering up at the rocky slope ahead. "It's a long way to climb for 'I think.'"

"Varo?" Maya said. "That fold, there. With the big rock sticking out above it. Like—like it was described to us, right?"

"It does seem like the right place," the scout said. "Of course, that's what my friend said when she went down to the river to meet her lover. She stripped off and dove right in, and an eel the size of my arm bit her right on the—"

"*Varo*," Maya said. "Yes or no?"

"Yes," he said promptly.

"Did she die?" Sarah said. "Your friend."

"No," Varo said, "but after that she never trusted any water bigger than a bathtub. Not that I blame her."

"All right," Maya said. "It looks like we can cross to that ridge and follow it from there. Shouldn't be too steep."

Gyre nodded agreement. "Not too steep" might be stretching the truth, but at least it didn't look like they'd actually have to scramble up a cliff face. And there was an indentation in the mountainside that *might* be the beginning of a tunnel, although it could just as easily be only a dimple in the rock.

It was only midmorning, and everyone was already sweating in spite of the chilly air. The mountains of Khirkhaz were hardly the Shattered Peaks—they were old and worn, smoothed by eons into bumps instead of jagged spires. This one was a *big* bump, though, and the tree cover made it hard to see far enough to get a sense of where they were going. Finally, they'd broken through to a rocky promontory that gave a good view of the ground ahead, and Maya had been able to nail down exactly where they were supposed to be going.

Maya. Last night had almost overwhelmed him, quite unexpectedly. Sitting together beside the fire, he'd managed—just for a moment—to forget about the haken hanging at her hip, about what she'd become. He'd pictured the *old* Maya, the little girl he remembered. She'd talked about Jaedia, and the life they'd led, and then...

What did you do after you left the farm, Gyre?

Starved. Shivered. Fucked for a few coins. Slit throats for less. Made friends and watched them die. Went into the mountains looking for a myth, and when I found it...

Enough. They were close now, and the climb demanded his attention. They made it to the ridge Maya had pointed out, a narrow, twisting saddle of rock with a steep slope on either side, winding its crooked way toward the rounded peak of the mountain. Gyre dropped back, looking for Elariel, who wasn't as sure-footed as the others. But Sarah was already with her, their arms linked, so Gyre let them be and walked beside Kit's pack-laden construct.

"You kept watch last night?" he said.

"No, I thought I'd take in dinner, a late show, and finish up with an orgy at Lord Spankbottom's club," Kit said. "Of course I kept watch. There's fuck-all else to do."

"And? Any sign of this Prodominus, or any Republic forces?"

"None that I could see, but that doesn't mean much. You could hide an army a kilometer away in these woods."

"Yeah." Gyre pursed his lips. "Let's hope that means they'll have trouble following us, too."

"Gyre!" Maya, up in front, cupped her hands to her mouth. "I think this is it!"

"Still not happy about that 'think'!" Gyre called back, to a chuckle from Kit.

He worked his way forward again, scrambling over a rocky outcrop and onto a stone ledge. A few stunted trees clung on in the cracks, including one bent and twisted specimen right at the edge of a steep cliff. Across from it, Maya stood by a fold in the rock. As he got closer, Gyre's silver eye let him see that it ran much deeper into the mountain than had been visible from below, ending in an unnaturally smooth stone wall.

They waited, taking shelter in the lee of the rock from the now-constant wind, while the others caught up. It might not be the Shattered Peaks, but Gyre was missing some of the cold-weather gear he'd assumed he wouldn't need in the south. Kit's constructs clattered in, and finally Sarah and Elariel, the arcanist with one arm around the shivering ghoul.

"There's definitely an arcana mechanism here," Maya said. "*Probably* it just opens the door, but be ready for anything." She paused, looking at Gyre. "Also, if Prodominus *is* following, he'll be able to feel this if he's anywhere close. Be on guard."

Gyre nodded. Maya turned to the door, placing her fingers against it and her other hand on her haken. As she looked away, Sarah gestured him over, and he went to squat beside her and Elariel, keeping one eye on the slope.

"How's she doing?"

"I'm worried," Sarah muttered.

"Just c-c-cold," Elariel said. "Be fine. But listen. Something's wrong."

"Wrong?"

"This is supposed to be a *Chosen* site," Elariel said, voice dropping to a whisper. "But there are...markers. Put here by *my* people."

"Markers? Where?"

Elariel nodded to the stunted tree near the entrance. "It looks natural, but it's not. It's been changed with *dhaka*, made to carry a message. It's like...I don't know. Imagine laying a trap for some animal, then scratching a sign on the rock so other hunters wouldn't fall into it. It says *danger*."

"What *kind* of danger?" Gyre said, looking over his shoulder at Maya.

Elariel shook her head. "If there was anything more specific, it's lost now. It's been four hundred years."

"If the Chosen buried some machine here," Sarah said, "wouldn't the ghouls naturally consider that a danger?"

"Or else, like she said, they set a trap," Gyre said. "And didn't want any of their own people falling into it."

Something *crunched*, and a deep rumble went through the mountain.

"It's opening," Maya said.

"Stay close," Gyre said, getting back to his feet.

A slab of stone as thick as a hand slid aside, opening into a long corridor bored straight as an arrow into the rock. Gyre let his hand drop to his sword, but apart from the door, nothing moved.

"This is it," Maya said.

"Any sign of Prodominus?" Gyre said.

Maya shook her head slowly. "I thought I felt something, a little while back, but it's gone again. Maybe he never came after us, or lost the trail."

"Or maybe he's hiding," Gyre said.

"We should be safer inside," Maya said. "This place has been sealed a long time."

She beckoned the others forward, and they started down the corridor in a tight group, with Varo taking the lead and Gyre and Maya close behind him. Kit's constructs spread out, a couple of the smaller ones rushing ahead, while the large one brought up the rear.

The corridor had once been featureless, no doubt cut directly from the surrounding stone with *deiat*, but the centuries had rounded its sharp edges. In one spot, water ran in through a crack in the ceiling, dripping from a stalactite at head height and coating one wall in shiny mineral deposits. Another, wider crack in the floor admitted a long, curling root sprouting countless blind tendrils. Up ahead, Gyre could see the lumpy shapes of irregular boulders.

"So much for being sealed," Gyre muttered.

Maya frowned. "The Purifier itself should still be functional." She poked at the root with her toe. "I can't see how—"

"Gyre!" Elariel shouted, voice hoarse. "It's coming!"

A clattering, grinding sound filled the world, like a thousand millstones at once. The root *moved*, pulsing, and long cracks spiderwebbed across the floor. They widened as sections of rock shifted, as if they were on an ice floe that was rapidly breaking up. Beneath a half-meter layer of stone, dark ropes of muscle heaved, studded with hard nodules that looked very much like teeth.

"What in the plaguing *fuck*—" Maya stumbled sideways, grabbing for her haken.

It was a ghoul construct, that much was clear immediately, but like nothing Gyre had ever seen before. What he'd thought was a root was part of it, a tendril, and two dozen others snaked upward. Chunks of stone, falling into the churning mass of muscle under their feet, were pulverized into geysers of dust with a horrible *crunch*. The remaining slabs of floor tilted wildly, and Gyre staggered, grabbing the edge of the rock he stood on as it threatened to tip vertically.

It's like we walked into the gullet of a beast, and now it's trying to swallow. He mustered an instant of concentration, and his skull *clicked*, everything slowing down around him. Maya drew her haken, the blazing blade igniting instantly, and swung at a tendril rearing up in front of her as the floor tilted and threatened to spill her into the deadly maelstrom of flesh and teeth. Sarah and Elariel were clinging to Kit's largest body, which dug in its claws in a desperate attempt to stay upright. Varo, at the very front, lost his footing entirely and took a flying leap from the disintegrating remains of his perch to a ledge of solid rock at the far end of the trap.

He has the right idea. Varo fought for a handhold, pulling himself slowly up over the lip. *We have to get clear.*

"Maya!" he shouted. "Jump! Up ahead!"

"I'll be fine!" Maya slashed another tendril aside with her flaming sword. "Help Beq!"

The plate under Gyre's feet lurched, and he swore and let go, pushing away from it. Shadows stretched ahead of him, possible positions, alternatives for varying degrees of force and motion. He picked the one he wanted and his limbs responded automatically, grabbing hold of a tendril as he fell and using it to vault himself to another teetering slab near Sarah and Elariel. He held out a hand, and Sarah grabbed with her artificial one, her other arm wrapped around Elariel's waist. She jumped just as her own perch crumbled, assisted by a shove from Kit's body. Gyre's shoulder screamed with pain as it took the weight of both women, but he held on as they swung past and up onto another chunk of floor. Behind him, Kit's big construct toppled, falling among the twists of muscle. With a *screech* it was ripped apart like a limp rag in a meat grinder.

"*Beq!*" Maya screamed again. Gyre looked around for the arcanist and finally spotted her hanging by both hands from a slab of rock that had tipped on its side. She was doggedly trying to pull herself atop it, spectacles askew and smudged with dust, but another chunk was pressing in behind her, threatening to grind her between the two.

"I've got her!" Gyre shouted. "Help Sarah!"

Maya hesitated for only an instant. Then she shifted, her own perch rocking, and reached out for Sarah and Elariel. Gyre gathered himself and leapt again, once more watching the shadows his augmentations sent rolling ahead of him. Every path seemed to lead to disaster—he saw his shadow-self fall short, over and over, or reach Beq only to be ground like grist in a mill between the converging rocks—

There! One shadow, one slender thread. *One way through.*

He grabbed a tendril with one hand, feeling it squirm as he used it to swing against a canting rock and leap off in the opposite direction. Beq, still struggling to pull herself up, turned her head in time to see the second stone coming, and she flinched away from the impact, instinctively throwing out a hand.

At that moment, Gyre soared over her head, grabbing her outstretched arm and planting his feet on the craggy top of the stone. He lifted her clear, an instant before the two rocks came together with a resounding *thud*, and jumped as his perch began tipping over, one arm around Beq. They landed on the ledge in a cloud of swirling dust. Gyre pushed himself to his feet, while Beq curled up, coughing. Sarah and Elariel were huddled together by Maya, while Varo had finally pulled himself up.

"Beq?" Maya stumbled through the dust, haken still in hand. "Are you okay?"

"Shoulder hurts," Beq wheezed between coughs. "But I'm okay."

"Sorry," Gyre said.

She looked up at him through dirty spectacles. "Better than being turned into ground vulpi."

"Chosen fucking defend." Maya looked at the tunnel behind them, where only a few bits of rock remained above the still-churning tendrils. "What *is* that thing?"

"A trap," Gyre said.

"Obviously," Maya snapped. "But—"

"Hate to interrupt," Varo said, "but we're not in the clear just yet."

The grinding of stone on stone got louder. In front of them, one of the boulders was cracked like an egg, unfolding itself to reveal a humanoid figure wearing the outer shell of stone like armor. *This*, at least, was horribly familiar.

Maya

Beq was coughing, cradling her injured arm, but she was *alive*, and that was more than Maya had thought any of them would be a minute before. Gyre had grabbed her in the bare instant before two rock plates had come together—Maya had been *certain* he wouldn't make it, her mind already drowning in despair.

I've never seen anyone move like that. His speed was quite simply inhuman. She'd known that, from fighting him, but this brought it home all the more clearly. His eye was glowing with its eerie green light. *What did they* do *to him?*

"—we're not in the clear just yet," Varo said, and Maya snapped around. A horror of dark muscle and stone unfolded in front of her.

"Back!" she shouted, haken igniting with a *whoosh* of flame.

"There isn't any *back*!" Sarah shouted. They were pressed nearly to the edge of the remaining floor, with nothing beyond but the crushing coils of the monstrosity.

Maya lashed out with *deiat*, flames washing toward the thing, but they guttered and vanished. She swore violently and squared off with her haken. It took a heavy step forward, the ground shivering. When it swung a stone-plated fist, she ducked and slashed upward. Her counter-stroke took a chunk out of the thing's arm but didn't sever it, and its momentum kept it bulling forward. Beq rolled aside, to the edge of the cliff, and Sarah and Elariel shuffled in the other direction. Varo had his blaster pistol out, but his bolt had as little effect as Maya's fire. Gyre, fading around to the side, sliced another slab off the creature's flank.

"Gyre!" Maya shouted. "Around behind it, keep its attention! Get it away from the others!"

He gave a nod, blurring into motion. The creature swung another fist at Maya, and she dodged again but didn't strike back. Instead, Gyre launched a blindingly fast series of thrusts, his silver blade slipping past the stone armor and sinking into the black muscle beneath. Maya had no idea if the thing felt pain, but it could at least recognize a threat, because it lumbered around, one heavy arm sweeping in a broad arc to drive Gyre back. He gave ground, and the creature went after this new threat, shuffling away from the cliff.

Maya followed it, running past the rest of the boulders. Gyre danced through the dust, slipping away from the creature's blows, but he wasn't doing enough damage to really slow it down. Maya raised her voice to be heard over the tumult.

"How do we kill it?"

"No idea!" Gyre shouted back. "Last time I saw one we dropped the roof on it and ran!"

Maya thought of the tentacled horror behind them and shook her head. *Not an option.* "In that case," she said, "I'll try cutting its fucking head off! See if you can get it to stop moving!"

Gyre gave a nod, face coated in sweat and dust. The next time the creature came at him, he ducked, letting its fist whistle centimeters over-head. Falling into a split, he slashed at the back of the thing's knee. It sank toward him as the joint gave way. Maya jumped and grabbed the top of its backplate with her free hand, swinging herself up to get a foothold on the rocky armor. As it tried to straighten, she put both hands on her haken and pulled hard on *deiat*. The blade lengthened, going from orange-red to a brilliant blue-white, and when she sank it into the base of the monster's neck it passed through stone and muscle like wet paper. Maya twisted her blade in an arc, and the creature's armored head fell free, narrowly missing Gyre as it hit the ground with a *crunch* and a spray of black blood.

Maya jumped down, skidding to a halt on the dusty ground. The creature collapsed toward her. She kept her haken at the ready, but it didn't move again.

"Cutting its head off," Gyre said, panting, "seems to have done the trick." The green glow in his eye faded, and he pulled the canister at his belt away and replaced it with another from his pack. "Nice work."

"Likewise," Maya said, straightening up. She let the blade of her haken vanish. "Everyone all right?"

"I think so." Varo staggered out of the fog of pulverized stone. He waved at the boulders around them. "But are there *more* of them?"

There was a short, profound silence, and then a *chorus* of cracking, grinding stone.

"You just *had* to fucking ask, Plagueluck!" Maya shouted, backing up rapidly. Gyre, the glow back in his eye, stood beside her. "Any ideas?"

"Dropping the ceiling on them and running is starting to look better all the time," Gyre said.

Sarah stepped up beside the three of them, an alchemical in each hand. "I can drop the ceiling," she said, "but there's nowhere to run."

"In that case," Gyre muttered, "I think we're fucked."

No. Maya looked back and forth across the phalanx of stone-clad monstrosities, then back at the living deathtrap behind them. *There has to be something.* She started pulling in *deiat*, felt the heat in her chest as the Thing responded. *There has to be a way out—*

Elariel stepped in front of her, hands raised, and spoke a word.

It was a word in another tongue, a liquid, raspy one Maya didn't understand. But it rippled out with all the force of a shouted command on a battlefield, and its effect on the monsters was immediate. They froze, half-unfolded. There was a long, silent moment, the only movement the eddies of the dust.

Elariel strode forward, into the swirling cloud. Maya exchanged a look with Gyre and found silent agreement.

"Stay close," she told the others. Step by step, flaming blade ahead of her, she advanced into the cloud. Gyre matched her, the green glow from his eye filtering through the dust. They passed between the silent creatures, which gave every impression of being merely strange statues. Something moved, fast, at Gyre's feet, and Maya nearly blasted it before she recognized one of the little spider-constructs.

Beyond the row of boulder-creatures, a tall archway led into a much larger space. Maya passed through, cautiously, and found herself in a circular room with a high, vaulted ceiling. Sunstones set into the walls brightened as she came in, throwing rays of light through the fading dust cloud. One side of the room was occupied by a massive arcana, a bank of unmetal cabinets full of crystal-and-wire constructions of unfathomable complexity, each linked to the next by cables as fat as Maya's wrist. More Chosen devices sprouted from the opposite wall, seven long, meter-high unmetal walls like the spokes of half a wheel, converging on a pit in the center of the room. Each wall ended in a tube the size of a man's head that plunged into the pit.

Amid all the strangeness, there was one thing Maya recognized. Beside the enormous device was an empty archway, thick at the bottom but tapering to a strand a few centimeters wide. *A Gate.* Elariel stood in front of it, turning in a circle to take everything in, before finally facing the rest of them.

"All right," Maya said to her, as the others came through the arch behind her. "Thank you, I think. But I need to know how the *fuck* you did that."

"Maya—" Gyre hissed.

"She's right." Elariel stepped forward, and Maya raised her haken protectively. Gyre, frowning, stepped between them.

"So what were those things?" Maya said, not lowering her blade.

"Traps," Elariel said. "Ghoul traps. Since the front gate was sealed, I suspect they were put here by tunneling in through the side of the mountain."

"Wonderful," Maya grated. "And how, exactly, did you manage to stop them?"

Elariel gave a weary shrug. "Because I am a"—a word in that other language Maya didn't understand. "You would call me a ghoul."

Chapter 22

Gyre

"Elariel?" Gyre muttered. "What are you—"

"A ghoul." Maya's eyes narrowed, and she took a step forward, blazing haken crackling. "She's a *ghoul*?"

"I thought ghouls looked...different," Beq said. She and Varo had bunched up behind Maya, while Sarah hurried to Elariel's side. "More like...monsters."

Elariel bared her lips in a snarl, and Gyre hurriedly said, "She was altered with *dhaka*. Exiled—"

"You knew about her?" Maya said. "And you brought her here?"

"You don't understand," Gyre said.

Maya raised her blade a fraction. "*I* don't understand?"

"You don't." Gyre met her gaze squarely. "You've never *met* a ghoul, you've just swallowed what the Order has taught you about them."

"Gyre—" She bit her lip. "I should have known. They've been using you from the start."

"No one is *using* me. I had to fight to be here, and Elariel was nearly *executed*. We're not working for anybody."

"Who told you that?" Maya flicked the tip of her blade at Elariel, sparks falling from it to sizzle on the stone floor. "Her?"

"*Fucking plaguefire,*" Gyre said. "Would you put that fucking thing down and listen to me?"

"She won't," Elariel said. "Now that she knows who I am, she can't risk the threat to her great project."

"Then *why did you tell her*?" Gyre snarled over his shoulder.

"Because we can't let her do it," Elariel said. "My people put those traps out there for a reason, Gyre. This place, this thing, they were *afraid* of it. They never wanted it to be used."

"Of course they never wanted it to be used," Maya said. "The ghouls would do anything to keep the Plague from being destroyed. That's why they sent you here in the first place."

Elariel's eyes went very wide.

"We can figure this out," Sarah said. "If Beq and I do a little investigating, I'm sure we can understand what this place is for."

"If it will really wipe out the plaguespawn," Gyre said, "even the ghouls should want it used. You told me yourself that plaguespawn have nothing to do with your people—"

"She didn't say *plaguespawn*," Elariel said. "She said the *Plague*."

"That's..." Gyre looked at his sister, watching her eyes. "Maya?"

Maya, blade trembling slightly, said nothing.

"I don't understand," Gyre said slowly. "The Plague died out with the Chosen, four centuries ago."

"No," Elariel said. "The Plague infects humans and Chosen both. But it only *kills* those with the ability to wield *deiat*, those who have Chosen blood. The stronger the power, the more severe the illness."

Maya's mouth fell open slightly, and her off hand went to her chest, as though there was a sudden pain there.

"That's what this place is," Elariel said. "The *Purifier*. A way for the

Chosen to destroy the Plague that was killing them. But they didn't finish in time, did they?"

"So what's the point of turning it on *now*?" Sarah said.

"Oh, that's obvious," Elariel said. "She and her Order friends are trying to help the Chosen return."

For a long moment, there was silence.

"We don't *know* any of this," Gyre said weakly. "Not for certain. Maya—"

But when he met her eyes, the truth was written on her face. Gyre's chest went tight, and his hand drifted toward the hilt of his sword.

"You lied to me," he said.

"Not...exactly," Maya said. Her voice was weak. "The plaguespawn will be destroyed—"

"At the price of making slaves out of all of humanity?" Gyre's voice rose to a shout.

"Fucking *look around*, Gyre!" Maya said, equally loud. "It's been four centuries of decay. Four centuries of loss, of watching civilization crumble. I've *been* to Skyreach. I've seen the Chosen towers, and I've seen the slums. I've seen the Forsaken Coast! In four hundred years, how much has *humanity* accomplished? *We need them.*"

"You—" Gyre bit off his retort. "I never should have trusted you. The Order has their hooks in too deep."

"This isn't about the *Order*, Gyre. Please—just listen—"

"No. We escaped slavery once, for better or for worse. You won't put the chains back on." Gyre drew his sword, the light of Maya's haken dancing along the bright silver edge. The thing in his head went *click*. "I won't let you."

Maya

Maya had let her blade drop. Now, slowly, she brought it back to a guard.

Elariel—the *ghoul*—backed away, Sarah tugging at her arm. Behind her, Maya was peripherally aware of Varo and Beq also getting out of the way. But her eyes were fixed on Gyre, his silver sword raised, a green light slowly brightening in his left eye.

No. Maya's throat was very dry. *No, no, no. We're so close.*

"I don't want to hurt you," she said.

"Then walk away," Gyre growled. "Take your girlfriend and your scout and go."

And give up our only chance at a better world. "I can't."

"Then you're going to have to hurt me," he said. "If you can."

Maya's free hand shot up, and she let out her frustration in a scream and a blast of white-hot fire. It parted and flowed around Gyre like water around a rock, but the sheer force pushed him back. Maya followed the flames in, haken swinging. He parried, *deiat* against the silver sword, the raw fire of creation spitting and crackling against the metal. Maya shoved with all her strength, trying to force him back, knock his blade away, but Gyre held his ground. Then, foot planted, he shoved, and it was Maya who slid back.

The opening was enough to let him spin away, so fast her eye struggled to follow. He came in from the side, slipping around her parry, his blade drawing a line of white-hot pain along her ribs. She slashed viciously, giving ground, but he parried again, letting her momentum drive him into another spin. This time he feinted low, then came in high, opening a gash in the meat of her shoulder. Maya stumbled backward, blood flowing freely. Dimly, she heard Beq screaming.

"*Give up*," Gyre said. "Please."

My brother. For a moment, abruptly, it *wasn't* him. It was the Eldest, and Nicomidi, and Tanax, and Hollis Plaguetouch, and everyone else who'd ever expected her to give way. *Deiat* poured into her, and the Thing grew hot, pulsing like a fever through her chest.

"No," Maya said.

"Maya—"

"*No!*"

She drew in a torrent of power and sent it spewing out again in a mass of brilliant fire. Even protected by his *deiat* shield, Gyre staggered. The stone around his feet started to glow a dull, sullen red. The Thing was a hot coal pressed against Maya's skin. Abruptly, she shifted the flow, producing a wall of blue-white fire between them. Gyre's image dissolved in the brilliant glow.

"Beq!" Maya screamed.

"Maya!" Beq came forward, one arm thrown across her face, fighting the waves of heat.

"Beq, *I need the nullifier now!*"

"But—"

Maya turned, face bloody and streaked with tears, flames whipping around her in a halo. Beq went pale. She reached into her pack and tossed Maya a small pouch, coming as close to the fire as she dared. Maya pulled it open, gripping the small, hard bit of arcana inside.

In the wall of fire, dark shapes resolved into a human figure. Gyre, arms crossed in front of his face like a man walking into the teeth of a storm, but coming closer.

Maya took the arcana Beq had given her and snaked it up under her torn shirt, pressing it against the Thing. It snapped into place with a *click*, like a pair of magnets coming together. All at once, as though someone had dunked her in cold water, the heat in her chest faded away. The pain from her ribs and shoulder vanished, too, and in its place she felt *power*, flowing into her body from a bottomless well. Movement felt light, effortless.

Gyre emerged from the curtain of flames sword first, eye glowing fiercely. Maya raised her haken, her crimson hair snapping back in an intangible wind. He was still faster, slipping around her blade, but when his sword came close she raised her off hand to block. Power *bled* from thin air, forming a disc of brilliant plasma that seized his weapon and held it fast. Gyre jerked back abruptly, unable to get his sword free. When her haken swept around, he let go of it and dove aside. He hit the ground shoulder-first in an awkward roll, popping back to his feet at once.

Maya let his sword fall and stalked after him, leaving a trail of blazing footprints. She felt euphoric, riding on an ever-cresting wave of
deiat. It reminded her of the first time they'd been reunited, back in
Raskos' warehouse in Deepfire. And *that* brought another thought
worming out of the recesses of her mind.

The Plague. Not just *resident* in humans and deadly to Chosen,
as Ashok had said, but killing *anyone* with the ability to touch *deiat*.
Chosen blood. Suddenly things fell into place. Her childhood fevers,
getting worse as she got older, until they'd implanted the Thing. The
illness that had come over her after Deepfire, after fighting the Eldest,
when the Thing had been hot enough to burn, struggling to contain
her power.

Basel knew I was too strong. Too strong to *live*, above the threshold
where the ever-present Plague turned from a harmless passenger to a
deadly pathogen. *He gave me the Thing to keep me alive.* And ever since,
whenever she pushed too hard at its boundaries, the Plague had come
for her.

It was in her now. Beq's little arcana had disabled the Thing entirely,
and for the first time in her life Maya was drawing on *deiat* at her full
potential, stronger than any centarch since the war. Ashok had warned
her she'd need that strength to activate the Purifier. But it came at a
price, and she could already feel it building. Her breath rattled in her
lungs, and her heart thundered triple-time.

Which means, she thought, as Gyre drew a pair of alchemical bombs,
I don't have time for this.

He threw them. Maya raised her hand. A lance of pure brilliance
picked him up and hurled him backward, snuffing the bombs' explosions in its greater flame, slamming him against the far wall of the cavern. Without the *deiat* shield, there would have been nothing left but
his bones. As it was, Maya allowed herself a single moment to watch
and make sure he still breathed before she turned away.

The Purifier was waiting. She could feel the potentiality of it, the
colossal energies harnessed through the seven Spires, all feeding power

from earth and sky through underground passages into the heart of the mountain. Deep below them, the body of the great machine lay in a silent, airless tomb, awaiting the surge that would bring it to life. All that was needed was a catalyst, a flood of *deiat* that would begin the chain reaction.

Maya walked to the main console. Beq and Varo were huddled against one wall, and Sarah had run to where Gyre had fallen. Elariel, however, stood directly in her path, clinging to the Purifier, her hair whipping wildly in the wind from Maya's flames.

"You can't," the ghoul croaked. "It's not what you think. *They* are not what you think."

"Move," Maya said.

"You—"

Maya coughed, suddenly, a stab of pain nearly doubling her over. She slapped her hand to her mouth and felt something hot and wet splash into it. When she fought free of the spasm, her palm was stained with black and red slime.

No time.

"Move," Maya grated. "Or *burn*."

Elariel met her eyes for one defiant moment, then ran.

Another step forward, tremors already running through her limbs. She slapped both hands on a single large crystal, following the paths that led from it in her mind's eye, tracing the flows of *deiat*. Nothing complex was needed, just raw power. And, for now, raw power was what she had. She took a breath, feeling sputum bubble in her lungs, and pulled in every thread of *deiat* she could reach. The energy of creation flooded into her, suffusing her, so brilliant and powerful that for a moment she couldn't feel the agony of her infested flesh. When it seemed like she was on the point of igniting herself, rupturing into a blaze of purest flame, she thrust the accumulated power *outward*, down into the crystals and along the wires into the depths of the machine.

The Purifier came to life. Deep in the mountain, it began to whirr and spin, focusing the power into every facet of a massive crystal chamber. Maya could follow it in her mind, riding the energy as it slammed inward in a carefully timed burst, converging from all sides on a single point of nothingness that *squeezed* inward until it could go no further, and then—

All over Khirkhaz, lightning crackled downward from a clear sky, hitting every Spire at once. The hidden cables *thrummed*. In the forests animals shrieked and gibbered, and birds fell twitching from the branches. Ghostly curtains of energy shimmered and danced above the mountain.

Across from Maya all the complex arcana went to work, guiding the power, tweaking and modulating it, pressing it into a shape that would blaze out like an all-devouring flame and never stop. For an instant, all that energy coiled like a spring, and she thought the mountain itself would give way. The wave built higher, and higher—

And burst. Ghostly white light slashed through the room, too fast to see. Maya felt it pass through her body, felt it rearrange her on a microscopic scale. Every dark, throbbing particle of the Plague, bathed in that light, resisted for a bare instant before bursting in a tiny explosion of its own, sending the wave on to the next particle, and the next. Every one added strength to the outgoing tide. It was happening to the others, too—Beq and Sarah, Varo, and even Gyre—the Plague living harmlessly in their bodies converted into pure white light, adding to the ripple that spread out through the rock of the mountain. From there it stretched out farther, reaching the camps and towns, the castles and the cities, every human body spreading it farther and farther until it passed beyond even Maya's mental vision. It would continue outward as long as there was Plague to feed it.

It's done.

Maya slumped across the console and vomited, a tide of dark bile streaked with crimson that washed over the already-dimming crystals and puddled on the floor. She slid to her knees, coughing, speckling everything in front of her with black and red.

"Maya!" Beq landed on her knees beside her. "Chosen *fucking* defend. Maya!"

"I'm—" Maya paused to hack up another glob of foulness. "I'm... all right."

"No you're *fucking not.*" Beq shoved a tablet of quickheal between Maya's lips. "Chew! Now!"

Maya obeyed, weakly, and medicinal numbness spread down her throat. But while her lungs burned, she felt *better* than she had moments before, the Plague no longer tearing her apart from the inside.

"Chosen above, fucking *plaguefire,*" Beq muttered, searching through her pack. "I knew we should have tested that thing. I knew it might not work—"

"It worked"—she spat another mass of black and red on the floor—"perfectly. This is...was...the Plague. And it's gone." Maya took a deep breath, ragged and painful but still somehow clean. "It's *gone.*" She grinned at Beq, who smiled back, though her eyes were streaming with tears. "I'd kiss you, if I weren't still vomiting blood."

"That's...all right," Beq said, chuckling weakly.

"The resonator. We have to tell Ashok."

Beq pulled the little arcana from her pack, and Maya fed it a stream of *deiat*, marveling at how easy it felt. It was like she'd been wearing weights on her limbs her whole life, unknowing, and now they'd fallen away. The image flickered to life, and Ashok beamed out at her.

"It worked," she said. "The Purifier. I could feel it. It *worked.*"

"I can feel it too," Ashok said. "You've done well."

"Now you can come through," Maya said. "And fix everything."

Ashok's smile widened, and his image flickered out. Across the room, the Gate activated, filling with swirling white mist. Maya stared, fighting to keep another coughing fit at bay. The resonator in her hands began to hum, shivering against her fingers.

Ashok's face became visible first, handsome as a statue, with dark skin, red eyes, and slick, golden hair. Then his bare shoulders, his chest, hairless and well muscled, his arms crossed. And then—

—a nightmare.

At the level of his waist, Ashok's body changed, his smooth skin ending in a ragged, torn fringe spreading out over dark, striated flesh. His humanoid trunk sprouted from a massive oval body the size of a thickhead, all rippling muscle and protruding bones made of black iron. A half dozen legs on either side looked more like mechanical apparatuses than anything alive, tendons stretched over a metal armature. More limbs coiled around his midsection, intertwined or dangling obscenely, some close to humanoid and others more like tentacles.

It looked, Maya thought in that stunned moment, as if someone had taken the top half of a handsome man and combined it with a truly enormous plaguespawn, one of the monsters they'd seen in the valley outside Leviathan's Womb. As he emerged from the gate, she could see bundles of thick tubes, pulsing with black fluid, sprouting from the top of the oval body and plugging in to his humanoid half at the base of his skull. They swung and rippled with every step, twining around one another like snakes.

The resonator in her hands was buzzing like a bee trapped under a cup.

Someone was screaming. *Beq*. And possibly Sarah as well. Maya would have screamed, but she didn't have the breath. Ashok's face contorted into a too-wide grin.

"Yes, indeed." There was a bubbling wetness to his voice. "You've done *very* well, *sha'deia*."

"You." Maya pushed away from the control console. "The Eldest said someone would come for it. Its father. It was *you*?"

"An admirable deduction," Ashok said. "If somewhat late in the day. As for the Eldest..." He shrugged, the many limbs below his waist horrifically mimicking the motion. "My children begin as mirrors of my own mind, but once I dispatch them in the world they tend to... diverge. No doubt it had become quite strange over the centuries."

"And Jaedia." Maya pushed away from the console, clinging to the resonator with one hand and fumblingly trying to draw her haken with the other. "Your...*thing*, the spider that left Hollis Plaguetouch, it *took* her. But she was too strong for it."

"Yes, indeed," he said. "Most unexpected. But, ultimately, not a significant setback. The Leviathan in Naumoriel's hands would have been...unpredictable. And you survived, obviously, long enough to make it here."

"Why?" Maya felt her eyes brimming with tears and shook them furiously away. She felt empty, hollowed out, unable to truly come to terms with the monstrosity in front of her. "What *are* you?"

"I told you the truth, more or less," Ashok said, taking another rippling step closer. "I needed you to activate the Purifier. Inconveniently, the level of *deiat* affinity it requires is higher than a human can possess without triggering the Plague. Most such children die in infancy. The strongest survive long enough for me to find them. There have been a few who have come close over the years, but none have done what you have, *sha'deia*. I am, truly, grateful." He gave another multilimbed shrug. "As for who I am, I told the truth there too, more or less. I am the last of the Chosen. I survived, isolated, while the rest choked and died."

"You told the *truth*?" Maya shook the buzzing resonator at him. "You're no Chosen. The Chosen weren't—"

"Monsters?" Ashok gave his too-wide grin again. "We were, you know. But it's true the rest didn't rise to my level of perfection. I have worked hard, over the centuries."

More figures were coming through the Gate, smaller than the massive Chosen. They looked like the humanoid plaguespawn Maya had fought on the Forsaken Coast, the Eldest's creations, but clearly refined and perfected. They moved with a smooth, natural grace, and the backs of their arms were long, curved blades. Their heads bore a circular mass of eyes, a dozen or more, but no other recognizable features.

"No," Maya said. She took a long, shaky breath and spat a mouthful of blood on the floor. "You're not going anywhere. I'm going to stop you, right here." *For Jaedia.*

"You won't, you know," Ashok said. "For all that our blood runs in your veins, you are still a human, and I am one of the Chosen. A child might as well hope to outrun a swiftbird. You could throw all your power against me, and I could still crush you with a wave of my hand." He grinned again. "Amusingly, however, I don't even need to do that much."

He took another step forward, and the resonator in Maya's hand exploded. Shards of crystal and hot metal slashed outward, opening cuts all along her arm and across her cheek. She got an instant's look at her left hand, a twisted ruin of torn flesh and gleaming bone, before the pain overwhelmed her and she sank to her knees with a desperate scream. There was something black mixed in with the welling tide of crimson, spatters of the "transmission medium" that had been at the heart of the arcana. It was cool, tiny spots of numbness amid a crashing wave of agony, but somehow Maya could feel it seeping into her skin. Dark spots swam in front of her vision, and she slumped forward.

"Sorry about that." Ashok's voice was the last thing she heard. "Sweet dreams, *sha'deia.*"

Chapter 23

"Gyre!" And cold, slipping into his veins like a mountain spring, water pushing back the heat that cracked his skin and drove the breath from his lungs.

He opened his eyes, real and silver, and saw Elariel standing over him, her fingertips pressed to his forehead. The cold flowed from there. *Dhaka.* His clothes were torn and scorched, and he smelled nothing but burnt hair. At his side was a fresh energy bottle, and beside it the one he'd been wearing, scorched so badly it had cracked in two.

"Wha..." Gyre coughed and swallowed. "What happened?"

"You sister nearly fried you alive," she said.

"I remember that," Gyre said, struggling to look past her. "Is she still here?"

"She activated the machine." Elariel shivered. "I felt it. Now she's talking to someone."

"Sarah?"

"Hiding behind one of those conduits," Elariel said.

"Help me up."

"You're badly hurt," Elariel warned. "I've taken your pain away, but I can't heal you so quickly. Remember last time."

Gyre gave a weary nod. The ghoul reached down, pulling his arm around her shoulder. He rose just in time to see the monstrous *thing* that came through the Gate, half-human, half-plaguespawn, like an inversion of Naumoriel's war-construct. From the screams, Gyre guessed this wasn't what Maya and her friends had expected. Elariel was abruptly shivering, nearly letting Gyre fall.

"It's him," she said, followed by a long string of words in her own language he assumed were profanity. "We're dead. We're all dead."

"It's *who*?"

"The Corruptor," she hissed. "The father of plaguespawn. The exile."

"I thought you said he was a myth."

"I thought he was," she said.

The Corruptor stalked closer to Maya, who was struggling to stand. Gyre shuffled forward.

"Gyre!" Kit's voice, one of her tiny spider-constructs climbing up to his shoulder. "What the *fuck* is going on?"

"No idea," Gyre said. "But we need to get out of here."

"One of me is with Sarah, and she agrees," Kit said. "She wants to know how, exactly."

"It'll have to be back the way we came," Gyre said, heart dropping. "Maybe—"

Something in Maya's grip exploded with a shattering *boom*. Gyre saw his sister stagger backward, blood spraying from her maimed hand, before she collapsed in a heap at the foot of the console. The Corruptor stalked forward, a satisfied look on his face, while behind him constructs with bladed arms and strange multiple eyes poured from the misty surface of what could only be a Gate.

"As for the rest of you," the Corruptor said, his wet, bubbling voice rising. "I'm afraid you're going to have to die. No need for complications at this stage, and more flesh is always welcome. So—" He paused, head cocked. "Well, well."

Another figure came into the room, a big man with a wild thatch of red hair, blending his beard and mustache into a shaggy mane. He had a haken, the blade a crazed, twisting mass of purple lightning, writhing like a trapped insect.

"I thought I would have to hunt you down," the Corruptor said. "But you've saved me the trouble."

"And you," the man said, "are significantly uglier than I expected." He glanced at Gyre. "You Silvereye?"

Gyre pulled away from Elariel and gave a cautious nod. The bearded man considered this for a moment, then spat on the floor.

"Strange times make for strange friends," he said. "Can I trust you to get your sister and the rest out of here?"

Gyre looked between him and the Corruptor, then nodded again.

"Good. The corridor's mostly collapsed, so you'll have to take the Gate." He spun his haken lazily, purple lightning arcing out from it to everything nearby, crawling across the floor and shimmering through his beard and up his arm. "I'll buy you all the time I can."

"How much, exactly, do you expect that to be?" The Corruptor's smile was fading. "I am one of the *Chosen*. And you are—"

"I am Kyriiarch Prodominus Scatterbolt," the man interrupted. "And I know a few tricks."

"Then by all means, let's see them."

The Corruptor raised one hand and a beam of light lanced out, much like the one that had pinned Gyre to the rock. It scythed through the spot where Prodominus had been standing before detonating against the back wall with a terrific *crump* and the rumble of falling stone. But Prodominus was no longer there—in a crackle of purple lightning, he was suddenly right beside Gyre, still nonchalantly spinning his blade.

"I give it a minute before he squashes me, lad," the Kyriiarch hissed. "Maybe two. Get your sister to the Gate and I'll retarget it while he's distracted. Take her to the Forge and tell her to find Xalen. She's the only one you can trust for sure."

Then, in another crackle of lightning, he vanished again. Curving lines of white light slashed across the chamber, drawing tracks of destruction. Violet energy shimmered and crashed against the Corruptor, breaking against a sphere of pale white that flickered into being around him. The huge creature turned, legs rippling.

"The thing is," Prodominus' voice boomed out, "I'll bet you haven't had a proper fight in *centuries*. Whereas out here"—a cage of flickering lightning sprang up around the Corruptor—"we've been practicing."

Gyre turned away from the fight and grabbed Elariel, who was staring with the wide-eyed terror of a rabbit facing down a wolf. She blinked and shuddered.

"Get Sarah," Gyre said. "Get her to the Gate."

"But—" Elariel gestured helplessly at the maelstrom of strobing energies. Monstrous constructs swarmed around the archway.

"Our *deiat* shields will keep the worst of it off." *I hope.* Gyre had no idea if his own even still functioned. "And I'll clear a path. Just get there." Seeing the despair on her face, he grabbed her shoulders and forced her to look at him. "*Please*, Elariel. We have to try."

The ghoul blinked and gave a quick, frightened nod. She ducked behind one of the conduits on the floor, staying low, and hurried toward where Sarah was hiding.

"Kit, can your other body get to Beq and Varo?"

"Probably," Kit said from his shoulder, "unless one of them decides to fry me."

"Do it, and tell them we're going for the Gate. Tell them I'll try to cut through, but I need someone to get Maya."

"They may not listen to..." Kit's spider-construct gestured at itself with its forelimbs. "Me."

"Tell them it's the only way any of us get out of here alive, including Maya," Gyre said. "Beq will listen."

"On my way," Kit said. "Now what?"

"Now," Gyre said, digging in his pockets, "let's see if we can thin these plaguing bastards out a little."

At the base of his skull, something went *click*.

* * *

Prodominus, flickering from place to place in a halo of purple energy, had drawn the Corruptor away from the Gate and the main console. Most of the constructs had followed, but the rest were spreading out, casting about with their weird, multi-eyed gaze. They looked up, blinking, as two small spheres hurtled over their heads to smash against the floor behind the Corruptor. Flames erupted instantly, the alchemical powders blazing wildly where they met the air. Several constructs staggered out of the inferno still ablaze, but soon collapsed as their muscle blackened and peeled away from their iron skeletons.

Another pair of bombs landed among the remainder, just ahead of Gyre himself. These were stunners, producing a light so bright it would send a normal human reeling. Gyre hoped that anything with so many eyes would be vulnerable. He hit the ground in a crouch, drew his sword, and slashed through the closest creature, cleaving it neatly from hip to shoulder. As it fell in a wash of black blood, the others closed in, their shadows leaping ahead of them in his silver eye.

Gyre's world was abruptly a maelstrom of shimmering, clashing images, and he struggled to find a clear path. The things were fast, even with his augmentations, their shadows ripping through the air with frightening speed. And they were stronger than any human, even a glancing parry sending him stumbling backward. He ducked, letting another pair of blades pass over his head, and spun to the left, taking a leg off the nearest construct as he went. The rest followed, spreading to either side, working as a pack.

They talk *to each other.* The things made no sound, but they functioned like parts of a single organism, some coming at him head-on while others covered his escape routes. Gyre ducked, dodged, ducked again, carved a construct in two and spun into the gap it left, only to find two more behind it closing in. With his free hand, he hurled an alchemical at them, and the blast knocked them off their feet. Even downed, they were dangerous, bladed arms flailing as he danced past them. He hurled his last flamer into the heart of the pack, and a half dozen of the things blackened and tumbled.

There's still too many. The first two incendiaries had cut off half the room, but the creatures that remained between him and the Gate were enough to make a wall of black flesh and iron bone. Gyre drove his sword into a construct's head and it dropped twitching to the ground, even as two of its fellows stepped over its corpse. His only hope was in constant movement, keeping them from surrounding him and closing off every possible route of escape. The pack surged around him.

"Gyre!" He felt a pressure on his shoulder as Kit's tiny body leapt off, launching itself into the face of a construct trying to skewer him from behind. The thing staggered back for a moment, then crushed the little spider between its blades. Gyre beheaded it an instant later, black blood spraying while the body wobbled and fell. He gave ground as more of the things closed in, pushing him farther from the Gate—*have they figured out what we're trying*—

A volley of blaster bolts *zipped* over his head, detonating among the multi-eyed creatures with deafening *cracks*. Beq and Varo charged toward Gyre, pistols in hand. Gyre attacked with renewed vigor, ignoring the constructs that tried to flank him. Varo gunned them down, one by one, while Beq dropped to her knees beside Maya's still form and started wrapping her maimed hand in a bandage.

Another *crack*, off to Gyre's left, indicated Sarah had joined the battle as well. A half dozen constructs split off to attack her, but she hit the first with a punch from her artificial arm strong enough to throw the thing completely off its feet and back into its fellows. Elariel, following the artificer, tossed a bomb into the pile and they all went up in a pillar of flame. Another of Kit's bodies scuttled beside them.

"That is *enough*," the Corruptor growled. "I will not be toyed with by a *human*."

"Oh no?" Prodominus flickered into being just in front of the massive creature. "Then stop playing around, plaguepit."

"*Gladly*," the Corruptor snarled. Limbs unfolded from around his midsection, tentacles snapping out and curving toward the Kyriliarch. Purple lightning crashed, and Prodominus vanished, but a moment later he appeared again, caught in the nexus of four converging limbs. "All you have are tricks of the light."

"You can get a long way with tricks of the light," Prodominus gasped.

Purple lightning slashed down, a single massive stroke that slammed into the Corruptor's spherical shield and outlined it in coruscating light. For a moment the white was invisible beneath sheets of crackling purple. Then the lightning faded, and the opalescent sphere beneath was intact. The tentacles holding Prodominus lifted him off the ground, to a level with the Corruptor's face.

"A fine effort, for one of *you*." The limbs around Prodominus tightened, and there was an audible *snap* of bone. The old man's face was a rictus of agony. "What shall I craft from your rendered flesh, hmm?"

Something crackled, just by Gyre's ear, and he heard the whisper of the Kyriliarch's voice. "It's done. Go!"

Only a thin line of constructs blocked the Gate. Gyre charged, and Varo and Sarah charged with him, both firing their blasters until they gave the whine of empty sunsplinters. Sarah holstered her weapon and slammed her fist into a construct, crushing it against the complicated workings of the Purifier and sending broken bits of wire and crystal pinwheeling away. Varo drew his sword, parrying the first construct that reached him and sinking his riposte into its midsection. It staggered on, blades raised, but before it could strike, another of Kit's bodies launched itself into the thing's face. It collapsed, writhing, and one of its fellows skewered the tiny spider. Gyre stepped in front of the scout and cut the constructs down.

Then the Gate was only a meter away, the space inside its narrow, twisted arch swirling with pearly fog.

White light scythed down, slashing in front of the Gate and leaving a line of bubbling red-hot stone in its wake. Gyre had already been slowing, not wanting to leap through without the others. If he'd continued at full speed, the burst would have cut him in half.

"Clever little bugs," the Corruptor said. He had maneuvered his huge shape around to face them, Prodominus hanging limp in his tentacles, more constructs swarming around his legs. "But no. You won't be leaving that way. And you won't be taking my *sha'deia*." He smiled beatifically at Maya. "She still has important work to do."

Beq, with Maya in her arms, was just behind Gyre with Varo. Sarah, the sleeve of her artificial arm shredding to reveal the construct beneath, stood beside them, her real hand pressed over a cut to her side. Elariel clung to her, wild-eyed. And Kit—

—was creeping across the floor toward the Corruptor, her last little spider-body dragging a sack larger than it was. A sack Gyre recognized. *That's where Sarah keeps her alchemicals.*

Gyre's head snapped up, meeting the Corruptor's eyes.

"Let me work for you too, then."

The thing's red eyes gleamed as it cocked its head. "And why would you do that?"

"Given what you did to the Kyriliarch, I assume you'll be fighting the Order." Gyre straightened up, sheathing his sword. "Destroying them is what I've been working for my whole life."

"Gyre—" Elariel said, then stopped as Sarah poked her.

"And what exactly could you do for me, human?" The Corruptor leaned forward. "I don't need the toys you've got buried in your skull."

"I can take you to where I got them," Gyre said. "The last city of the ghouls. That has to be worth something, right?"

"Gyre!" Elariel broke free of Sarah's restraining hand. "You can't!"

"Relax, creature," the Corruptor said. "He's merely buying time for this little thing to execute some ploy."

He shifted forward, one huge foot coming down on Kit's back, punching straight through her fragile body and pinning it to the floor. Her legs wriggled weakly, shifting the sack a few centimeters farther.

"Kit!" Gyre said, taking a step forward.

"Don't be an idiot," she said. "I'm not really here, remember? I'll... catch...up..." Her voice faded to nothing, and the little spider stopped moving.

"Curious," the Corruptor said, bending to examine it. "What manner of—"

Gyre dug an alchemical from his pocket. It wasn't much, another stunner, enough to produce a brief pulse of light and a quick shock wave. He tossed it underhand, right at the Corruptor's foot, beside Kit's still body and the leather sack. Its thin clay shattered, and it burst with a *whump*—

—and Gyre squeezed his eyes shut and threw his arm across his face, just in time.

Every alchemical in the sack went up at once—burners and stunners, bigger bombs and powders for shattering rock. Flaming bits of clay fountained upward, engulfing the Corruptor, and the blast wave nearly knocked Gyre off his feet. Prodominus fell to the stone, tossed by a wildly flailing tentacle.

The whole front half of the Corruptor's body had been shredded, several legs removed, other limbs hanging by threads of gristle. His humanoid shape had bloody wounds all across its front, and a chunk of shattered stone had sheared off part of his scalp. The enormous thing collapsed into a heap, black blood spurting in a dozen places.

Gyre blinked spots away from his eyes and ran to Beq and Maya. His sister looked like half a corpse already, spattered with black and red gore, a stain already soaking through the thick bandage around her hand, her skin several shades too pale. Gyre grabbed the stunned Beq by the shoulders and wrestled her up, pushing her toward the Gate.

"Get her through!" he said, shouting. "All of you, get through! *Now!*"

"Ow." The Corruptor's voice was a bubbling mess. "You are really starting to irritate me."

The wounds on his humanoid body were closing before Gyre's eyes, rents healing as though they'd never been, blood sloughing away in dry, powdery flakes. Great ropes of muscle whipped out of his lower body, limbs twisting as they thickened and became whole again. Long, ropy tendrils took the place of the missing legs, hardening rapidly to flesh and bone.

"You can't escape, you know," the Corruptor said as he regained his feet. "Wherever you go, I can follow. I will get my *sha'deia* back, and the rest of you will discover new frontiers of suffering." His voice was still pleasant, conversational. "Depend on it."

Beq was through the Gate, and Varo. Sarah and Elariel, arm in arm, supporting each other. Gyre backed to the threshold and threw a guilty look at Prodominus. The Kyriliarch had levered himself halfway up, both legs clearly shattered, blood dripping from his lips and down into his beard. He lifted his haken. The blade ignited, purple lightning crackling.

"*Go*, boy," he said. "And remember who you can trust."

"Don't be a fool—" the Corruptor said, in sudden understanding.

But he moved too late. Gyre stepped back through the Gate, and the last thing he saw before the mist closed over him was a concentrated bolt of shimmering lightning leaping from Prodominus' blade, shattering the thinnest part of the arch. There was a high, inhuman screech, and then everything went white.

Epilogue

Corruptor

The expression on Nial-est-Ashok's face, as his features knitted them-selves back together from pulverized black goo, was one of mild irritation.

Well. That was ... unexpected.

The destruction of the Gate while still charged with *deiat* had unleashed a sudden flux of uncontrolled power. It had wrecked one end of the Purifier control room, sending spidery cracks through solid rock and reducing the delicate equipment to so much twisted junk.

That was all right; the machine had served its purpose. The air that filled Ashok's reconstructed lungs was completely, gloriously free of the infernal phage that had kept him prisoner for four centuries, defying his every attempt to cure or filter it. The world that the ghouls had turned implacably hostile to his kind welcomed him once again. *At long, long last.*

The centarch Prodominus, who'd broken the archway, had been closest to the blast. There was little left of him but ash and the fused, blackened remains of his haken. That was mildly vexing. Ashok had expected to amuse himself stripping information from the man's living brain before rendering him into parts. *Ah well.*

The damage to Ashok himself and the destruction of dozens of his constructs barely signified. His body repaired itself without his conscious intervention, drawing on internal stores of energy. They would need to be replenished in time, but the need was not urgent. *And there are always more constructs where those came from.* So many more now, since his supply of materials was vastly expanded.

No, the cause of Ashok's annoyance was not the blast, but the fact that it was now more than a hundred kilometers to the closest Gate, with all the resulting implications for his timetable. After planning for so long, hitting a snag right from the start rankled. A reminder that the real world was never *quite* as perfectly under control as he would like it to be.

But that's why I'm here, after all. To fix things. And while some parts of the plan might have to be delayed, there were others that could proceed at once.

He concentrated his mind, attuning it to the thrumming power that filled his misshapen body. The principle of his resonators required *dhaka* and *deiat*, wielded in unison—no wonder it had never been discovered even during the glory days of the Chosen. The transmission medium, nothing more or less than Ashok's own blood, hummed with the same power whether it was in his veins or a thousand kilometers away. An image projector sprang to life, showing the centarch on the other side what Ashok wanted him to see, the handsome image of the man he'd once been.

"Begin preparations at Skyreach at once," he said. "I will give you the signal when I am ready."

He shifted focus before the centarch could answer, activating more resonators, giving more instructions. Then he turned his attention to his children, the tiny copies of himself that had been his window into the larger world for so long. They needed no resonator to hear him—the blood that ran through them was his own, and it sang his words directly into their minds.

When he was nearly finished, he paused for a moment, listening to the inaudible hum. There was something else, not a child or a resonator but echoing to his power nonetheless. Faint, but there. A mind, dark with pain, lying in fitful slumber.

Ashok realized who it was and broke into a slow smile. Echoes of power carried his whispers down a link forged from a spatter of blood.

"Sweet dreams, *sha'deia*," he crooned. "See you soon..."

The story continues in . . .

Emperor of Ruin

Book 3 of Burningblade & Silvereye

Coming in 2023!

Acknowledgments

I find these sections get shorter as a series goes on, not because I am any less indebted but simply to avoid repeating myself. *Ashes of the Sun* includes my thanks to everyone who helped plant this idea in my head, and they all deserve my gratitude once again.

Some names, of course, absolutely *should* be repeated. Brit Hvide provided excellent editing from outline to final draft, and writing *Blood of the Chosen* was a considerably less fraught process than *Ashes of the Sun* because of it. My thanks as well to the rest of the Orbit team: Laura Fitzgerald, Ellen Wright, Angela Man, Paola Crespo, Alex Lencicki, Stephanie Hess, Lauren Panepinto, Bryn A. McDonald, Rachel Hairston, and Tim Holman. I am also indebted, as always, to my agent Seth Fishman and his team at the Gernert Company—Jack Gernert, Rebecca Gardner, Will Roberts, Nora Gonzalez, and Ellen Goodson Coughtrey—for all their work in getting these words into your hands. And, of course, my wife, Casey Blair, helped me work through the most tangled of plot snarls.

Finally, my sincere thanks to everyone who picked up *Ashes of the Sun* and gave it a read. Without you, none of this would be possible.

Glossary

agathios (pl. agathia)—a person in training to be a **centarch**. The **Twilight Order** searches out children with the ability to touch *deiat* and trains them as agathia from a young age. Agathia become full centarchs on being granted their **cognomen**.

alchemy—the process of refining and recombining ghoul **arcana**. Even broken, rotten remnants of the ghouls' organic "machines" can be rendered down into useful by-products, from which an alchemist can create **quickheal** and other medicines, bombs, powerful acids, and a variety of other tools depending on the materials available. The **Twilight Order** forbids alchemy and considers its products *dhak*, so the practice is more common in the **Splinter Kingdoms** than in the **Dawn Republic**. A few alchemicals, like quickheal, are so useful that the Order considers them legal, **sanctioned arcana**, provided they are made by a few carefully controlled suppliers.

arcana—any tool or implement of **Elder** origin, from rare and powerful weapons like **haken** or **blasters** to **alchemical** creations like **quickheal**. Common people generally have little understanding of the differences between types of arcana.

auto—a **Chosen** ground vehicle. Oval-shaped with a curved bottom, it floats half a meter above the ground and has seats for four to eight passengers. It requires a **sunsplinter** to power itself, and it can only function on a **repulsion grid**. In the present day, they are used only in **Skyreach**.

Auxiliaries—one of the two major branches of the armed forces of the **Dawn Republic**, along with the **Legions**. The Auxiliaries are by far the larger force but, unlike the Legions, carry no **arcana** weapons and armor, relying on ordinary human-made swords, spears, and bows. They are responsible for policing, keeping order, and local defense against bandits and plaguespawn, under the command of the local **dux**. Sometimes called by the derogatory nickname "Auxies," especially by criminals.

banners—the subgroups of the **Khirkhaz Commune**, rebels against the **Dawn Republic**. Named for their use of the Commune's flag in colors other than the main group's red: Whites, Greens, and Blacks. Famously fractious and prone to rivalry.

bird—Ordinary birds are common, but the term often refers to the large, flightless varieties used as beasts of burden. See **loadbird**, **swiftbird**, and **warbird**.

"black spider"—Maya's name for the creature—construct or plaguespawn—that controlled first Hollis Plaguetouch and then Jaedia. Resembling a fat-bodied spider or tick, the creature attaches to the back of a human's neck and is apparently able to control their actions and use *dhaka*, though not make use of *deiat*. The host retains consciousness and some autonomy, and Jaedia was able to resist temporarily under extreme conditions. When removed, it leaves behind poison that kills the host, though Maya was able to prevent this in Jaedia's case. Maya destroyed the spider, but it is not known if it was the only one of its kind.

blaster—an **arcana** weapon that uses *deiat* in a crude fashion, firing bolts of pure energy that explode on impact. Like any arcana making use of *deiat* on its own, blasters are powered by energy stored in **sunsplinters** and useless once the energy is expended. The **Legions** use blasters as their standard ranged weapon. Pistol and rifle variants both exist, with the latter having greater range.

Since charged sunsplinters can only be acquired from the **Twilight Order** or occasionally scavenged from ruins, functioning blasters are very expensive and a mark of status.

centarch—one of the elite warriors of the **Twilight Order**, capable of wielding *deiat* through a **haken**, unlike all other **humans**.

Chosen—one of the **Elder** races, along with the **ghouls**. All Chosen could use *deiat*, without the aid of tools like **haken**, and this power made them unchallenged rulers of a continent-spanning empire for centuries, with **humans** serving them. They were wiped out by the **Plague**, but in their final years, they founded the **Dawn Republic** and the **Twilight Order** to help humanity survive in their absence.

cognomen—**Humans** in the former **Chosen** Empire have either only a given name or a given name and a family name for city dwellers and elites. In addition, some people have a cognomen, a third name that describes some aspect of their history, character, or appearance. Cognomen are granted by general acclamation, not chosen, and trying to pick one's own cognomen is the height of arrogance and opens one to mockery. Cognomen are not always complimentary but can be very hard to shake once applied. They are often two-word compounds: Rottentooth, Boldstep, Halfmask.

For **centarchs**, cognomen have a greater significance. They are granted, not by the centarch's peers, but by the **Kyriarch** Council when an **agathios** reaches the status of a full centarch. The cognomen matches the way the centarch manifests *deiat*, and the Council often chooses names held by past centarchs, with the oldest names conveying the most favor and honor.

Commune—The **Khirkhaz** Commune is a rebel organization trying to free Khirkhaz from the political control of the **Dawn Republic**. It was created by Apphia Kotzed, who convinced several independent rebel movements to come together and declare a single purpose. The individual groups retain a great deal of independence, and central control is often nominal.

construct—a semiorganic autonomous servant created by the **ghouls** using *dhaka*. Constructs come in a huge variety of shapes and sizes, but many are roughly humanoid, with specialized construction for their particular role, such as armor, weapons, or extra limbs. They are typically built of artificial muscle layered over a metal skeleton, and resemble **plaguespawn**, although the latter are much more chaotic and strange. A device called an analytica provides the construct's ability to understand instructions and make decisions, but only the ghouls understood how these function.

Dawn Republic—a nominally democratic state created by the **Chosen** as their numbers dwindled during the **Plague**. Originally, the Republic encompassed all the land that had been part of the Chosen Empire, but in the four hundred years since the Plague, much of the territory has broken away, forming smaller polities collectively known as the **Splinter Kingdoms**. Even so, the Republic remains the most powerful nation in the known world, with its capital at the old Chosen city of Skyreach.

The Republic has a sometimes uneasy relationship with the **Twilight Order** and its **centarchs**. The Order was charged by the Chosen to defend the Republic and humanity, but not to rule it, and so normally stands apart from the daily running of Republican politics. However, the centarchs collectively wield unmatched power, and the Republic's elite military forces, the **Legions**, rely on Chosen-built weapons and armor that only the Twilight Order can maintain. The upshot is that the wishes and suggestions of the Order carry considerable weight with the Republic government, and centarchs are legally empowered to dispense justice and commandeer any necessary resources in pursuit of their missions.

The Republic is ruled by a Senate, which is theoretically elected, but the franchise is restricted to the wealthy, and senators almost always come from a small group of powerful families. The Senate elects two consuls every year to serve as chief executives. The Senate appoints a dux as military commander and chief magistrate to the various regions of the Republic, typically one per major city. The **duxes** command the **Auxiliaries**, who handle policing and local defense, with the Legions retained under the consuls' direct control or seconded in small detachments as needed.

Deepfire—a city deep in the Shattered Peak mountains. Deepfire is an exclave, considered **Dawn Republic** territory in spite of being far outside the Republic's borders, connected by a **Gate** under the **Chosen** fortress known as the Spike.

Originally, the mountain that stood where Deepfire is now hosted a major **ghoul** city—perhaps the ghoul capital, though stories are conflicted. The Chosen deployed a weapon of unparalleled destructive power against it. While the nature of the weapon is unknown, it blasted the mountain into a kilometers-wide crater and left a giant fissure in the rock known as the Pit. Immediately afterward, the Chosen forces began a systematic purge of the surviving ghoul tunnels.

As the Chosen died out, the **Twilight Order** continued the purges. Humans from the surrounding areas flocked to the crater, since heat from the Chosen weapon—still burning at the bottom of the Pit—kept it warm in the depths of winter, and the Order and **Legion** presence provided protection from **plaguespawn**. Scavenging in the tunnels eventually became a major industry, and the Order maintained their presence to manage it.

Modern Deepfire is a divided city. The crater has long since been filled with buildings, and the edge of it marks the formal boundary of the Republic. Beyond that, the mountain is riddled with tunnels, and the people who live in them are called tunnelborn. Tunnelborn are not Republic citizens, and manufactories set up to exploit their cheap labor have become the city's second primary industry. Tension between the tunnelborn and the Republic citizens living aboveground is common, exacerbated by the plentiful opportunities for smuggling and corruption available to Republic officials.

deiat—the power of creation, the fire of the sun. The **Chosen** could draw *deiat* energy to accomplish a wide range of spectacular feats, from destructive manifestations like balls of flame or bursts of raw force to defensive barriers and more. It could also be used to create unnatural substances, like the indestructible **unmetal**. More advanced uses of *deiat* required specialized tools, now called **arcana**. These devices, when powered by a *deiat* wielder, could accomplish wonders—the **Gates** that wove the Empire together and the skyships and skyfortresses that hovered overhead are notable examples, in addition to more mundane tools like **blasters**, watch charms, water treatment facilities, and so on.

Deiat does have limits. It manipulates physical objects and properties—force, temperature, and so on—and does not interact with biological systems at any level except the crudely destructive. *Deiat* tools also require a continuous flow of power, either from a wielder or a storage device like a **sunsplinter**, and cannot operate without the will of the wielder. In particular, the autonomous **constructs** used by the **ghouls** are impossible to create with *deiat*.

With the Chosen wiped out by the **Plague**, the only wielders of *deiat* remaining are the **centarchs** of the **Twilight Order**, who can use their **haken**—themselves a *deiat*-created tool—to draw *deiat* power, though more weakly than the Chosen could. Why some **humans** have the ability to wield *deiat* and others do not is unknown. Centarchs are typically limited to a particular class of effects—fire, ice, force, and so on—although all can use *deiat* to power arcana such as Gates and **panoply** belts. Only the most primitive of construction techniques are still practiced, but existing unmetal can be reforged and reshaped, allowing the creation of the armor of the centarchs and the **Legions**.

dhak—Originally, this term referred only to **ghoul arcana** produced using *dhaka*. In the centuries since the **Plague War**, its meaning has expanded, and it is now synonymous with unsanctioned arcana—arcana not in the very narrow categories approved for safe use by the **Twilight Order**. Possession of *dhak* is illegal in the **Dawn Republic** and grounds for immediate imprisonment or even execution, at the discretion of the arresting official.

dhaka—a form of supernatural power, distinct from ***deiat***, originally wielded by the **ghouls**. *Dhaka* allows a wielder to influence biological systems and processes, to accelerate, change, or even give a semblance of life to nonliving things. It can heal wounds and alter living creatures and was used by the ghouls to create a great variety of living and semi-living tools—light sources, weapons, even vehicles. The most noteworthy were **constructs**, automata that could accept orders and act independently, a type of creation impossible even for the **Chosen**.

Any **human** can learn to wield *dhaka*, though the practice can be very dangerous and much knowledge has been lost. After the **Plague War**, the dying Chosen created the **Twilight Order**, and one of its central commandments was to stamp out the knowledge and practice of *dhaka* forever. This has proven difficult, and the Order pursues ***dhakim*** down to the present day.

dhakim—a human wielder of ***dhaka***. Illegal under penalty of death in the **Dawn Republic**, and even in the **Splinter Kingdoms**, often shunned and likely to be hunted down by **centarchs**. *Dhakim* are widely seen as mad, conducting gruesome experiments and creating horrible diseases. Adding to this perception is the fact that *dhakim* can exert influence over **plaguespawn**, bringing the mindless creatures under their command. Very occasionally, a *dhakim* will establish a reputation as a healer and come to be accepted by their community.

dux—a military governor appointed by the Senate of the **Dawn Republic**, in charge of a major city and its surrounding region. Commands the **Legion** and **Auxiliary** forces within their area of authority. Sometimes an outsider to the region, sometimes drawn from local elites, depending on political requirements.

Ehrenvare—a **Splinter Kingdom** to the west of the **Dawn Republic**, ruled by a king and a military aristocracy, who fight as **warbird**-riding lancers.

Elder—something of the time before the **Plague War**, approximately four hundred years ago, when the **Chosen** ruled an empire and the

ghouls lived underground. As most common people are hazy on the distinction between various types of **arcana** and ruins, Chosen and ghoul remnants alike are often referred to generically as Elder.

Flitter—a small, relatively inexpensive flying vehicle of the **Chosen**. It resembles a small boat with a curved bottom and typically carries four to six passengers. Powered by a **sunsplinter**, it requires far less *deiat* energy to operate than a true **skyship**, but it can only function over a **repulsion grid**. In the present day, they are used only in **Skyreach**.

Forge—the headquarters of the **Twilight Order**, a mountain fortress not far from **Skyreach**. Built with the help of the **Chosen** at the Order's founding, it is a colossal complex, large enough to accommodate the entire Twilight Order even at its height. As the numbers of **centarchs** have shrunk over the centuries, the Forge is now largely empty. It has three **Gates**, the only location to house more than one. The Order's training, storage, and support facilities are located here, as well as the seat of the Council.

Gate—a **Chosen arcana** that allows instantaneous transport from one location to another. A Gate looks like a freestanding **unmetal** arch big enough to admit a wagon. When activated and powered with *deiat*, it fills with a silvery curtain and connects to a target Gate, allowing free passage between the two simply by stepping through.

Because Gates require *deiat* to power them and set their destination, only a **centarch** can activate one, and the Gate network is exclusively used by the **Twilight Order**. Many Gate locations are kept deliberately obscure to prevent enemies of the Order from setting ambushes. In times of extreme danger to the **Dawn Republic**, the Order has used the Gates to transport the **Legions**, giving the Republic military unmatched strategic mobility.

Geraia—the ruling council of the **ghouls** of **Refuge**. Theoretically chosen by acclamation, but in practice a gerontocracy, with the eldest ghouls presiding. Prone to long-winded debates, and famously slow to action, and especially reluctant to do anything that poses the smallest risk of the city being discovered.

ghouls—one of the **Elder** races, along with the **Chosen**. They are basically humanoid in form but fully covered in fur, with wide big-pupiled eyes adapted for very low light and long pointed ears that express their emotional state. They are masters of *dhaka* and produce many **constructs** and biological **arcana**. With the advanced medicine made possible by *dhaka*, ghouls can live for more than four hundred years.

Once spread throughout the Chosen Empire, ghouls were mostly wiped out during the **Plague War**, and **humans** believe them to be extinct. All surviving ghouls live in the city of **Refuge** (known as **the Tomb** to humans), a carefully concealed underground safe haven beneath the Shattered Peak mountains. Ghoul society is almost completely self-contained and egalitarian, with manual labor performed entirely by constructs. Leadership is provided by the gerontocratic **Geraia**, but most decisions are made by slow consensus.

The Chosen taught, and most humans believe, that ghouls began the Plague War with their rebellion, then created the **Plague** and the **plaguespawn** during the conflict. Most ghouls deny this, though the truth of what happened is kept secret even among themselves.

glowstone—an inexpensive light source resembling a glassy stone, producing a dim blue light when shaken hard. An **alchemical** creation and generally **sanctioned arcana**.

Grace—a **Splinter Kingdom** to the north of the **Dawn Republic** and also the capital city of that kingdom, ruled by a monarch known as the Red Queen. The city is built under the canted wreck of the **skyfortress** *Grace in Execution*. **Alchemy** and other *dhak* are legal in Grace, and the **Twilight Order** is forbidden. Smuggling *dhak* into the Republic is a major industry.

haken (pl. haken)—the most powerful **Chosen arcana** and the signature weapon of the **centarchs**. Haken resemble bladeless swords, usually adorned with crystals. In the hands of a **human** with the right potential, they allow access to *deiat*. The wielder can generate a blade of pure energy, shaped according to the manifestation of their talent—fire, wind, force, and so on—and draw power to create a variety of effects or activate other Chosen arcana.

The haken were created by the Chosen in their final days to arm the **Twilight Order** and allow human civilization some access to *deiat*, and the secret of their construction has been long since lost. Fortunately, the centarchs have an instinctive ability to sense haken in general and their own in particular, so when they are lost the Order can generally recover them.

hardshell—a tortoise-like creature used as a beast of burden. Hardshells resemble common tortoises, but on a massive scale, standing nearly two meters tall at the shoulder and three meters at the top of the shell. They are rare and expensive and have to be trained from the egg to be responsive to their handlers' commands. Though slow, they can pull enormous loads and are capable of subsisting on little water and poor forage. They are mostly used in deserts and other badlands where fodder is difficult to find.

human—Humans have always formed a vast majority of the population, both in the former **Chosen** Empire and beyond. After the **Plague War** and the extinction of the Chosen, humans are all that remain, apart from the hidden **ghouls** of **Refuge**.

In the lands formerly ruled by the Chosen, the human inhabitants display some differences from baseline humans in the rest of the world. They display a much wider range of hair, eye, and skin tones, are highly resistant to disease, and heal quickly. Women have control over their fertility and must consciously invoke it in order to conceive.

A tiny minority of humans have the ability to wield *deiat* with the assistance of a **haken**, and these are sought out as children by the **Twilight Order** to be trained into **centarchs**. Humans are capable of learning *dhaka*, though the Order works to suppress this as much as it can.

Inheritance, **the**—the founding text of the **Twilight Order**, written by the **Chosen** to provide guidance after their extinction. It gives a brief history of the Chosen, the **Plague War**, and the destruction of the **ghouls**, lays out the ideals and precepts of the Order, and establishes its basic structure and laws.

Khirkhaz—a region in the southwestern part of the **Dawn Republic**, between the Worldspine Mountains and the coast. While not a **Splinter Kingdom**, it has a traditional local independence under the **Lightning Barons** and the local aristocracy, and it often proves troublesome for the Senate to manage. Currently the home of the **Commune**, a group of rebels against the Republic.

Kyriliarch—one of the twelve members of the Council that leads the **Twilight Order**.

Legions—one of the two branches of the **Dawn Republic** military, along with the **Auxiliaries**. The Legions are small in number but highly trained and equipped with **arcana** weapons and armor. They use **blaster** rifles and distinctive white **unmetal** armor, giving them power that no conventionally armed force can match.

Though they form the core of the Republic's military and can be concentrated against notable threats, the majority of the Legions at any given time are dispersed, sweeping for plaguespawn. The much more numerous Auxiliaries handle local defense, policing, and other duties.

Since only the **Twilight Order** has the ability to recharge **sunsplinters**, reshape unmetal armor, and perform other maintenance, the Legions are ultimately dependent on the Order's **centarchs** to sustain themselves. This makes the Republic as a whole reliant on the Order, which has sometimes rankled Republic leadership. Legionaries are often seconded to the Order for duty combating **plaguespawn** and *dhakim* when the centarchs are spread too thin.

Leviathan—a massive war-construct built by the **ghouls** in the last stages of the **Plague War**. It was intended to be a land-based equivalent to the **Chosen skyfortresses**, and an enormous underground facility dubbed Leviathan's Womb was created to build it, but it remained unfinished at the war's end. Naumoriel assembled the remaining parts to activate it, especially the Core Analytica that serves as its "brain."

Too complex to be controlled by a traditional construct intelligence, the Leviathan had a facility to transfer the mind of a living being into its analytica, for whom it would then serve as a body. In addition to the gargantuan Leviathan itself, it has a swarm of smaller semiautonomous constructs linked to the same controlling intelligence, intended to serve as gatherers for organic material to fuel the Leviathan. Though the Leviathan was crippled by Gyre, Kit's mind was transferred from her dying body to the analytica, and its construct swarm is under her control.

Lightning Baron—one of seven nobles who traditionally rule **Khirkhaz** from the seven **Spires**. Named for the lightning storms of their fortress-homes. There are currently only six Lightning Barons, with the Kotzed family declared traitors to the Republic and their Spire taken by the rest.

loadbird—The most common beast of burden in the former **Chosen** Empire, loadbirds are large flightless birds capable of pulling plows or wheeled vehicles. They look something like emus, standing roughly four feet tall at the shoulder, with a long neck that raises their undersized head much higher. Their legs are overdeveloped and heavily muscled, and their wings are small and vestigial.

Like their cousins **warbirds** and **swiftbirds**, loadbirds are controlled by a combination of reins, whistle commands, and tongue clicks; the better trained and more amicable a bird is, the more likely it can be directed by whistles and clicks alone. Loadbirds can be ridden but are slow and uncomfortable. Bred for strength, they can pull heavy weights alone or in teams.

Loadbirds eat mostly seeds and insects. They dislike **thickheads**, and clashes between the two species are notorious for causing problems.

nyfa seed—The ubiquitous nyfa bush is a hardy shrub, capable of growing under just about any conditions. It produces acorn-sized oily seeds continuously throughout its growing season. While the seeds are not edible by humans, **loadbirds** and **swiftbirds** love them and can subsist on them indefinitely. **Warbirds** will eat them as well but require insects or rodents to stay healthy.

Order—the **Twilight Order**.

panoply—a type of **Chosen arcana** that creates a defensive barrier, called a panoply field, around the user, absorbing incoming attacks. A panoply needs a constant supply of *deiat* to operate and so is not useful to anyone other than **centarchs**. It will deflect any energy blast or fast-moving object, drawing *deiat* energy from the user in the process.

A centarch using a panoply is impervious to normal weaponry, and the field will even stop **blaster** bolts or the blade of a haken. However, the energy drain to maintain the field in the face of a sustained attack will quickly exhaust the centarch's capacity to draw on *deiat*. Drawing too much power in too short a time will render a centarch unconscious and leave them unable to access *deiat* for several hours. Duels between centarchs are typically fought wearing panoplies, with the loser being the first to be knocked out in this manner.

Physically, the most common form of panoply is a broad belt of thin silver fabric, worn around the midsection, but other varieties exist with the same function.

Plague—a virulent illness that affected the **Chosen** during the **Plague War**. It was supposedly released by the **ghouls** in their rebellion against Chosen rule, and in spite of enormous efforts at combating it, ultimately proved completely fatal to the Chosen, although it had no effect on humans. It is commonly associated with **plaguespawn**, who appeared around the same time, but the connection is not understood.

plaguespawn—unnatural creatures created with *dhaka* that have afflicted the former **Chosen** Empire since the **Plague War**. It is commonly believed they were originally created by the **ghouls** as living weapons during the conflict though the surviving ghouls deny this.

Plaguespawn have almost infinitely variable forms. They appear as an assembly of organic parts in a vaguely animal-like shape, mostly muscle and bone, from a variety of mismatched sources. They can be as small as mice or as large as elephants, and there are stories of even bigger monsters. In spite of their hodgepodge, ramshackle appearance, they are universally vicious, fast, and deadly.

While they use animal matter in their bodies, plaguespawn are not biological creatures in the normal sense, and they are powered by *dhaka*. They do not eat, excrete, or reproduce as true animals do. Instead, their sole drive is to find and kill animals, the larger the better, and humans above all others. After killing its prey, the plaguespawn disassembles the corpses using *dhaka* and incorporates them into itself, sometimes completely altering its own form in the process. Plaguespawn thus grow larger the more they kill, though there may be an ultimate upper limit on this process.

It's not well understood how new plaguespawn come into existence. Small plaguespawn have been observed to "bud" from larger ones, and areas infested with plaguespawn tend to become more infested over time. On the other hand, areas swept clean for years can suddenly be subject to plaguespawn outbreaks. One theory is that the **Plague** itself is still present in the atmosphere and periodically causes plaguespawn to form spontaneously. The **Twilight Order** maintains that plaguespawn outbreaks are caused by *dhak* and *dhakim*, and hunts them relentlessly.

Dhakim do have a connection to plaguespawn through *dhaka*, and can exert control over them. Absent this control, the monsters are nearly mindless, driven only to hunt and kill. The more powerful the *dhakim*, the more and larger plaguespawn they can control.

The threat of plaguespawn is ubiquitous throughout the former Chosen Empire. In the **Dawn Republic**, a large part of the **Legions** at any given time are engaged in plaguespawn sweeps, repeated at multiyear intervals throughout Republic territory. Along the borders, the **Auxiliaries** keep constant watch for incursions. This keeps Republic territory reasonably safe from plaguespawn attack, though the effort involved is enormous and periodic outbreaks still occur. In the **Splinter Kingdoms**, with their lesser resources, such sweeps are impossible and plaguespawn attacks are a fact of life. Towns and villages are walled, houses are fortified, and travelers go well armed. Fortunately, the mindlessness of plaguespawn means they are usually no match for the well prepared.

Plague War—the conflict that brought about the destruction of the **Elder** races and the fall of the **Chosen** Empire. The specific events of the war have largely been lost in the chaos of the times, but an outline is preserved in the histories of the **Twilight Order**. The **ghouls** rebelled against the rule of the Chosen, and when their rebellion was suppressed they unleashed the **Plague**, which eventually wiped out the Chosen completely. The dwindling Chosen, however, were able to exterminate the ghouls in turn, and then founded the **Twilight Order** and the **Dawn Republic** to help their human former subjects survive in the wreckage of their empire.

The surviving **ghouls** of **Refuge** contest this version of events, but the truth is a well-guarded secret even from their own people.

pony—a small equine sometimes used as a mount or beast of burden. More expensive and less capable than **loadbirds**, **thickheads**, or **hardshells**, ponies are relatively rare, and primarily used as status symbols by the wealthy.

quickheal—an **alchemical** creation that functions as an anesthetic, prevents infection, and promotes rapid healing. It can be made either in a liquid form or as waxy, chewable tablets. **Sanctioned arcana** when produced by an **Order**-approved alchemist.

Refuge—the last **ghoul** city, buried deep under the Shattered Peak mountains. Ruled by the **Geraia** and protected by an army of constructs, its inhabitants are determined to avoid contact with the outside world.

Republic—the **Dawn Republic**.

repulsion grid—a **Chosen arcana** that allows for relatively cheap and easy flight within the grid's boundaries. **Autos** and **flitters** don't require the full power of a **skyship** to stay aloft, but "push" against the buried grid. The only known functioning repulsion grid is beneath the city of **Skyreach**.

sanctioned arcana—**arcana** or **alchemical** products approved by the **Twilight Order** for general use, including **quickheal**, **glowstones**, and other staples. All other arcana and alchemical products are considered *dhak* by the Order. Sanctioned arcana is always expensive and in limited supply, which creates constant problems with smugglers selling *dhak*.

skyfortress—the largest class of **skyship** created by the **Chosen** Empire. Only eight of these massive vessels were ever built. During the **Plague War**, they were used to deliver the most devastating of the Chosen's weapons against the **ghouls**. Of the eight, three were lost over the sea in a last-ditch attempt by the Chosen to find land outside their continent-wide empire, in the hopes of escaping the **Plague**. The other five were either grounded and eventually destroyed, or crashed due to mishap or ghoul attack. One, the skyfortress *Grace in Execution*, overhangs the city of Grace and was the original reason for its settlement.

Skyreach—the capital of the **Dawn Republic** and former capital of the **Chosen** Empire. The heart of Republic wealth and power, and the home of its Senate and ruling class. The huge Chosen buildings that form the heart of Skyreach would be impossible to inhabit, and indeed unstable, without a continuous supply of **sunsplinters** charged with *deiat*. Only here, with the cooperation of the **Twilight Order**, is something like the Chosen's old standard of living maintained. Living in such a tower is a mark of extremely high status, only available to the hugely wealthy and powerful.

skyship—any of the wide variety of flying vessels used by the **Chosen**. These ranged from small one-man skiffs to the massive **skyfortresses**, generally taking the form of flattened teardrops, with the pointed end being the bow. They were some of the most advanced and complex **arcana** the Chosen created. Many were destroyed in the **Plague War**, and while the **Twilight Order** maintained a few during the first few decades of its existence, they quickly broke down beyond human capacity to repair. No operational skyships are currently known to exist, though there are always rumors among scavengers.

Spire—one of seven **Chosen** structures in **Khirkhaz**, each a single tall tower with a surrounding wall. The towers are topped by hundreds of long rods, giving them a bristling appearance. Every day at dawn and dusk, violent lightning storms hit the Spires, with many bolts earthing themselves on the protruding rods. No one is certain of the Spires' original purpose, but they are now the seats of the **Lightning Barons** who rule Khirkhaz for the **Republic**.

Splinter Kingdoms—portions of the former **Chosen** Empire that have broken away from the **Dawn Republic**. After the **Plague War**, the Republic asserted authority over the entirety of the old Chosen Empire, but maintaining control over such a vast area proved impossible in the face of rebellions and **plaguespawn** attacks. Some regions were abandoned as the **Legions** retreated to a perimeter they could keep clear of plaguespawn, while other cities declared themselves independent under local rulers or ambitious warlords. The Republic crushed some of these rebellions, but strained resources meant others had to be accepted.

Life in the Splinter Kingdoms is generally more dangerous than in the Republic, without the **arcana**-armed Legions to keep order and suppress plaguespawn. However, this varies greatly from polity to polity. In spite of their name, not all the breakaway states are monarchies—there are free cities, republics, and other political experiments, sometimes changing rapidly as they war with one another. As a general rule, the farther from the Republic they are, the smaller and less stable they become, with larger kingdoms like **Grace**, Meltrock, and Drail stabilized by trade with the Republic.

While ***dhak*** is illegal in the Republic, its status in the Splinter Kingdoms varies. Some attempt to maintain the Republic's ban, while others, like Grace, embrace *dhak* and encourage its creation and sale. Smuggling across the Republic border is a major business. The **Twilight Order** asserts that its centarchs have the right to go anywhere in the old Chosen Empire to hunt *dhak* and ***dhakim***, but as a practical matter some Splinter Kingdoms are openly hostile to Order agents, and they must move secretly there.

sunsplinter—an **arcana** device that serves as a ***deiat*** battery, storing power for future use by other arcana. Most notably used by **blasters** as a power source. Only someone with a connection to *deiat* can refill one, so fully charged sunsplinters are rare and expensive.

sunstone—an **arcana** light source, powered by ***deiat***, which produces bright white light. Controlled by *deiat* and requiring periodic infusions of power to keep operating, so used only by the **Twilight Order** or Republic elites.

swiftbird—a cousin of the **loadbird** and the **warbird**, specialized for riding. Generally resembles a loadbird, but with longer, leaner legs. Contrary to its name, the swiftbird specializes not in speed but in endurance. A warbird might outrun one over the course of a short charge, but a swiftbird can keep up a rapid pace for ten to twelve hours a day with sufficient food and water, allowing riders to cover long distances.

thickhead—a large reptilian creature used as a beast of burden. Thickheads resemble giant lizards, with short tails, tough, scaly skin, and bony protrusions around their skulls. They are tremendously strong and can pull very heavy loads, although their fastest pace is not much more than a walk. They are also very sure-footed and can traverse almost any terrain. Slow and expensive to maintain compared to **loadbirds**, they're used for particularly heavy burdens or as pack animals over bad roads.

Though thickheads look fierce, with their beaks and spiked skulls, they are pure vegetarians and display almost no aggressive behavior.

Their smell tends to rile loadbirds, who sometimes snap at them or shy away. When threatened, a thickhead lowers itself to the ground and puts its forepaws over its face, protecting its vulnerable eyes and belly and relying on its tough hide to repel an attacker. Once hunkered down, they are notoriously difficult to get moving again.

"Thing, the"—Maya's name for the small **arcana** implanted in her flesh above her breastbone. Baselanthus put it there when she was a little girl, telling her it would prevent the regular illnesses that threatened her health. He and Jaedia taught her to keep it secret, since it could be viewed as *dhak*. During her emotional fight with Gyre in Deepfire, Maya found the Thing growing hot enough to sear her skin, and not long afterward, she was sick with a violent fever.

Tomb, the—human name for the legendary last city of the **ghouls**, assumed to be extinct, which is full of fantastic treasure. See **Refuge**.

Twilight Order—an organization created by the dying **Chosen**, in the last days of the **Plague War**, to give humans the ability to use *deiat* and sustain civilization after their extinction. Key to this purpose are the **haken**, Chosen **arcana** that allow the few humans capable of drawing on *deiat* to wield its power.

The purposes of the Twilight Order are to defend humanity as a whole, especially from plaguespawn and ghouls; to suppress knowledge of *dhaka* and destroy *dhakim*, as part of that defense; and to make sure the power of *deiat* is wielded for the common good. These themes are laid out in a book called the *Inheritance*, which details the history of the Chosen and the Plague War and explains the goals of the Order.

The core of the Order are the **centarchs**. Every **human** capable of wielding *deiat* that the Order can locate is brought to the **Forge** to become an **agathios**, a centarch trainee under an experienced teacher. When they are deemed ready by their master, usually by their early twenties, they receive their **cognomen** and are declared a full centarch. Apart from the **Kyriliarchs**, all centarchs are theoretically peers, and free to choose their own path, though in practice a great deal of deference is paid to seniority. Centarchs, wielding *deiat* through their haken, travel throughout the **Dawn Republic** and beyond, fighting plaguespawn and hunting *dhak* and *dhakim*.

The governing body of the Order is the Council of twelve **Kyriliarchs**. Generally senior centarchs, these members are nominated by the other centarchs, approved by the Council, and serve for life. Only a majority of the Council can issue directions that centarchs are bound by the laws of the Order to accept. The Council sets broad policy for the Order, directs centarchs to particular areas of trouble, and rules on intra-Order disputes and transgressions.

In addition to the centarchs, the Order includes support staff of several sorts. The Forge is maintained by hereditary families of servants, who do manual labor in the fortress. An extensive logistics service handles supplies and tracks the vast storehouse of arcana the Order maintains, and a courier service uses the **Gates** to provide rapid delivery of information. Arcanists help maintain equipment and work with centarchs in the field to research arcana. Another group, euphemistically called scouts rather than spies, support the centarchs directly on missions and maintain outposts and intelligence-gathering operations throughout the Republic and the **Splinter Kingdoms**, working undercover where the Order is not welcome.

While the Order is not in charge of the Republic, nor subject to the instructions of the Republic Senate, the two groups maintain an uneasy but close relationship. The *Inheritance* instructs the Order to stay out of mundane politics, to preserve their independence and reduce the temptation to corruption. But the Order has traditionally been willing to intervene when the Republic is threatened, and the power of the centarchs is the ultimate guarantor of the Republic's continued status as the most powerful nation in the remains of the Chosen Empire.

unmetal—a material used by the **Chosen** for a wide variety of purposes. Unmetal is lighter than steel but enormously stronger, essentially indestructible except against *deiat*. Even *deiat* takes significant time and effort to damage it. It can have a variety of colors and finishes but is usually identifiable by its iridescent sheen.

With the fall of the Chosen, the means of creating unmetal has been lost, but large amounts remain from various Chosen ruins. Modifying and repurposing them is obviously a challenge, however. The **Twilight Order** retains a limited capacity to reforge unmetal, which they use to create equipment for themselves and the **Legions**.

vulpi (pl. vulpi)—a livestock animal raised for meat, with a unique life cycle. They are omnivores and will eat nearly anything, but can thrive on grasses and weeds. Vulpi are born small and helpless, but rapidly grow into boisterous, playful creatures resembling both pigs and weasels. This yearling phase lasts for approximately their first year or two. Toward the end of it, they mate repeatedly, and females store enough sperm to last for the rest of their lives. They then mature into breeders, nearly doubling in size and becoming squatter and ill-tempered. For the following year or more, the females will give birth to litters of pups every eight to ten weeks.

Finally, the mature vulpi enter their final stage of life, during which they are called terminals. They become sessile, increase enormously in size (up to tenfold if provided with plenty of feed), and their legs atrophy and are eventually lost in the vast bulk of their bodies. In this phase they are extremely efficient eaters and produce little waste. On their own, terminals simply die of starvation, but properly tended and eventually slaughtered they produce large amounts of high-quality, pork-like meat. Vulpi is a staple throughout the **Dawn Republic** and the **Splinter Kingdoms**. Culled at the yearling or breeder stage, they can also provide useful leather and other by-products.

warbird—A rarer cousin of **loadbirds** and **swiftbirds**, warbirds are large, flightless birds bred for combat. They resemble loadbirds but retain larger wings, which they flap for stability while kicking. Unlike their more docile cousins, warbirds have long talons on their toes and a sickle-like claw on the back of their foot, and are capable of tearing an unarmored human to shreds.

In battle, warbirds are typically equipped with armor and have blades affixed to their beaks, while carrying an armored rider who fights with a lance or spear. Outside the **Republic** (where the **Legions** with their **arcana** weapons remain the dominant force) warbird-riding cavalry is often the preeminent military arm.

Warbirds are more difficult to train than their cousins, and more expensive to keep, eating mostly large insects and rodents. They are therefore expensive, and owning one is usually a mark of status.

About the author

Django Wexler is the author of the Shadow Campaigns novels. He graduated from Carnegie Mellon University in Pittsburgh with degrees in creative writing and computer science, and worked for the university in artificial intelligence research. He is also the author of a series of middle-grade fantasy novels, *The Forbidden Library*, *The Mad Apprentice*, and *The Palace of Glass*.